LIGHT AND STILL SECRETS

LOVE AND OTHER SECRETS

Sarah Challis

WINDSOR
PARAGON

First published 2009
by Headline Review
This Large Print edition published 2009
by BBC Audiobooks Ltd
by arrangement with
Headline Publishing Group

Hardcover   ISBN: 978 1 408 42893 1
Softcover   ISBN: 978 1 408 42894 8

British Library Cataloguing in Publication Data available

Printed and bound in Great Britain by
CPI Antony Rowe, Chippenham and Eastbourne

For Dan and Inger, with love.

CHAPTER ONE

It was pitch-dark and blowing hard. Jane was terrified by the sound the wind made as it roared down the lane. The hedges seemed to rear and heave on either side as if something wild and furious were trying to break through. Fallen branches went skewing across the road, and under her boots there was a litter of twigs and stones washed down by the earlier rain. It was hard work pushing the pram into the wind and she had to bend her head and use all her strength.

She'd left the dog at home. It was easier without him in the dark and she hadn't far to go. She was nearly there now. The double gates were open, which was strange. The wind must have forced the catch that held them closed.

She knew where to go. She didn't need a torch, but the dark looming house frightened her, and when she stepped out of the wind it was worse, listening to it howling through the trees at the back.

She had the key ready in her pocket and opened the door without a problem. The light switch was just to the right. Her fingers felt across the rough cement of the wall and it was a relief to turn the light on and be able to see again, everything familiar and in its place, and to push the door shut on the wild night.

She was so unprepared for what happened next. Her back was turned when she heard a familiar noise. It was a door opening and, whirling round, her heart leaping in her chest, she saw someone standing at the top of the steps from the house.

Instantly she knew she had to get out, to escape, but the woman had come down the steps and taken hold of the pram and was shouting loudly, and Jane had to struggle with her, in terror and desperation, to make her let go. She pushed her hard in the chest and the woman let go of the handle and took a step backwards, and with flailing arms went down, her short length crumpling on the concrete floor.

Jane was gone in that instant, hauling the pram behind her through the outside door and then running through the crashing night the way she had come, a sob of panic in her throat, looking over her shoulder in terror that she was being followed.

It wasn't until she was back in the cottage with all the doors bolted and the curtains drawn that she began to piece together what had happened and then a worse fear took hold. The fear of what she had done.

*   *   *

Jane lay for a moment in the grip of the horrible dream before she realised that it was morning and that it was 1 April, April Fools' Day, the day on which Florence was due to have her baby. From the start it had seemed an inauspicious date, especially for the birth of a baby planned with such precision as this one evidently had been.

She wished that the day had not begun like that and it was a while before she shook off the feelings that the dream had stirred. As she drew back the curtains, she found herself looking for signs or

2

portents that might mark this day as special or significant, but everything outside her bedroom window appeared normal. The garden below was a neat square of grass dominated by a large, silvery-trunkcd flowering cherry tree. Its fat, sugar-pink blossoms were tossed by the same mean, squally wind that had fretted at them yesterday and the day before, soiling their delicate edges with ugly brown stains before throwing them to the ground, where they collected in spoiling pink drifts, blotting out the path that led in a straight line to the garden gate. Across the road an identical tree bobbed and ducked in the garden of the neighbours' almost identical house, a 1930s mock-Tudor villa with black-beamed gables and leaded windows, and further up the curve of the quiet suburban road the crown of tossing, candyfloss pink was repeated between the other substantial detached houses of The Avenue. All that lovely blossom, thought Jane, should be reaching up into a blue spring sky like a celebration, not battered to the ground by a shivering winter wind.

With the birth of the baby so imminent, Jane examined for the hundredth time how she felt as the prospective grandmother. Excited, obviously, and anxious, because, despite the fact that Florence was a senior registrar and her baby was to be born in a gleaming new hospital on the edge of a Midlands city, giving birth always had its inherent risks and Flo was considered old to be having a first baby. At thirty-five she had told her mother that she was termed an elderly primigravida or something that sounded worryingly geriatric, and the birth was therefore at greater risk of complications than if she had been more youthful.

3

'You realise that when you had me, you were the optimum age,' Flo had informed her. 'Teenage mothers are physically the best suited to give birth.' After a pause, she added, 'If not in other ways.'

No, not in other ways, Jane had thought. That went without saying, as it always did, and always had. She did not need her daughter to remind her. Now as she stared down at the cold spring garden where the daffodils lay battered by the wind and rain of the previous night, she thought of the suicidal despair that she had felt when she discovered that *she* was pregnant. In fact the whole business of Flo's pregnancy had served to highlight the difference between mother and daughter in a way that Jane had been surprised to discover was disturbing and painful. She had expected to have put all that behind her, *moved on*, as people now would say. After thirty-five years, her eighteen-year-old self had little to do with the person she had become, and yet seven months ago when Flo telephoned to tell her that she was pregnant, she found herself being propelled backwards in time to exactly the moment that she could no longer keep her pregnancy a secret from her own mother. They were inextricably linked, grandmother, mother, daughter, like a set of Russian dolls, each one complete as an individual and yet fitting snugly within the body of the next in size. Whatever they might feel about it, they belonged together.

There was one obvious similarity in that Flo wasn't married and, it appeared, had no intention of becoming so. In fact her partner, Ha, seemed so incidental to the announcement that Jane hardly liked even to mention him by asking if he was pleased by the news.

'Actually,' said Flo, as if the question were irrelevant, 'I haven't asked him if he's *pleased*. This baby was my decision.'

'Oh, I see,' said Jane meekly. She was fond of Ha, a good-looking and good-natured orthopaedic surgeon of Vietnamese immigrant parents, and a colleague of Flo's at the hospital. He seemed to know instinctively how to manage her daughter in a way that Jane had never learned. When she was argumentative or moody he defused the situation with a display of oriental calm and detachment.

They had been together, on and off, for five years, but even now didn't co-habit in any formal sort of way, choosing instead to live independently. In Flo's case this was in her own new flat in a rejuvenated area of the small city in which she worked, while Ha shared a chaotic house with some other young doctors. Jane found this puzzling: if you loved someone enough to have their baby, surely you wanted to live with them too. The home-making instinct, which had always been so strong in her, seemed to have been bred out of her daughter. When she expressed her surprise to Enzo, her husband, he said, 'It seems quite common, these days—these sorts of no-strings-attached relationships. They call their partners "fuck buddies".'

'What a horrible expression!' said Jane, making a face. 'What has happened to love and romance?'

'Oh, they haven't got time for all that nonsense,' said Enzo. 'They just look for compatible partners to meet a biological need. They don't want the complication of emotional attachments.'

'Is that what you would have wanted when we

5

first met?'

'It has a certain appeal—to a man, I suppose,' he teased, 'but I could see that it wouldn't be a popular idea with you, so I didn't pursue it. You know very well that I wanted to marry you on sight. I could hardly wait to carry you over the threshold.'

Privately, Jane wondered if the advent of a baby might alter Flo's living arrangements. Maybe she and Ha would buy a house together, set up home properly and make a family for the baby, but this did not seem to be the moment to ask. 'Treading on eggshells' was the phrase that came to mind in all her dealings with her daughter. Quite often a perfectly innocent enquiry or comment was turned about and used against her.

As she absorbed Flo's announcement, she had felt it was safe to say, 'Well, darling, how *lovely*. What exciting news! May I tell the others, or would you rather do it yourself?' She referred to the wider family: Enzo, whom she had married when Flo was ten, and their two sons, Alessandro and Marco, Flo's half-brothers. Both were university students and travelling abroad in the long summer vacation, but due back now that it was September.

'Oh, Mum, I don't mind. What does it matter who tells them? You can, if you want.'

Flo's indifference was studied. Jane could hear the effort she was making to disguise her excitement. She recognised the smile in her voice and was glad.

'Are you pleased?' Flo could not resist asking, and Jane could not respond in any way other than by saying, 'I am thrilled. Absolutely thrilled.'

'You'll be a grandmother,' said Flo unnecessarily.

'Yes. Wonderful!' It *was* wonderful, miraculous almost, because Jane had often wondered whether Flo would ever want to be a mother. In many ways she was one of the least maternal people that she could think of, but often brusque, seemingly tough women made magnificent, fierce mothers. All the same, as the weeks went by, Jane often found herself thinking, poor baby, and wondering whether she had failed in her maternal duty in producing a daughter who seemed so ill suited for motherhood.

*   *   *

Seven months later, Jane felt that Flo's pregnancy had been going on for years, like an elephant's, and it was hard to remember what life had been like before, when she hadn't been carrying a baby. Modern mothers seemed to make so much more of pregnancy than Jane or her generation had ever done. They tended to be older, and maybe it was years in the workplace that made them take the whole thing up as if it was a cause, or a project, rather than just get on with it in a state of semi-ignorance. No stone seemed to be left unturned, no avenue unexplored, in the quest for the perfect pregnancy. Foods that Jane had happily eaten on a regular basis throughout her pregnancies were now on the banned list, and these days if you drank or smoked you were considered unfit to be a mother. Now it was all about doing antenatal Pilates exercises to a background of tantric chanting, and worrying about how much the use of disposable nappies would wreck your standing as an eco-warrior. The sixties hippie mothers had been

7

bonkers enough, lugging their babies to love-ins and pop festivals, but surely Flo's generation of super-mummies were even more unhinged?

Swallowing enormous iron tablets had been the only change that Jane could remember being asked to make when she was pregnant that first time, and any other alteration to her lifestyle had been because she suddenly couldn't bear the smell of coffee or had a yearning for Vesta dehydrated chicken curries—extraordinary desiccated morsels rattling about in a box, with bullets of bright green peas, and no doubt packed with banned additives. Having a baby seemed much less of a performance back then, when even saying the word 'pregnant' had been embarrassing, and women wore vast balloon-shaped maternity dresses to conceal their condition instead of flaunting their swollen bellies in skin-tight Lycra.

Now on this cold, blustery morning with a lowering sky full of busy, racing grey clouds, Jane found it hard to believe that Flo's long-awaited baby would be born. It had been arranged that unless she went into labour within the next few hours, she would be admitted to hospital to be induced. She didn't hold with the inconvenience of a completely natural birth—not for herself, at any rate—and she and Ha already knew the sex of the baby—a boy. Flo had shown Jane the intrauterine photographs, the blurred broad bean shape with its bowed head and splayed reptile hands. 'See,' she said, pointing at a tiny pale shoot, 'a penis!'

So this baby, oblivious to what awaited him, swimming in his warm, private world, was already a male person with a name. He was to be called Tintin. How could you give a real person a comic

8

strip name? Again, it seemed unwise to ask, especially when Jane had called Florence after a children's television character from *The Magic Roundabout*, not because she liked the name but because she'd had to think of something when the midwife asked her—that horrible, bullying midwife who had made her push until she tore nearly in two. Not to have a name ready only served to emphasise the irregular and shaming origins of the newborn baby, so Florence she became.

Oh, Flo, thought Jane, turning from the window to gather up the clothes she would wear for the day ahead. She felt a rush of love and womanly sympathy for her daughter, who, despite all her medical and scientific knowledge, could not really be prepared for what this baby would mean or how it would change her life for ever. It didn't matter who or what you were, or how old or young, rich or poor, educated or ignorant, you could not escape the knock-out impact of having a baby. Jane could remember so acutely the sense of suspended time and place as the huge burden of a new order of love and responsibility hit her with a force that she had never anticipated. Nothing, nothing, could prepare a first-time mother for the almost unbearable tenderness, and the terrible anxiety that she would be unequal to the task of keeping the tiny, barely breathing, little creature alive, not just for an hour or a day, but for ever.

To Jane it had seemed as if her life was set within a glass-domed snow scene, which Flo's birth had shaken so thoroughly that when the blizzard subsided the landscape had changed irrevocably and the tiny scrap mewling in the hospital crib was the centre of an altered universe.

9

It wasn't just the emotional and hormonal changes either. Flo might know all about giving birth from a medical perspective but did she know how unlike herself she would feel in those first days, when her bruised, stretched and bleeding body was returned to her after the delivery, to inhabit like a stranger? Jane remembered gazing with dismay at her swollen, veined and leaking breasts and the puckered, flabby stomach, hanging in front of her like an empty bag. How could this be the slim, youthful body she had surrendered nine months earlier?

And then there were the early weeks when it seemed almost impossible to do anything else than be a wetnurse; still in her Laura Ashley nightdress at midday, feeding, changing, burping, changing, and then maybe an hour of peace before the process started all over again. She remembered her hair hanging long and lank, impossible to wash when she was so numb with tiredness that the idea of putting her head under the tap seemed like torture, and anyway the water was cold because the temperamental boiler had gone out.

As long as Flo lived, the ties of bone and blood would hold her, and with each decade would come new challenges. The dangerous toddler years, when just preventing disastrous and tragic accidents would seem to take over her life; and then the agonies of starting school and learning to be a social being, when she would offer herself up for torture to spare her child suffering at the hands of the bullies or an unsympathetic teacher who sent him home from school with a face crumpled with misery. So it went on, and each phase would throw up its own dramas, and Flo would find herself ever more helpless to intervene, until finally Tintin was an adult and she would have to stand to one side and watch, still loving and anxious, but no longer able to influence anything very much.

Thinking all this, Jane had a vision of Flo, with her expensive haircut and her glasses on the end of her nose, lounging in one of her pale leather armchairs with a stack of newspapers and magazines at her feet, reading about the stock market or which wine to buy in Waitrose. It was difficult to imagine a baby anywhere in the picture—even in the wooden Shaker crib bought from a London designer shop for nearly eight hundred pounds.

'Is it really practical, though?' Jane had asked doubtfully. 'Won't the baby get its head stuck between these bars?'

'Oh, Mum! Don't be silly. Do you really think they could market something that was unsafe?' Maybe not, thought Jane, but daft, all the same, to spend a fortune on what looked as if it had been knocked up by a nineteenth-century American pioneer out of apple boxes, especially when the baby would outgrow it in a few weeks.

'You slept in a drawer at first, you know,' she said a bit wistfully, and was rewarded with a fierce look.

'Oh, please!' Flo could not bear this sort of nostalgic observation. She had always hated talking about herself as a baby, as if she couldn't bear hearing about herself when she was dependent and vulnerable.

As she put on her make-up in the bathroom, not really seeing her face, certainly not as a canvas for

11

imaginative application of lip pencil and eye shadow, Jane thought of the exhaustion of the broken nights and lack of sleep that her daughter would now have to live through. She remembered how she had become familiar with peculiar World Service radio programmes, as she padded about at two and three and four in the morning with a sleepless, bawling Flo in her arms. No wonder they were called 'small', those hours when no one else in the world seemed to be awake and when she looked out of the cottage window there was no other light to be seen to make her feel less alone. People talk of 'some unearthly hour' and that is exactly what it felt like during those desperate early morning vigils: 'unearthly', as if she and her baby occupied a strange floating planet of their own.

Face done in the usual way, age-reversal moisturiser—some hope—grey eyeliner, pink lipstick, Jane saw her acceptable, daytime self look back at her, but this very day it would become a grandmother's face. She smiled brightly at her image in the glass. 'Goodness, you don't look old enough to be a granny,' she told herself. Would people say that? She doubted it, because she *did* look old enough. Her face was pouching and sagging and lined. Smiling, she looked all right, but you couldn't keep smiling all the time or you were mistaken for a mental defective. When she wasn't smiling the downward lines from the corners of her mouth made her look sad and dissatisfied, which wasn't how she felt. Weren't you supposed to end up with the face you deserved? It was not a comforting thought.

Downstairs in her tidy bright kitchen, Jane was

greeted ecstatically by her dog, a large brindled mongrel called Chipper, part Lab, part collie and a large part unknown. He was a burly, heavy-coated creature with a broad square face. His adoption from the dogs' home had been the reason for one of Jane and Enzo's rare disagreements, which had gone on for several days before Jane got her way through sheer, unwavering obstinacy.

'With the boys off our hands what do we want a dog for? It's just a tie, when we could be free to do what we like, when we like,' Enzo had argued. 'Why do you want to saddle yourself with something else to look after?'

Because that's what I'm good at, thought Jane, and because the woman at the rescue centre had explained that Chipper was a cruelty case who had been found tied to a shopping trolley and thrown into a river. He required a quiet home without other pets or young children, where he could regain confidence in humankind. Jane saw a well of sadness in his gentle, puzzled eyes and made up her mind to take him. That was three years ago and now even Enzo had to agree that he was a wonderful dog, obedient, loyal and loving, and because he was a vigilant guard dog, Jane pointed out that she was never nervous when she was alone in the house. This had become something of a consideration in a neighbourhood like theirs, in the prosperous suburbs of a Staffordshire country town where poverty and drug-taking were endemic.

She unlocked the back door to put Chipper out in the garden and was met by a gust of cold wind that wrapped her skirt round her legs, and brought with it the smell of wet leaves, wet grass, wet earth.

She closed the door hurriedly behind him and began to put together her breakfast and think about the day ahead.

For the past decade, Jane had worked four mornings a week as personal assistant to an ageing, knighted pop star at his country estate, generally running his affairs and executing a trust he had set up to provide holidays for disadvantaged children. Sir Tommy was best remembered for his outrageous behaviour through the sixties and seventies, particularly his personal mission to ingest a large proportion of the national product of Colombia. These days he had thinning hippie hair and still wore his trademark flamboyant clothes, the skintight trousers emphasising the stick-thin legs and the famous strut, which had begun to look less provocative and more arthritic. In fact, Enzo had suggested to him that he was an ideal subject for the keyhole knee surgery that he had so successfully pioneered.

Sir Tommy was now not only a father of six, but also a grandfather three times over, and had a new, aristocratic young wife—the daughter of an impoverished Irish earl. He had taken up shooting, and his wife was Joint Master of a smart pack of Derbyshire foxhounds. It amused Enzo that this icon of anarchic youth should have metamorphosed into a supporter of the Countryside Alliance, but they were all the same, these survivors of Flower Power, who had managed to emerge from a pall of drugs and dissolution with well-lined pockets and right-wing tendencies. Look at Tash and Denby, he pointed out, thinking of Jane's sister and her husband, who had been devout hippies in the sixties but were

14

now ensconced in their country pile, growing knobbly organic vegetables and herding their flock of rare-breed sheep like a pair of Marie Antoinettes. They were great friends of Sir Tommy, from their days in an ashram in India, and it was through them that Jane went to work for him in the first place.

The kitchen was calm and quiet, and as Jane made a pot of coffee and fetched the newspaper from the hall, she thought of how much she had looked forward to these three days while Enzo was away delivering a paper on hip replacement at a medical conference in Munich. His absence was like a special sort of holiday during which she could do exactly as she liked and eat as irregularly as she wished, and go to bed at eight o'clock with a sandwich and a glass of wine if she wanted. Glancing at the kitchen clock as she sat down with her cup of coffee and the pleasure of having first look at the newspaper, she reckoned that any moment he would telephone, as he did daily, and his voice would echo with the loneliness of the bleak breakfast buffet and long empty corridor back to the isolation of a hotel bedroom.

She always felt guilty that she enjoyed it when he was away and did her best to convince him that she missed him, which she did, but in a positive sense. To relish someone's short-term absence is not necessarily a bad thing, she thought, as she got up to get some yoghurt from the fridge. It allowed her a temporary break from being the sort of person she felt she owed to Enzo, as his wife. It was the sort of relief that taking off her corsets must have been to a wasp-waisted Victorian lady. She could just slump and *be*, and watch rubbish programmes on the television and read trashy novels and ring up her girlfriends and talk and gossip for half an hour at a time. She could let her standards drop because there was no one to care, or notice that she was really a slob.

Of course, she would hate being alone if it was a permanent state, and by the time Enzo's taxi stopped by the gate she would be eager to see him again, to sit with their elbows on the kitchen table sharing a bottle of wine and talking about the time they had spent apart. Not gossiping, because he wasn't that sort of man, but sharing news of work and family, and generally retuning to each other's wavelength. She would be back in character again, getting up to make the coffee or unpack the dishwasher, sorting out his suitcase and putting his dirty clothes into the washing machine, planning the next day's meals in her head.

The telephone rang—the expected call was on cue—but when she picked it up it was her sister's voice that she heard on the other end of the line.

'Oh, it's you, Tash. I thought it would be Enzo.'

'Oh, sorry. Well, as you can hear, it's not.'

'He's away, delivering a paper. He usually rings at this time, but it's never anything important. He always wants me to feel sorry for him, staying in a five-star hotel in some exotic location, only this time it's Munich, which sounds rather dull.'

'You should be glad he keeps in touch and isn't too busy seducing the chambermaid.' Tash's own husband, Denby, was unerringly unreliable. 'Anyway, I rang because today's the day, isn't it? D-day? Or B-day, I suppose. I don't mean to be unkind, but really, you would think Flo's was the first baby ever produced.'

'Oh, but they are all like that today!' said Jane, feeling moved to defend her daughter.

'Yes, but Flo is a doctor! You would think she would show a bit more, I don't know, professional restraint. This baby has been her sole topic of conversation for months. I'm surprised she hasn't arranged for a five-gun salute in Hyde Park by way of announcing the birth.'

'I know what you mean,' said Jane, feeling disloyal. 'She told me last week that she is going to have a doulas at the birthing. It's called a birthing now—like bringing a ship into port.'

'What the hell is a doulas? It sounds like something you'd eat in Greece.'

'It's a labour assistant; one of her girlfriends who has been chosen to accompany her throughout the birthing. It's a Red Indian practice—or some South American tribe, I don't remember exactly. The most recent thinking is that the father is not necessarily the right person to have beside you as you push. Well, we could have told them that, couldn't we?'

They both chuckled, Tash thinking of Denby, who fainted at the sight of blood and suffered from post-natal depression after each of their four babies, and Jane because when Flo was born she had no one to hold her hand. With Enzo, it had been different. Although he sounded Italian he was actually born and bred in Lowland Scotland of an ice-cream dynasty, and the hot Mediterranean blood in his veins had been cooled by the bleak climate of his home town of Musselburgh on the Firth of Forth. He had sat by her bed when Alessandro was born, reading the newspaper and eating toast brought to him by nurses more

17

interested in his welfare than that of Jane. He'd missed Marco's birth entirely, following Chelsea at an away match in the Netherlands.

'So it *is* today? The birthing.'

'Yes. I imagine Flo and her obstetrician got their diaries out and found the most convenient day. A window in their busy schedules.'

'It seems cold-blooded somehow, doesn't it? Or am I totally out of date?'

'Out of date, I think. Flo would argue that it is more efficient and safer this way. She won't be on a bus, for instance, when her waters break.'

'Flo? On a bus? Please! Flo hasn't been on a bus since she was in school uniform. But I can see her point. In case of emergency. They're too old, in my opinion, these professional women—wanting it all, and leaving it so late to have their babies. My advice is to crack on and get your breeding out of the way in your twenties. It's obvious that thirty-five is terribly late to start. After all, the female body is designed to have babies from about twelve years old, isn't it? The equipment is bound to have seized up if it's left lying idle all those years. I had the whole of my lot by the time I was thirty and then I was able to dust off my hands and say, that's one job out of the way, and get on with other things.'

That was Tash's attitude to everything, thought Jane, who had sometimes wondered if her children weren't made to feel that they were exactly that—a job to be got out of the way. She had taken secret satisfaction at the hours they had spent as teenagers in her own kitchen when Tash was busy building a mail-order clothes business with Denby. She saw it as evidence that Tash's many successes and formidable energy did not extend to concentrating much on her home life. Sabrina, the younger daughter, had once given herself a complete Goth makeover, with black hair and lips, and Tash hadn't even noticed.

Tash had always been dynamic, which was what allowed Denby to be more of an ornamental sort of husband, although these days, with his receding hair and large tummy, he was hardly that any more. Jane noticed that he had even given up calling himself the 'ideas man' of their business. She supposed he had come to realise that most people who knew him felt that 'idle sod' would be more accurate. She was fond of him, though, because he was good-natured and kind. Really, thinking of Ha, and with regard to her immediate family, it was the men who were long-suffering and, in a way, easier and nicer characters.

'I was going to ask you and Enzo to lunch on Sunday,' Tash went on. 'I can't say I'd forgotten about Tintin's imminent arrival—I mean, who could?—but I hadn't factored it in, as it were. I suppose you'll be on duty, doing the granny thing?'

'Actually, Flo hasn't asked me.' Jane kept her tone breezy. 'You can't imagine her ever needing help, can you? And she'll have Ha on stand-by, I expect.'

'Will you come, then? We've got our latest Indian manufacturer over to discuss non-toxic clothing and sustainable design, and for some reason he's brought his wife with him.'

Oh, I see, thought Jane. I'm needed to talk to the wife. 'Well, we'd love to.' Enzo enjoyed poking fun at her sister, and liked Denby. She knew that he wouldn't mind her accepting the invitation. 'Do you want me to bring anything? Shall I do a pud?'

'No, thank you! Puds are completely out. Denby is such a porker these days and dreams of nothing but treacle suet sponges, but I'm not letting him have them. Our business is about lifestyle—he can't be the frontsperson of an eco-aware clothing company looking as if he lives on pie and chips. It gives totally the wrong impression to have him photographed for our promotional material alongside our Indian production workers, who are naturally very slight and malnourished-looking.'

Goodness, poor Denby, thought Jane. One of life's fairly innocent comforts denied him. Tash could be so fierce about some things.

The sisters continued with arrangements for Sunday and enquiries about each other's children until, looking at the clock, Jane said, 'I must go. I'm working this morning and I planned to call in and see Aunt Joan on the way.'

'You're too good to her. She doesn't deserve your devotion,' said Tash. 'Sour old cow.'

'Oh, she's not. Not really. And after all, she's all we have left of Mother's generation.'

'That may be, but I live in dread that the care home will telephone to say that she's been thrown out and will we go and collect her. I honestly don't know how they put up with her, although of course they charge her enough. She's a cash cow, in fact.'

'She's our only link with the past. I enjoy talking to her about the old days—when we were young. She has a remarkable memory for things that happened forty years ago.' Being charitable was another thing in which Jane had learned to specialise. It had become a habit to try to tone down Tash's more inflammatory opinions.

20

'Well, rather you than me. I certainly don't want to be reminded of growing up. It wasn't exactly sweetness and light, was it? I can't remember a time when I wasn't at loggerheads with Mother. It was different with Daddy, of course.'

They paused, thinking of their post-war childhood—ordered, secure, well provided for. They had never doubted that they were loved, but their relationship with their mother had been curiously lacking in the warmth and spontaneity that they both felt they enjoyed with their own children.

Jane sighed. She couldn't share Tash's toughness towards the past. Their parents were long since dead, killed in a car accident, and she couldn't see the point of criticising them from afar. It only opened up old wounds, and anyway wasn't there always a feeling of opposition between generations in their attitudes to child-rearing?

'We must both dash. Let me know, won't you, when there's any news of Florence?'

'I will.'

'See you on Sunday, usual time. I'll be able to introduce you as a grandmother. You can sit in a corner nodding your old grey head wisely over your knitting and saying you can't eat rich food.'

'Grandmothers aren't like that any more. Nowadays they wear ankle chains and short skirts, and pick up toyboys when they go abroad on holiday.'

'Is this what you plan? Has anyone warned Enzo? Give my love to Tommy, the dear old smack-head.' And she was gone.

* * *

21

Cedar Lodge was a self-important-looking country house set behind a park-like wall on the edge of the town where Jane and Enzo lived. It was the sort of red stone Edwardian building that sprouted towers and decorative gables, built by a Midland industrialist to demonstrate his newly acquired fortune, and to distance himself from the factory chimneys and mean streets of the city wherein it was amassed. A new conservatory now stuck out at the front, in which an assortment of old people slept in armchairs amongst dried-out potted plants.

The house wore an air of disappointment, as if it expected better things than conversion to a residential home for the elderly, and the atmosphere reminded Jane of *The Sleeping Beauty*, as if time had somehow been arrested, although, in this case, not the ageing process. It was an absence of hope that collected in the heavy, soporifically warm rooms.

The carers, in their semi-medical uniforms, moved about with an air of tranquillity and calm. Nothing happened very fast, of course, when even with an arm or walking stick to lean on, the top speed achieved by the most agile of the residents was a shuffling creep. It was as if a slow-motion button had been pushed, and the home was one of the few places where Jane felt herself wind down.

This is what life amounts to, she often thought. You worry and fret about the things that seem so important, and all the time you are heading towards this—just a state of being, when not much matters any more. In her case, she might like to believe that fifty was the new forty, but eighty-eight or ninety was not the new anything. However, she

22

sometimes felt a certain longing to be parked in an armchair with her hands in her lap, waiting for lunch, with nothing whatever expected of her.

This morning she found Aunt Joan in the smaller of the drawing rooms, sitting bolt upright in one of a circle of armchairs, each with a protective pad on the seat. Her iron-grey hair was fastened back on either side of her long gloomy face with combs, and she was dressed oddly in a floral summer skirt worn with heavy brown tights. Her legs had grown stout in old age, with thickened ankles and feet pushed into modern-looking Velcro-fastened shoes. Her cardigan and blouse were recognisably her own, exactly what she would always have worn as a high-ranking secretary in the Home Office. She was peering at the crossword on the back page of the newspaper she held in her hand, and she looked up as Jane dropped a kiss on to her head.

'Oh, good morning, Jane. What are you doing here? Don't you have work to go to?' This was fairly typical of the level of welcome to be expected, usually with something of a reproach thrown in.

'I'm on my way. I thought I would call in as I went past because it's a special day. Flo is having her baby today! The next time you see me, I will be a grandmother!'

Aunt Joan looked at her beadily. 'A baby? Whatever does she want a baby for? Isn't she too old? And she's not married, as far as I am aware.'

She spoke as if Flo's pregnancy was news to her, while the truth was that Jane had told her months ago and spoke of it at almost every visit. Acting as if surprised every time it was mentioned meant that Aunt Joan could get far more mileage out of her unfavourable reaction. She was like a dog returning time and again to a juicy bone.

'Being married isn't a consideration these days,' said Jane lightly. 'Florence is thirty-five, you know. She thinks it's time to start a family. Her biological clock is ticking away. I imagine she felt it was now or never.'

'What's wrong with "never", I should like to know,' sniffed Joan. 'In my day, "never" was considered appropriate if one was single. Hasn't she been trained for years to look after other people's children? Why can't she be satisfied with that?' She kicked out her feet impatiently as if she was personally affronted.

Jane reached into her bag for the striped packet of pick-and-mix sweets she usually brought with her. Going to see Aunt Joan was like visiting a bad-tempered horse and feeding it sugar lumps in order to be allowed to stroke its nose. But why shouldn't she be crabby? Why shouldn't old age relieve you of the tedious obligation of being nice all the time? Not that Aunt Joan had ever made much effort to be unnecessarily pleasant. She took some pride in having been thought of as a 'terror' amongst the other secretaries and typists in her department. Not suffering fools gladly had been a source of satisfaction to her all her life.

'Here you are,' Jane said, passing over the bag of sweets. 'All your favourites. I chose them specially.' She watched the old face light up with greedy pleasure, like that of a very ancient child. She would keep off the subject of the baby for the time being, but then Jane heard herself saying, unwisely, 'Did I tell you that Flo knows that she's having a boy? She's going to call him Tintin.'

'What?' barked Joan, and Jane had to repeat the whole remark in a louder voice, which she regretted. How silly it sounded. She glanced anxiously at the two other old people sitting in adjacent chairs. One was fast asleep with a large blue teddy bear clasped on her lap, and the other elderly lady was poring over the pages of a tattered copy of the *Racing Post*.

'Timothy? Did you say Timothy?'

Jane nodded feebly. She felt she didn't have the stamina to spell out the absurd real name.

'After your father, I suppose, although why Florence should ever want to call a child of hers after *him* is hard to imagine!'

Oh dear, thought Jane, but it was too late, she had set Joan off on one of her specialist subjects—the shortcomings of her long-deceased sister and brother-in-law. Of course, she did have a point, given that Jane's father had done everything he could to pressurise Jane into having an abortion when she was pregnant with Florence, and had provided little support after she was born. If he had had his way she would have been adopted at birth.

It was Aunt Joan who had stepped in to help Jane, both financially and in providing her with somewhere to live. For the last six months of her pregnancy she had stayed in London, in the spare room of Joan's Marylebone garden flat. Aunt Joan put a jelly baby into her mouth and Jane caught a glimpse of the little pink body chomped by long tawny teeth.

'It was shameful,' Joan suddenly said in a loud voice. 'Shameful the way your parents treated you.

Anyone could see you had made a terrible mistake and that you weren't a bad, immoral sort of girl. They were selfish parents, Timothy and Eileen, and I say that even though Eileen was my only sister. Far too wrapped up in themselves to take a proper interest in you and Natasha. Oh, yes, you had everything you wanted, but that's not what I mean. People should be prepared to make sacrifices if they choose to have children, and they never did that.

'Eileen always treated you as if you were an inconvenience. Oh, Natasha was all right because she was headstrong and went her own way, but it was hard on you. When they were killed, on that road in the South of France, I always felt that they should never have been there. Off on holiday on their own in that sports car, like a pair of lovers, even though they were in their fifties.' She spoke with scorn and contempt.

It's what you have never had, thought Jane, looking at her aunt's cross, ugly old face. Aunt Joan didn't know what it was like to be utterly engrossed in someone else, as Jane's mother had been in her handsome, vain father.

'Tash and I never had anything to complain about,' she said stoutly. 'They were very good parents in lots of ways, and my getting pregnant was their worst nightmare. I let them down terribly. But it was all so long ago, and we've done all right, haven't we, Tash and I? We've got lovely families of our own. And I had you when I needed someone.' She took one of Joan's hands and squeezed it warmly. 'You know that I'll always be so grateful for how kind you were.'

It was Joan's turn to brush away at the

conversation with an impatient gesture. 'Don't be silly. I couldn't see them turn their backs on you as they did and have you turfed out onto the street. I was in a position to help and you were so young, still a child . . .' An expression resembling fondness crossed her face. In old age there had come about a softening of the iron control that had prevented displays of emotion throughout her adult life.

They sat in silence for a moment, each with her own memories.

It's strange, thought Jane, that Florence giving birth should bring the past back to us all, the awful time when I got into trouble, as they called it in those days. For years and years I haven't thought about it, and now I can think of little else.

'I must go,' she said, consulting her watch. 'Sir Tommy will be wondering where I've got to.'

Joan leaned forward to speak in a confidential tone. 'Before you go, Jane, dear, they've asked me to return to work, you know,' she said. 'To run the department. It's gone to pieces since I retired. Ministerial leaks and scandals, mismanagement of resources, inappropriate use of stationery. The list goes on and on.'

'And are you going to accept?' asked Jane, getting up and smoothing out her skirt.

This was another of her aunt's favourite subjects on which her mind seemed to dwell with increasing frequency as she got older and more muddled. Joan made a satisfied face, pulling down her mouth in a circular motion. It would only require a passing member of staff to fasten a nosebag round her ears to complete the picture of an ancient horse put out to rest. 'I am considering it,' she said. 'Although, of course, I don't know how they would manage without me here.'

'No, neither do I,' said Jane, leaning forward to kiss the hairy old cheek. She glanced at the crossword in her aunt's lap and noticed that the puzzle was nearly completed. 'Eight down,' she read. 'Tart ingredient, tame recipe? (9).' In wobbly letters Joan had written 'MINCEMEAT'.

*   *   *

As Jane drove away, her aunt's remarks about her parents went round in her mind. Even though what Joan had said was partly true, she did not find it in her heart to blame them for anything very much. She could see now that they had always been as kind and as loving as their particular personalities, and the nature of their own relationship, had allowed. As a middle-aged adult herself, exactly the same age as her mother, in fact, when she had died on a twisting French Riviera road, she felt that she had a better understanding of their marriage. She could see that at the heart of it was her mother's desperate need to preserve and defend her relationship with her husband against all comers, which included her children.

When they were small she passed Jane and Tash into the care of village girls and au pairs—she would not have wished for the intrusion of a full-time nanny. In today's climate of overindulgent childcare, when babies seemed to have turned into mini-dictators and to have their parents totally under their thumbs, it seemed a peculiar way to bring up children, but back then it was not unusual. Jane couldn't remember ever feeling that she was brought up any differently from most of her friends

28

from the same sort of middle-class background. She knew boys from perfectly satisfactory families who were sent to boarding school at seven years old, and other parents who left their children at home when they went away on adult holidays. Children usually ate in the kitchen with the domestic help and hardly ever entered the drawing room without permission. It was as if childhood was a parallel but separate existence, which only at designated times interacted with the adult world of their parents. It was not until they were teenagers, almost adult social beings, that the boundaries started to dissolve.

The problem with her mother, Jane thought, and what made her different from other mothers—and which in retrospect she could see coloured their growing-up—was that Timothy, their father, loved having daughters, and Tash and Jane were attractive enough to gain his attention. Their mother did what she could to prevent this happening as if in any way it might threaten to displace her as the number one female in his life. It was as if she believed that his love was of a finite quantity, which if expended in one place would run thin in another—if he was interested in them, then he was less interested in her. If he complimented Tash on her long coltish legs in a tiny miniskirt, her mother took it as a slight, or an implied criticism of how she looked.

Jane realised now that the sudden explosion of sexy youth in the sixties came at exactly the wrong time for her mother, when she must have been anxious about losing her own good looks. She certainly wouldn't have been able to compete with Tash, with her skintight jeans and ironed-straight hair and eyes outlined in thick black kohl, and she did everything she could to stop her blossoming into the head-turning beauty that she would inevitably become. From puberty on, Eileen and her elder daughter were at war.

Did she realise what she was doing, Jane wondered, and thought that probably she did not. Self-knowledge was not one of her mother's strengths, and no doubt she told herself that the battles she fought over what Tash should wear were in some way for her own good. It wasn't 'appropriate' for a young girl to look so openly sexual and challenging. It wasn't safe to attract the attention of men. She would have told herself that she was only trying to protect her daughter from a world she was too young to understand. In many ways Jane could sympathise. To an extent it was what every mother of a teenage daughter would feel.

But she could see now why Tash's teenage friends were made to feel unwelcome when they came to the house to try on the tiny corduroy miniskirts that Tash was already running up on her mother's sewing machine. Jane remembered how on Saturday mornings her father was about, laughing and teasing and calling them into the sitting room to show him how they looked. He sat in an armchair, smoking, his long legs crossed, with the newspaper on his lap. She could picture him wearing a check shirt because it was the weekend, with a cravat tied round his neck and his brown hair smoothed straight back. Tash's friends would blush and giggle and push at one another and then run shrieking back upstairs to lie on Tash's bed and lift their thin arms over their heads and say,

'Your dad's really super! He's so handsome, he looks like Gregory Peck!'

Jane, usually reading in her own room across the landing with the door open, would sense that the atmosphere in the house was charged with something she could not explain or identify, like a current of electricity. The older girls felt it too, tossing their long hair, and flashing their eyes, and talking in high, light voices while their sideways looks glanced off each other and sought something out of sight.

It wasn't long before Tash was told by her mother that while her friends could come on week-night evenings, they were not to come to the house on Saturday mornings because 'it's not fair on Daddy when he's at work all the week to have his home taken over at weekends'. Jane could remember quite clearly the row that followed, the shouting and banging doors and Tash screaming, 'OK, you'll drive me away, then? Is that what you want?' If her father had been present she would have turned to him imploringly and he would have made a face and shrugged his shoulders. Like a small boy he didn't like to be in trouble with their mother. It was easier to agree. But of course this row would never have taken place in front of him because that would have been to draw the battle lines out in the open and their mother was much too subtle an operator for that.

Oh, yes, Jane could see it clearly now and understood why the visits had to stop. Her father enjoyed them, that was why. He enjoyed them a bit too much.

Jane at the same age was a different proposition. She was rather a plodding, secretive

31

teenager and certainly didn't have the stylish friends that might have caught her father's eye. With her it was his interest in her education that had to be deflected. If he spent too much time talking about history or helping her with a project on something he was particularly interested in, like the D-Day landings or the British in India, her mother would find a reason to make them move from where they were sitting, or demand attention in some distracting way, or even, quite blatantly, say something like, 'It makes me feel so stupid and ill-informed, hearing you talk like that. My parents, you see, didn't believe in educating girls. That is why I was so determined that you should have the chances that were denied to me. You and Tash have been so blessed, having parents willing to make sacrifices for you.'

'I don't know how you can talk of your husband like that,' she once reprimanded a newly married Tash, who was complaining about Denby. 'I have never once criticised your father, and do you know why? Because I thank God every single day of my life that I still have him. If you had gone through the war, as we did, when we knew that every time we said goodbye it could be for ever, you would be the same. That is, if you love Denby as I love Daddy.' Her tone said that she doubted it.

Aunt Joan was right when she said that their parents behaved like lovers and made little effort to adjust their relationship to include their children. But Jane couldn't blame them for how they were, because they were kind and dutiful in other ways, and her mother was conscientious about bringing them up properly and seeing they had what she termed 'a good start'. In fact, if any

32

blame was to be attached to anyone, it was to her, the daughter, who was stupid enough to get pregnant at eighteen. She was the one who had wrecked her mother's hopes.

CHAPTER TWO

It was supposed to be the Swinging Sixties, when young people made love, not war, and wafted about wearing caftans in a cloud of dope, but don't you believe it, thought Jane, it wasn't all like that, not in her family, and not in the semi-rural West Midlands.

After the war and before Jane was born, her father, Timothy Kindersley, had come out of the army and taken up the position that had been waiting for him as sales director of the small, family-owned steel foundry in West Bromwich. As the country struggled to get back on its feet, the foundry was under contract to make components for the burgeoning Midland car industry. With financial help from his father, he bought a handsome red-brick Georgian house on the High Street of a large village on the edge of Wolverhampton. Here he was sufficiently distanced from the foundry for his new wife, Eileen, fresh from the southern Home Counties, to be able to dissociate herself from the grimy source of their wealth, but close enough for him to motor into his office at a leisurely nine thirty each day.

During Jane's childhood the directors of the company rewarded themselves generously, and at the same time there were suddenly things to buy in the shops, undreamed of by earlier generations, and miraculous after the austerity of the war and its immediate aftermath. Eileen Kindersley, who had a good eye for colour and style, set to work to spend, and furnished the family home with pale, fitted Axminster carpets and interlined glazed chintz curtains and polished inherited furniture. She made weekly trips, wearing hat and gloves, to a newly revamped department store in Birmingham, returning home with glossy carrier bags of her purchases. The larger items would be delivered next day by one of the store's own fleet of vans.

The weekly grocery order was brought to the back door in a cardboard box and the meat from the village butcher was delivered by a boy on a bicycle with a basket on the front. There was a daily cleaning woman and a gardener, and Timothy drove a Jaguar, and Eileen, a sporty Triumph Herald. They played bridge and belonged to a golf club, and drank pink gin and opened a bottle of wine at lunchtime on a Sunday.

Upward social mobility became the aim and purpose of Mrs Kindersley's existence, and she took the trouble to understand exactly what was needed to propel her daughters into the upper middle classes, whom she aped and admired, and on whom the ravages of the war and loss of traditional incomes had forced a broadening of entry qualifications. If a pretty girl from a well-off middle-class family was given the chance to meet the right people, there was nothing to stop her marrying considerably above herself.

Two years older than Jane, Tash was destined to pioneer this campaign, but by the mid-sixties she was far from malleable material and had already devoted herself to exploring all that the new decade had to offer. It was hard to see from where she had got this inspiration, given the Kindersley girls' careful and protected upbringing, but she set about her rebellion with the tactics of a guerrilla fighter. Naughty and self-willed at school, she was only interested in art and pop music and fashion, and refused, at seventeen, to go to be 'finished' at Winkfield Place in Berkshire. Her mother, who did her research thoroughly, had discovered that smart, dim girls with no O levels were sent there, on residential courses, to learn cookery, deportment and etiquette, and to meet other girls' eligible brothers, before being released as finished products on the marriage market.

Eileen Kindersley saw sending Tash away as her chance to wean her from her 'ordinary', provincial friends, rid her of her deliberately cultivated Midlands accent, and show her what it took to attract the right sort of young man. It was the first step towards being photographed for *Country Life* wearing a string of pearls and a smug expression, having successfully hitched herself to some junior cavalry officer from a solid family with a double-barrelled surname.

Tash was having none of it. She was too bright, and despite her lack of application passed too many exams, and in her last year at school she appeared to be concentrating on a future career as a streetwalker. She grew her hair long, dyed it buttercup yellow and ironed it dead straight under a piece of brown paper spread on the ironing board. She wore her school skirt so short you could see her knickers when she bent over, and long boots and skinny-rib jumpers, her green school

35

raincoat rolled up in her duffel bag. When she and Jane stood at the bus stop together in the mornings on their way to the private girls' school they attended in Tettenhall, one of the posher suburbs of Wolverhampton, male drivers tooted and waved, and she gave them the finger in return. At weekends she wore jeans so tight that she couldn't bend in the middle and which cut her neat little bottom into two separated orbs. She wore a defiant donkey jacket covered in CND badges and associated with beatniks, hippies and peace marchers, declared she was an atheist and would no longer be accompanying the family to church— surely a good thing, thought Jane, looking as she did. She started going out with an astonishingly handsome and virtually inarticulate farmworker called Alan, and sat outside the house snogging him in his old van in full view of passers-by on the village High Street.

Then, one day, with her eyes blacked out in kohl, and with her splashy, colourful artwork in an enormous portfolio, she caught the train south and was successfully interviewed for a place at the London College of Fashion.

Her parents let her go with only a show of resistance. She might have wrecked her mother's plans for her, but she was so aggravating to have at home that it could only have been a relief to have her out of the way. They agreed that she could take up her place provided that she stayed, as a paying guest, with a 'nice' family her mother knew of in Richmond.

Off Tash went with her psychedelic clothes thrown into a trunk decorated with giant daisies, wearing a huge black floppy hat, and smoking a

36

Gauloise cigarette for effect. Her sense of style was already set and was defined by being as far as possible from that of her mother, who favoured neat dress and jacket ensembles bought at Aquascutum, summer shirtwaisters and petal hats, all worn with a double string of cultured pearls.

Within a few weeks, Tash had met up with four other girl students and was living in a flat above a shoe shop on the King's Road, then the centre of Swinging London, thus contravening all her parents' rules and conditions, and making the final break with home.

Jane, left behind, plodded on at school and dreamed of escape. Although she was banned from reading *Honey* or *Jackie*, the new teenage magazines aimed at her age group, with their pages full of romance and fashion and advice on boyfriends, she was not unaware of what was going on in London, but it all seemed as far removed from her life as if it had been taking place in Outer Mongolia. Most of the girls incarcerated in the sixth form at her school were the same, and hardly different from their mothers in outlook. The teenager was a fairly recent invention and an American one at that, and parents in general were opposed to everything that the term came to represent—politically radical, sexually wanton and work shy. They did what they could to keep their daughters well away from rebellious teen culture and contamination by what they saw as a dangerous breakdown in solid, middle-class, Christian values. They disapproved of the current loud, clashing, anarchic music with suggestive lyrics; the provocative, uninhibited, dancing; the white lips and sooty eyes of the insolent-looking

37

girls in their tiny skirts, and their exaggerated, backcombed hairstyles; worst of all, the sexual freedom that they believed would come with the Pill.

The Pill? The newspapers were full of the effect it would have on the nation's morals, but where was it to be found? How did you get it? Stuck in a village where the chemist's counter was manned by an elderly man in a white coat, who made buying make-up or sanitary products pure embarrassment, Jane had no idea. She had learned from a plump, promiscuous girl in her year called Paula James, who had already gone all the way with her spotty boyfriend from the secondary modern school, that boys had to take responsibility for birth control and should wear a rubber. A rubber? Where? In their trouser pocket? What difference could that possibly make? Jane was truly mystified. Other sorts of birth control were only available through family doctors, and only for married women, as far as she knew.

Of course she understood about reproduction— for that was how sex was taught—and she had drawn neat cross sections of the male and female reproductive organs, copied from the blackboard drawings of Miss Maws, the biology teacher. Any discussion was out of the question. Miss Maws was at least seventy, in the view of Jane and her classmates. She had white hair in a round bun and wore thick lisle stockings and polished brown lace-ups. Any girl caught wearing nail varnish was sent to her to be dealt with. Armed with a wodge of cotton wool and a bottle of acetone, she rubbed at each offending fingernail, her face contorted with distaste into an expression that said, 'So you are *that sort of cheap girl!'*

Miss Maws' carefully labelled diagrams bore no resemblance whatever to anything Jane was ever to come across in real life, and the mechanics of sex remained a mystery. Inserting a Tampax was difficult enough, squatting in the lavatory cubicle at school, white cardboard tube in her hand, studying the instruction diagram as she poked away between her legs, while her friends spoke words of advice and encouragement from outside the door. Then there was all the anxiety of losing it up there, in the velvety, slippery, seaweed-smelling interior that her mother told her was dirty to touch.

The Swinging Sixties might have been rampaging elsewhere but until she was seventeen Jane continued to play hockey and tennis, wear the ghastly school uniform with its absurd tricorn hat and hideous coat, do her homework, go to church with her parents, and dream of getting married and having a home of her own. The most rebellious things she ever did were to smoke on the bus on the way home from school and get reported to the headmistress by some busybody informant, and to roll over the waistband of her bottle-green uniform skirt until the hem arrived at a few inches above her knees. Otherwise, she managed to by-pass the whole decade and what it stood for: drugs and sex and easy living.

She explored the new teenage shops with her friends on Saturday mornings, especially a boutique in Wolverhampton called FabGear, where pop music poured out of the op art-painted shop front, and the department store where her mother sometimes shopped opened a section for teenagers called Birdcage. Although she enjoyed the Beatles and the Rolling Stones, and dancing at parties where girls outnumbered boys and the fruit punch was made more exciting with ginger ale, it was all mild and unrebellious stuff. Screaming at pop concerts, buying the *New Musical Express*, watching *Top of the Pops* to pick up the latest dance craze from the Go-Jos didn't interest her. Unless you went looking for it, it was perfectly possible to remain more or less unaffected by the explosion of youth culture.

She did want a boyfriend, though. It seemed to Jane that it would be wonderful to have someone love her in a romantic way, to write her sonnets, and admire and compliment her on her prettiness and brains. Having felt so very ordinary—with a sister like Tash that was easy—she longed for someone to find her special.

Other girls at school managed to acquire boys. They found them through their brothers, at parties, or the Pony Club, or because they were sons of friends of their parents. These were ordinary, unremarkable girls, unlike scandalous Paula, who was in a league of her own in terms of sexual experience, and was anyway considered common because her father was in trade, the owner of a garage in Wolverhampton. They came to school on Monday mornings bursting with the news of what had befallen them at the weekend, because the course of true love was inevitably full of rollercoaster ups and downs. Misty-eyed and dreamy, or bursting into storms of heartbroken tears, they reported the delicious agonies of being in love. Some secretly showed off the livid love bites on their necks, or discussed in whispering

40

corners exactly how far they should let their boyfriends go because, of course, sex itself was not an innovation. These girls, however, had every intention of preserving their virginity for marriage. It was what was expected of them and they had all been warned by their mothers that boys could not be trusted in this department because their urges were uncontrollable. It was the duty of girls to be sensible and good. 'Getting into trouble' was the worst possible fate for a nicely brought-up girl, and even those who had only allowed their boyfriends to undo their bra straps and feel their breasts worried themselves sick if 'the curse' was a few days late.

What kept them in line was a mix of fear, Christian teaching, ethical mumbo jumbo, and social and parental pressure. But it only took a strong-minded and brave girl like Tash to knock this aside and do what she pleased amongst other more liberated young people who were busy exploring new freedoms themselves.

It didn't seem like that to Jane, who felt the whole burden of her parents' expectations, and weighed down by her sense of duty. She was starting to hate school and to feel miserable at home. Without Tash to liven things up, and keep her company, she felt lonely and isolated. If only she had a real, live boyfriend, she could escape the stultifying boredom of school and weekends at home.

Twice she went to see Tash in London, who was now living in a squat with Denby. Jane could almost have fallen in love with him herself, with his immaculate velvet suits and flowing Byronic hair. Instead she lay on her bed and read novels, huge

41

sweeping romances of the Napoleonic era, Thomas Hardy, Jane Austen, and dreamed of love. In these fantasies the male role was not taken by the sort of boys she knew, like gangly Hugh Bywater, who lived next door, or the sullen, self-conscious brothers of her friends, but older, experienced men, who swept her off her feet with their charm and sophistication; men like Simon Templar from *The Saint*, which was one of her favourite television programmes.

'Why don't you *do* something?' her mother complained, standing at the bedroom door, hands on hips. She didn't count Jane's reading or revising for her A levels as an activity. 'Don't you have any friends? Why don't you go to the cinema? Or join a badminton club? Or make a cake for Sunday tea, if you don't want to go out? I've never known such an apathetic girl as you. You won't meet people, or get asked to things, you know, lolling about on your bed like that.'

Jane closed her eyes to shut out her mother's presence. Leave me alone, she pleaded in her head. 'Perhaps I'm ill,' she offered. 'Perhaps I've got a debilitating wasting disease, or something.'

'Don't be silly! Although I suppose you could possibly have glandular fever. Maybe I should make you an appointment to see Dr Chamberlain.'

'I was joking,' said Jane. 'I feel perfectly all right. Please, just leave me alone.' She closed her eyes again. Her mother went to the window and twitched the curtains in irritation—blue striped cotton, the design she had chosen to look fresh and pretty in a popular girl's room that would be the envy of all her friends, with its white paintwork and yellow candlewick bedspread.

'Well, if you're not ill, you must get up and come downstairs and find something to do. It's not normal to spend so much time on your own at your age. When I was seventeen I was out all the time, at the tennis club or Young Conservatives, or bicycling with my friends. You have to make an *effort*, you know, to be popular. No one likes a droopy, dull girl with nothing to say for herself.'

'What's the point? I'll be going to teacher training college in a few months. I'll be forced to meet new people then.'

'Oh, really, Jane! You are the most maddening girl. I don't know where I went wrong with you and Tash. You're both equally aggravating. There's you, who behaves like a recluse and won't go anywhere or do anything, and Tash, who couldn't be kept in at any price, and goodness knows where she got to, or who with. How could you be so different?'

Jane didn't know. 'Perhaps one of us was swapped in the hospital at birth?' she suggested.

'Oh, don't be so irritating!' snapped her mother. 'Hugh's at home from school,' she added, looking out of the window towards their neighbours' house. 'I saw his mother this morning. He's got study leave or something before his A levels begin. Why don't you call round and see him? Ask him to lunch, if you like. Go for a walk, or get him to take you out for a drive.'

'You've just said he's supposed to be revising,' Jane pointed out, more to annoy than anything else.

'He can't work all the time, can he?' Knowing Hugh, Jane thought it was highly unlikely he would be working at all, but she could see there was no

43

escape. Her mother was relentless. Jane swung her legs off the bed and stood up. She really did feel tired and thick-headed and her limbs seemed too heavy to lift. Maybe she was ill after all, or maybe it was just the leaden weight of chronic boredom.

'OK, OK,' she said.

'Don't OK me in that tone of voice,' her mother snapped.

'OK.'

She slumped downstairs behind her mother, who was wearing a close-fitting shirtwaister and sling-back shoes. She had taken to having her hair coloured and it was now a burnished gold and set in a backcombed, stiffened bubble shape around her head. Jane was told, at home and at school, to keep her own thick brown hair off her face, and took to wearing a wide elasticated hairband, which she hoped made her look like Audrey Hepburn, although she could see that with her round face she had some way to go to realise that particular dream.

All right, she would go round to see if Hugh was at home if it would keep her mother quiet. Although he was rude and patronising to her, he was the only boy she could count as a friend because she had known him all her life. They had endured the same terrible dancing classes and been to the same children's parties, where Jane was too shy to speak to anyone, and Hugh fought other little boys, ate too much and was usually sick.

He was the only boy she knew at all, really, because she couldn't count the grammar school boys on the debating team, or the one or two others she met through friends, who had never been remotely interested in her and left her tongue-tied and self-conscious. At least, with Hugh, she felt confident enough to be herself.

Nevertheless, before she went she put on some mascara, spitting onto the solid dark brown block and working it into a paste with the little brush. Her lashes, already long and dark, clogged together in spiky clumps. She squirted herself from her bottle of Elizabeth Arden's Blue Grass, which was currently her favourite scent. Hugh might not be romantic material but he was still a boy and these days grown tall and shaggy and more mysterious. A bit of effort had to be made.

The house next door was set back down a semi-circular drive and behind a high red-brick wall. It was an imposing house, calling itself Foreland Lodge, and Hugh and his three older brothers lived there between school and university terms with their solicitor father and doctor mother. Dr Diana Bywater was one of the very few mothers that Jane knew who actually worked and didn't have a rest on her bed after lunch to listen to *Woman's Hour*, or have her hair washed and set once a week and dried on little rollers under a freestanding, dome-shaped dryer, in a row of other women, leafing through magazines or having their nails manicured. Instead, she was brisk and energetic and had wild, wiry grey hair cut short and square. She was a full-time partner in a practice in Wolverhampton—darkest Wolverhampton, Jane's mother called it—where nearly all her patients were West Indian or Pakistani. As a result her house was neglected and chaotic, wondrously untidy, and provided Jane with a fascinating glimpse into an alternative way of life.

This afternoon, Hugh answered the door. He

45

was barefoot and wearing a pair of wide bell-bottom jeans and a T-shirt, and eating a slice of toast. He was so tall and thin that his chest seemed to cave inwards and the points of his elbows were as sharp as knives. His shaggy hair hung in his eyes although the back was shorter, as a nod to his boarding school rule regarding length of hair and back of collar. This was the most rebellious style his housemaster would let him get away with. Infringements of hair regulations generally took up a great deal of time and energy, it seemed to Jane.

'Hello,' he said. 'I'm having breakfast. Are you coming in?'

'Yes, please. Mummy said you were at home.' She followed him through the stoneflagged hall, in which the table under a large, elegant mirror was laden with a collection of books, keys, a hairbrush, gardening gloves, secateurs, seed catalogues and hats of various types. The floor under the table continued the theme of carelessly discarded possessions, which one day someone would shout about losing.

'What's the matter with you?' Hugh asked, leading the way into the kitchen, which was in a state of untidiness that Jane still found astonishing. It would have been hard to find the space on the kitchen table in which to put down a teacup.

'What do you mean, matter?'

'You look awful. Hideous clothes as usual. You can't think those trousers with those elastic stirrup things are trendy? And why is your hair scraped back like that? It looks very peculiar.'

'Oh, shut up! I don't care about trendy. Anyway, why should I tart myself up for you? I *am* quite miserable, actually, or more fed-up. My mother

46

sent me round here because she wants me to be out having a super time all the time.'

'What's wrong with that? Mine's the opposite. She wants to keep me under lock and key because of revising for bloody A levels.'

'And mine's always telling me I work too hard. And you should hear the sort of thing she wants me to be doing! Badminton club! Young Conservatives! She doesn't get it that I'd rather be on my own than forced to be sociable.'

'Oh, dear me. You're not exactly Miss Congeniality, are you? You can come to the flicks with Jem and me, if you like.' Hugh tipped a striped cat off the kitchen table and started to hack at a loaf to toast on the Aga. Jem was his best friend who lived a few miles away. They had been at nursery school together and had homed in on one another from the first day their mothers had dumped them there. *'Tom Jones* is still on. It's got to be my favourite film ever. I've seen it twice already.'

'I don't think I should. I've got an essay to write.'

'Well, don't then. I don't care. You're boring anyway.' They bickered on like this in an amiable way. 'Fucking exams,' observed Hugh, spreading honey on his toast with a dirty knife he fished out of the sink. 'It's too fucking boring at home on my own. I just stay in bed all day.'

Was it true, Jane thought, or just boasting? Exams so terrified her that she worked terribly hard, stayed up most of the night revising; most girls did, as far as she could tell, although Tash had been an exception, as she was in most things.

'Have you decided what you're going to do when

47

they're over? When you leave school.'

'I'm going to France for two months with Jem—picking grapes and things. Getting stoned, one hopes. Then, if I scrape two As and a B I'm going to UCH. What about you?'

'I don't know. Mummy wants me to do a typing course in Wolverhampton for a few weeks in the summer holidays. She says I should have a skill, as if I was handicapped or something. Like weaving baskets or making those crinoline lady lavatory-roll holders. After that I might go away somewhere, if I get around to organising it. Eurorailing, I suppose. Some girls at school are going to Italy for a few weeks and I could join them. Mummy and Daddy are off on a cruise and Mummy doesn't want me hanging about here while they're away. Then I go to teacher training college in Cambridge, if I get the grades, which I won't. I know I won't.'

'Of course you will. You're too swotty by half,' said Hugh. 'It's not a good thing in a girl, but I suppose you can't help it. It goes with being so boring.' He lifted an arm as if to fend off an expected attack.

'You are foul. I feel bad enough about myself without you saying things like that.' Jane leaned on the counter and watched Hugh eating. 'Do you feel like I do?' she asked him thoughtfully. 'As if you are waiting for proper life to start because this can be all there is? No, I don't think you do. You're like Tash, sailing on, not bothering about what you get told is right for you to do.'

'Haven't you noticed that four out of six in this family are doctors, or training to be, and I am about to be the fifth, if I pull myself together as The Grunt says?' The Grunt was Hugh's housemaster. 'What's that if it's not conditioning? I'm only doing medicine because I'm marginally less bad at science and it saves me from having to think of anything else I want to do. I can't imagine ever being a doctor. I loathe children and old people. I'll want to give them fatal injections all the time.'

Jane considered this alarming piece of information.

'However did you get through the interview? Isn't the selection process supposed to weed out lying psychopaths?'

'Oh, I can do the spiel,' said Hugh airily. 'I knew what the interviewers wanted to hear, and it makes a huge difference that my mother trained at UCH. They love that "generations of doctors in one family" garbage. I fooled them with my pretended sense of vocation.'

'Don't you feel bad about that? About having to pretend.'

'I'd have to pretend about wanting to do anything.'

'That's exactly how I feel. How are we supposed to know what we want to do with the rest of our lives? I hate school but I'm not looking forward to going to college either. I'm only being a teacher because I can't think of anything else to be. Everything is, you've got to do this, or be like this, so that you can get to do this or be that, so that eventually, if you're good and lucky and work hard, you can do something else. I can't see an end to it. When do you get to the point where you arrive at wherever it is, doing or being what you want, when it all makes sense and you suddenly think, this is it. This is what life is for?'

'Oh, dear me!' said Hugh in a loud, army major sort of voice. 'Typical teenager! Confused, lack of direction, low motivation. Bring back National Service, I say. Have you got a boyfriend yet?' he asked in his normal voice. 'Oh, don't bother to answer. One look at you tells me all I need to know. You're still on the shelf.'

'I don't want one, thank you,' Jane lied.

'Oh, yes you do. You're desperate, I'd say. If you were more beautiful I might consider going out with you, but you're not, so that's that. I'm not one for charitable acts. You're useless, actually. You are one of the few girls I really know, but you don't even introduce me to your sexy friends.'

'If I had any, they wouldn't look at you.'

'Why not? I'm terrifically attractive to the opposite sex.'

'What makes you think so?'

'Because girls are always queuing up to enjoy my body. Everywhere I go.'

Jane laughed. Hugh was weird-looking, with his long thin face and his John Lennon glasses, and rather spotty this morning, and not dreamy boyfriend material at all.

'So, describe your ideal girl,' said Jane. Talking to Hugh was always useful as an information-gathering exercise.

'Julie Christie or Susannah York. Tall, blonde, leggy and posh. Not too much to ask, is it?'

'They're so obvious,' said Jane. 'What about Jane Birkin?'

'Oh, no. Too thin and goofy-looking for my taste. Come on,' he said, slinging plate and knife in the sink. 'Go and take off those appalling trousers and come to the flicks with Jem and me. He's picking me up in half an hour. It'll cheer you up to be seen out with the two heart-throbs of the West Midlands and it will give your mother hope that you might not be a social misfit after all.'

'OK,' said Jane, laughing. 'Thanks, Hugh. You're so horrible and rude, but you always cheer me up. My mother will be pleased too.'

'That's the whole point of me,' said Hugh. 'To be a little ray of sunshine in the lives of the less fortunate.'

It *was* the point of him, and was the main reason that it was Hugh whom Jane telephoned seven months later to tell him she was pregnant. She fed coins into a public call box on a rainy Cambridge street corner while from the other end of the line she heard young male voices in his hall of residence shouting for him to come to the telephone.

'Jane?' he said, sounding as if he had just woken up. 'What do you want?'

'I'm pregnant,' she said in a small expressionless voice. The momentous words seemed to drift on a white cloud of her breath above her head. He was the first person she had told, other than two of the girls she had made friends with in her college.

'You can't be. Not you, of all people. Immaculate conception springs to mind!' His voice was light and jokey. Slowly it dawned on him that she was serious. 'Shit! Are you sure? It's easy to get it wrong, isn't it? Those kit things aren't that reliable.'

'I'm sure. I've done the test three times.'

'Holy Moley! What are you going to do?'

'I don't know.'

'You can have an abortion, you know. It can be

51

arranged.'

'I don't know where or how. I haven't that kind of money either.'

'I can find out. Doesn't Tash know how it's done? She must do.'

'She's in India. She's there for a year. I can't contact her except by letter, which takes about six weeks.'

'Shit! I assume you haven't told your parents?'

'No. I've only just found out. I'm only two months gone.'

'I imagine that they're not going to be very thrilled. What does the boyfriend say?'

'I haven't got a boyfriend.'

'What? Have you been dumped?'

'Not exactly. I don't know who he is, you see. I can't remember much about him. One of my friends has made some enquiries because her boyfriend is at the same college, but it turns out nobody can be sure exactly who was there, at the party thing I went to. No one seems to have heard of him at the college where, you know, it happened.'

'Oh shit! A one-night stand? You're the last person . . . you should have stuck to being a Sunday school teacher, shouldn't you?'

'I know.'

There was a pause. 'I'll have a think. Ask about. Do you want to come to London this weekend? We could talk about it then. You don't sound very hysterical, though. You're not blubbing down the phone or anything.'

'I've thought of killing myself, actually.'

'Don't do that. Too messy.'

'Not as messy as living through this.'

'Heh! Come on.' The pips went and Jane put more coins in the box.

'Thank you,' she said. 'Thank you for asking me to London. I'll get the train. Could I come on Friday evening?'

'Yeah, you do that. I'll see you then. Come to my room. I'll be here after six o'clock. I'll wait for you. And, Jane, cheer up. It could be worse.'

'Could it?'

*   *   *

She put the receiver back on its cradle. The telephone box smelled disgusting and there was an ominous stain glistening on the floor. She pushed the door open and collected her bicycle from where it leaned against the wall of the Catholic church, which stood, sombre and menacing, on the corner of the road, its spire an accusing finger pointing into the sky. It was dark, and a bitter biting wind from the Fens fretted dried leaves and a scatter of litter about her boots. The shops further along towards the city centre were bright with Christmas lights and late shoppers crowded the pavements, well wrapped against the cold. Students, bundled in scarves and coats, cycled slowly past in twos and threes, their heads bent into the wind, the lights of their bicycles wavering faintly.

Jane felt completely detached from her surroundings, from the city and the university, from her college, and her few new friends. Instead she was aware of being absolutely alone, an isolated little figure moving against the tide under the great dark winter sky. She got on her bicycle and pushed away from the kerb, away from the city centre, her feet working hard against the pedals, her thighs straining, her hands gripping the handlebars. She struggled along with the wind against her and felt the cold hitting her cheeks and nose, and the itch of the woollen scarf on her neck. She wished that this moment could go on for ever; bicycling through the night, never arriving, never having to face the mess she was in.

How could this have happened to her? She asked the same question over and over again. The evening had begun innocently enough. She had been persuaded to go to the freshers' party in the second week of her first term by other girls who had rooms on the same corridor in her all-girls college. They had set out for the evening in high spirits, with their freshly washed hair and new short skirts, full of hope and anticipation.

They had arrived too early and had stood in an uncertain little group, ignored by the boys, who must have been equally awkward and self-conscious in their bell-bottom trousers and Chelsea boots, with their hair bushily outgrowing the styles that had been enforced by the schools they had recently left. They laughed and joked and drank from cans of beer, and passed round cigarettes and made no attempt to approach the girls or even look in their direction. When the music began the bolder girls, who knew that they were pretty and that the boys were aware of that fact, began to dance the twist together, and gradually boys joined in and couples started to form.

For a long time, after the dancing began and the lights were turned down, Jane had taken refuge with the other less bold girls in a little gaggle in the kitchen, picking at the French bread, and cocktail sticks of cubes of Cheddar and pineapple. Later they moved to sit on the stairs, singing along to the Monkees and Sandie Shaw, chatting and sharing cigarettes and trying to pretend that they didn't mind that no one wanted to dance with them.

Just when Jane thought that she had never ever spent such a miserable and pointless night in her life, a tall boy with shaggy hair parted in the middle lurched over and asked her to dance. He was already quite drunk and seemed to need her as a support, hanging on to her tightly and drooping over her, his face snuffling at her neck, and then kissing her on the mouth, forcing his tongue between her teeth. It was the first time that she had been kissed like that, and although it was a horrible experience—how could a tongue be so hard and pointy, and his mouth tasted of beer and cigarettes—she was still glad that it was happening to her. She had never been held like that either, so tight that she could feel his hard body grinding against her. The experience was exciting and thrilling, not because it was sexually arousing, not in the least, but because it meant that she had crossed a divide. This was what it was all about; the pop music, the clothes, the hours spent ironing her hair into smooth swinging curtains. To be here in this dark room thick with cigarette smoke, kissing a boy, was the first sure step to gaining membership of the cult of shining youth, to belonging, to being privy to the mysteries of love. She had been rescued from the ranks of the rejects, and for that she was grateful.

Later, when her head was pounding from drink

55

and smoke and the party had disintegrated into couples snogging in heaps in the corners of the dark room, she had said that she had to find the bathroom, and stumbled upstairs. When she came out a few minutes later, the boy was waiting for her on the landing and, putting his arm round her, pulled her into a dark room and pushed her backwards onto an unmade bed heaped with clothes. That's when it happened. It was first of all surprise, followed by not wishing to be rude, that was her undoing. She was too polite to tell him to stop what he appeared to want to do so very urgently. He scrabbled at her clothes, lying heavily across her.

'No!' she said faintly. 'Please, I don't think this is a good idea.' She tried to push him off but his weight held her down and he was groaning in a most alarming way. He's ill, she thought. He's having a heart attack or a fit, or something. He seemed to be entirely unaware of her, lost in a drunken world of his own, as he heaved and shoved. A moment later he collapsed on top of her and she fought to move her head to one side so that she could breathe. He's dead, she thought. Oh God, he's dead.

A moment later, he seemed to recover, and rolled off. He staggered towards the door and fumbled to find the handle, and then ricocheted across the landing into the bathroom from where Jane could hear the sound of him being sick. Hastily, she readjusted her clothing and checked the time. Unless she left immediately she would be late back into college. She tapped lightly on the bathroom door but there was no reply. She hesitated and then went back into the bedroom

56

and turned on the light. The room sprang into all its sordid detail, the rumpled bed, the soiled clothes on the floor, the dirty plates and mugs piled on the table. She scrabbled about in the mess and found a biro and a piece of file paper. 'Had to go,' she wrote, and then added 'Luv you, Jane xxxx' and then her telephone number. She slid it under the bathroom door and ran downstairs to where the party had broken up. The room they had danced in was empty, save for a boy sitting on the floor playing a guitar and a girl weeping in a corner.

Jane collected her bicycle and cycled back to her college through the city streets, minus her virginity, and with a sense of shocked relief. So that was it. That was what all the fuss was about. She would no longer have to pretend that she had a boyfriend because tonight she had acquired the real thing. She wasn't sure of his name but it didn't matter because he had whispered into her smoky hair that he loved her, and it followed that now he would want to take her out on dates and have her round to his room to drink coffee and talk about interesting films and books, and all the other things she imagined boyfriends did. She supposed that they would repeat the sex part, and so she would have to go to the Brook clinic for birth control advice. She had seen leaflets about the Pill lying around in the college common room. It was all perfectly straightforward to be a modern sort of girl.

Of course, she never saw him again. Later on, as the weeks went by, she came to the conclusion that he must have woken up the next morning with the sort of hangover that left only a vague memory of the night before. She was either clean forgotten, or remembered and regretted. By the end of the term, when she knew she was pregnant, she couldn't recall what he looked like and could have passed him in the street without recognising him.

A sense of unfairness and self-pity overwhelmed her. Her foolishness, the inadequacy of the sexual encounter that had brought her to this terrible point in her life, the incidental nature of it all, prevented her from really believing it could be true. It was like doing fractions, the only maths she had ever enjoyed, where one side of the equation had to equal the other. How could her stupidity, a few too many glasses of wine, her reluctance to deny the boy what he wanted because it seemed rude, come to equal pregnancy, a ruined life, an unwanted baby? If she had changed just one thing on one side of the equation—less to drink, or sitting on the stairs with her friends and going home when they did, or not going to the party at all—then it would all be different. Her life would not be ruined. She had read somewhere that 'if only' were the saddest words in the English language, but they were the words that were constantly in her head, since she had found out.

She had done the sums. The baby was due in July, when she would be nineteen years old. A teenage mother. A tart, a slut, a bad girl. If she cycled until her heart thumped, or jumped off the stairs, or drank gin or took scalding baths, maybe she could dislodge the egg that had taken root and was growing inside her. Maybe Hugh would find out about a backstreet abortionist who could hook it out with a bent metal coathanger, and set her free? She promised she would never be so stupid

58

again. Never. She would be a nun, anything that God wanted of her, if only she could escape her present fate. Maybe she would die on the abortionist's table. It happened, she knew. She had heard stories of girls collapsing in pools of blood on bathroom floors, but at least that way she would never have to tell her parents, and they would be sad and forgiving at her funeral.

The person she needed most was Tash, who by being away in India had let her down. She would have known what to do, and that's what Jane wanted: someone to take over her life and make decisions for her, exactly as her mother had always done.

How different her story would have been if Tash had been in London, smoking dope with Denby and hanging out with their sophisticated, swinging friends, the musicians and artists and aristocratic shopgirls. The address of an abortionist would have been found in a trice and the necessary money begged or borrowed. Tash herself had used an illegal clinic when she forgot to take the Pill and got pregnant in her second year at art college. It had been nothing. She said it had been nothing. Just an injection and then an uncomfortable hour or so. Just an injection could change her life.

*　　　*　　　*

Unfortunately for Jane, or so it seemed at the time, Hugh and his friends, although full of bravado, were too young, too newly arrived in London and too inexperienced to help her get rid of the baby. They did not have the necessary contacts to know the competent gynaecologists and anaesthetists who, for a fee, would undertake to deal with the embarrassment of illegitimacy in safe and hygienic surroundings. Nor were they streetwise enough to know the telephone numbers of the practitioners, semi-qualified, or not qualified at all, who made a business of relieving women and girls of the unwanted contents of their wombs in grubby bathrooms and kitchens across the city.

Jane returned to Cambridge from London not much cheered by Hugh's company. He had got his own rackety student life going at full swing, and although he was kind, he was also self-absorbed and preoccupied with pursuing a girl medical student whom he said he fancied something rotten.

Jane had felt a bit like the Ancient Mariner. Her pregnancy hung like an albatross round her neck, and she knew she was condemned by Hugh's friends as a living example of what they all dreaded—getting a girl banged up, and ruining their own lives as a result. They treated her as if she was a retard—how could she have been so stupid, so dumb, so dangerously ill-prepared for student life? Didn't she know about the Pill, for God's sake? You should have got on the Pill, girl, before you had sex with some bloke you didn't know at a party, was what no one said but what she knew they thought.

Back in Cambridge, she continued the term in a trance, half believing that perhaps it wasn't happening to her, after all. She felt so normal. She had looked up pregnancy in a medical book in the college library. She should be feeling sick, her breasts should be tender, she should be feeling *something*, surely, if it was really true.

Another month went by, and on the day that her period should have begun, she found a few drops of blood on her knickers. She was so relieved that she leaned on the lavatory door and wept. She had been spared. Her ordeal was over. But the days went by and nothing more happened. Her fervent gratitude was short-lived, and by now the waist of her jeans was growing tight and a soft little mound had appeared where once her belly had been smooth and flat.

'You must tell someone soon,' advised her friends, both less inexperienced than she was. They were nice, middle-class girls who privately viewed Jane as foolish and irresponsible. Although at the beginning they had been warmly supportive, now they were more critical. Jane had been stupid and now she was being pig-headed. Eventually the college authorities would have to know and when the scandal broke they wanted to put a little distance between them. Yes, she was a friend, but they were at pains to make it clear that they were not at all the sort of girls who would get themselves pregnant. One of them, Judith, the daughter of a Yorkshire builder, already had found herself a steady boyfriend, whom she rigorously denied sex. 'If you hand it all to them on a plate,' she said, 'why should they hang around? Take it and run, more like.' She was set on course as a professional virgin, at least until there was an engagement ring in sight. She had done well for herself. Her boyfriend was the son of a big Lincolnshire farmer. She had already bought herself a waxed jacket and had started to go out beagling. She was grooming herself for the role of country wife.

Jane's other friend was Rosie, a gentle girl from

Norfolk, who really wanted to be a teacher and had a boyfriend at home. She had already slept with him in his parents' creaking double bed when they were away on holiday, but she didn't drink—not a drop—and birth control was exactly that, controlled by her, in a methodical, businesslike way. She found it hard to understand how Jane could have been so careless.

'You should see a doctor. You must make plans. They won't let you stay at college if you are pregnant,' they advised.

'I will, I will,' Jane promised. But where could she go for help? She thought of telling her mother, but rejected it as the worst possible option because her reaction to the news was what Jane most dreaded. Her doctor at home? Dr Chamberlain was a fumbly old man who had known her since she was a baby and called her 'young lady'. His surgery was in a converted shop between the butcher's and the library, where there was always someone she knew in the waiting room and there was an expectation that you shared your symptoms as you waited to be called for the consultation. Impossible. Hugh's mother? She would be sensible and kind, but she was a devout Catholic and Jane didn't know how she could bear the shame of admitting to her that she had had sex with a boy at a party, and did not even know his name. In some countries girls got tied to a stake in the sand and stoned to death for such a crime. In Ireland they got put in homes run by nuns and treated like criminal scum, their babies taken from them at birth.

She would have to do something, she knew, but each day she got up and got dressed and went

62

down to the refectory to eat slabs of thick white bread for breakfast. She wanted to eat and eat, piles of stodge, filling her body and brain with heavy, numbing, bland dough, before she dragged herself to lectures and then lay on her bed in the afternoons, sleeping or reading, her skirt unfastened, or the zip of her jeans undone.

It was after Christmas, when she was at home for the holidays, that she was forced to face what was happening to her. One morning she went up to her room with a pad of Basildon Bond writing paper and, in her careful, neat handwriting, composed a letter to the principal of her college in which she said that she could not return for the next term, owing to 'family circumstances'. She addressed the envelope and took it to the postbox in the wall of Mrs Jessop's house opposite. She was anxious going out of the gate and crossing the road, feeling as if the curious eyes of the elderly neighbour were on her from the windows and perfectly capable of reading through the envelope and exclaiming over the contents.

Meanwhile Hugh had told his mother, who, when she knew that Eileen Kindersley was out playing bridge, called to see Jane. She had asked a colleague to cover her antenatal clinic for her and had come home early especially. She knocked at the door and waited for Jane, who came to answer it, pale-faced and with unwashed hair, wearing an oversized sweater of her father's.

'Look, Jane,' said Diana Bywater briskly, recognising the wretched misery on her face, 'Hugh has told me. He says you need help, and I thought that because I am a doctor and a friend, I could offer you some advice. May I come in?'

Jane took her into the kitchen where she had been eating yet another bowl of cornflakes, and, utterly tongue-tied, listened to what was said to her with a blank, shut-off expression.

'You must tell your parents immediately,' said Diana, 'and if you find the idea of that as difficult as I imagine you might, I am willing to tell them for you, or to be here to support you when you do.' She had a dim view of Eileen and Timothy Kindersley as parents and was not unaware of the social pretensions and pressure to conform within the family. She could imagine the reaction when they heard Jane's news.

'I can give you advice about where to go to have the baby. There are many Church-run homes for unmarried mothers, but I wouldn't want you to go to one of those—they tend to be very weighted towards guilt and a bogus sort of morality. A London clinic would be better, from where you can arrange for the baby's adoption, but first of all you need to see a doctor and have the pregnancy confirmed and a proper health check. I can understand you might not want to see Dr Chamberlain and I can arrange for you to become a temporary patient somewhere else.' This is not a stupid girl, she thought, but why is she just standing there with that mulish expression on her face? 'Jane,' she said again, firmly, 'you have got to face up to this, and do something. The pregnancy will start to show very soon. You can't hide it from your parents for much longer.'

Jane rubbed at her eyes with both fists and then blinked. 'Why do I have to?' she said in a small voice. 'Why do I have to tell them? Why can't I just go off somewhere where no one knows me and get

64

this thing over?'

'Don't be silly,' said Diana, more gently. 'You can't run away. Now is the time that you need support from everyone who loves you, and your mother and father are first on that list. You need someone to take care of you. You can't do this on your own.'

'But I've decided,' said Jane. 'I've decided what I will do. I've written to college and told them I'm not coming back. I posted the letter yesterday. Term starts in a week, but instead I'll catch the train to London and get a job, and when I have to, I'll find somewhere to have the baby. My father pays me a living allowance. I can live on that, for a while at least.'

Diana looked at her for a moment without speaking. It was a brave stand, she thought, to try to go it alone. She couldn't force Jane to tell her parents and she could understand why she didn't want to. 'At least let me persuade you to see a doctor,' she said. 'Let me arrange that for you. I have quite a few friends who are London GPs. I can find someone sympathetic, who will look after you well.'

'Thank you,' said Jane, 'but only if you promise me that you won't tell my mother.'

*   *   *

In the end no one had to tell Eileen Kindersley that her daughter was pregnant. A few mornings later, she walked into Jane's bedroom and discovered her standing naked except for a pair of knickers, looking down at her swollen stomach with distaste. A swift glance at her breasts

65

confirmed Eileen's suspicion.

'Oh my God!' she said, sitting down heavily on the end of the bed. 'I don't believe it. Tell me it's not true. You haven't just put on weight, have you? You're pregnant!'

Even now Jane could hardly bear to remember what followed—the shouting and tears and recriminations. Her mother's anger was incandescent, erupting like a volcano at the sight of her. Jane had only to walk into a room to spark off another tirade, while her father skulked about looking utterly miserable and went to work early and came home late.

'Jane, Jane,' he said, more sad and defeated than angry, 'how could you do this to us?' Had Jane been more of a smart-arse, she might have said, 'Easily, actually. It took about three minutes and I can't really remember much about it.' Instead she burst into tears, which made her mother even more furious.

'Too late to be sorry!' she spat. 'No use crying now!'

Although her mother frequently sat with her head in her hands and wailed, 'Where did I go wrong with you? How could you have been so stupid?' Jane knew that she did not feel it was her fault. She had done her job as a mother but Jane had wilfully broken the rules and now she would pay for it. It wasn't only that she was throwing away her college place, but by leaving it too late to have an abortion, she was deliberately wrecking what was left of her future.

Then the planning began. She would have to be sent away somewhere to have the baby and it would be immediately put up for adoption. They

66

would then arrange for her to go abroad for six months, possibly as an au pair to an army family posted in Germany. This would give her time to get over the experience of giving birth and to regain her figure. 'If you work hard at it,' her mother told her, 'you could be your pre-baby weight in six weeks. I managed it with both of you, but then I am a much more self-disciplined person. You really must stop stuffing yourself with all this food. There is absolutely no need to put on all this blubber.' She looked at her daughter with distaste.

Her father promised that he would do all he could to secure her a college place that she could take up the following year, preferably where she knew no one.

'A fresh start, darling, that's what we'll try and do for you,' he said with tears in his eyes. 'You can put this dreadful mistake behind you, and in a few years even those people who know about the baby will have forgotten it ever happened.'

'Of course, if you find someone acceptable to marry you, it will be another matter,' said her mother, grimly. 'It distresses me very much, because what nice family will welcome a daughter-in-law who has had another man's child? I mean, what does it say about the kind of girl you are, or what kind of home you come from? Really, it breaks my heart when I think how you and Tash have had everything, everything, handed to you by me and Daddy, and you have thrown it back in our faces.'

It was a horrible winter, anyway, with an outbreak of foot-and-mouth disease rampaging through the countryside and images of pyres of burning cows on every news bulletin. Many of the

Kindersleys' friends were farmers, or country people who had had their hunting or racing disrupted. Everything, as her father said, was 'utterly bloody'. Things were not going well at the foundry, where there were strikes and threatened walk-outs. According to the Kindersley management, the unions had the industry in a stranglehold and were bleeding the company dry.

Bowed down with guilt and shame, Jane made sad little attempts to please. She baked cakes and cleaned her room while she waited for her parents to decide where to send her. One thing was made clear; that she couldn't stay on at home, growing fatter by the minute for everyone to see.

It was then that Aunt Joan stepped in, offering Jane temporary refuge in her spare bedroom in London. For the time being she could get a job and would then be booked into a hospital to have the baby, which would be adopted at birth. Meekly, Jane accepted that the crisis in her life was being dealt with by the grown-ups. She could not see there was an option to do things differently.

CHAPTER THREE

Florence was in love. For the first time in her life she felt overwhelmed with emotion for someone other than herself, and she couldn't take her eyes off Tintin's screwed-up, little red face. Had she not been so besotted, she would have realised he was a perfectly ordinary, rather hideous baby, resembling a little old man, or a freshly skinned rabbit, but with a pointed head embellished with a crest of wispy black hair and a gummy, out-of-focus blue gaze. In her current condition he was the most beautiful infant ever born. With one well-manicured finger she stroked his downy crown and watched the blood pulsing under the soft fontanelle of his unformed skull.

She couldn't get enough of it, the miracle of this first physical encounter in the outside world with this miniature human being who for months she had only known inside her womb. She stroked his silky, pink cheek and marvelled at his little rosy mouth that turned instinctively towards her touch. She uncurled one tiny furled fist and took in the long, delicate fingers and transparent shell-like nails—clearly a sensitive boy; a future violinist, an artist, maybe—and dropped a kiss on his head. His breath was so slight, just the smallest snuffle, and then his blotchy eyelids closed again and he slept.

The birth had gone entirely to plan, the epidural kicking in at exactly the right moment when things had started to get tough. Alice, her best friend and birthing doulas, had been a wonderful support and shared every moment, wiping Flo's brow with organic lavender water and encouraging her to push. They had clung to one another with tears of joy as Tintin gave his first hearty cry, and it was Alice who took the birthing photographs that were soon winging their way onto the mobile telephones of Flo and Ha's friends all over the world.

Alice had now left to go home to collect her own child from nursery school, feeling utterly worn out and with a crashing headache, while Flo touched up her make-up, combed her hair and, wrapping the cashmere baby blanket closer round Tintin's warm shape, held him against her shoulder. The most intense happiness washed over her and she gave a deep sigh and leaned back on the pillow of the hospital bed. Lying on the sheet next to her, her mobile telephone bleeped messages, which she would ignore for the moment.

Ha, sitting beside her, furtively trying to read the newspaper lodged on his knee, looked up. 'Shall I put him back in the crib thing?' he asked. 'You could have a bit of a sleep, then.'

'Don't you want to hold him again?'

'Yeah. Sure.' Ha didn't particularly. Babies had never been his thing and so far he did not find Tintin an exception, but he could see that non-involvement was not an option. He held out his arms, took the wrapped baby and held him in what he thought was the approved manner. He looked down at the little face peeking out from the folds of blanket. God, he thought, he's not very pretty. Tintin seemed to have inherited none of his own features. He looked almost entirely European, in fact, with a shapeless potato face, a large nose with flared nostrils on which a scattering of white spots sprouted, and a receding chin. His head was weirdly shaped, like a Martian in a comic strip. It was a good thing he was a boy, looking like that.

Florence must have read his thoughts from the expression on his face. She looked up from her mobile telephone on which she was reading congratulatory text messages. 'What's the matter?' she demanded.

'Nothing,' said Ha quickly. 'It takes getting used to, doesn't it, holding your own baby for the first time?'

'Isn't he beautiful? Absolutely perfect.'

Ha was saved from answering by a stout nurse

70

pushing open the door with her backside, her arms full of Cellophane-wrapped bouquets. 'Look,' she said to Flo. 'Aren't you the lucky one?' She laid them on the bed, took Tintin out of Ha's arms and plonked him back in the plastic crib.

'You need to rest now,' she said to Florence. 'I'm going to take Baby away for routine tests. After Mr Terence has come round this afternoon and checked you out, you'll be able to go home if you want.'

Florence anxiously watched Tintin being wheeled away.

'He's fine, though, isn't he?' she said to Ha. 'Anyone can see that. A whopper too. Nearly three kilos!'

'Of course he is. He's perfect. Clever, aren't we? Good at making babies!' Ha bent to look at the cards pinned to the bouquets and read the messages out loud. ' "Welcome, Tintin, and love and congratulations to you both, from all your friends at the hospital." '

There were several others like this and then, attached to a bunch of pink stargazer lilies, 'Well done! So proud of you, and longing to meet our grandson. Much love, Enzo and Mum.'

'It's kind of everyone, isn't it? What do you want me to do with all these? It looks like a florist's shop in here.'

'Oh, take them back to the flat and put them in water in the sink,' said Florence indifferently, without looking at the flowers. The champagne that Ha had poured for them both was making her head ache. 'I'm feeling terribly tired suddenly and the stitches are bloody sore. I think I might just have a little sleep.' She was already missing Tintin.

71

She wished that the nurse would bring him back.

'You do that.' Ha leaned to drop a kiss on her blonde head. 'I'll see you later,' and he gathered up the bouquets, slipped out of the room and quietly closed the door behind him. He felt oddly excluded from all of this performance, but he was quite a favourite with the nurses and confident that he would be offered a cup of tea and celebratory chocolate biscuits on his way out.

Florence settled herself more comfortably and closed her eyes. She had been given a private room off the main ward as a special concession because she was on the medical staff, and it was peaceful and quiet. She longed to sleep but the sky outside the plate-glass window was full of racing grey clouds and every now and then a blast of quite hot sunshine smote her eyelids and disturbed her. She wished that she had asked Ha to close the blinds but she wasn't getting out of bed to do so now. She felt too sore and bruised and was conscious of a flow of blood that she didn't want to encourage by standing up. Her breasts were heavy and she felt generally battered, increasingly more so now that the effects of the epidural had worn off. She slid her hands over her stomach and was dismayed to discover it felt only slightly flatter than before giving birth. There seemed so much of it left, even after Tintin's departure. She could pick up the mass of it with both hands. She would have to get back to the gym as soon as possible and pull all the slack, stretched muscle back into shape. In her overnight bag she had brought a pair of velour tracksuit bottoms to wear home, but thought longingly of the tight jeans that she should fit into in a few months.

As she dozed she thought of all the goodwill messages that she had received. Everyone was so happy for her. The safe delivery of a healthy baby was such a lovely thing to celebrate. She wished that she had managed to speak to her mother, who had left a message on her mobile saying that she was sure that she would want to rest and that she would wait to hear from her. She wouldn't want to be a nuisance, thought Florence. She was always like that: tentative and half apologetic if she telephoned, as if Florence's life was far busier and more important than her own. Florence found it rather annoying although at the same time she recognised that she hated to be disturbed at home in the evenings if she was tired after a busy day at work and that she might have conveyed this from time to time in her voice or manner.

Now Florence would really have liked to tell her herself how wonderful it all was. There was something she wanted to ask her that had never occurred to her to ask before. She had never enquired what it had been like when she was born. She had always been too full of resentment at the circumstances of her birth to care much about how her mother had felt. In fact, she had never even thought about it before. Now she wondered if Jane had loved her from the start. Had she been overwhelmed, bowled over with love for the new baby in her arms? Had she? Flo doubted it. She had been so young, just a kid who had made a terrible mistake, but all the same, first babies were pretty awesome. She must remember to ask her. She closed her eyes and slowly her thoughts slipped away and she slept.

73

Timothy Kindersley drove Jane down to London, with her belongings in the back of the new Jaguar. It was understood that she would not be returning home until after 'the event', as her mother referred to the birth of the baby. She had wept again as Jane said goodbye and given her an envelope with twenty pounds in it. 'You'll need maternity clothes,' she said grimly. 'Although I hope you'll try and make do with as little as possible. You should look in the *Lady* magazine. There are often advertisements for second-hand maternity wear belonging to nice sort of women who have completed their families.' Jane thought of these clothes with a sinking heart. She imagined frumpy tweed skirts with elastic panels, and ugly smock tops.

Her aunt, Joan Metcalfe, a spinster aged forty-seven, lived in a garden flat off Marylebone High Street, which had a shabby, village feel about its small shops, which included independent butchers and grocers. The flat consisted of two bedrooms, a small poky kitchen, bathroom, and a sitting room with a dining area. The large front bedroom was taken by Joan and furnished with heavy antique furniture inherited from her parents. The back bedroom was small but sunny, looking out at the little square of garden. It had a narrow single bed, a flimsy hanging cupboard containing a row of the suits Joan wore to work, and a chest of drawers filled with her summer clothes neatly folded with tissue paper and mothballs. She emptied one drawer to take Jane's things, the rest of which Jane kept in her college trunk, which was too large to fit under the bed, and had to sit in the middle of the floor, giving her occupation of the room a temporary feeling. There was a small gas fire set into the wall and an upright chair and folding card table under the window.

The room could never feel like hers, because the presence of Joan was too heavily imposed upon it, but when Jane put her Indian bedspread on the bed and the small rug, which six months ago she had bought to take to college, in front of the fire, it made it a little less spinsterish and grim. Later on she would buy a bean bag, she decided, and spend evenings curled up, reading. After all, there was going to be nothing much else to do with her time.

After Joan went to work on the first morning, Jane washed up their meagre breakfast things, returned to her room and closed the door. A weak winter dawn was only just creeping across the sky and the flat was cold. She lit the fire, which hissed and popped as the flame turned from blue to gold, and sat as close as she could. The flat was so cold that she felt her bones had turned to ice.

Although it was a relief to be away from her parents and the atmosphere at home, she felt terribly alone. The long day stretched out in front of her and apart from shopping for one or two items that Joan had written on a shopping list, and preparing a simple supper, she had just two things to do, both of which she dreaded. The most important was to go to her afternoon appointment with a doctor recommended by Diana Bywater, and the other was to look for a job. She didn't care what she did—any menial work that she could keep on until nearer the time that the baby was due.

The flat was very quiet. The occupants of the two upper floors made hardly any noise, just the soft thud of a door closing, and from time to time the distant rush of drawing water. Jane sat close to the fire, watching her very white shins turn pink and begin to itch. Loneliness invaded the room, which, even as she sat there, seemed empty and lifeless. She could collect her things and go out of the front door and nothing of her would remain. She felt she was becoming a transient, insubstantial person, while the baby was swelling up inside her, pushing her out of her own life.

It was an effort to think about what she was going to wear, to pull on her knickers, which had started to feel as if she was wearing them back to front, and the jeans that she couldn't do up. On top she wore one of her father's checked shirts, and then pulled her shoulder-length hair into a ponytail. There was no point in thinking about what she looked like when she was as fat as this, and growing fatter by the minute, and everything that was fashionable was designed for stick insect teenagers like Twiggy.

Before she went out she tidied the flat and pushed the carpet sweeper over the sitting-room floor. The evening before, she and Aunt Joan had spent only a short time sitting opposite one another on the uncomfortable straight armchairs before Jane had excused herself and gone to bed. It was hard to tell what Joan did in her non-working hours. There was a bookcase of history books and biographies but no lighter reading material lying about, except for the daily newspaper, which Joan bought on the way to work and carried home in her briefcase in order to sit with the crossword after supper. There were only two photographs on display, one of an old-fashioned wedding, all cloche hats and ankle-length dresses, which Jane assumed was of her maternal grandparents, and the other of a youthful Joan arm in arm with a pretty young woman who was laughing into the camera as they walked along a seaside promenade. Jane picked it up to look more closely and realised the girl on the right, with her fair hair blowing from under a felt hat, was her mother. She looked about eighteen, about Jane's own age, and she had a carefree air, which Jane found hard to recognise. Turning the photograph over, she read 'Cromer 1939'. Doing some mental arithmetic, she realised that this photograph would have been taken at about the time that she met Jane's father, her future husband. Perhaps that was why she looked so happy and was clutching her sister's arm because she knew that she was not going to have to rely on her company on holidays and days out. Joan looked amazingly the same, with her long face and a gloomy expression. She didn't look much fun, not as though she would have rolled down her stockings and paddled in the sea, or eaten a dripping ice-cream cone in public. Perhaps people don't change that much, thought Jane. Maybe when you are eighteen you are set for life, you have already made your own future and your happiness is decided. Just by a quick glance at the two girls in the photograph you could tell which sister would go on to marry a handsome and successful man and which would end up a spinster, living alone in a small London flat and working in a dull office for a living.

If that was so, then Jane felt that she herself was

already destined for a sad and lonely life, having, as her mother constantly reminded her, thrown away all her chances. Worse was that for the rest of her life she would carry about with her the burden of having sinned, because surely to conceive a baby who would never know its father and then to give it away at birth was a dreadful thing to do. Jane tried her very hardest not to think like this but more and more it occupied her mind, especially as the baby had started to move within her. She had felt strange fluttering movements as if a tiny, frail creature, no bigger than a butterfly, was batting its weak little arms and legs, trying to attract her attention, or to escape. Poor little thing, Jane said to it. Nobody loves you, or wants you, or is excited about your coming, except perhaps an unknown woman who desperately wants a baby, any baby, and who will one day be your adopted mother. It seemed to her quite a dreadful thing that this baby should be growing in an atmosphere of tears and recriminations. A vale of tears, she thought, liking the dramatic weight of the words. Poor little thing, swimming in its own sealed sea. Perhaps it could sense her misery and despair and knew already, informed by its developing tissues from her tissues and bones from her bones, that its very being was a disaster that had wrecked its mother's life. What sort of person would it grow into, knowing that? Poor baby, Jane thought, and wished it could be otherwise with all her heart.

Carefully double locking the front door and putting the key into her duffel bag, she went down the steps and onto the pavement. It was a cold grey February morning, and a gloomy, yellowish fog blotted out any distant view. This was a quiet residential street with little traffic and few pedestrians, just identical large three-storey houses, uniform behind their railings, facing one another across the road with cars parked on either side. Glancing up at the house fronts, Jane could see no signs of life. The windows were all closed against the cold, and sometimes curtains remained shut as well. There was no sound of radios playing or children laughing or the chink of china floating from within, and no smell of breakfast bacon or brewed coffee reached her. What a solitary place a street packed with people's homes could be. Then a door opened in front of her and a man came out onto the steps wearing a long dark overcoat and a bowler hat. He and Jane almost collided by the wrought-iron gate and he glared at her in irritation just as she was about to say 'Good morning', as she would have done to anyone she met out and about at home.

Instead he strode away, swinging his furled umbrella, and Jane trailed behind, following Aunt Joan's instructions to go to the top of the road and turn right onto Marylebone High Street where she would find the shops she needed and also the newsagent that displayed cards advertising situations vacant.

She found the grocer's first and went inside to buy a quarter of cheese and Bath Oliver biscuits, tinned tomatoes, macaroni, and butter. She was relieved to see that the shop had been laid out as a supermarket and that she could walk up and down the short narrow aisle and choose what she wanted without having to talk to the foreign-looking man behind the till. He was small and dark-skinned, with a mouth of gold teeth and slicked-back hair.

She didn't understand what he said to her as she took the basket to him, but she smiled and nodded, and then blushed because she felt so stupid. She put her groceries into the oilcloth shopping bag that Aunt Joan kept hanging behind the kitchen door, and wandered further along the street. She paused outside a coffee bar with an Italian name. The smell of hot fresh pastries was overwhelming and Jane realised that she was terribly hungry, as if her stomach had been turned inside out. There were several people sitting at small square Formica-covered tables, including two young women with a toddler in a pushchair. She saw at a glance that there were no young people her age, who, in groups, made Jane feel unaccountably afraid. Summoning her courage she went in and sat near the women and ordered a frothy coffee and a large warm pastry, fragrant with almond paste and plump raisins.

The women were both blonde and pretty, with long straight hair, and Jane realised that they were foreign, gabbling away in what sounded like Dutch, and that the child, parked so that he faced away from them, towards where Jane was sitting, was of little interest to them. They must be au pairs, she thought, noticing that neither wore a wedding ring. The child, a boy of about two, was pretty, with brown curls and large blue eyes. He had dropped a little plastic car onto the ground and was trying to pick it up but was restricted by his harness and it remained just beyond his little stretching fingers. He fixed Jane with his blue gaze and she smiled at him and leaned forward to retrieve the toy and hand it back to him. One of the two women stared at her with open hostility and manoeuvred the chair so that the child was facing towards them, and snatching the toy from the little boy placed it on the table. He began to cry, screwing his little hands into fists and rubbing them into his eyes.

Jane could hardly bear it. How could the woman, who looked so pretty, be so unkind, she thought, trying to swallow the pastry, which clogged her mouth. She drank her scalding coffee and stood up to leave, only to be called back as she went out onto the street because she had forgotten that she had not paid her bill. Blushing furiously, she fumbled with her big woollen gloves and dropped one on the floor, feeling the contemptuous eyes of the two women on her.

'Oh, sorry,' she said to the waiter, who stood with outstretched hand. 'I'm so sorry. I forgot I hadn't paid.' He said nothing, but after she had dropped some coins into his palm and turned to go, he made a remark to the two women and all three looked after her and laughed as if they knew something that she didn't.

Jane blundered along the pavement with the shopping bag banging against her legs. She felt close to tears. She could never go in that café again and she expected everywhere else would be the same, and that she would always feel intimidated and awkward, but after she had walked for a few minutes she realised that she had given the waiter five shillings and had left without her change. No wonder he laughed at her. She had made a fool of herself.

She knew that she was going to hate London. She could see it could be exciting if you were with a crowd of friends shopping in the new boutiques on King's Road or Kensington High Street, or going to a show or a concert, but it was no fun on your own. She thought of the great city stretching away in every direction, mile after mile of houses and offices, shops and schools, churches and hospitals, palaces, cathedrals and castles, and apart from Aunt Joan and Hugh, she knew no one and no one knew or cared about her.

Ahead of her she saw an empty red telephone box and felt a longing to go inside and stand for a moment in the small square of protection it offered and put its four glass walls between herself and the rest of the city. She tugged at the heavy door and went in and automatically lifted the black receiver and heard the familiar dial tone. She wished that there was someone she could telephone but there was not a single person she could think of. Her mother had told her on no account was she to contact any of her old school friends. The fewer people who knew about her disgrace, the better. The dial tone vibrated in her ear and she leaned against the red-framed glass panel beside her. How thick and treacly red the paint was; even the drips had dried hard into immovable droplets. It made her think of blood, and then suddenly she was overcome with a suffocating fear of what was ahead of her and was unavoidable, the awful ordeal of pain to be got through. She thought of all the screaming and blood-soaked sheets that accompanied any fictional birth she had ever read about or seen on the television, and bowed her head in misery and self-pity. Then with shaking fingers she dialled the number of her father's office. He would understand how she felt, alone and unhappy and miles from home. He had hugged her last night before he left to return home, and said, 'I'm always here if you need me, darling. Don't ever feel abandoned. This is for the best, you know. That you should come here. Your mother is quite right about that.' Jane hadn't been able to stop herself from crying as he tightened his arms around her and he had looked stricken and lifted her chin with a hand and pleaded, 'Oh, please, don't. Don't make it harder than it already is. You must be a brave girl.' Now she just wanted to hear his voice again, and some words of reassurance that everything would be all right.

She had the coins ready to shove into the slot when her call was answered by Mrs Weston, her father's secretary, and she made an effort to sound bright and normal as she asked to speak to him. Mrs Weston, with her strong Midlands accent, so deplored by Jane's mother, sounded warm and friendly and pleased to speak to her. Jane longed to wail down the line, 'Please, help me. I'm so frightened and unhappy,' but she was too afraid of doing the unthinkable, of letting the side down even further than she had already, if that were possible. Her mother's mantra was that people should not know her shame, and to spread news of it through the factory would be unpardonable.

'Wait a minute, love, he's in a meeting, I think. No, it's all right. They've finished. I'll get him to come to the phone. You all right, love? You sound a bit faint.'

'Me? No, I'm fine, thank you. It must be the telephone. It is very crackly.' She fed in more coins and then her father was on the line and the sound of his voice started the tears welling and for a moment she could not speak and when she did, her

83

voice was congested and wavering and she heard her father say, 'Jane? Not now, darling. I really can't speak to you here. Telephone this evening and speak to your mother. You're perfectly all right, aren't you? Well, that's good. We'll speak to you this evening then. Goodbye, darling. Chin up.'

Jane put down the receiver and stood gulping, with her red face pressed against the misted glass of the box. She had never felt so alone or so miserable. There didn't seem to be anyone in the whole world to whom she could turn for comfort.

I've got to just get on with it, she told herself, pushing open the heavy door. It's all my fault and I must stop feeling sorry for myself. She stood on the pavement blinded by tears, trying to remember in which way lay the newsagent.

When she found it she saw that a board in the window was full of hand-written and typed notices for everything from a two-door oak wardrobe for sale, to a wedding dress (worn once) and situations vacant and wanted. She spent a long time reading every one but there didn't seem to be much that she could do. There appeared to be a dearth of hairdressers and plumbers, carpenters and house painters, bookkeepers and mother's helps, but each one said 'experience essential'. No one seemed to need a cleaner or shop assistant, but there were plenty of people offering their services as 'domestic help'. A nursery school wanted an assistant, so she wrote down the telephone number even though it said 'experience preferred', and a firm of solicitors offered the position of junior clerk with typing. Surely she could learn to type? It couldn't be that difficult. She wished that she had been to the sort of school that taught girls something useful like office skills.

Oh dear, it wasn't looking very hopeful. She reread them all, hoping that she might have missed something, and then a grey-haired man put his head in the window and shifted the board so that he could add a new card. 'Assistant wanted in small bookshop,' read the wavering capitals. 'Hours by arrangement.'

*   *   *

Later that afternoon, when it was already dark, although the day had been so murky that really it had hardly been light at all, Jane sat beside the gas fire in her bedroom with a mug of tea and a packet of digestive biscuits and started a letter to Rosie and Judith. She had promised that she would write to them and up to now there had been nothing to tell, but today was different.

Dear Rosie,

When you've read this please pass it on to Judith. I'm sorry I have been so slow to write and tell you what's become of me, but really nothing much had happened, until yesterday when I got shipped to London to stay with my Aunt Joan (a hairy old spinster) in her flat in Marylebone. This is to get me away from home and avoid anyone that my parents know finding out about the baby. It's all right being here and better than being at home with my mother, who can't bear the sight of me. I don't blame her, really. I know I am a disgrace to the family name, and all that.

My aunt goes out to work every day and so

at the moment I have the flat to myself but today I went looking for a job and I think I have found one! I had an up and down sort of morning, and felt pretty lonely and miserable for the first part. I don't know anyone at all in London and so I have to learn to go about on my own and I can tell you that it is very large and quite scary and extremely easy to get lost. I have Aunt Joan's *A to Z* in my hand all the time and I feel such a twit, standing on the pavement, peering at it every few yards. No one else seems lost or a stranger, like me. People sweep past, always in a hurry, and it is hard to find someone who has the time to tell me where I am and point out where I should be going.

The good news is that I have already found a job working in a small bookshop within walking distance of my aunt's flat. I saw a situation vacant card in the newsagent's window and I went straight round to the shop. The owner is quite an old man, a foreigner of some sort, who is quite hard to understand and he hardly asked me any questions and didn't seem to mind that I haven't had any experience. I have to unpack stock and put it on the shelves and dust and things like that, and I will have to learn how to work the till and give people change—and you know how hopeless I am at mental arithmetic. I can see me getting in an awful muddle. Anyway, I start on Monday and it will be strange to be shut up with Mr Kowalski all day, but he seems friendly and kind. The last assistant was his sister, who died, which is a bit sad—

filling a dead sister's shoes, sort of thing. I don't think he has bothered much about the shop since then and there are piles of books everywhere, and the place looks as if it needs a real spring clean.

I didn't tell him about the baby and I feel rather guilty about that because he'll have to find someone else in the summer when I get too big to fit in the shop. I will be knocking over the piles of books and the postcard stand when I turn round. I will earn £7.10 shillings a week, which seems quite a lot, and I am going to try and save as much as I can.

In the afternoon I had to go to a clinic about the baby. This was the worst part of the day. The surgery was somewhere horrible on the dirty old Euston Road and the receptionist looked me up and down as though I was a piece of rubbish because there I was at a prenatal clinic and I was not married and I hadn't brought what she called 'a sample' with me, so she could tell I was a hopeless case. I bet she has read my notes and on the front page I expect it says 'UNMARRIED MOTHER'.

The waiting room was full of Indian and Pakistani women, looking frozen nearly to death in their beautiful saris with ugly nylon coats on the top. In their delicate sandals their bare feet were navy blue with cold.

They didn't speak at all, but some of the big, white English women tried to be friendly and wanted to talk about 'the little 'un', pointing at my belly, and I didn't dare say that I didn't want it and was going to give it away as soon as poss. Of course they saw that I wasn't married and some of them were nice about it. The woman next to me said that she was expecting her sixth baby (can you imagine?!!) and that her husband had got her in the family way before they were married and so he had to marry her. A shotgun wedding, she called it. I didn't have the courage to tell her that I don't even know who the father of my baby is.

Then I was called by the nurse to be weighed, right in front of everybody, and I've put on 10lbs. Can you think of anything more depressing? So that was something else to feel ashamed of and I suppose I must stop eating quite so much toast.

Then I had to wait again to see the doctor. He is a friend of someone we know at home and so he was quite kind and understanding and I didn't have to explain it all to him because he already knew. Instead, he hummed and hahed and then examined me which was . . . well, just think of the worst and most shaming thing, and it was like that. Far, far worse than going along the street with your skirt tucked in your knickers. He put on rubber gloves and the horrible nurse came in and glared at me from the foot of the bed. All women who've had babies have to go through this, I told myself. Even the Queen and Princess Margaret have to endure the rubber fingers of Mr Pinker, the royal gynaecologist. Somehow that was a comfort.

But it was horrible and I just held my breath and stared at the cracks in the ceiling.

It would have helped if I had been drunk, I suppose. They should give women a tot of rum in these places, like 'going over the top', in the First World War.

After the nurse had gone, the doctor asked me quite kindly about where I was intending to have the baby and I said I didn't know and he recommended the Marylebone Hospital where most of his patients go, and then I had to fill in forms about the baby being put up for adoption at birth. The Church of England's Children's Society will take it away. He said that newborn babies were the easiest to get adopted. Everybody wants them. (Except me and other teenage mothers.) I am starting to think 'poor little thing' and hoping it finds a nice home. I nearly asked if I could choose who got it, but I didn't like to, because I can see that I should be grateful that it is all being taken care of, and not make things more difficult. I could tell this is what the nurse thought.

Anyway, the doctor said that I was fit and healthy and that having a baby so young is really a good thing in some ways and that I should have an easy time! Ha! Ha! He told me I had got to take iron pills and come back in a month, and that was that.

I even managed to catch a bus back from the clinic and get off at the right stop. Tonight I have made macaroni cheese for supper but something has gone wrong with it and it looks like a lump of knobbly concrete and smells like an old gym shoe.

I don't know my aunt that well and I don't

somehow think she is going to be much fun to live with, but maybe I am not in a position to expect things to be fun.

Please, please come and see me some time. I often think of you at college without me and wish that I was there and none of this had happened. At least I seem to have stopped crying, which is a good thing, and also I haven't been sick once. Getting a job has cheered me up quite a lot.

Lots of love,
Jane

CHAPTER FOUR

Tash heard about Jane's pregnancy nearly four months after she had left England. She sat cross-legged in a loose white tunic and trousers under a tree in an ashram in Rishikesh in Northern India, sorting through the packet of blue air-mail envelopes, which had been waiting for her and Denby at the poste restante in the busy town on the other side of the Ganges. Since they had arrived in India Tash had chopped off her long bleached hair and it had grown into a short dark bob, like a boy, and she was very tanned. Her silver bracelets slid up and down her brown arms as she picked out the envelopes addressed in Jane's tidy handwriting. She would read those first when she had them in proper chronological order.

Jane wrote as she spoke, and several times Tash smiled as her sister described things that had happened to her, and her experience of leaving

90

home and starting at teacher training college. To begin with, thought Tash, she had evidently been a bit lonely and homesick. She must have been, if she had nothing better to do than write to her sister every week.

Every now and then Tash looked up and gazed into the distance, to the heavily forested slopes of the hills and the distant Himalayas, and then turned her attention back to the letters. She had been away long enough to make it hard to recall how it was to be in the England Jane described. She tried to remember what it was like to feel numb with cold, and the heavy weight of winter clothes. She thought of pinched white faces and people passing each other in the street without lifting their eyes. She thought of boiled cabbage and the smell of thickened gravy. She thought of restrained middle-class English voices and cold handshakes and chilly bedrooms and bus queues and London traffic and how in November there were days when the light failed altogether and there was a dingy grey shroud over everything from gloomy daybreak to dusk.

From where she was sitting in a grove of shady sal trees she could see the rope bridge that crossed the Ganges, crowded with a steady two-way procession of pilgrims, tourists, orange-robed holy men and cows. This was as far as the old minibus that she and Denby had driven from England could go. It was parked up near where she sat, full of the bundles of cotton clothes she had picked up on their travels, and boxes of beads and belts and silver jewellery. Piratical gangs of monkeys swarmed over it, trying to unscrew the one remaining wing mirror, and doing their best to

91

break off the windscreen wipers. One of the sliding windows would not shut and every now and then Tash had to jump up and chase the monkeys away as they tried to break in. A small crowd of dark-eyed ragged children had gathered round her and she indicated that if they guarded the van, she would give them a handful of rupees. After that they clapped and shouted and threw stones and looked back over their thin little shoulders to see if she was pleased with their efforts.

Denby was somewhere over the river, where ashrams dotted the hillsides and holy men lived in caves. He was trying to find the ashram where the Beatles were holed up. He couldn't resist a bit of glamour and razzmatazz, but as far as Tash could see, their presence meant an end to the tranquillity and spiritual enlightenment that she and Denby had come to seek.

She put the letters from her parents to one side to read later. It was quite shocking to find how difficult it was to bring to life an image of her mother and father. She sat for a moment looking across the hills and tried to conjure up their voices, but they wouldn't come to her. Over the clamour of the children, all she could hear were the mewing cries of the enormous wide-winged birds that rode the currents of air high above the river, and the tinkling of bells in the distance. She could remember her mother's scent, though, and her method of sitting down and crossing her legs in one movement; how her fingers lit a cigarette and how she leaned back a little and narrowed her eyes as she exhaled the smoke. She thought of the smell of her father, of aftershave and cigar smoke, and remembered how she had once seen him from a distance, across a room crowded with people, and how he stood out, taller than most, sleeker and superior-looking as if he was of a different, higher species.

Tash turned back to the letters. There was only one more envelope from Jane, written just after Christmas, and when she opened it she saw that there was something different about the handwriting. It was untidier and sloping, and there were crossings out and no funny faces or little flowers drawn in the margins. Tash saw at a glance that it was written from home, not college, and then the first line sprang out at her. 'Darling Sis, I hardly know how to write this, but I have to tell you that something terrible has happened to me . . .'

She read to the end and then started again at the beginning. Some of the children who had come to squat beside her watched her face. They saw that something had altered her mood and that her happiness had turned to dust, like the dirt that they stirred with their fingertips where they sat. When she had finished she folded the letter and put it back into the envelope and got to her feet, stooping to gather the other envelopes, which she was no longer interested in.

Going back to the van she shoved the whole bundle onto the driver's seat and leaned against the door, her head in her hands. Oh God, she thought. Poor little Jane. Poor little sister. If only she had been there, she could have helped her. It was ridiculous that she hadn't had an abortion. She could have arranged it for her so easily. It was so stupid, stupid to have a baby, as if she was a wronged maiden in a Victorian novel. Why the hell hadn't she got proper advice? Why hadn't anyone told her what she should do? She felt hot with anger towards her parents. Why hadn't they helped her? Jane wrote that they were trying to decide where she should go until the baby was born. It was typical of them that they wanted to hide her away somewhere to cover up the pregnancy. Social shame would matter more to her mother than anything else. How dare they ship her off somewhere, like an outcast?

Unwanted pregnancies could be dealt with. There was no need for all this misery and *Sturm und Drang*. After all, abortion might still be illegal, but everyone knew that was going to change. The mindset was already in place. The Act had been passed. Unwanted babies should not be born. Girls and women should have a choice. The bad old days were supposed to be over.

She would have to wait for Denby to come back from exploring the other side of the river and then she would insist that they go back into town and she would try and put through a call home. God knows how long he would be or how long it would take her. The place was so crowded with press and photographers it was nigh impossible to get near a telephone. She didn't care what the time difference was. It would serve her parents right if she woke them up in the middle of the night.

When she and Denby had arrived the evening before they were in time for the divine light ceremony on the banks of the river. Tash had felt so completely at peace watching the pilgrims lighting little oil lamps and floating them on the surface of the dark water while the air trembled with the chanting voices of the monks. She knew

94

that this ceremony of Aarti was the time when the stress of ordinary life was cast off and thanks were given for the blessings of the day and great calm descended on the sombre hills.

Now that sense of spiritual sublimity had gone completely and she felt agitated and angry. When a young European couple drifted past hand in hand and garlanded with flowers, she was too cross to reply to their greeting of 'Hari-Om'.

Oh, shut up and fuck off, you morons, she thought, giving them a fierce glare. Where the hell was Denby?

*   *   *

Jane's days in London began to follow a pattern. She would wake early, immediately conscious of the icy cold of her bedroom, and as soon as she had gathered courage, make a dash to light the gas fire and crouch beside it as she dressed. One Saturday afternoon she had taken her wages and bought two swirly patterned, tent-shaped minidresses from a fashion shop called Biba, full of amazing and cheap clothes, and although she wasn't convinced they were decent, she wore them nearly every day with thick tights underneath and shoes with sturdy stacked heels. Their shape concealed the bump of baby, which was now becoming more obvious and causing her misery as she put aside her too-tight jeans and skirts.

As soon as she was dressed she went to the equally freezing kitchen and lit the gas stove to warm it up a bit, and put the kettle on to boil. She dragged the wooden ironing board from the kitchen cupboard and, with the heavy old steam iron, pressed the flannel blouse that Aunt Joan had put out to wear that day, paying particular attention to the stiffened collar and cuffs.

Meanwhile, she could hear her aunt splashing about in the icy bathroom, having what she called an 'all over' wash. Baths were taken only twice a week, when the alarming gas water heater was lit for the occasion. Later, Joan would emerge in her pale blue candlewick dressing gown, her face shiny with Pond's vanishing cream and her hair tightly wound on pink plastic curlers, spiked with hairpins, and collect the blouse draped over the back of a chair on her way to get dressed.

Flattening out yesterday's newspaper on the kitchen table, Jane then set about polishing her aunt's court shoes, either brown, black or navy, using little glass pots of appropriately coloured shoe cream and sets of brushes. An old pair of interlock peach-coloured camiknickers was provided for the final shine.

By the time Aunt Joan reappeared in one of her severely tailored work suits, her hair was freed from the curlers and now resembled the tight florets on a head of cauliflower. Her shoes were lined up on the floor beside her chair, waiting for her feet in their American Tan 40 denier nylon stockings, and Jane had made a pot of strong tea and got out the tin of Rich Tea biscuits with a picture of the Coronation of Queen Elizabeth II on the lid.

Jane had taken to helping her aunt 'get off' to work by performing these little lady's maid tasks. Aunt Joan liked being waited on, and Jane was happy to oblige because she felt it was a way of showing she was grateful without constantly having to say as much. These mornings were usually companionable although conversation was kept to the minimum. It was the freedom from condemnation, outright or implied, that Jane most appreciated. The atmosphere in the kitchen was entirely neutral, exactly what it might have been between two flatmates, each preoccupied with the working day ahead. Aunt Joan simply accepted her niece's condition as something to be got on with, with the minimum of fuss.

This didn't mean that she wasn't often irritable and snappy, and sometimes Jane felt that her presence was an annoyance in itself, and on these mornings she crept away with her mug of tea to her bedroom. But Aunt Joan's grumps were nothing more than that, and were not charged with emotion or even really directed at her personally. They were just part of who she was, and really, thought Jane, it was no wonder, considering that the routine of her life seemed so joyless.

On the better-tempered mornings, Jane would stay in the kitchen and they would drink their tea together and eat the two biscuits each, which constituted Joan's breakfast, while she applied her make-up using the mirror of her powder compact, tilted towards the electric light over the sink. A thick panstick in the same colour as the biscuit went on first, followed by a furry coating of face powder and then a slash of orange Elizabeth Arden lipstick called Coral Fire. Licking a finger she would smooth over her brows and then colour them in with a brown pencil. Jane watched, fascinated by the difference between her aunt and her mother, whose morning routine was undertaken wearing a towelling turban to protect her hair and was as extensive as Joan's was brief, and involved cotton wool, make-up brushes and a drawerful of pots and lotions.

Aunt Joan approved of Jane's job in the bookshop. She did not hold with idleness of any sort, but further than that, she passed no judgement whatever, either on how Jane occupied herself in her spare time, her appearance, or the money she had spent on the new clothes. This lack of critical scrutiny came as a great relief. Jane felt as if she was free for the first time in her life, away from her mother's strictures and criticisms.

'Just look at that girl with those great, fat legs in a short skirt,' or, 'One should never wear turquoise, it's terribly common,' or, 'That colour of lipstick isn't suitable on a girl your age.' Her mother's rulings ordered the whole world into what was approved of and what wasn't, and it took more bravery than Jane possessed to challenge her judgement. She had never felt up to it, having observed the epic struggles between her mother and Tash, which were only resolved by Tash leaving home for good.

The evenings in London followed a similar pattern. Aunt Joan rarely went out on a week night, maybe once a month to a concert or a play, and on the evenings spent at home she would change out of her work clothes and put on a pair of what she called slacks—quite daring for a woman to wear corduroy trousers—and a sweater relegated to second division after years of office wear, and a pair of quilted bedroom slippers. Her poor feet suffered terrible punishment from the court shoes worn for so many hours in order to clip about in a professional manner in the office.

Jane, who was home earlier, had fallen into the habit of preparing something for supper, and since Aunt Joan abhorred extravagance and waste and had what she called a delicate stomach, food was kept very simple and eaten at the little round table in the sitting room with proper silver, good china and a white lace tablecloth.

'Of course, your mother made sure that she got the best family pieces,' Aunt Joan told her, picking up a solid silver serving spoon, and Jane, feeling awkward, tried to look apologetic. She had grown up with a very different version of how things had been divided.

After she had cleared away and washed up, they would watch selected television programmes on the black-and-white set or listen to the wireless while doing the crossword, Aunt Joan reading out the clues when she got stuck. At ten o'clock it was time for cocoa and bed. We're like a couple of old spinsters, thought Jane, but she had settled into the routine and her unhappiness had grown much less acute. It felt right that she should be living a nun-like existence, considering her circumstances.

Her work in the bookshop was what had made the difference. She got up every day with a purpose and had begun to feel that she was useful, in an undemanding way. Mr Kowalski did not appear to expect much from her, apart from being there within the opening hours of ten to five thirty, and on Saturday morning. He was vague about her exact tasks, waving a blue-veined, bony hand towards the shelves as if that was explanation enough, and she began to plan for herself, deciding when the window display needed a change, or the shelves reorganising and dusting. It became clear that all Mr Kowalski really wanted was someone to man the front of the shop while he sat undisturbed in the back room, by the electric fire, drinking strong black coffee and smoking endless cigarettes. The room was dark and cheerless, with brown paper glued over the small window, and a single light bulb hanging over the table where he worked. All round the walls were shelves of second-hand books, faded tomes of military history in many different languages, and much of the day Mr Kowalski filled out index cards in his beautiful spidery handwriting and entered the books in a catalogue. There was a threadbare dusty carpet on the floor, on which teetering towers of books were stacked, and two old chairs with the horsehair stuffing bursting through the worn velvet upholstery. It was impossible to distinguish between the books already catalogued and the piles of those that were awaiting his attention, and from the first day Mr Kowalski told Jane that she should not disrupt his system.

'Your work is in the shop,' he said. 'In here, it is just an old man, undisturbed. Do you understand?' and Jane nodded, relieved, because she found the atmosphere in the small room oppressive, as if there was not enough oxygen for the two of them.

Mr Kowalski was a small, dainty man with a tiny frame upon which was set a large, leonine head with slicked-back, longish, grey hair. He had unhealthy-looking skin the colour of skimmed milk, so pale that it was almost blue, and his face was a series of sharp planes that coincided at the arc of his beaky nose. His eyes were sunk in bruise-coloured dark shadows behind his half-moon glasses and he had a thick, mid-European accent that Jane could not place. It was several weeks before she felt she knew him well enough to ask where he came from and learned that he and his sister had moved from Poland at some time during the war.

'Jews, I expect,' said Aunt Joan, when she told her. 'Poor things. They would have come here to escape the pogroms. Goodness only knows the suffering they would have endured.' Jane wondered if she was right because Mr Kowalski seemed to have made no effort to integrate into ordinary English society. His only regular caller was another small, grey Polish man in a long overcoat, who came once a week to join him in the back room. Once Jane had needed information on a book ordered for a customer and had knocked on the door, and when she opened it, saw that on the table, lying on a grease-marked paper wrapping, was a long brown sausage as thick as her wrist, and a large jar of pickled cucumbers. Beside the sausage was a tall, green bottle and two tiny cut-glass tumblers filled with colourless liquid. Mr Kowalski and his friend were enjoying a little mid-afternoon snack of some food and drink that reminded them of home. Would Jews eat sausage? Jane didn't think so. Perhaps he was a lapsed Jew. He offered her a piece on the tip of a knife, a pink slice glistening with beads of white fat. The room was very warm and smelled overpoweringly of garlic, cut by the sharp vinegar of the cucumbers. She had to accept because it would surely be churlish to refuse.

'Delicious!' she said, nibbling at the edge. 'Delicious. Thank you so much!' The taste was meaty and pungent as if it was manufactured from

101

unspeakable bits of dead pig. Afterwards she went to the tiny lavatory and wrapped what was left in a fold of paper and put it in her bag. For the first time since she was pregnant she felt sick.

Mr Kowalski did not live in the flat above the shop, but locked up at half-past five in the evening and disappeared slowly down the road in an identical long overcoat to that of his friend, carrying a string bag of meagre shopping, a few books in brown paper under his arm ready for posting on his way to work the following morning. He took with him an air of melancholy and suffering nobly borne, and after a few weeks Jane tried to think of ways to brighten up his life. Telling jokes and being loud and cheerful were obviously non-starters. The conversations that they shared were always serious—there was never any playful banter—in fact behaving in a jokey way in the sombre atmosphere of the shop was unthinkable. So instead Jane took to buying a fresh pastry on the way past the Viennese bakers and presenting it to Mr Kowalski with a cup of his very black coffee in the middle of the morning.

The patisserie was unlike anything she had ever seen before. Chubbs, the bakers in the village at home, sold fat pink iced buns known as Big Berthas, heavy sugared doughnuts filled with imitation red jam and Chelsea buns, heavy and lardy and solid, alongside pallid pastry sausage rolls containing a finger of grey-pink blobby meat. Here, at Lotti's, the window was full of glazed jewel-coloured tarts and crispy flans, chocolate tortes and strudels, liqueur-soaked sponges decorated with preserved fruits. She drooled and lingered over her choice.

'What is this?' exclaimed Mr Kowalski on the first occasion, when she stood at the door of the back room with a golden brioche, sitting on a saucer, in her hand. 'For me? Oh, my dear girl! You are too kind. How good it smells. But you must share it with me, Jane, my dear.'

Horrified, she saw that his hand trembled and his eyes behind his glasses filled with tears. Oh, no, she thought. The cake is having a Marcel Proust madeleine effect, but reminding him of awful, rather than happy, times in the past.

After talking about him with Aunt Joan, she was quite sure that there were terrifying memories lurking behind those sunken dark eyes. But he so evidently enjoyed the little cake, breaking it between his bony fingers and popping the crumbs into his mouth like a bird, that she felt she had begun a tradition, and each day she tried to bring him something different, if only a polished apple when her funds were low at the end of the week.

As she acquainted herself with the shop, Jane discovered an eclectic collection of classics and foreign language books, with few popular modern novels. There were no Ian Fleming or Alistair Maclean thrillers, no science fiction, and no romantic novels that might attract women readers into the shop. The sort of books that Jane's mother read, by Georgette Heyer, Agatha Christie or Elizabeth Jane Howard, were not on the shelves and Jane wondered how the shop kept going at all when further down the road there was a much livelier bookstore with its window crammed with modern paperbacks. When she knew him better, she persuaded Mr Kowalski to stock Penguin copies of *The Forsyte Saga*, which she displayed in the window and which sold out almost as soon as she put them there, thanks to the adaptation of the novels, which had recently been serialised on television.

In the long hours that she was unoccupied, perched on her chair behind the till, she discovered Iris Murdoch novels, with their dark suggestiveness and strange psychological insight into the complex nature of relationships, and she read Tolstoy and Dickens, and Giuseppe Tomaso di Lampedusa's *The Leopard*, and everything she found by Graham Greene and Evelyn Waugh. She was surprised to discover a whole shelf of novels by D. H. Lawrence, and read *Lady Chatterley's Lover* in her lunchhour, without ever understanding what the fuss was about. While her own life had seemed to come to a standstill, or was temporarily diverted off course, she devoured the drama of fictional characters. It was another way of not thinking about the baby.

*   *   *

As the winter crept on into spring, Jane had two visits from her mother, who used trips to Harrods and the dignified shops of elegant Regent Street to check up on her daughter. What Jane most wanted to know was if there was any news of Tash.

'I've written to her loads of times using the poste restante addresses that she left, but I've never had a letter back.'

'Oh, yes,' said her mother vaguely. 'Yes, we have heard from her once or twice but the post seems very unreliable and takes weeks and weeks. She sent her love to you, of course, and was concerned that you were all right. She seems to be fine and is travelling about the country in that clapped-out old minibus she and Denby bought. I don't think she has much time to write. She never was good at keeping in touch. If anything serious happened, of course, she would telephone, so we are not worried. You're looking well, darling,' she added as they shared a tray of tea and delicious sandwiches at Browns Hotel. 'Only three months to go and then we can get your life back on the rails. Look what I've bought you!' She delved into the glossy green and gold carrier bag and shook out a Courrèges-inspired cream wool dress with white PVC panels across the shoulders. 'A little shift dress from Way In, as an incentive to lose the weight after the event.'

The dress was so youthful and desirable that it made Jane feel she might burst into tears. This was what her mother wanted to turn her into—a sleek, reinvented and improved version of her pre-baby self.

'Daddy sends his love. He's having a beastly time at the works with these ghastly shop stewards. They're all Communists, you know. They should be taken out and shot. This terrible Labour government is ruining the country. And after everything that Daddy fought for in the war. Really, it breaks my heart.' Obviously, thought Jane, uncharitably, a little light shopping at Harrods helped.

*   *   *

Later in the evening of the day that Tintin was born, Florence took him home. He was wrapped in

105

his cashmere blanket and wore a tiny pale blue cap on his downy, newborn head. Ha walked backwards down the hospital corridor capturing the historic occasion on a video camera, and Florence, with her face prettily made up, looked radiant and composed, while behind her, like a lady-in-waiting, plodded a ward assistant bearing more bouquets of flowers.

There was only a moment of tension when Ha was slow to unlock the door of the car and the cold wind blew in gusts across the sodden car park. Florence turned her body to shelter the sleeping baby. 'Get a move on, Ha,' she snapped. 'Surely you know which is the bloody key by now?'

The infant carrier had to be slotted onto the seat belts in the back seat, all made awkward by the difficulty of clambering in and out of Ha's sporty two-door car. Eventually they were ready to go and Florence sat in the back with Tintin, trying to fight the waves of panic that she felt as they turned into the swooping evening traffic. He was so small, so frail, so vulnerable. She saw tearing jagged metal in her mind, heard screeching brakes. 'For heaven's sake, drive carefully!' she implored, glancing nervously out of the windows as uncaring drivers hurtled past.

The enormity of what she had done by giving birth swept over Florence as she touched Tintin's cheek with a finger and gently rearranged his little cap. She knew that her life would never be the same again. The thought was as terrifying as it was elating. For the first time ever she felt unsure of how capable she would prove to be. Mothering skills were supposed to come naturally, a combination of instinct, intelligence and common sense, but she felt nervous and panicked by the responsibility.

He drove easily, switching lanes and glancing in the driver mirror.

'Everything OK?' he asked. 'Are you feeling all right?'

'Yes, of course,' said Florence. 'Just a bit tired and battered.'

'That's to be expected,' he said. 'It's not so easy for older mothers.'

'Thanks,' said Florence without a smile.

Ha thought he was being funny. He leaned over to play a CD. In that one gesture, left over from their life as it had been before yesterday, when they always drove with music, which they selected for one another, Florence knew that her feelings about Tintin werc not shared. Ha was his old self, unchanged, perhaps more ebullient than usual, but certainly not overwhelmed, fearful, exhausted and strung up all at once. It made sense. It wasn't he who had had the baby or who was genetically wired to undertake its nurture. He was the one who was supposed to be in tiptop condition to go out hunting the woolly mammoth so that they all could eat. Fatherhood was something quite different.

Flo hadn't imagined it would be like this. Surrounded by well-wishers and the love and concern of friends and family, she had never thought that she would feel so alone. The thought of her quiet, tidy flat waiting for her return, of the silent nursery and the waiting crib with the neatly folded baby blankets, the plastic baby bath and the butterfly mobile, the new white painted chest of drawers piled with tiny new folded clothes—all of them filled her with a cold fear. In twenty minutes

107

or so, if they survived the journey, she would take Tintin up the stairs and open the door and carry him in, and from then on there would be no escape.

CHAPTER FIVE

'Are you coming with me today to meet Tintin?' Jane asked Enzo as they sat at breakfast on the first morning he was home from his conference.

He looked up from the newspaper with a quizzical expression on his face. He was a small man with a full head of curly silvery hair and deep-set brown eyes, a large aquiline nose, and a sensitive full-lipped mouth.

'Did Flo invite me?' he asked, his voice deeper than one might have expected from his stature, and with a trace of a Scottish accent.

'Well, of course she did. When she asked me, she meant you as well.'

'When are you going?'

'This morning. She wants me to come as soon as possible. She can't wait to show him off and I can't wait to see him!'

Enzo hesitated. His relationship with his stepdaughter had become warm and cordial over the years as she gradually got over her early resentment of him as the unwelcome intruder in her relationship with her mother. In fact, the reason that Flo had followed medicine as a career was largely due to his influence and the respect that she had for him.

However, Enzo had always taken the line that

he was not Florence's father, and did not try to act as if he were. He had come into her life when she was ten years old and he had never assumed that because he had married her mother, Florence should be expected to love him as well. Because he respected her feelings, Florence eventually learned to trust, and then like him.

'Why don't you go on your own this first time?' he suggested. 'I expect she'd like to have you to herself to go over all the gory details, and I've got a lot of notes to write up.' Enzo was a workaholic and headed a pioneering orthopaedic department in a teaching hospital in Birmingham.

Jane considered. 'Well, perhaps it would be best this first time. I expect Florence still feels a bit shell-shocked. I don't intend to stay long and I am going to take a casserole which she can put in the freezer if she and Ha don't want to eat it straight away. Oh, I can't wait to see the baby. She says he is absolutely adorable.'

'Ah!' said Enzo, drily. 'That's good. Otherwise she might have asked for a refund.'

Jane smiled. 'She sounds completely besotted, and there I was, worrying that she might not bond with him, or whatever it's called. I just couldn't picture her as a mother, somehow.'

'Hmm.' Enzo had always taken a neutral and non-critical stance towards Flo. When she had behaved appallingly as a ten year old, he had, wisely, simply ignored her and made no attempt either to win her over or discipline her. It didn't take Florence long to learn that her tantrums had no effect whatever on him and she grudgingly gave them up.

When his own sons were born in fairly quick

succession, he took trouble to make sure that she did not feel in any way displaced. She was a clever and solemn little girl, and Enzo, who came from a large, extended family, knew exactly how to make her feel valued. He agreed with her that babies were boring companions and together they went to the library every Saturday morning to choose books, and on Sunday afternoons he took her with him to watch cricket or rugby. In a completely natural way, he allowed her to know that he valued her company. Jane watched with gratitude as her sullen and uncooperative daughter lowered her guard and started to become a likeable and loving child again.

Jane would always love Enzo because of it. There were all the other reasons to love him, of course, but how he treated Florence came pretty near the top of the list. She would never have married him had she not been sure that he would be a good stepfather, but all the same, he had really been more sensitive and thoughtful than she could ever have hoped.

Enzo was a man who was entirely *'bien dans sa peau'*, as the French would say. From a working-class background he had won scholarships, first to Edinburgh Academy and then to University College, London, to study medicine. He moved effortlessly between his Italian family in Scotland and his largely middle-class English friends at university. Because he was bright and a good sportsman, and shrewd and amusing company, he was successful and popular everywhere he went, without ever making any effort to compromise who he was, or where he came from, in order to belong. He was his own man and respected for it.

Jane had met him at a club rugby match that she had been taken to watch by Denby on a freezing Saturday afternoon in February when Florence was eight years old. Tash, who was heavily pregnant, had told Denby he had to look after their two children, toddlers of two and four, while she had a rest. Ever resourceful in devising ways to make his life easier, Denby had persuaded Jane to go with him because he knew that she would take care of the children and Florence would keep them amused, chasing about on the touchline.

Watching rugby would not exactly have been Jane's choice, but she had nothing else to do, it was free, and she liked it that Florence had contact with her cousins and felt part of a larger family. She even took a bit of an interest in the match and noticed the short, dark young man playing at scrum half for the UCL side. He was swarthy, with a mop of long black curly hair and twinkling brown legs, and he seemed to be everywhere on the pitch, playing with a verve and tenacity that rattled the opposition.

'Take out that scrum half!' shouted a well-wrapped supporter of the other side.

'That's dreadful! How can he say that!' Jane complained to Denby, and the next moment there was an illegal tackle and a terrible collision of bodies, and the little player was left lying flat on his back, winded and dazed.

Enzo always said that when he came round the first thing he saw was Jane bending over him with a look of great concern on her face, and that was that, he had found the woman he wanted to marry. It was the bang on the head that did it. 'But I know you!' he cried, as he was carted off protesting.

'You're Jane, aren't you? I've met you before! In hospital, on the maternity ward! You'd just had a baby girl!'

Jane racked her brains. That was eight years ago. She couldn't remember the doctors at all. 'I was a student,' he went on excitedly. 'A friend of Hugh Bywater. He was a friend of yours too. Can't you remember? We came to visit you!' Jane could remember, now she thought about it, but it was so long ago, and she would not have known him again. 'I've never forgotten you!' he cried. 'I always wondered what happened to you!'

'Just keep quiet, will you?' said the stretcher-bearer. 'You're supposed to be lying still till you've been seen by the doc!'

'I am the doc!'

At first he thought she was Denby's wife and he was so hugely relieved to find that wasn't the case that he asked her out on the spot. Of course she couldn't go, she had Florence to look after, but Enzo was not a man to be thwarted and he took her telephone number and kept trying until she agreed. Two years later they were married.

Meeting Enzo like that was the greatest piece of good luck in her life, Jane always thought, with having Tash as a sister a close second. It entirely reversed the view she had formed of herself at nineteen, as someone who had thrown away her chances. The fact that she had 'a past', as her mother put it, with Flo always on hand as evidence, bothered Enzo not at all. Times and attitudes had anyway changed over the eight years since Flo was born, and one of Enzo's sisters had two children out of wedlock—dearly loved and indulged children, who were brought up by their grandparents at the very centre of the family.

When they finally married at a register office in London, Enzo's whole family came down to London on an overnight coach from Edinburgh and took over a friend's Italian restaurant for the reception. Jane's mother was torn between relief that her daughter was marrying a newly qualified surgeon and horror at the noise and exuberance and vulgarity of the in-laws. Jane remembered fondly how much her father had enjoyed the occasion and how handsome he had looked as he gave her away. Enzo's beautiful young female cousins, all flashing dark eyes and tossing hair, fought to dance with him when they pushed the tables back after the wedding breakfast and the three-piece band started to play.

Enzo's father, a short, square man with a face the colour of salami, and a wide brown-toothed smile, sweating profusely and wearing a startling satin waistcoat, insisted on dancing with her mother. He held her close and then slid a large brown hand to cup one of her buttocks. She towered over him wearing an expression of utter distaste beneath her feathered hat, looking like a furious chicken.

'At least you won't have to *see* them, will you, dear?' she said to Jane later, as she stood on the pavement waiting for a taxi to take them back to their hotel. 'I mean, thank goodness they live in Scotland!'

In fact, Enzo's great, warm tribe had been one of the greatest pleasures of Jane's marriage. There had never been an occasion when she felt alone or unsupported after she had become his wife.

'You don't mind, do you?' Enzo asked, now. 'If I

113

don't come with you?'

'Of course I don't mind. You're probably right about going on my own this first time. We'll go together next week, shall we? When Ha is likely to be about. It's easy to overlook his part in all of this, and Tintin is his baby as well.'

'That sounds a good idea. You'll give Flo my love, won't you? I've got something for her, actually. A necklace I saw in an antique shop in Munich. It's only glass and silver, but pretty. I thought it would be a nice way to mark Tintin's birth.'

'How thoughtful! Flo will be thrilled. So you'll be working at home today? That's good. I won't have to worry about Chipper.'

From his basket under the window the dog lifted his head at the sound of his name and thumped his tail.

'There's cold meat and stuff in the fridge for your lunch,' said Jane getting a casserole out of the freezer and putting it on the table to take with her. 'I think I might just call in at Cedar Lodge and see Aunt Joan on the way, to tell her the good news. I've given up trying to speak to her on the telephone. The bellowed conversations don't really go anywhere. She's too deaf to hear properly and then she gets irritated and confused. Sometimes I feel she doesn't even know that it's me on the other end of the line.'

Enzo nodded, already thinking about something else. Jane's commentaries tended to run past him in the mornings.

'I did tell you, didn't I, that we are going to lunch with Tash and Denby on Sunday?'

'You did.'

'They've got their Indian production manager over. Tash didn't want me to take a pudding because she has put Denby on a diet.'

'Ah!'

Jane glanced at Enzo, who was rummaging in his briefcase. He's not listening, she thought. My voice is like background noise. Going through to the utility room to get an insulated bag for the casserole she saw that he had left a load of dirty washing on the floor, a jumble of shirts and underwear that he had taken to Munich. He was a man used to having women looking after him. First his mother and his sisters, then Jane, and all the theatre sisters and anxious little nurses who were at his beck and call at the hospital. Jane imagined them passing him instruments during operations, their eyes wide above their masks, scanning his face for the slightest signal that he wanted something, eager to anticipate his every wish.

When she went back through to the kitchen he was gone, ignoring the debris of the breakfast things on the table. By just getting up and leaving things as they were he seemed to suggest that lowly tasks were exclusively her department. He could make a small effort to help, she thought. A gesture, at least, if only to show her that he realised that she did all these things for him. At the same time, she knew she was really to blame because if he had even picked up a coffee cup she would have said, 'Oh, don't bother with that. I'll do it.'

She'd have to take Chipper out before she left for Flo's. It was no good expecting Enzo to do so. He would already be up in his study reading or writing something significant and, probably,

115

ultimately life-saving. It wasn't difficult to see that while her time was spent performing mundane tasks for people, his was the important work, but all the same, as she put on an old coat and collected Chipper's lead off the hook behind the kitchen door, she still felt mildly irritated.

It was a bright morning, still cold, but with a weak, watery sun wavering through the thin grey clouds, and as Jane walked down the road she looked over her neighbours' hedges and fences and noted the various signs of the end of winter, the drifts of daffodils, the bright crocuses poking through the newly green grass, and the sharp little green points of new leaves on the hedges.

It was a prosperous neighbourhood, middle-class, middle-aged, with houses set well back from the road with wide drives on which shining cars were parked. There were no plastic toys littering the lawns, no bounding dogs, no lines of flapping washing, no toddlers on tricycles, no young mothers with prams. All was quiet. Whatever life went on behind the leaded glass of the mock-Tudor windows and the oak-studded front doors was hidden from the prying eyes of passers-by. How little we know about each other, Jane thought. She and Enzo and the boys had lived there for nearly twelve years and she could name only about six of the householders in The Avenue and recall only having spoken to her immediate neighbours perhaps three times in the last month.

Anything could happen, anything could be going on, she thought, and we wouldn't know. There was a Pakistani family living at the next house she passed. Apart from incongruous lime-green net curtains at all the windows, it looked no different

116

from any of the others, and yet there had been rumbles of concern when they had arrived two years ago, the portly father buttoned into a three-piece suit and the shy wife in a gold embroidered sari. Would they let down the standard of the road, people asked. Would there be offensive cooking smells and rowdy goings-on? Would they understand that gardens must be maintained, lawns cut, paths swept, houses painted? They needn't have worried. The house looked immaculate and as much like a fortress as any of the others. Only the area at the front was a little strange, tarmacked over so that it looked more like a car park, with the obligatory cherry tree sticking up out of a round hole left for its trunk. The high gates were electronically controlled and tightly shut.

What on earth went on in there, Jane wondered. Was the security system to keep people in, or out? Nobody knew what the man did for a living. There were rumours he had a market stall, that he owned a jeweller's in Birmingham, that he was the landlord of a string of rented houses in the city.

When Jane and Enzo had first moved in there was concern about them too, because of the strange, foreign-sounding name. 'We didn't know, you see, dear,' said Mrs Maple from next door, standing at her oak garden gate in hat, coat and gloves, her pink face eager to talk, 'quite what to expect. You just don't know these days, do you? So it's a lovely relief to see that you are all, well, English, and your husband a doctor too!'

She thought we might be black, thought Jane, amused.

'And it's two lovely boys, you've got?' went

on Mrs Maple, beady-eyed, poking about for information like a blackbird in a flowerbed.

'That's right,' said Jane. 'And a daughter who has already left home.' No need to go into stepdaughters, half-sisters. No need for Mrs Maple to start doing sums, wondering, working out the truth.

Enzo loved living here. It was as far removed as possible from the noisy, cramped house where he grew up in a dour grey Scottish town and he liked the space and quiet and anonymity. He dealt with people and their problems all day, he said. He certainly didn't want to be made conscious of his neighbours when he got home. The boys had enjoyed it too, just an easy bike ride from tennis courts and swimming pool, and with the school they attended only fifteen minutes' walk away. Now they were hardly at home, their lives taking off in different directions. They still had the two big attic bedrooms at the top of the house, with their schoolboy posters peeling off the walls and their untidy shelves of books and magazines, but apart from returning at least once every holiday to dump their possessions, eat some favourite meals and cadge a bit of money, they no longer really lived there. They took after Enzo and were bright, confident young men. Home was a springboard for the rest of their lives, not a place in which to linger.

The house had never been home to Florence, and Jane always felt a bit sad that when she used to come to stay when she was a medical student, she slept in the tidy spare room, as if she was a visitor. Now, with the arrival of Tintin, Jane wondered if she should reorganise things and create a nursery on the first floor, a room specially for when he came to stay. She planned to buy a second-hand cot and a baby buggy. She imagined pushing him, sleeping and contented, up The Avenue where she was walking now, to the small patch of woodland at the top. It was a little bit of pretend countryside where squirrels ran up and down the oak tree and violets and primroses grew in the bank. She could sit on the bench provided by the council and rock the pram with the toe of her shoe while Tintin slept.

Although she had pushed the boys in their strollers not so many years ago, it was Florence as a baby that Jane remembered now. The battered old coach-built pram with chipped cream paint and brown folding hood suddenly seemed as real as if she had the worn handlebar between her hands and she was pushing it up the road in front of her. She remembered the weight of it, the creak of the springs, the worn plastic lining, which she had scrubbed clean but which remained cracked and discoloured. She remembered Florence asleep with her golden curls poking out from her little knitted hat, her hand in a pink mitten against her cheek. She remembered many things that she wished to forget, which had lain hidden for a long, long time.

Chipper, running ahead, turned back to wait for her. Jane shoved her hands into the pockets of her coat and strode purposefully up the road. She shouldn't be dawdling along thinking about the past when she had a busy day in front of her.

*   *   *

When Jane was six months pregnant she had an

119

interview with the adoption society that her parents had arranged would take her baby. It took place when she went for her first appointment at the hospital antenatal clinic. At least sixty women were called to attend at two o'clock in the afternoon, and they were instructed to announce their arrival and then sit in order on rows of plastic chairs in a large waiting room, each clutching a sample of urine brought along in anything from a fish paste pot to a milk bottle. Jane, who had had to ask for time off work, was dismayed to find a long queue in front of her when she arrived.

'Terrible, this place is, love,' said the woman behind her, who had tight blond curls and a raddled face. To Jane she looked far too old to be pregnant but she was wearing a smock top over a considerable bulge of baby. 'Your first time, is it? Unless you get here half an hour early, you're here all the afternoon. Bloody cheek, I call it, treating us like we've got nothing else to do. I have to send me other kids round to their nan's because I know I won't be back at teatime.'

Each woman in turn was called forward to the nurse's desk and their notes retrieved from a trolley of folders containing hundreds of similar buff files. They were then directed to a double row of curtained cubicles where they were told to remove their underwear, climb onto the couch and wait for the consultant to examine them. Meanwhile, everyone else got up and moved up one place. It looked as if it would be a very long wait and Jane wished that she had brought a book to read. A lot of the other women got knitting out of their bags and started clacking away, poring over patterns for tiny matinée jackets or little white bootees.

Jane was relieved to see that there were one or two girls who looked even younger than she was. She tried to see if they were wearing wedding rings because they seemed bold and unashamed. Listening to the conversations going on round her she found that the older women were full of advice and information for those expecting their first babies. They seemed to have strong views to air on everything from nappy rash to breast-feeding, which they were very opposed to. The bottle was all the thing. 'Then you can get your old man to feed the baby!' said one. 'You must be bloody joking!' said another from the row behind. 'There's only one sort of bottle as far as mine's concerned, and it's not a bloody baby bottle, neither!' It was like a large, cheerful club and Jane felt that the sickness and heartburn and swollen ankles and high blood pressure that they complained of were made bearable because of the camaraderie of this sisterhood. They were all in it together and there was nothing to be done but get on with it. She didn't want to have to tell any of them that she wasn't going to be keeping her baby.

Later, she lay on the narrow bed in the curtained cubicle, trying to distance herself from the unpleasant nature of the examination and the curtness of the doctor. Any moment the nurse with a face like a turnip would be back to take a blood sample, but when the curtains were pulled aside it was a grey-haired woman in a neat tweed suit who stepped in, holding a clipboard and carrying a handbag over her arm. She managed to look non-medical, but still official.

'Miss Kindersley?' she asked. 'I'm Mrs Daniels,

from the adoption society. I always try to see my girls at about this stage of their pregnancies to have a little chat. It's so much better when you know a little bit about the adoption process.'

Jane nodded dumbly, completely taken by surprise.

'Let's see,' said Mrs Daniels, consulting her notes. 'Baby is due in July, in three months, so this is the right time to start the procedure to allocate him to his new family. We have a very long list of couples wishing to adopt a baby. Some have a long wait before one becomes available. Of course, newborns are always the most sought after. Older children are harder to place, for obvious reasons. So your baby will make a woman who is unable to have her own children very happy and that's something nice for you to think about, isn't it? We try to give the adoptive parents as much time as possible to make preparations for Baby's arrival so when we have completed the paperwork and the consent forms, I will be able to give them the news which they have been waiting for.'

Jane struggled to sit up on the narrow bed, and pulled the cellular blanket over her knees. She felt at a terrible disadvantage. It was like being interviewed, half-naked, by her headmistress.

'We are a Christian organisation and we screen our couples very carefully. I can assure you that Baby will have a loving and secure Christian home. I know how important that is to you.' She looked down at Jane with a bright smile and then leaned forward to pat her hand.

'It is not uncommon for young women to feel a little weepy and upset at the thought of parting with their babies. It's only natural that you should,

122

but you understand that you are doing what is best for Baby and for yourself, because you are not in a position to offer a proper start in life, or have the necessary means of supporting a child.'

Jane nodded. She was finding it hard to breathe or swallow. Her face was on fire.

'Will I know who has the baby? Will I know where he has gone?'

Mrs Daniels shook her head. 'Oh, no, dear. By law we have to maintain complete secrecy to protect both you and the adopting parents. That is why Baby will be removed immediately after birth and you will have no further contact with him.'

'I won't be allowed to see him?'

'No. It is much better not. Better for you, that is. In our experience, mothers get over the parting with very little trouble if it is done this way. He will be taken by the midwife to the nursery where he will be looked after and started on a bottle-feeding schedule. You will remain on the ward until you are ready to go home.' She smiled again. She had large teeth that seemed too big for her mouth and her breath smelled very faintly of fish. She turned to her clipboard.

'Now, shall we just go through these forms, Miss Kindersley?'

Jane took the sheets of paper in a trembling hand. 'Now? Do I have to do this now?' she asked. 'Only, I don't feel all that well. I'd rather—'

'You can take them away with you, if you prefer, but they are quite straightforward and only require your signature. I have prepared them with your name and other details.' Mrs Daniels got a pen from her bag and held it out to Jane.

'I see. But I really don't want to do this just yet. I

123

imagined that it would be later on, nearer the time.'

Mrs Daniels paused. The brightness of her smile faded and was replaced by a look of doubt and concern. 'I hope that you aren't going to be difficult, Miss Kindersley,' she said in a regretful tone. 'I think you need to remind yourself of the wishes of your parents. You have caused them a great deal of anxiety, as you know. I see from my correspondence with them that they request an immediate adoption. It seems,' she consulted her notes and gave a sad little sigh, 'that the father of your baby is unknown.'

Jane nodded, unable to speak. She twisted the blanket between her hands and willed herself not to cry. This woman was of the sort that she had always tried hard to please; like other people's mothers or teachers. It would have been so much easier to take the offered biro and comply with her wishes, but there was a stubborn little core in her heart that would not let her do it. She didn't have time to wonder why she was resisting, but it seemed to matter very much that she did.

Mrs Daniels gave her another long look and then put her pen back in her handbag and closed it with a snap. 'Of course, I can come to see you at your next appointment here in a month's time, if you prefer. By then I hope you will be ready to complete the paperwork. It will give you a chance to show that you have become a more responsible person, and in your circumstances it should be a great relief for you to know that Baby's future is secured.' She gave Jane a last grimace of a smile, and went out through the curtains.

Jane heard a whispered conversation with

someone outside and guessed she was speaking to the nurse and that her obstinacy was being discussed. What could they expect? She was a bad girl, behaving badly.

*   *   *

All the way home on the bus, Jane sat on the top deck with her hot face pressed against the cold window. Why am I being like this, she thought. Why am I making everything worse? Haven't I caused enough trouble already? Why do I hate the thought of the nice Christian couple waiting to take this baby away? After all, I don't want it. It's ruined my whole life, so why should I care?

And all the way home the baby kicked and turned somersaults inside her. Being poked at by the doctor seemed to have thoroughly woken him up. Why does everyone call him 'he', Jane thought, and suddenly it seemed to her that this wasn't a boy baby at all.

*   *   *

Jane found Aunt Joan in her usual chair in the drawing room of Cedar Lodge. She stood for a moment watching her sitting there with her chin nodding onto her chest, her bony hands clasped on the shelf of her stomach. She looked so incredibly old and withdrawn, as if she was already adjusting to leaving the world and everything in it. Was she asleep? As Jane drew closer and then gently touched her arm, Joan snapped open her eyes and was instantly alert.

'Jane? What are you doing here? Not at work?'

'No. I've taken the day off to visit Flo and her baby. I think I told you she knew it would be a boy? Born the day before yesterday and absolutely perfect and healthy in every way. She's thrilled with him.'

'Of course, I remember you told me. I don't forget everything, you know. I might be senile but I've still got a little brain left in working order.'

Jane drew up a chair, conscious that if she sat on it, she would present her back to another elderly woman sitting opposite, but when she glanced in her direction she saw that she was quite unaware of her presence, staring into space, her face blank.

Jane turned back to Aunt Joan, who said, 'I suppose I should ask you how heavy he is, as if he were a salmon. That's what everybody always wants to know about babies, although I've never quite known why. It's not a question ever asked again in life, is it?'

'Oh, he's whopping! Flo's been terribly careful about diet and so on, for maximum nutritional value and special foods for his brain development! He's bred to win, this one! How did our babies ever turn out moderately normal, mine and Tash's, when we drank and smoked non-stop throughout our pregnancies? Nobody told us not to, in those days. Now we'd get reported to the social services!'

Joan snorted. 'Is she at home? Back at that flat of hers?'

'Yes, they don't keep you in hospital any more unless there are complications. I was kept in for ten days when I had Flo. It was like a prison sentence. I remember looking out of the barred ward window and weeping with longing to feel fresh air on my face.'

126

'I remember,' said Joan, and Jane thought, of course you would, and she took her aunt's old hand in hers. It been Aunt Joan who had come to see her every evening after work, clipping across the polished linoleum to her bedside in her painful court shoes with a string bag containing fruit or a book or a bag of sweets, and one evening a pack of postcards from the National Gallery of a Renoir painting of a rosy girl playing with a chubby, laughing baby. She laid them on Jane's bed with a book of postage stamps and said, 'You can write and tell your friends about Florence.' By doing so she was taking up her stand against Jane's mother, who wanted the very existence of this baby denied.

'Give me my bag, if you would,' said Aunt Joan, poking at it with her stick where it sat on the low table in front of her chair. Jane passed it to her and watched as she fumbled to find what she was looking for: a small green leather box. She handed it to Jane and said, 'There, that's for the baby. I made them get it out of the safe when you told me it was going to be a boy. Have a look.' Jane opened the box and inside found a pair of old gold cufflinks. 'They were your great-grandfather's. Goodness knows why I've kept them all these years, but I'd like Florence's boy to have them.' Jane held the links in the palm of her hand. The gold was pale and the two rectangular sides of the cufflink, each one stamped with the initials 'J.S.', were joined by a delicate chain.

'They're beautiful,' she said. 'What do the initials stand for?'

'James Stafford.'

'Tintin will love them when he's old enough to appreciate them.'

'Tintin? I thought you said his name was to be Timothy?'

'No, it's Tintin, I'm afraid.'

'Well, thank God for that!'

'It's a terrible name!' said Jane, laughing. 'I hope that they have second thoughts about it and change their minds! It seems the Belgian comic-book character was Ha's favourite when he was a boy.'

'Better than Timothy!' Aunt Joan could never let it go, thought Jane, that old feud with her father. She couldn't see where the dislike could spring from because he was never a bad man; ineffectual and weak, perhaps, but surely not deserving of this lasting contempt.

*   *   *

Later, when she stood up to go, Jane was suddenly aware that the elderly woman opposite was now watching her with an alert interest, and she turned and acknowledged her with a smile. A look of great animation crossed the old face.

'Oh! We're great friends, Joan and I!' announced the old lady in a sweet, girlish voice. 'We have *great* fun, don't we, darling? Out dining and dancing every night! What high jinks!'

And to Jane's surprise Joan responded kindly, smiling back and saying, 'Yes, we do, Enid. *Great* fun!' before turning to Jane and raising her eyebrows.

Jane walked back to her car thinking that even in extreme old age, and in the most unlikely person, human kindness did not necessarily run dry and still made the world a nicer place. It was touching that the source, in this case, was crabby old Joan, who was not a woman who had engendered much affection in her life, and now was stuck in a home because there was no one willing to look after her. I suppose, if I was a better person, I would have had hcr to livc with us, Jane thought, but it wouldn't work for five minutes. She'd drive me to murder.

*   *   *

The hour's drive to the small cathedral city in which Florence lived and worked took Jane through open countryside where sheep and lambs grazed in bleached brown fields, untouched as yet by the freshness of spring, and the earth of the ploughed land was as dark as chocolate. This was prosperous, Midlands farming country with big, red-brick farmhouses, four storeys high, sometimes set back from the road by railed paddocks in which horses grazed, still wearing thick winter rugs. In some of the fields enormous farm machinery moved slowly, like giant, brightly painted toys, followed by wheeling flocks of seagulls.

Jane disliked the country, the wide open spaces, the naked-looking sky, the long empty views. Instead of a sense of freedom, she felt threatening loneliness and isolation. Remains of villages flashed by, heartless places without shop, post office, or church, where cottage doors opened onto the busy road and juggernaut lorries rattled the windows and blackened the brickwork.

The verges on either side were worn and dirty, the grass matted and grey, littered with shredded

129

plastic and other rubbish, old shoes, a man's tattered jacket blown against the fence, a large piece of twisted metal, then a length of flattened, gingerish fur—a fox, a cat?

The countryside petered out into a semi-built-up area of industrial units, garages, car showrooms, factory outlets selling garden furniture and carpets, then supermarkets and DIY stores and fast-food restaurants. The road was slow, clogged with traffic, crawling between sets of lights and roundabouts and then, thankfully, Jane reached the turning for the motorway that would speed her all the way to Florence.

It was only a few minutes from the exit at the other end, past the bus station and then a triangle of park with flowerbeds of daffodils planted in straight lines, past the red stone clock tower erected by a nineteenth-century factory owner, and then under the railway bridge to the canal street on which Florence lived in an old warehouse converted into flats. There was private parking at the rear of the building and Jane spotted Florence's car with a baby seat already in place and a sticker in the rear window warning that a baby was on board. What are other car drivers supposed to do, thought Jane. Decide not to have an accident? A few minutes later, her arms full, she was knocking at her daughter's door.

It took a long time for Florence to open it. Her face, devoid of make-up, looked young and without subtlety, her skin rather shiny, and with dark smudges under her eyes. She was dressed in a pair of baggy track trousers and an outsize sweater, but her smile was brilliant. Without saying a word, she relieved her mother of the casserole and plastic bags and then turned back to embrace her. They did not kiss, but rather held each other quite tightly, which was not something that Florence, as a rule, was keen on. A fleeting kiss on the cheek was her usual greeting, and Jane wondered at a new tenderness between them.

'Come!' said Florence, holding out her hand to lead Jane further into the flat, and then, 'Wait here!' A moment later she returned with a shawl-wrapped bundle and with great solemnity placed Tintin in his grandmother's arms.

CHAPTER SIX

'Oh, Tash, he really is a lovely baby!' sighed Jane a few days later as she stood in her sister's enormous kitchen, chopping parsley. 'I didn't know what to expect as a grandmother. I wondered if I would feel that instant rush of love that I did for my own babies, and I did! Flo put him in my arms and he opened his big blue eyes and gave me the once-over—a very serious assessment—and then he yawned, scrunched up his little face, and did a thunderous fart, and closed his eyes again, as if to say, "Yes, I feel safe with you." I really felt the connection between us very strongly. It was wonderful, miraculous! He's so plump, he doesn't seem newborn and he hasn't got that raw, half-cooked look of some babies. His skin is a lovely pale biscuit colour—like a Rich Tea biscuit—and he has these big blue eyes, but slightly almond-shaped with long dark lashes and a mop of black hair. Ha said he couldn't see it, but there is

131

definitely an oriental look about him. And he's so good and contented, although Flo says she has no time to do anything at all between feeds and nappy changes. You know how it is with a new baby. Can you remember how you were often still in your nightdress at lunchtime? Of course, the telephone never stops ringing, and just when he had gone to sleep after lunch and Flo was having a rest, the community nurse arrived to see how they are getting on and they both had to be woken up.'

Tash looked across at her sister and thought she was looking prettier than usual. Jane never made much effort with her appearance, and hadn't for years, and Tash, for whom clothes were such an important expression of her own personality, found it hard to imagine what it was like to not care much what one wore. Looking reasonably tidy and being comfortable were Jane's guiding principles, although to be fair there had been times when she hadn't the money to spend anything on herself.

Today she was wearing a long woollen skirt that Tash knew to be at least five years old, and a cashmere sweater she had given her one Christmas. In fact, the earrings and necklace had been a gift from her as well, and the boots were those she had passed on last year when she decided that they weren't right for her. The tassels did not work for the gaucho look she was assembling back then.

It wasn't that lack of vanity made her sister unattractive. In fact, Denby was always saying that Jane was 'womanly', by which he meant beddable. There was something wholesome about her pink and white complexion, and her thick brown hair,

132

which these days she was colouring to cover the grey. She looked as she always had, thought Tash fondly; older, obviously, but essentially like the girl she had once been with a face that was still somehow open and easy to read. Today it was lit with excitement about Flo's baby.

'You *are* smitten!' she said, taking Jane's hand for a moment. 'But I'm not at all sure I want to enthuse over babies just yet. It seems only ten minutes since I finished with my own. I shall start taking a proper interest in Tintin when he is about two and can hold a sensible conversation. Did Flo get the parcel I sent?'

'The organic baby clothes? Yes, she did. They arrived the morning I was there. She was delighted with them because, naturally, Tintin must have only the best!'

'Good. Did you see the sample of our new cot bedding? Tell you what, if Tintin is really such a stunner, we could use him in our catalogue. The fact that he's slightly ethnic-looking would be perfect for our company profile.'

Jane smiled at her sister, who had turned to stir a pan on her enormous Aga and was then whisking away to gather bright pottery plates from a distressed, lime-washed cupboard, which extended the whole length of one wall. She had spotted it in a derelict Italian farmhouse last year and had it shipped home in pieces—a process that a less determined person would have found overwhelming.

Tash was still slim, with none of the middle-aged padding that Jane recognised had settled on her own hips, and had let her thick shoulder-length hair go completely grey. Jane realised this was a

133

statement about something or other. She couldn't quite remember whether it was the exploitation of women by the beauty industry, a protest against stereotyping or attitudes to ageing, or the chemicals in hair dye. Probably all of them and a few more, because Tash was a great embracer of causes.

From the back, the grey mane could have made her look like an ancient *Macbeth*-type crone had she not been dressed in her own clothing designs— in this case very tight black trousers and a pale lavender-coloured woollen shirt with a velvet waistcoat. Her arms jangled with silver bracelets as she moved about, adding this and that from the herb rack to the saucepan. And that was the other thing about her, thought Jane—the speed and energy with which she did everything. She was never still for a moment. She had set the huge kitchen table for lunch at a run, darting backwards and forwards to the cupboards with armfuls of cutlery and handfuls of glasses.

Having grey hair seemed to enhance the beauty of her face, the delicate bone structure even more pronounced in middle age, the signature dark red lipstick on her wide mouth, her eyes still ringed with kohl as they had been since she was fifteen, and the whole lit by the animation and liveliness that she had always possessed. Both sisters were blessed with good skin—that was something to thank their mother for—and Tash's complexion had benefited from the care she had taken to look after it. She had developed her own natural skin products years before they became fashionable, melting honey and smashing herbs in a pestle and mortar in her first tiny London kitchen while the little box fridge was full of mashed avocados and pulped fruit. Nowadays her whole new range, endorsed by models and superstars, was produced in a stainless-steel factory unit in Wales, while Tash and Denby flew round the world sourcing wonder ingredients as well as growing what they could at home.

Through the open door to the garden Jane could see Enzo and Denby walking about with the Indian guests, Denby leading the way, gesturing grandly to right and left. Being so tall and recently grown quite stout, he cut an impressive figure. Gradually, over the years, he had reverted to type and now looked the English country gentleman he had been at such pains to leave behind in his youth. Given that he and Tash had recently moved to this large country house, complete with walled vegetable garden, in a park-like setting, with iron railings down the drive, a ha-ha and fine old cedar trees, his appearance was appropriate. This morning he was wearing moleskin trousers, brown boots, a striped cotton shirt, and a checked waistcoat such as a nineteenth-century squire might well have had in his wardrobe.

'Are the Singhs cold out there, do you think?' asked Tash, coming to stand beside her sister for a moment. 'Denby gets terribly carried away explaining his garden plans. He's completely replanted the parterre. He went to Holland last week to bring back some special dwarf box. He's planted it with golden variegated and purple sage in a sea of *Festuca glauca*—you know, that lovely grey-leaved grass.' She spun to the huge American fridge and got out a bottle of champagne as she talked. 'Here, let's get this open. We can get

135

started by wetting the baby's head together.'

'No, they won't be cold,' said Jane, still standing at the glass doors and trying to picture what Tash had just described. She and Denby carried such sweeping schemes in their heads that it made her feel very pedestrian by contrast. 'They look very well wrapped up and it's actually quite warm this morning.'

'We had to lend them proper outdoor clothes. Poor Mrs Singh looked blue with cold when she arrived but she was quite resistant to wearing my shearling coat. I had a sudden awful feeling that she might think it was made out of some forbidden, unclean animal. I must admit that it's a bit of a concern that she and Rashid seem to dress entirely in man-made fibres, which hardly makes them ideal ambassadors for our grand new organic, sustainable cotton factory. Her sari is one hundred per cent nylon and crackling with static electricity. I think I may have to have a little chat about it.' She eased the cork out of the bottle with a satisfying pop.

Jane looked at her sister in amazement. 'For heaven's sake, Tash, you can't do that! You don't own your employees, and certainly not their wives! You can't dictate what they wear!'

Tash looked up from pouring the champagne. 'It would only be gentle pressure I had in mind. I was thinking of offering a clothing voucher scheme for the workers, as well as making them company shareholders, which we do already. It would look good in the catalogue, wouldn't it, if we could say that the whole workforce wears the ethically approved clothes that it produces? It would give the factory and the people who work in it a philosophical unity.'

'That may be, but in this instance you can't and mustn't say anything. It would be as bad as all those awful, bossy missionaries in the last century making African women wear bras. Perhaps the Singhs don't want to wear Western clothing, and how do you know that her sari material isn't made from recycled tyres, or something very environmentally sound?'

'Jane, our clothing isn't "Western"! The whole point is that our designs transcend cultural and ethnic differences—and aren't gender exclusive, either. Mr *or* Mrs Singh could wear what I've got on today, for instance!'

Jane had to laugh. Her first impression was that the Singhs were small and round and highly unlikely to want to go about dressed as Tash. She could see that Mr Singh had on what looked like a three-piece suit, and probably wore a fob watch. Suddenly Tash saw the absurdity of her argument. 'Well, perhaps not! OK, sis. Denby would agree with you. He's always telling me I have the tact of a rhinoceros.'

'Well, he's right in this case!'

Tash handed Jane a glass and lifted her own. 'To Tintin!'

'Tintin!' They smiled at one another over the rims. Tash took a gulp and then put down her glass. Her face took on a slightly strained look.

'Oh, by the way, I had a medical last week. A boob scan. Apparently something showed up.'

Jane looked at Tash in immediate concern but her sister, catching sight of her face, gave a careless little laugh. 'Don't look like that. I'm sure it is nothing. Nothing they're particularly worried about, but I've got to go back for another check. I just thought you should know. I haven't said anything to Denby; he's such a terrific one for flapping. He'll imagine me dead and buried in no time at all. In fact, he'll probably start designing a garden of rest with me in a tasteful urn!' Tash laughed another short nervous bark.

'I'm so sorry,' said Jane, catching hold of her hand. 'Can I come with you to your appointment? I'd really like to.'

'Oh, God no! It would be a waste of your time and I don't need support just yet. I'm expecting to get a clean bill of health.'

Jane could not drink her champagne now. The celebratory atmosphere had entirely gone. She put down the glass and put her arms round her sister. Despite the huge energy she radiated, she felt very small and frail. She was a hard person to embrace because she was rarely still long enough to hug, but this time she leaned into Jane's body and allowed her head to drop onto her shoulder. But it was only a moment before she extricated herself and went to look out of the window.

'We have to do what Churchill advised,' she said. 'Keep buggering on.'

*   *   *

After her guests had all gone home and Denby was asleep in front of the television, Tash put on a coat and a pair of boots and went for a walk. Although it was after six thirty it was still light and she felt that if she met anybody she would be compelled to have the sort of springtime conversation that ran on the lines of, 'Aren't the evenings drawing out?

138

Look, it's still light!'

She walked down the drive towards the lodge cottage in which their current 'couple' from South Africa were living in return for helping around the place. There was no sign of life as she opened the small iron gate next to the cattle grid over which vehicles rattled on their way to the big house. Glancing up at the windows of the cottage she saw that the curtains were all drawn tight. Probably still in bed, she thought. Probably never have got out of it today, on their day off. They were a young couple, tall and brown and healthy-looking.

The thought made Tash feel old and sad. She had a vision of Denby, noisily asleep in his armchair, and herself, walking alone on a Sunday evening, perhaps carrying with her, under the padded cotton coat she was wearing, the speading roots of a fatal disease.

Don't think it, she told herself sternly, but she couldn't help it. Who could, in her situation? It had even been hard telling Jane, who was the one person to whom she could tell everything. She felt that by speaking of this dreadful thing, she was casting a burden on those whom she loved and who loved her in return, and it was not a situation she was used to. She had always been the strong one. Or at least, she had got used to thinking of herself as being like that. The rock at the centre of things.

As she walked down the lane she turned back to look at the house. She was proud of how imposing it was in the twilight, like a great house in a romantic film; Manderley or Tara, or somewhere like that. I've got used to thinking of my life as a success, she thought, because I've achieved almost everything I've ever wanted. It's been like a film in which I star and direct and write the script, and suddenly it seems as if there's a new scriptwriter who threatens to take the whole thing off in another direction.

Of course there had been hard times and painful times but she had always survived. She had survived Denby's infidelities when at one time she would have thought his treachery would have wrecked their life together. She had learned to forgive and even to understand, and these days she could look at the old rogue with the deepest affection.

I'm going to get through this, she told herself, whatever it is. If it's bad news, I'll get through that as well. I'll deal with it and be strong for Denby and the kids. We're a pair of tough old birds, Jane and me. That's one good thing we have inherited from our mother.

She thought of Jane as she had been today, brimming with happiness about Flo's baby. Who would have thought that things could have turned out so well, when at one time they had looked so black? Jane had survived, and so would she.

* * *

The day after her visit to the hospital Jane was forced to accept that the time had come to tell Mr Kowalski the truth. Although she often kept her coat on, saying it was cold in the shop, or wore the big shapeless jumper belonging to her father, it was getting increasingly hard to disguise her condition. She caught her own reflection in shop windows and could see that she was looking decidedly rotund.

140

On her way to work she stopped at the patisserie and bought two apricot pastries, and at the Italian delicatessen for a small packet of ground coffee, despite the fact that it was one of the few things that made her feel sick and which she could no longer drink. Mr Kowalski had not yet arrived and so she let herself into the shop and went through to the back room to switch on the electric fire and put the kettle on to boil. The room was so bleak and cold with its bare light bulb, its papered-over window and general disarray, but she put the pastries on saucers and washed the two small cups and the coffee jug in the small basin in the lavatory across the passage. She had everything ready by the time she heard a key turning in the front door of the shop.

Mr Kowalski came shuffling in, wearing his long overcoat and muffler and his foreign-looking black felt hat and with his string bag in his hand.

'Ah! My dear,' he said, 'you are here early this morning.' He looked round the room, seeing the pastries and coffee pot. 'What is this? A celebration? A birthday?'

'No, not exactly. Mr Kowalski, I have something I must tell you.' Jane's voice wavered with nerves.

'Not something grave, I hope? Your face looks very solemn.'

'Well, yes, it is serious. Mr Kowalski, I expect that you have noticed, or maybe, wondered . . .' Jane faltered. She felt she had made a bad start. She didn't mean to suggest that he took an interest in her body or would have realised that it had changed shape. 'Anyway, I feel that I have to tell you that I'm expecting a baby!' There, all in a rush she had done it. 'I realise that I'm letting you down

141

and that I should have told you when you first interviewed me, and I'm really sorry about that.'

Mr Kowalski had sat himself at his table, still wearing his coat. She hadn't given him time to take it off. 'Oh, my dear!' he said, smiling at her. 'A baby is always to be rejoiced over!'

'Well, no! Not in this case. I mean, it was a terrible mistake. You know that I'm not married, or anything.' Jane flushed furiously. Her hands were shaking as she poured out the very dark coffee and passed the cup to her employer.

'I must correct you. A baby is always to be rejoiced over, whatever the circumstances. It is a wonderful gift, a joy and a great responsibility. I have observed you at your work. You are gentle and patient, and you are a healthy young woman with a good life in front of you. You will be a wonderful mother for this baby.'

'Oh, but you don't understand. I'm not going to keep it, Mr Kowalski. I can't, you see. My parents won't allow it. I am too young and I'm supposed to be at college, and it's all arranged for it to be adopted as soon as it's born. It will go to a really nice family who can't have their own children.'

'You are giving your baby away?' Mr Kowalski's face was suddenly very grave. 'How can this be?'

'Well, I've got to. Everybody says that it's the best thing, you see. Best for the baby. It will go to people who can give it a much better life than I ever could.'

'But how is it better? Better for whom? Better in what way?'

'Better for the baby. And for me. It was a terrible mistake, you see. Me getting pregnant.'

'No, I do not see. I do not see how a mother can

142

give up a baby or how your parents can wish this to happen.'

Jane fell silent. She hadn't expected this. She was prepared to apologise for the inconvenience caused by her pregnancy, but not to defend her decision. She had never had a personal conversation with Mr Kowalski before and yet here he was, challenging everything she said, challenging the decision she had been led to believe was best.

'They are thinking of me too, you see. They say that I'm much too young to have the responsibility of looking after a baby. My mother thinks I am still a child myself. I have got to get my life back on track and take up my college place.'

'This is more important to you than your child?'

'Well, no. Of course I want to be sure that it has a proper home and everything. The adoption society promise that they check everything very carefully.'

'How can you know this? When you give it away to strangers? How can they measure the love that your baby will receive? This is the most unnatural thing I have ever heard of.'

He spoke so sharply and with such feeling that Jane's knees began to tremble and her breath fluttered in her chest in an alarming way. Without being invited she pulled out the chair from the opposite side of the table and sat down and put her hot face in her hands. It was all too much—the hospital visit, Mrs Daniels and her forms, and the baby moving about inside her as a reminder of the new life she had created and was preparing to give away. A huge wave of self-pity engulfed her. It's not fair, she thought. It's not fair that this

143

should have happened to me. If only she had someone to talk to, who would understand and sympathise. Aunt Joan did not invite confidences. She preferred to ignore Jane's situation as something unfortunate, best got on with, and Rosie and Judith, busy on their first teaching practices, did not respond to her messages to telephone her, to write, to come to see her in London.

Mr Kowalski sat looking at her in silence. Even with her eyes covered, Jane could sense that he was not apologetic for having upset her. The atmosphere still seethed with his indignation. Then he pulled a clean, folded handkerchief from his jacket pocket and handed it to her across the table.

'You must not cry,' he said in a kinder tone. 'I have something to show you,' and he reached to an inside pocket and took out a worn leather wallet. He fumbled through some tiny scraps of folded paper and then laid two small black-and-white photographs on the table.

'Here,' he said. 'My wife and children.'

Jane gulped and picked up the first of the small snaps. The photograph had a snowy backdrop and showed a heavily wrapped-up young woman standing holding the hand of a child of about two of indeterminate sex. Behind them was a forest of birch trees iced over with white. It was impossible to determine the young woman's features or expression. The photograph was unremarkable in every way and Jane could think of nothing to say except, 'It looks very cold.'

The second showed the same young woman with the child on her knee, sitting on a bench on what looked like a station platform. She was wearing a scarf over her light-coloured hair and squinted into the sunshine. She had a pleasant, unremarkable face and the child—a girl of about three or four, with blonde plaits—was holding the mother's hand in both her own small hands, and looking up at the photographer without smiling.

'Elzbietta, my wife, and Ewa, my daughter,' said Mr Kowalski.

'You said "children"?'

'Elzbietta was pregnant in this second photograph.'

With a terrible sense of foreboding, Jane guessed what was coming, but she knew that she had to ask. 'And?' she said in a small voice. 'What happened to them, Mr Kowalski?'

'During the war, my sister and I were couriers for the Polish Home Army—the underground resistance. While I was absent, the Germans came to our flat in Poznan and took my wife and child. The neighbours saw them go but did not know where they were taken. I never saw them again. These photographs are all I have to remind me that they ever existed. Later, many years after the war ended and I was here, in England, the Red Cross helped me to trace what happened to them. Fortunately they died early on in a concentration camp in Poland. They were not deported as so many were, and they did not suffer for too long. The baby, when it was born, was another girl. The camps kept meticulous records, but I do not even know what my wife called her.'

'It's a terrible story. I am so sorry. I see why you feel like you do. I am so, so sorry.' Jane knew her words were feeble.

'Forgive me,' sighed Mr Kowalski, picking up

the photographs and putting them back in his wallet. 'I speak to you from the heart because of what I know, what I have experienced, but now it is a different time and a different country, and every good girl should follow the advice of her parents. But believe me,' he added, 'think very carefully before you give this baby away into another woman's arms. It will be harder than you think and you may regret it for the rest of your life.'

Walking home that evening after the shop was shut, Jane noticed that the sky was still light. A glimmer of brightness lingered to lighten the gloom that gathered around the streetlamps. The year was creeping towards spring. Just as imperceptibly it would move towards summer and the birth of the baby and then after that she could get her life back. All day she had thought about what Mr Kowalski told her. The war and the atrocities of which he spoke were not her world. They had nothing to do with her or the future of her baby. She could have had it aborted months ago, if she had been smarter, better informed. It would have been nothing more than a blob of pink jelly flushed down a drain. It was stupidity that meant that she was now carrying the baby she cared nothing for. If she could have disposed of it so easily at the beginning, why shouldn't she give it away after it was born? She should not allow herself to be influenced by the tragedy of an old man from a foreign country. She did not want this baby and she was going to part with it. She couldn't keep it, just because she felt sorry for an old Polish man whose own children had died in gas ovens.

Jane remembered the lovely dress her mother had bought her from Way In, which was hanging on the back of her bedroom door at Aunt Joan's. It was the first thing she saw when she opened her eyes every morning. With the baby gone, she would go on a diet and get slim and start behaving like a young person again. She remembered the swish of her long hair on her bare shoulders as she sprayed herself with Blue Grass before going out with her sixth form friends. She remembered dancing to the Beatles and Sandie Shaw and the Monkees at eighteenth birthday parties, before her youth was cut short. She had never had a chance to be a young woman, to have a boyfriend, to share a flat, to have a job, to learn to drive. Her father had promised her a Mini when she left college. That was the world that awaited her—young and fun and exciting—not this half-life with Aunt Joan, living like a middle-aged spinster, and spending her days mouldering away in a grotty bookshop with a tragic old Pole.

She tried to imagine what Tash would say to her. She would give her a proper talking-to, sort her out, tell her what was what. She missed her so much. It was awful not having heard from her except being told that she sent her love. It was so unlike Tash not to have written to her when she heard about the baby. She would have called her a fool, of course, but she would have made her feel better, cheered her up.

As she turned into Aunt Joan's street, she realised that she was ravenously hungry, as she often was these days, and she thought about supper of tomato soup and then sardines on a plateful of toast. Mr Kowalski's wife and little girl had probably starved and yet the new baby managed to survive the pregnancy. What could it have been like to give birth in such conditions, knowing that your baby and little girl were sure to die? Jane could not bear to think about it. Really, he shouldn't have told her the terrible story. It wasn't fair.

*   *   *

Over the next weeks, London suddenly seemed to be full of babies. Everywhere Jane went they were there; on the bus, in queues at the shops, carried in their mothers' arms, in pushchairs and prams, on hoardings and billboards, in parks and gardens. She watched their faces, sleeping, smiling, crying, and how their mothers, while still talking, or paying the bus fare, or loading their shopping bags, would touch a cheek or stroke the little fold at the back of a fragile neck, or rearrange a tiny cap so deftly, so tenderly, and she felt her heart ache that she would never be like this with her own baby, she would never feel its warm weight on her shoulder, or hear the little snuffling noises and cat's yawn as it woke from sleep.

One Saturday afternoon when she felt that she had to get out of the stuffy, over-furnished flat, she found herself wandering past Mothercare, a shop she had never noticed before, and staring hard in the window at the white painted cots piled with teddy bears, at the carrycots and neatly folded piles of snowy white nappies tied with pink and blue satin ribbons.

She pushed open the door, went in and wandered down the aisles, fingering the tiny white and blue and pink and lemon-yellow Babygros on hangers no wider than the span of her hand. These strange garments, which looked as though they might be worn by a rabbit in a Beatrix Potter story, must be a new invention—didn't babies still wear long flannel nighties, folded up at the end to keep their feet warm? There were bootees and mittens tied with tiny satin ribbons and snug little bonnets and lacy cardigans. Entranced, she touched the weblike knitted wool, so soft and light.

Somewhere, she thought, there was a woman who would soon be buying all this stuff for her baby. She could be anywhere—up in the north of England where Jane had never been. She could be in Norfolk, living in a black and white cottage on a flat lonely Fenland road. Jane imagined the line of washing flapping in the cold wind off the dykes— the white nappies bucking and dancing in the wind, her baby sleeping in a pram in the garden.

She could be here in London, living close to Aunt Joan's flat. Jane could pass her own baby in the street without ever knowing that it was hers. The woman could be rich or poor; the adoption society did not measure wealth as a deciding factor in who should get a baby. Mr Kowalski's words would not leave her. How could she be so sure that her baby would be loved as she would love it? How could Mrs Daniels ever know, really know, what went on in a family, however suitable it might look on paper?

Jane had only ever met one person who was adopted—a girl in her class at school. Claire was a tall, gentle, shy girl, who said that she had always known that her adopted parents were not her own. They had never pretended otherwise, and she clearly loved them and was loved in return. Jane remembered seeing them at parents' meetings: a small grey-haired couple, anxious and nervous, older than other people's parents, wearing old-fashioned clothes, and more tentative and hesitant, following their gangly daughter about the hall, like small birds who had reared a cuckoo and couldn't quite believe it.

Just say she kept her baby, how could she ever look after it? Quite apart from the fact that she knew nothing, absolutely nothing, about babies, how could she afford to live? Her father was adamant that he wouldn't go on helping her, and she had never been remotely independent in her life. Apart from a few holiday jobs where her meagre earnings were for pocket money to spend on herself, she had never had to pay for anything. How could she buy food and clothes? Her small wage from the bookshop seemed to disappear by the end of the week, frittered away on this and that—a magazine, chocolate, shampoo, a new pair of boots. How could she ever pay rent, if she had a baby to look after and couldn't go out to work? She couldn't ask Aunt Joan if she could stay with her. It had always been made absolutely clear that the arrangement was only temporary and would come to an end after the baby was born.

Her mother, who thought the Welfare State was the ruination of the country, was always complaining about unmarried girls who got in the family way and then demanded council housing and National Assistance. Did she actually know any of these feckless girls, thought Jane. Was she speaking from experience? It was more likely that she read about them in the *Daily Mail*. How did these girls manage it? What was the system that allowed them to claim benefits, and live in council flats? She had heard of Family Allowance—her mother had drawn it every week at the post office with a coupon torn from a booklet. I am not too proud, she said, to claim what my husband has already paid for, but Jane did not know if she would be eligible, and anyway, she was sure it would only be a fraction of what she would need to live on.

It was impossible, impossible, she told herself, while the stone of misery in her throat seemed to grow each day and threaten to choke her. Perhaps it was just the stage of her pregnancy, she thought, that made her feel so emotional and tearful. The nurse at the hospital had given her a booklet called 'The Next Six Months' and it was full of warnings of how hormonal changes in the middle months might make expectant mothers 'weepy', and that it was nothing to worry about, and how their husbands must be understanding. 'It can be a difficult time for him,' advised the writer. 'He may well wonder what happened to the wife he knew and loved. You can reassure him that he will get the "old" you back after the birth of your baby.'

Jane put the booklet in the wastepaper bin.

When the shop was quiet, she sometimes sat behind the till and wished with all her might that she had had the sense in the early weeks to find out how to get a termination, and then the next minute, feeling the baby kicking and turning within her, she would wonder how she could think such a thing. It would have been like murder, treating the baby as if it was no more important than an unwanted kitten, drowned in a bucket.

One afternoon she felt so low that she asked Mr Kowalski if she could use his telephone and

151

rang Hugh, just to hear a friendly voice, to speak to someone who was busy with what she thought of as a proper life, but he wasn't in, of course, and she left him a message to ring her back. When he did it was nearly five thirty and she was just about to start shutting the shop, but she stayed and talked to him for twenty minutes, or rather he talked to her, going on and on about the student demonstrations he had got involved in, against the war in Vietnam.

Her mother had told her when she had last telephoned Aunt Joan's flat that, to her huge disapproval, Hugh's activities were supported by both his parents, who had gone by coach to London the previous weekend to join him in Trafalgar Square.

'They are really the most extraordinary people,' complained Mrs Kindersley. 'Fond as I am of them, you could mistake them for Lefties or even Communists, the way that they talk, while living in that large house and educating the boys at public schools. In Daddy's view they are "champagne socialists" and traitors to their class. I don't know what is happening to this country, what with these bra-burning women and you young people and your free love and drugs.'

Listening to Hugh banging on, Jane felt completely indifferent towards the present Labour government or US foreign policy. Being actively engaged in the adult world was impossible when she was powerless to alter anything around her and she could not see beyond the birth of the baby. She had nothing in common with all the angry young people with their long hair and placards, 'Make Love not War', 'All You need is Love' and

152

'PEACE', whose photographs appeared on the front of the newspapers.

'How are you, anyway?' said Hugh, at last. 'Everything going all right?'

'Yes, I suppose so,' said Jane, feeling that it was a mistake to have telephoned him. What did she expect of him? What was there that he could possibly understand?

'You feeling OK?'

'A bit like a human incubator.'

'Cheer up, mate. Only a few more months and you'll get your life back. You can come on the demos then.'

*   *   *

The seventh month of Jane's pregnancy coincided with the blossoming of a soft spring, which greened the ugly, stunted London trees and filled their branches with singing birds. She had succumbed to wearing maternity trousers, which her mother had sent her, constructed with a hideous nylon front that stretched to accommodate the bulge of the baby. She bought two cheerful sprigged cotton smock tops from the new Laura Ashley shop in South Kensington, and felt better, younger, even a little hopeful. In pregnancy her hair had become more lustrous and she wore it long and loose on her shoulders. It's possible that I can be pretty again, she told herself, and experimented with a pale pink lipstick and dark eyeliner.

'Everlasting Love' played non-stop on the pirate radio stations, and then Cliff Richard's 'Congratulations', and she sang along as she listened to her little transistor in her bedroom and

153

hummed the tunes when she was alone in the shop.

'You are happier, yes?' asked Mr Kowalski one morning as she put a slice of apricot strudel in front of him.

'Hmm.' Jane stopped to consider and realised that yes, she was. 'It's a lovely day, Mr Kowalski. The winter's over. The sun is shining and that always helps. You wouldn't realise in here, with the windows all papered up.'

'You are looking well. A woman carrying a baby is often very beautiful at this time.'

Jane flushed. The remark seemed much too personal in the small space of the back room, but when she glanced at Mr Kowalski he had looked down and was absorbed in his book list, breaking the strudel into small pieces to dab quickly into his mouth. She had observed the odd way in which he ate—almost guilty, in little rushes—and of course, she understood now, since he had told her about his family. To be in the position of enjoying food himself was hard for him when the horror of starvation must never be far from his mind.

Then a remarkable thing happened, something that changed everything, for ever.

'Actually,' Jane heard herself saying in a confident tone, 'I am going to keep my baby. I have decided that I am not going to give it up for adoption.' The words seemed to come from nowhere. They leaped from her mouth and hovered in the air of the dusty room. Was that me? Did I really say that? It was as if she was the subject of a visitation, or had been possessed by the spirit of a passing angel. She was as shocked as if another person had used her voice, but now she had spoken, what she had said gathered weight and

154

conviction. At the same time she experienced a new lightness where her heart had once been heavy with unhappiness. It's true, she thought. It's true. I *have* decided.

Mr Kowalski looked up, and a gentle smile lit his face.

'This is good news, my dear. It is not my business to influence you when you have told me of your parents' wishes, but I am so glad because I know that you are right. However hard it may seem now, this is a wise decision and one that you will never regret.'

*   *   *

Easier said than done, Mr Kowalski. The row that erupted when she later telephoned her mother from the shop was stupendous. Far, far worse than when Mrs Kindersley found her daughter was stupid enough to get pregnant at eighteen. By insisting that she was going to keep the baby, her mother claimed that she was deliberately wrecking any chance to salvage what was left of her future.

'We simply won't allow it!' she screamed down the telephone. 'If you insist on going through with this madness you won't get a penny, not a penny of support from us! You will be entirely on your own! Do you understand what that will mean?'

Even thinking about it now made Jane feel faintly distressed. She wondered that she had the resolve to stick to her guns when she was terrified of the future, and deeply ashamed of her stupidity in getting pregnant.

'*That* could be put down to your inexperience, your naïvety, and that dreadful boy taking advantage of you,' her mother cried into the telephone. 'But this is defiance and wilful disobedience, and if you go ahead with it, you will ruin your life and condemn your child as a bastard. It is the most stupid and pig-headed thing I have ever heard.'

'Jane, Jane,' cried her father when he telephoned the flat later that evening. 'What are you thinking of? There is absolutely no question but this wretched baby is to be adopted. You are causing your mother and me a great deal of distress by behaving in this inconsiderate and selfish way. Now be a good girl and stop this nonsense.'

Jane sat, mute and determined, quaking but resolute, with the telephone receiver in her lap. There was no need to put it to her ear to hear her mother's background shrieks: 'Tell her! Tell her! She will never come home again. Never! She'll be cut off without a penny! Is that what she wants?'

Aunt Joan, coming in late from the office, her face etched by fatigue, caught the tail end of the blast. She plonked down on the hard hall chair, still wearing her outdoor coat and headscarf. When Jane replaced the receiver, there was a moment of silence between them.

'They rang *me*,' said Jane eventually, unable to meet her aunt's eye. 'I didn't make the call.' Even now, at this moment of high personal crisis, she felt the need to explain that she was not behaving inconsiderately by making trunk calls on her aunt's telephone.

'I am not concerned with that,' snapped Aunt Joan. 'I am much more upset to find that you have made a decision without consulting me. While you

156

are under my roof, you are effectively in my care, and it would have been sensible to discuss this with me first.'

Oh God, thought Jane. She was under attack from every side. Tears came easily and slid down her cheeks. 'I have only just made up my mind,' she blurted out. 'Just today, and I had to tell them at once. I had to get it over with while I felt strong enough.'

'You are keeping the baby, I gather?'

'Yes.'

There was another long silence in which Jane studied a print of *The Last Supper* on the wall beside her.

'Do you really know what you are doing?'

'Yes, I think so.' Her voice was now wavering and without conviction. The truth was that she didn't know if she did or not. How could she know? She was acting on impulse, on instinct. It was easier to be sure of what she couldn't do—which was to part with the baby.

'In that case, you are a brave girl. I didn't know that you had that sort of spirit. The path you have chosen will be lonely and hard. I expect your parents have told you that they won't support you?'

'Yes. You must have heard. They have made that quite clear. Mummy said if I keep the baby, I am never to go home again. She and Daddy will cut me out of their lives, she said.'

Aunt Joan shook her head, with a grimace, as if she were not surprised. 'I imagine you realise that it will not be easy to bring up a child alone, and in poverty?'

Jane sighed. Did her aunt think she was too stupid to have understood that? In fact, the future was such a pressing anxiety that she couldn't bring herself to consider the implications of her decision. She clung to a vague notion that somehow she would find a way.

'Yes, I do, but I *can't* have the baby adopted. It's as simple as that. It may seem selfish and everything, but I suddenly felt: stop, this is wrong, it's my baby—more mine than anything else in my life, and I'm the only real parent it will ever have. I've made such a mess of everything so far, but I can do my best from now on. I don't want this baby ever to believe that its father is unknown and that its mother didn't want it. I can't explain properly, but I feel that this is the most important thing I will ever do, even if my mother thinks it is wicked of me.'

She had never spoken to Aunt Joan like this. The anguish of her situation helped overcome the natural restraint that existed between them. Her aunt's moustache, her forbidding underwear drying on the clothes horse in the bathroom, her sniffing disdain for 'silliness', made any intimacies seem impossible. Their conversations revolved around the daily meagre shopping list, the bath rota, the mice in the larder, and it had been fine like this; a welcome relief from the over-emotional atmosphere of home.

But now here she was blurting everything out in the chilly, narrow hall, under the yellowing, fly-spotted lampshade of the centre light, which illuminated little except a circle of dun-coloured carpet and the grey fur of dust on the legs of the chair on which Aunt Joan sat.

I am going to remember this day for ever, thought Jane. The few minutes that they sat in the

158

hall, contemplating her future, seemed to lengthen into an age, while her thoughts ranged wildly. *The Last Supper*—what a lot was going on in that painting. She had always imagined that it was like a school photograph with Jesus and the disciples all sitting in a row smiling into the camera, but it was chaotic, she noticed now, with people leaning across one another and pointing and gesticulating and whispering, some looking angry and suspicious, and the table a wreck. That's it, she thought. That's what life is really like. Nothing is straightforward. Even Jesus couldn't control things.

'We had better have something to eat,' said Aunt Joan, finally. Her voice sounded tired. 'And maybe a drink. I think perhaps we should have a glass of sherry.' Jane glanced at her aunt and saw an unexpected kindness in her face. Their eyes met and Aunt Joan smiled faintly. 'Come along,' she said. 'I don't suppose it is good for your baby—all this upset.' She got wearily to her feet and led the way into the sitting room, taking off her coat and scarf and dropping her briefcase onto a chair as she went.

Later, over the tomato soup and flushed by the drink, Aunt Joan said, 'I don't know what has influenced you to make this decision but I can quite understand how a mother, however young, would want to keep her baby. I shall never have a child of my own, but I am not without imagination. Bringing a child into the world is the most important thing a woman can do, and I see no reason why you should not be an excellent mother, Jane. I will give you whatever support I can, at the expense of losing my sister's goodwill. However,

159

after the birth, you understand that it won't be possible for you to remain here? Much as I have enjoyed your company, it isn't entirely convenient and couldn't become a permanent arrangement. We must look for somewhere suitable for you and a baby, and possibly the opportunity for some employment, somewhere with a crèche, for instance, or perhaps work that you could do at home.'

Jane had a vision of herself as a Victorian outworker, making lace or shuttling a weaver's loom in an earth-floored cottage. She would be joining a long tradition of women struggling to keep themselves and their children out of the workhouse, or free of the Social Services. She felt a wave of something like elation. She knew that it was all going to be dreadfully difficult, but it was exciting and, what was more, she was convinced that everything would be all right. She couldn't help her parents and their anger. It was what she expected and they had every right to feel that way, but she wasn't going to change her mind because of them. They might say that she couldn't ever go home again, but soon Tash would be back from India, and that was much more important. Tash was family enough for her.

Maybe later on, when he had had time to get used to the idea, she would telephone her father at his office and try to explain how she felt. Surely his love for her could not be cut off for ever? Eventually he would come to forgive her and understand why she had to keep her baby.

160

CHAPTER SEVEN

Early on the morning of 6 April, Tintin's fifth day in the world, a grey fog descended on Florence. Alice should have been with her these first few days to help her—that's what they had planned because that was the whole point of a doulas—but her own child had gone down with chickenpox. Bloody bad timing, but Florence could hardly complain.

A few friends from the hospital had dropped round the night before with two bottles of champagne and it had turned into an impromptu party, with pizzas ordered after eleven o'clock and a lot of talking and laughing. Tintin was awake for most of the evening, passed around and exclaimed over by the two women, both of whom were married but, as yet, childless. Flo lost count of the number of times she had tried to feed him—at least every two hours, or so it seemed. By the time everyone had gone home and Ha had flopped into her bed and gone straight to sleep, Tintin was wide awake and crying furiously.

Flo had never felt so tired. It was two in the morning as she stood barefoot in the kitchen waiting for the kettle to boil. The dishwasher was full and needed to be unpacked and the sink was full of dirty plates, with wine glasses stacked on the counter. The pizza boxes were piled on top of the overflowing kitchen bin that was too slim and stylish to conceal much rubbish and was already full of Tintin's nappies.

She felt so, so tired. If she leaned against the

161

counter she could go to sleep, but over the noise of the kettle, she could still hear the insistent cries on and on, working up in a red-faced, furious crescendo.

'Leave him,' said Ha, appearing briefly in the kitchen for a glass of water, bleary-eyed, hair on end, wearing only a pair of boxer shorts. 'He can't be hungry. It won't hurt him to cry for a bit. Come to bed.' But she couldn't leave him. There must be something wrong. He was clean and dry and fed and lying in the approved position in his Shaker crib with the mobile of antique Venetian glass artfully made into butterflies over his head, wrapped in his blanket and lying on a natural sheepskin baby fleece. A night-light glowed in the corner and she had checked the temperature of the room several times.

Of course babies cried, she knew that. She was a doctor, after all, who gave young mothers advice when they came to her clinics. Crying is perfectly natural, she told them. You must learn not to be upset by it. You can be sure that if your baby is fed and winded, with a clean nappy, is not too warm or too cold, and shows no other symptoms of illness, then he is crying for no particular reason and you can afford to ignore him. He will eventually settle, or perhaps you could bring forward his next feed and you will find that he will drop off after a few sucks. That was the advice she gave, and yet she now found it less than reassuring.

She would have to try to feed him once more, wincing in agony as he attached himself to her cracked nipples, but it did not seem to be what he wanted and it only shut him up for a moment. After a few sucks he turned his head away and

162

started to scream. She changed his nappy, fumbling with the adhesive tapes, and almost immediately had to go through the whole procedure again, warned by the look of concentration on his face and the ructions from below. Another dirty nappy to join the binful.

Damn. She had forgotten the whole winding performance, and she had learned from her few days' acquaintance with Tintin that if she didn't get a burp out of him he would not settle. He was crying now because he didn't like being changed and she was worried that there looked to be a red patch on his little pointed bum, which might just be nappy rash. She did up all the poppers on the tiny sleepsuit and found she had one left over, so that she had done them wrong somehow, and she had to start again, by which time he had spewed out a thin stream of milk, wetting the front. She got a fresh suit from the drawer, but then she realised that his vest was wet too, and so that needed changing. He was really screaming now, his face contorted and bright red, his little fists clenched.

'Come on, baby. Come on, baby!' she pleaded, but he was bellowing so hard that he wasn't listening. Oh God, have I hurt him? she wondered, struggling to get the vest over his head. She had to blunder on and get the dressing bit over with, and then she picked him up and held him against her shoulder and gently rubbed his cross little back. More milk gushed from his mouth into her hair. He was so full he was overflowing, or was there something wrong? Reflux, maybe, or pyloric stenosis?

At last the crying stopped and she heard the merest hiccup of a burp. Thank you, God, thank

163

you, she prayed fervently. A few more moments on her shoulder and then, very gently, she wrapped Tintin in his cashmere blanket, took him to his nursery and laid him down to sleep.

She wanted to go to bed but felt so ravenously hungry that she stood at the counter and wolfed a large bowl of muesli and half a packet of digestive biscuits. This was not the way to lose the excess baby weight, but exhaustion made the urge to stuff food into her mouth irresistible.

The kettle boiled and she made a mug of chamomile tea and took it with her to the bedroom, tiptoeing past Tintin's door. Ha lay on his side, sleeping soundly, and Florence realised that he had turned off the baby alarm, which lay buried beneath a pile of clothes on a chair. She got into bed and lay stiffly beside him, feeling angry. How dare he interfere with her arrangements like that? He turned over and threw a heavy arm in her direction, which she pushed off. She felt nothing towards him but irritation. Even his breathing offended her.

Her obsession now was with Tintin, whose needs she was so clearly failing to meet. She could think of nothing else but him, and as she lay in the half-light of her bedroom, she relived the evening and recognised the anxiety and reluctance she had experienced when her friends asked to hold him, or picked him up from his crib. She had had to resist the urge to snatch him back, and say, 'Leave him alone. Don't hold him like that. He's mine!'

The next moment she fell into a black hole of sleep, but within what seemed like a few minutes the cries started again, quietly at first but building to a persistent, screaming climax. She would have to do something. Stumbling on legs wooden with fatigue, she got out of bed, furiously dragging the duvet from Ha as she went. She rushed into the nursery and picked up Tintin, whose face was scarlet and contorted, newborn yet infinitely knowing. The moment he felt himself lifted to his mother's shoulder, the bawling subsided.

Florence nuzzled his sweet-smelling head. He just wanted me, she thought, with a rush of purest love. He needed me. She went through to the sitting room and, collecting a cashmere throw, lay down on the sofa with Tintin resting on her breast. She knew that this was ill-advised but she was past the point of caring. She would do anything to get a little sleep.

Had Day Five been a battlefield there would have been no doubt who was the victor. Snuffling and hiccuping, Tintin yawned contentedly, and closed his eyes.

*　　　*　　　*

Ha woke her at half-past eight on his way to work. He was freshly shaved, smelled of his citrus cologne and looked handsome and rested. 'I've made you a cup of tea,' he said, dragging over a side table on which to put the mug. 'Is he still asleep?'

Florence hardly dared look, but Tintin was warm and solid against her chest, his half-moon eyelids tight shut and his tiny breaths only just dilating his delicate nostrils.

'Looks like it,' she said. 'I fed him again at six, but he went back to sleep afterwards.'

'Here, let me take him,' said Ha, leaning

forward to pick him up. 'Little monster. I'll put him in his crib thing, shall I? You can have your tea then.'

Florence had to stop herself saying, 'No, don't! He might wake up. Leave him alone.' She watched Ha take the baby out of the room and waited to hear the cries begin, but there was silence. She wondered if he had put him on his side and guessed that he wouldn't have bothered to tuck him in properly.

She knew her impatience with Ha was irrational. He hadn't done anything wrong, but for the moment it felt as if he was in the way—an unnecessary extra in a two-party relationship. She didn't want to have to consider him, or even have him there at all, with his masculine bulk, his male smell, his big hands and feet, his clumsiness when he held the baby. There wasn't room for him. Her flat felt too small for three of them.

Of course, she was familiar with all of this. Every textbook ever written warned about the tumultuous feelings of new mothers, the overwhelming possessiveness towards the baby, the danger of excluding the father. She had seen countless sullen teenage fathers in her clinic, slouching in the hospital chairs, hands thrust deep into jeans pockets, baseball caps pulled down; alienated, superfluous, marginalised, while their equally young girlfriends handled their baby with deft and practised hands, their faces solemn with motherhood, transformed by the experience into teenage madonnas.

How many times had she scribbled a note to social workers—'Father a worry—appears uninvolved, some signs of aggression—jealous of baby'? By the time the next visit came round, maybe a month later, the girl would be alone. 'We've split up, see, Shane and me. He wouldn't commit, like, to me and Chelsey. He was still going with his mates, all them lot that do drugs, and I wasn't having it. Not with the baby, like. Anyway, we're better on our own, aren't we, lovey? I'm moving in with my sister—she's got two of her own. It'll be better than the b. and b. where we are now.'

It upset Flo to think of it now. How cold she must have seemed, professional and capable, sitting there behind a desk, making notes. She took care to appear non-judgemental but privately she lamented the attitude of these girls, with their unrealistic expectations, their irresponsibility in getting pregnant in the first place, their assumption of a lifetime of welfare. 'Bloody teenage mothers,' she complained later to her colleagues. 'Who the hell do they think they are? Bloody well versed on their rights, all on income support, and the first to complain about the NHS, when they contribute precisely nothing.'

To Jane and Enzo, Flo had always had frighteningly right-wing views. In turn, she called them woolly-minded liberals, typical products of the sixties, and viewed the Health Service, even though she worked for it, as an inefficient dinosaur, ill-equipped to meet the demands of a new society. 'People don't value what they don't pay for,' she claimed. 'You only have to look at the number of missed doctors' appointments to understand that basic fact, and when you're old—' she glared at them fiercely—'who the hell do you think will be around to look after you? You can't dole out free IVF treatment *and* look after an ageing population. I tell you, the whole thing will creak to a stop, go belly-up. In the end the monster will devour itself and it will be cheaper to send all our patients, including our elderly, abroad for treatment or residential care.'

Ha came back and moved her legs so that he could sit on the sofa beside her.

'So,' he said. 'What are your plans for today?'

'Plans? I don't have any *plans*. I just hope to survive it. The nurse is coming sometime this morning. She is going to show me how to bath him.'

'Why? Don't you know how?'

'Of course I do—in theory. Practice is rather different. I feel, like terrified, of everything at the moment. Even changing his vest scares the shit out of me. I thought I was going to rip an ear off or something. His neck goes all wobbly.'

Ha laughed. 'This doesn't sound like you, Flo. I've never known you daunted by anything.'

'I'm not *daunted*—I just feel, I don't know, sort of inept.' To her dismay, fat tears started to slide down her cheeks. She sat up and drew her knees in to her chest and hid her face.

'Baby blues!' said Ha, in a knowing voice, unadvisedly as it turned out, because Florence turned on him angrily.

'Don't say that as if I'm some bloody textbook case. You weren't up the whole night, or you'd feel exhausted, too. You wouldn't be so effing chirpy if you'd only had three hours' sleep.'

'No, OK, sorry.' Ha put a hand on her back. 'Perhaps you'll be able to catch up a bit today. Do you want me to bring anything back from the shops? I finish my shift at five o'clock.'

168

'I don't know. I can't remember what's in the fridge. You'll have to look.'

'You do *want* me to come back tonight?' There was hesitation in his voice.

'Yes. Of course I do.' Do I, though? thought Flo. She was too tired to think, but on the other hand she didn't want to be left alone. She felt scared of being alone with her baby—how ridiculous was that? It was all right when he was asleep but he would be awake and hungry at any moment and then perhaps he would cry and be fretful as he had been yesterday, and frankly, she didn't know what she would do.

'I'll cook supper. I'll bring back a chicken or something,' said Ha.

'Yeah, OK, thanks.' The evening seemed too far away to consider and she couldn't care about what she ate.

'I'd better go then. Why don't you have a bath while he's still asleep? You'll feel better then.' Flo appeared so downcast that Ha was alarmed. He hesitated. 'Flo?'

'Yes.' She was sitting with her face buried in her knees again, her blond hair tousled and sticking out in clumps.

'Look, love, it's normal to feel a bit all over the place. Don't beat yourself up about it. Just relax, sweetie. Go with it. It won't always be as hard as this.'

Flo rubbed her head and looked up with a small smile. 'Yes, I know. These first days are sure to be a bit difficult. We need to get a routine established.' It was what she would have said to any of the young mothers in her clinic, but she said it with a sinking heart. What have I done, a voice screamed inside her head. I will never, ever get my life back now.

Ha dropped a kiss on the top of her head. 'Call me,' he said. 'I'll come back if you want me. I'm on paternity leave officially, so I don't have to go in after today, anyway.'

'No, no, you go. I'll be fine. It's partly that the breast-feeding isn't going that well. It's agonising at the moment, and although my boobs are rock hard, I've no idea if he's getting enough milk. I mean, maybe that's why he cried so much yesterday. He kept coming off the breast and screaming. I just found it really upsetting.'

'Oh, come on, Flo. You know that nature will take care of that. The more he feeds the more milk you'll get.'

'Of course I bloody know, but that doesn't stop me worrying that I might be one of those women who just don't produce enough milk. It does happen.'

'Put him on a bottle then, if you're worried. Come on, it's a no-brainer. You don't have to be *upset* about it!'

'Of course I'm upset. I don't intend to bottle-feed him. Under any circumstances. I am totally committed to breast-feeding.' Her voice sounded almost hysterical in her ears.

'Then just relax and get plenty of rest and it will all be fine.'

'Yes.' Flo sounded far from convinced.

'Let's see these rock-hard boobs,' said Ha, in an interested voice.

'Oh, *please*! I'm wearing a bra that resembles a weapon of mass destruction. I'm not in the mood to provide you with titillation.'

170

'Heh!' said Ha, backing off, and holding up his hands as if in defence.

'Yeah—well!'

'OK. Sorry. You probably don't want to know that you look wonderful and more beautiful than I've ever seen you.'

'Piss off, Ha! I've never felt so hideous. Just piss off to work, for God's sake.'

Ha, hands still outstretched, backed out. It was true, in fact, he thought, as he loped down the stairs to his car. Florence really did look lovely. All soft and round and very, very feminine. If she had let him he would have liked to have lain with her on the sofa and stroked her tummy and breasts, but that was clearly not on offer. He had thought she would like to know how lovely and desirable she was to him as the mother of his son.

Jesus, thought Flo, lying back with her eyes closed—how wrong could men get it? How could Ha possibly think that she was interested in sex, or even what he found attractive, at a time like this? Then as the door closed behind him, she heard Tintin's first mewling cry and the tears started to rush down her cheeks. She would have given anything to be getting into her car and driving off to work. What have I done, she thought again. My life was fine before. Why had a baby seemed so important? She knew that it wasn't that she didn't love Tintin—rather the opposite. She loved him so much that it was immobilising and consuming her. It wasn't just her body that had gone to pieces, she seemed to have lost her mind as well.

She would have to get off the sofa. Tintin was crying, the flat was a tip and Vera, her cleaner, didn't come until Friday. There was a pile of dirty baby clothes slung in a corner of the bathroom that she would have to put in the washing machine before the community midwife arrived.

Flo sensed that Nurse Andrews disliked her. There was often a certain tension between nurses and female doctors, and she had seemed hesitant and almost unwilling to give advice or show her how to breast-feed. 'I need all the help I can get,' Flo had told her, trying to break down her reserve. 'It's not the same thing at all, you know—theory and practice.' Even so, the midwife had remained less than friendly and kept saying, 'I know I don't need to tell you, but . . .' and looking round the flat with an expression that seemed to say, 'It's all very well for some!'

Tintin's crying somehow seemed less urgent in the daytime, so before she went to him, Flo gathered up the piles of tiny clothes from the floor and collected her own stained and milk-encrusted things and shoved them all in the machine. When she turned the dial, nothing happened. She checked the plug—Ha was always pulling it out to use the socket for his espresso maker, but it was in place as it should be. She tried again—nothing. Shit. The effing thing would go wrong now. How the hell could she manage without a washing machine? She glared at it with real hatred and kicked it with her bare foot, which hurt. Slowly, she slumped to the floor, the pizza boxes around her feet, while Tintin's screams grew louder.

*   *   *

Throughout the seventh month of Jane's pregnancy, her parents kept up their offensive to

172

make her change her mind. Her mother twice took the train to London and subjected her daughter to what she called 'knocking some sense' into her. 'You'll live in a council house for the rest of your life! You'll be nothing better than a shop girl! You're denying your child a father and a future!'

Jane had no defence other than dumb obstinacy. There was no argument to meet her mother's opposition, so she simply tried not to listen, sitting with her head bowed in an attitude that provoked the utmost irritation and exasperation.

'I don't think you have taken on board that we will have nothing to do with you or the baby if you continue with this madness. You will be on your own, Jane. Just think what that will be like. You may imagine that Joan will support you in some way but she hasn't a penny to spare—I should know because Daddy has to help her from time to time. It will be no good coming to us when you find that you can't manage. Worst of all will be the social stigma—an unmarried, teenage mother! Think of it! The disgrace.'

On and on it went. Her mother did her best, Jane had to give her that. Then her father was sent to try a different tactic, which Jane found much more upsetting and difficult to withstand. He was so evidently distressed by her decision because of the grief it was causing, and she hated to hurt him by denying him what he wanted. 'I won't be able to go on paying you an allowance, you know,' he said sadly, stirring spaghetti round his plate in an Italian restaurant in Greek Street. 'Your mother won't allow it. All I can do is to transfer a little lump sum from time to time into your bank account, but God only knows how you will manage.

It breaks my heart to think of it. I don't want to lose you, but there it is, I shan't be allowed to see you.' His eyes filled with tears and Jane reached for his hand. This was the hardest cut of all.

'But I'll keep in touch. She can't stop me writing to you, can she? I can send you photos and things, and ring you at the office?'

He sighed, his handsome face downcast. For the first time Jane noticed the softness of his chin, the weakness of his mouth. She saw no strength or determination in his features, and realised just how dominated he was by her mother, frightened by her iron will.

'There's something else,' he said. 'Letters from Tash. Your mother wouldn't send them on to you because Tash, as you know, has always been openly rebellious and non-conformist, and they don't see eye to eye on anything very much. This hippie lifestyle she is leading in India, dope smoking, sitting at the feet of some yogi—she's lost all grip on reality. It's all very well for her to encourage you to keep the baby, but she doesn't have a clue how hard it is becoming in this country. I tell you, industry is held to ransom by the unions, and what with cheap foreign competition—it's all going down the drain, all that my family have worked for in the Midlands . . .'

'What do you mean, letters from Tash?'

'A bundle of letters for you—arrived all at once, six months' worth. Your mother decided not to send them on. She didn't think they would be, um, helpful, given Tash's attitude to most things . . .'

'So where are they?' Jane's heart had missed a beat. She had so longed to hear from her sister, had missed her so much. She couldn't believe that her mother had stolen her letters. There was no other word for it.

'I've got them here. I knew how much you would like to hear from her, how close you two are, but for Lord's sake don't mention them to your mother!'

'As if I would! What will you tell her if she wonders what has happened to them?'

Her father shrugged. 'I've no idea. I'm no good at deceiving her. I suppose I will have to admit that I brought them to you. Let's hope she doesn't notice that they are missing. She put them away in her desk; I don't imagine that she will check that they are still there, not just for the moment, anyway.'

'Thank you, thank you,' said Jane, seizing the bundle of pale blue air-mail envelopes, stuck with exotic Indian stamps. Each one had been opened.

'It's criminal, Dad, to steal someone's post and open it!' she cried. 'Did you know that? You can tell Mummy that if she kicks up a fuss.'

Her father shook his head. 'Don't be silly, darling. She's your mother! Whatever she does is for the best possible reason. It's only because she cares so much about you.'

Jane accepted this meekly. Tash would have said, 'That's how military juntas and iron-fisted dictators explain away their ghastly crimes.'

'There's something else that perhaps you should know. I've thought about telling you from the start of this dreadful business. I knew that Mummy would be horrified but I think it might help you to understand. The thing is, Jane, darling, your mother and I *had* to get married. We would have done anyway, we were very in love, but the fact

175

that she was pregnant made it imperative that we wasted no time. It was a wartime wedding—the end of the war, anyway—and I was still in the army, but as it happened, she lost the baby at three months, and then Tash didn't turn up for another year or so. Do you understand?'

'No! Why are you telling me this? Why is it important?' Jane couldn't take it in. The cinematic version of her parent's love story, the version of it that her mother had insisted upon, was suddenly looking quite different.

'We *had* to get married because of the pregnancy. We weren't even engaged at the time. That's what I am saying. It was so very, very important not to have a child out of wedlock. That's why your mother is so upset about your situation—that you don't even know the identity of the father, and so on. It brings back all the anxiety of that time for us. Knowing this may make you see why she cares so much about you, and feels so strongly that your baby needs a father.' Jane couldn't follow the drift of this information. Was it to make her feel better or worse? To recognise her mother's attitude, or to see it as hypocrisy? Whatever it was, it had cost her father a lot to tell her, and now he sat looking miserable and defeated and cornered.

'Dad? Thank you for the letters, and thank you for telling me about the other thing. I suppose it makes me see that Mummy is human after all, if you know what I mean. I'm really, really sorry to hurt you, but I can't change my mind about my baby.'

'No, I didn't think you would. It's madness, you know. Madness,' and he beckoned the waiter to

176

bring the bill.

*　　　*　　　*

Tash's letters—six of them, written over the last months in reply to the letters Jane had sent her— were nearly as good as talking to her sister face to face. They were funny and informative and full of descriptions of the colour and drama of India. Smoking pot and travelling by minibus round the country, she and Denby were having a wonderful time, but underneath the carefree, freewheeling lifestyle, there were serious intentions. Tash had established contact with leading cotton and clothing manufacturers and had begun to lay the foundations of her future business. She had arranged for a supplier to make up simple white cotton nightdresses to her design, as the first item in her mail-order clothing line.

The last two letters dealt with the news of Jane's pregnancy. 'Jano,' she wrote,

I'm really, really sorry that I'm not there to be with you. I can't bear to think of you wandering about London with no one to turn to. I could have got you sorted out in no time, but that's not much use to you now. Hugh was useless, by the sound of it—but I am glad that you didn't go to the wrong person to get fixed. A friend of mine from college nearly died last year. She ended up in hospital having blood transfusions. I still can't believe that this has happened to you of all people. Although in my opinion it's always the sweet, innocent chicks who get knocked up—not, as Denby

177

would say, hard-hearted, fuck-off girls like me. Anyway, don't be bullied into doing anything you don't want to do. You say it's too late for an abortion and that Mum has arranged for adoption. Personally, if I got to the end of the production line, I wouldn't give my baby up for all the tea in China (or India).

I'm trying hard to imagine your situation and how you only have two choices—either get rid of the baby at birth and get on with the life you had before, as a student, etc.—but forever trying to forget your dark secret. God, it's like a Victorian novel! Or else keep the baby, and rethink your future. You're the only one who can decide what is right for you but I can imagine what the pressure's been like at home. Either way, it's a tough choice. I'm going to get Denby to write his sister's address and telephone number on the bottom of this letter. She has a cottage in Sussex that will be empty for a couple of years while she and her husband are in Hong Kong. They don't want tenants because they plan to come back for a month every summer and are looking for someone to house-sit. If you need anywhere to go—you might want somewhere to stay after the birth, either with or without the bambino—it would be a start, at least. I don't know what it's like—a bit primitive, I think, because it's only a holiday cottage. They had a writer friend living there for a while but he turned out to be an unreliable smack-head, so I am sure that they would be pleased to have a wronged maiden instead. You'd be much less likely to chop up the furniture to light the fire, or pee out of the bedroom window on the postman.

At the bottom of the flimsy sheet Denby had written, 'Whoops! Silly old Jane to get up the duff! Here is the address and telephone number in Hong Kong of my sister and her boring husband. They are over for a month in June, but the cottage will be empty after that. Must go! Writing this is the most work I have done in six months. Lots of love, Denby.'

*   *   *

Jane might have known that even from India it would be Tash who sent her a lifeline. Now she had something to think about, and slowly the cottage took over her imagination. She saw the clean white nappies blowing on the washing line, the pram under the apple trees, the sunlit garden, the gingham-curtained cottage windows. She felt tremendously happy that she was going to be able to give this baby such a picturesque start in life.

She began to make practical preparations too. She wrote to her father at his office and asked him to send on her Post Office Savings book in which she had £500 of accumulated birthday and Christmas money, and she began to save what she could from her pay packet. She bought a second-hand McLaren pushchair and a wooden playpen, and began to trawl through bundles of baby clothes in Oxfam shops, collecting what she could from the list of baby essentials that the hospital clinic had given her.

Mr Kowalski allowed her to telephone Hong

Kong—a terrifying experience, because so much depended on it being a success. There was a strange echo effect when Denby's sister answered, so that Jane heard her own voice repeating everything she said, a moment after she had spoken. She stumbled over her explanation and Denby's sister, Caroline, sounded grand and offhand.

'Oh, I see!' she said. 'Well, we haven't really thought seriously about a house-sitter, not after the last one.'

'I am extremely reliable. I would look after everything for you.'

'You sound very young. How old are you?'

'Nineteen.'

'Oh dear. We wouldn't want teenagers hanging around the place, or some sort of student commune.'

'Oh, no! I'm not like that at all. I would live very quietly. Just me and the baby.'

'Baby?'

'Yes. I'm expecting a baby in July.'

'Oh, I see. I didn't realise that you're married.'

'Well, actually . . . no, I'm not.'

'Oh, goodness!' Caroline paused. Jane could imagine what she was thinking. 'I'm not sure . . . it doesn't sound very suitable, any of it. You're not a *hippie* or a *squatter*, are you?'

'Of course I'm not! You know I am a friend of Denby's. It's my sister that he's away with in India.'

'I'm not sure that being a friend of Denby's is a particular recommendation.'

Jane's heart sank. This wasn't working out at all as she had expected.

'I'll have to talk to Nigel about it. We aren't

offering any sort of payment, you realise? You would have to pay your own electricity and so on.'

'Yes, I understand.'

'I have to admit that it would be a relief to know that there was someone living there. There have been break-ins in the area, vandalism, that sort of thing. There seems to be some local feeling about places that are unoccupied second homes.'

'Oh dear,' said Jane. Caroline was making it sound as if she were in some way responsible. Or maybe, just people *like* her—unmarried mothers sort of people.

'Anyway, I will telephone you after I've spoken to Nigel. Just give me your number.'

Jane did and hung up, caught between hope and despair. It had been stupid of her to assume that it would work out just because Denby had said it would. She thought of the navy-blue pushchair she had cleaned with a damp cloth and which was now folded in a corner of her bedroom at Aunt Joan's, and the well-washed, second-hand baby clothes that she held up almost each night to admire and refold. How silly she had been to get so excited, to feel that things were going to work out.

She had even told Mr Kowalski that she had found somewhere to live and he had nodded his head and smiled. That was something she had noticed. After all the keen interest in her keeping the baby, he hadn't got any practical suggestions to make about how exactly she should go about it. She had nursed the faintest hope that he would help in some way, but in fact he hadn't even mentioned the subject again. There was news coming from Poland, with rumbles of rebellion and repression and perhaps if he ever thought about babies his mind was filled with images of barbed-wire fences and frozen snowy plains, of high brick chimneys billowing smoke into the grey Polish sky. He wouldn't know anything about modern British babies, with their tins of baby milk and list of requirements.

As it happened, Jane need not have worried. Nigel telephoned the next day from his office, and accepted her offer to be a house-sitter, provided everything was satisfactory at a meeting he arranged in June, to which she was to bring two references as to her good character and trustworthiness, and sign some forms accepting responsibility for damages and so on. He had persuaded Caroline that a single girl was likely to be a better bet than a man and, influenced by the unwelcome news that Nigel's two younger brothers wanted to use the place to entertain girlfriends at weekends, she had agreed. Having found sex with Nigel much less exciting than it had been before they were married, Caroline resented being reminded that other people were still having fun. Anything was better than having the cottage used as a knocking shop.

*   *   *

One afternoon when Tintin was just over a week old, Jane received a telephone call from Florence. She was surprised and pleased to hear her daughter's voice, and turned away from the quite tricky letter she was writing on behalf of Sir Tommy in relation to climate change. A pressure group had got on to the fact that he flew everywhere by private jet and was calling for him to justify this in the light of his concern for the future of the Siberian tiger and its rapidly diminishing habitat. So far she had written a page of quite heartfelt-sounding bullshit, which she was getting rather good at producing.

'How is everything going?' she asked. Florence's voice didn't sound very bright; not quite herself.

'Oh, all right. No, he's gorgeous, beautiful, but I don't know, Mum, these first days just seem so *hard*. Alice was going to be here every day to support me. She was my doulas, remember, but her kid's gone and got chickenpox, and I don't know anyone else who could come and help. Ha said he'd get his mother to stay for a few days, but I didn't want her. I hardly know her, for one thing, and this flat is too small, and after all, she had Ha and his brother over thirty years ago, so she's not exactly an expert on current practice. She'd have to come by train from Newcastle and she doesn't drive, so she couldn't go to the supermarket. There are no shops near the flat, you know. You have to get in the car if you want as much as a pint of milk, although I can get Tesco to deliver, but I just haven't got round to sitting down at the computer and getting it organised. Then the washing machine broke down and although it's hardly been used, it's out of its guarantee period. I can't get anyone to come and mend it until next week. Ha had to take a load of stuff to the launderette on his way to work . . .'

Jane listened without interrupting. Her mind had already formed an idea of what was to come. Any moment Florence was going to ask her to go to her, and help her with Tintin, and already she could feel a swell of pleasure and importance.

183

'So, Mum, I wondered—well, I completely understand if you can't—but I wondered whether you could come and be here for a bit? You're so good at organising things and it would be so great for me. I mean, I wouldn't worry about being a rotten mother if you were here.'

Florence needed her. For what was the first time since she was about fifteen, her daughter needed and wanted her.

'Of course I'll come, if you'd like me to!' she heard herself saying. 'I'll come tomorrow. I'll sort things out this end with Enzo, maybe call in and tell Aunt Joan where I'll be, and then I'll come.'

CHAPTER EIGHT

The next morning, sitting at his desk in his study at home, Enzo was conscious of Jane's very evident happiness at being summoned by Florence. The atmosphere in the house was charged with it. She had chatted happily at breakfast about what she was taking for the baby and how she would help to settle him into what she called 'a proper routine', so that Florence could get the rest she needed. She was going to shop on the way and planned to take over the domestic side of things and also try to involve Ha so that he shouldn't feel excluded. It was a typical Jane strategy, thought Enzo, listening to her making telephone calls, cancelling the rest of her life, and running up and down stairs organising things before she left.

For once he found it difficult to start work. This morning he had intended to begin on the

184

formidable paper that he was assigned to deliver to the symposium of orthopaedic surgeons in San Francisco in six weeks' time. He found that he was in a thoughtful mood when, as a rule, he was not a man much given to introspection. If he had considered it at all he would probably have understood that his particular buoyant and optimistic nature had something to do with his position as adored only son in a large, traditional Italian family, and that his smooth progress through life had been effected by a series of deft handovers from the care of one capable and devoted woman to another.

It surely wasn't just chance that when he met and fell in love with Jane he delivered himself into the arms of another nurturing sort of woman, who had a corresponding need to be needed. She was never happier than when she was being useful to someone in some way, which was not to say that she had a servile nature—not at all; there was a stubborn and independent core to his wife that Enzo learned should not be underestimated or ignored. However, she liked to be quietly helpful, and to do more for people than perhaps they deserved or expected. That, of course, was the reason that he could hear her downstairs singing in the kitchen and bustling about with a burst of energetic activity. She was delighted that Florence not only needed her, but had actually turned to her for help.

When he first met Jane, he had seen at once that she was a natural mother, and when their own boys were small there was plenty of opportunity for her to be selflessly devoted to the family. Then, as the years went by and there was less required of her at home, she had chosen a part-time job that required her to look after a man who in many ways was like an over-grown and spoiled child.

For the most part she was responsible for running his charitable foundations, which was doing what she was best at, but on a larger scale. She wouldn't have wanted to organise the clean water project on the ground in Somalia, or the children's clinics in Benin—that would have been more Tash's line, involving a lot of shouting down the telephone and general bossiness—but she worked gladly behind the scenes and, most important of all, kept Sir Tommy's other staff happy, avoiding too many eruptions or upsets when he behaved particularly thoughtlessly.

Enzo was respectful of this feminine drive to sustain and succour. In his professional work he had witnessed quite remarkable recoveries made by female patients who knew that they had to get back on their feet again because their families needed them. Women were generally stronger than men when emotional and physical demands were united.

Why Florence's call for help was significant, thought Enzo, and why it made Jane so happy this morning, was that as she had grown up—and Enzo had been a witness to this—Florence had made it a priority to be independent of her mother. It was as if Jane's devotion came at too high a price.

Florence had been a self-contained and typically truculent teenager, and although she'd been fine with him, she had turned her moods on her mother. Later, as she'd become an adult and begun her training as a doctor, there'd been a coolness in her behaviour towards Jane that Enzo

186

regretted on Jane's behalf. Florence made it clear that she did not need her mother's advice or approval, and would pointedly consult Enzo first if there was anything that she wanted to discuss.

He had never talked about this with Jane because she would have denied it and become defensive, but he knew it was the truth all the same. Once Tash, who had witnessed some careless slight inflicted by Florence on Jane, had said to him when they were alone, 'Florence has never let it go, has she? The illegitimacy. She is absolutely determined to see herself as a disaster who ruined Jane's life, and she can't forgive her for it. It's the old "I never asked to be born" thing. It makes me so mad because we all know how much Jane wanted her and how hard she had to fight to keep her. What lengths she went to . . .' She spoke so vehemently that Enzo was surprised. Of course he knew the story—how tough it had been those first years—but Tash's words were weighted with significance and when he looked at her he saw that her eyes had filled with indignant tears.

So part of the reason Jane was so happy to be going off and leaving him for an indefinite period, thought Enzo ruefully, was that the advent of this baby seemed to mark a turning point, and maybe would help to heal whatever wound Florence felt had been inflicted on her.

That was enough psychology for one morning. After all, an orthopaedic surgeon was a nuts and bolts man, the mechanical engineer of medicine, but still he could not settle to his work and decided that a cup of filter coffee would help. He also felt a nagging desire to see Jane, be in the same room as her, but when he went downstairs she was heaving

187

furniture about in the sitting room and the Hoover was thundering. She was wearing jeans and her hair was tied up in an elastic band, like a teenager.

'You don't have to do all this,' he said, standing in the doorway. 'I've got a busy week. I shall hardly be here.'

'I like to leave things properly,' she shouted back. 'It gives me peace of mind, somehow, when I'm away, to think that I've vacuumed behind the sofa. Sad, isn't it?'

Enzo shrugged. He could go out of the door and never, ever, consider what state the house was in, or care what it was like when he came back. However, it was a harmless enough compulsion, although he couldn't think why it was necessary when they employed a cleaner. Carole was a thin, blonde girl, who smoked at the back door and wore stiletto heels even to work. He was always finding Jane making her coffee and listening to the endless saga of her chaotic life.

'Well, don't bother leaving food. I can eat at the hospital, or pick up something on the way home.'

'Of course I will! I'll stock the fridge and make sure there is fruit and salad and so on.'

'What about the dog, more to the point? I draw the line at dog-sitting.'

'Honestly, Enzo! As if I would expect you to. You'd forget we *had* a dog, five minutes after I'd left.'

'What are you going to do with him? Send him to stay in a hotel?'

'I couldn't possibly put him into kennels after his dogs' home start in life. He might think I had abandoned him. No, I'll take him with me.'

'Is that a good idea?'

Jane stopped what she was doing and straightened up, tucking a loose hank of hair behind her ear. 'Well, I don't suppose Florence will be pleased, but if she wants me to drop everything and go and help, then Chipper is part of the deal.'

'Won't it be difficult, having a big dog in a small flat?'

'No, I don't think so. He's very well-behaved and it will be nice taking him for a walk with the baby. Look,' she turned to the window, where a splashy sunshine was moving across the garden, 'the weather has improved. It's really quite warm today. Quite warm enough to take Tintin out in his pram. There's nothing like fresh air for making babies sleep.'

'Buggy,' corrected Enzo. 'They don't have prams any more. It's buggies these days.'

'Buggy, then, know-all. Will you come at the weekend?'

'No, probably not. I think it's best I stay here and get some work done. Small babies in small flats aren't really my scene, to be honest. Tell Tintin I'll kick a ball about with him in five years or so. By the way, are you coming with me to San Francisco? I should be able to get your ticket on Airmiles, if you are.'

'I'd love to, of course, but can I tell you later?' Jane turned away to plump up the sofa cushions. 'There are various things I want to sort out before I commit myself.'

Tash, Jane thought, with a sudden memory of her sister. I need to make sure that Tash is all right. That is reason enough.

Enzo felt slightly aggrieved. First, Jane was leaving him for an indefinite period to go to

Florence, and now she was hesitating about San Francisco. He had assumed that she would jump at the prospect of a few days in an exciting and sophisticated foreign city. He shrugged again, but Jane had returned to her hoovering and did not notice. She hadn't even offered to make him his coffee. It was all very well, this do-goodery, but there was a limit.

'What about Sir Tommy?' he shouted above the roar. 'Is it all right with him if you have time off? Can Africa wait?' He quite surprised himself by taking this negative line towards her going away.

'Yes, it can. He's in Mustique until the end of the month and things are fairly quiet at the moment. There's not much on until his Hyde Park concert in August. Anyway, I can take my laptop and my mobile, so I can keep in touch and deal with anything that crops up.'

So that's that, thought Enzo. He supposed he *would* be all right without her. Certainly for a day or two he would enjoy the change of being at home alone. He had overheard Jane say as much, with a little laugh, about herself to her girlfriends. She didn't mean that she preferred life without him, he knew that, and he felt the same, but being briefly apart was fine for married couples. It created a little breathing space, a little room.

A week, though, was quite a long time. Maybe he would telephone some friends and try to arrange a round or two of golf, or get tickets for a football match. Yes, he'd be fine. Then he remembered how empty and echoing the house became when Jane wasn't in, how the quiet road began to depress him when he stood at his study window and felt inspiration draining out of him at the sight of the neat gardens, the blank windows with their discreet curtains, the tidily packed recycling bins at the kerbside, the total lack of exuberant life.

Maybe he would telephone the boys, see what they were doing at the weekend, maybe even drive up to Newcastle to visit Sandro, and call in at Durham to see Marco, fix to stay a night or two, take them out to a good dinner. In his mind's eye he saw the long haul up the motorway, and then the reverse drive on Sunday night and being alone in the car, rain on the windscreen through the black night, and he realised that he didn't want to go without Jane.

Of course he doesn't mind me being away, thought Jane with a little sadness, as she banged the Hoover under a chair. He's always been self-contained and self-sufficient. She imagined the hospital canteen and Enzo at the centre of a laughing group—his team, in fact—each carrying a tin tray on which there was a plate of solid brown food, shepherd's pie and baked beans, or Lancashire hotpot, looking for a free table so that they could all sit together. Most of his life is spent away from me, she thought. All the important stuff he does, anyway. A housekeeper could do what I do for him. He'll work late, and hardly miss me. It's Florence who needs me now. And she felt a pleasurable sense of purpose as she finished her housework. She didn't notice Enzo clattering about in the kitchen or stomping up the stairs with his coffee cup.

She would telephone the boys before she left. Marco had sounded a bit down the last time they had spoken. Jane suspected things were not going

191

that well with his girlfriend, a stroppy Irish girl who Jane privately thought was manipulative and controlling. When she got back from Flo's, she would ask him to come home for a weekend so that she could judge for herself. She might even mention her concern to Sandro, who as the older brother still kept an eye on Marco. Perhaps he knew what was going on. Maybe she could get them both home and ask Florence and Ha to come too, so that Tintin could be introduced to his family. What a happy occasion that would be. The house would be full again and she would cook an enormous joint of beef and make everyone's favourite puddings.

The two other people she needed to think about were Aunt Joan and Tash. Aunt Joan she would call in to see on her way up to Florence. She would take her a few small treats, like visiting a child at boarding school, and explain that she would be away for a week or so. She would telephone Tash before she left. Oh, Tash . . . she thought, turning off the Hoover and winding up the flex. Please, please, God, let her be all right. She would be, she knew it. Tash was invincible, but then she shouldn't think that. It was tempting providence.

*   *   *

Jane gave Enzo a proper cooked lunch before she left, and talked him through the contents of the fridge. He put his arms round her as she was trying to draw his attention to the spinach, salad, ready-prepared broccoli and carrots in the vegetable drawer and said, 'I'll miss you, you know. Don't be away too long,' and she turned in surprise.

'Will you? I think you only notice me if I'm not here, if you know what I mean.'

'Jane!' Enzo made an exasperated face. 'Don't say that sort of thing. It's so obviously not true.'

'You're always so busy, you have to admit. I'm not complaining. I understand it's the nature of your work.'

'Have I ever made you feel unimportant to me? Have I? Look, just this morning I was asking you to come to San Francisco and it was you who said you couldn't say "yes" without "sorting stuff out".'

'Well, that's true. I do have something to see to before I know whether I'll be free to come.'

'What? The dog?'

'Actually, no!' Jane felt anger rising. It seemed as if Enzo was mocking the trivial nature of her life, of her own unimportant commitments. 'It's exactly as I said. I won't know for a while if I can come. I might be, well, needed here.'

Enzo raised his eyes to heaven and lifted his hands in surrender. 'OK, OK!' He wasn't going to ask Jane what exactly was so important.

They had eaten lunch in silence, listening to the news on the radio, Jane feeling resentful and Enzo feeling hurt. How did these scraps occur, thought Jane, spooning out the apple crumble. After all these years of a happy marriage, how could a husband and wife run counter to each other, collide, spark off such animosity? She was confident that she was the innocent party. Enzo needed to be reminded from time to time that she did have a life of her own. She couldn't tell him about Tash, which was a pity, because it would make him see how self-centred he was being.

Enzo, for his part, felt that Jane had rebuffed his

193

warm embrace and declaration of his feelings for her. Well, if she wanted to be like that, he wasn't going to tell her again. Anyway, what could she possibly have to do that took precedence over him wanting her company? Family dramas apart, that is, and as far as he knew everything was all right on that front. Florence was obviously making heavy weather of this baby, but even Jane couldn't think that she had to sideline everything else and go to look after them both on anything more than a very temporary basis.

After they had finished eating, Enzo went straight back up to his study and Jane cleared up and put on the dishwasher. She didn't want to leave without making her peace with Enzo. Fate was so arbitrary that a terrible accident might befall either of them and they might never see one another again. When she had packed the car and Chipper was happily installed as a passenger, she went upstairs to say goodbye, and they hugged each other and kissed, without reviving the quarrel.

Later, as Jane drove away, Enzo came downstairs and stood for a moment at the door to wave her off. Our relationship is robust enough to withstand pettiness, thought Jane, waving back. We can forgive it in each other, and know that our love will last. It was a comforting thought.

Enzo went back upstairs thinking of nothing but hip replacements.

*   *   *

'I won't be long, darling,' she said to Chipper as she drew up outside Cedar Lodge. It sometimes

194

struck her as being very English and dotty to speak to her dog like this, but it didn't stop her.

It had fulfilled Chipper's wildest dreams, to be included in the expedition. All the packing up and activity had alerted him to his mistress's plans to be away from home and he had spent most of the morning sitting by her car with a desperate expression on his face. Now he lay stretched out on the seat with his head on his paws, sighing contentedly, with a week's grocery shopping stacked round him.

'I'll leave the window open for you,' Jane said.

He looked up, entirely at peace. He knew that the car was a safe place to be. She would come back to him if he waited patiently.

Jane picked out the bag of things she had collected to take to Aunt Joan and went across the gravel towards Cedar Lodge. The small pots outside the front door had been planted with tulips and daffodils, which nodded in the sprightly wind, and the brass plate and bell pull shone in the sunshine. Inside it was very warm and the hall smelled of lunch and disinfectant, somewhere between a boarding school and a hospital. A television played from the lounge, and as Jane passed the open door she glimpsed the elderly residents dozing in silence in armchairs arranged in a circle around the walls. Today Jane did not feel, as she often did, that she would like to go and sit with them, unnoticed, and spend the afternoon nodding off to sleep, untroubled by the outside world. Instead she felt brisk and purposeful, her head full of plans to avoid traffic blackspots on the drive ahead, and working out what time she would be with Florence.

She found Aunt Joan in her room on the first floor, not asleep, but working away at the crossword. As Jane drew a chair up to sit beside her she noticed that the lenses of her spectacles were filmed with dirt.

'Here,' she said, reaching out to take them off her aunt's nose. 'You'll find it easier to see if I give these a good clean.'

'Oh, Jane, I am glad that you've come because I have something I want to show you.' Aunt Joan began to scrabble amongst the papers on her table, the same one that she and Jane used to take their meals on in the sitting room of the Marylebone flat. She found what she was looking for and held out a postcard. 'I want you to see this. From Natasha. As you know, she has never been one for keeping in touch.' On the front of the card was a bright Matisse painting. Jane turned it over and read in Tash's exuberant handwriting,

I hear that you are well and comfortable at Cedar Lodge. I have to go into hospital next week for tests and I wanted you to know. Don't worry—it's probably nothing serious, but I'd like to think that you would pray for me. For the first time in my life, I feel frightened!
Love, Tash.
PS, I hope that you don't mind me asking you this.

'Of course, I have been worried,' said Aunt Joan. 'I take it she means cancer?'

Jane nodded, trying to work out why her sister had chosen Aunt Joan as a confidante when she

196

was usually so pitiless and condemning of her.

'I will pray for her, of course. I have plenty of time, you see, and I believe in the power of prayer.'

'Yes. I know that people often turn to prayer when there is a crisis in their lives, but I didn't know that Tash was any sort of believer, except in some sort of wafty Indian mysticism.'

'That doesn't matter. Christianity isn't a club. It isn't an insurance policy either.'

'But it can be a comfort, can't it? Thinking that there is Someone in charge. She's been terribly brave. She only told me about it the other day and wouldn't allow me to tell anyone else. She doesn't want it talked about until she knows one way or the other.'

'Like your mother.'

'What do you mean?'

'She thought that she had cancer, you know. Breast cancer. She discovered a lump just before they went off on that last holiday.'

'I didn't know that.' Jane frowned. She had reached an age when she thought of her parents' lives, so long in the past, as completed, judged, come to terms with, tidied up and filed away in a finished state. She did not expect to have to deal with revelations at this stage.

'I don't think anybody knew but me, and it was your father who told me, not Eileen. He was terribly worried about her. The specialist had discussed a mastectomy—well, you know what that would have meant to a woman as vain as your mother.'

'But how extraordinary that we never knew this—Tash or me. Why weren't we told? Why didn't our mother tell us? We were adults, after all.'

'As I say, she was adamant that no one should know. She dreaded old age and illness as people who have invested heavily in their looks and youthfulness often do. Of course, your father got better looking as he got older. Men of his type usually do, and go on attracting much younger women. You can imagine what that was like for her.'

Jane nodded. Yes, she could imagine. Her aunt's words cast a shadow on the happiness of her day. What was the point of delving about in her parents' relationship when they had been dead for years? Why dredge up hurtful and unsettling truths now?

'But we should have been told!' she said, a sudden thought occurring to her. 'If our mother had breast cancer, it puts Tash and me into a higher risk group. It makes this whole scare of Tash's more serious.'

'But she didn't. She didn't have cancer. The lump was benign.'

Jane stared at her aunt. 'How do you know?'

'Because the doctor's letter came while she was away. She told me that she was having an important letter sent to my address and she was going to telephone me to find out the result. Of course, she never did. The accident happened on the day the letter arrived.'

'And you never told us.'

'No. She hadn't wanted me to. She was vehement about it, and so I didn't. I thought that I could allow her that.'

Jane felt confused. Did it make any difference, knowing now, after all these years, that her mother

198

had gone on that holiday fearful that she might be seriously ill? Jane had visited her parents at home just before they left. It was the last time she had seen them alive. Somewhere from her memory she glimpsed a fragment from the past, her mother's bed covered with the colourful clothes she intended to pack for the South of France. She remembered picking up a high-heeled, gold leather sandal and dangling it from her fingers. There was a coral-coloured chiffon scarf. A pink and gold caftan, a little mound of costume jewellery to be slipped into a velvet pouch. She remembered the glamour of the clothes and realised now that her mother was defying the hideous cruelty of the threatened cancer.

'It's so strange, hearing this now, out of the blue. I thought that Tash and I knew everything about them.'

'Can you ever be sure you know everything about anyone? I don't think so.'

'No, I suppose that's true.' Jane considered her aunt. She had always seemed elderly—even when she lived with her and she could not have been fifty; younger, certainly, than Jane was now. It was impossible to think of her as a girl who might have had secrets of any sort, or as an old woman whose life had been anything other than transparently dull.

'Will you thank Natasha for her card,' said Aunt Joan, 'and tell her that I will pray for her as she asked? I should like to see her again. Perhaps, later on, she will come and visit me.'

'I am sure she will,' lied Jane. 'I'll tell her. And I'll let you know when I have any news of her.'

'I should like to see the baby too. Florence's

199

little boy. I gave him the cufflinks, didn't I? Eileen should be here to see him—her great-grandson. There was no need for her to die, no need at all. No need for Timothy to die. What a waste it was. Foolish and wicked.'

Jane leaned forward to take her aunt's unadorned hand, with its paper-thin, brown-spotted skin and thickened yellow nails. 'Don't be upset,' she said. 'Not about the past, anyway. It all happened so long ago.'

In Aunt Joan's mind, the events of ages ago appeared to be as fresh as today's news. Tash's brush with cancer was no more immediate than her sister's threatened illness of so many years ago. Jane could understand why it was more rewarding to dwell on the past. The dull monotony of the present as the lonely survivor of her generation, her own friends either dead or leading similarly restricted lives, was far less engrossing than the time when she had been busy and active and must have felt that she was at the heart of things.

'I'll bring Tintin to see you, I promise. No doubt I'll have him to stay when he's a bit older.'

'Timothy?' said Aunt Joan querulously. 'No. Not Timothy. He was Eileen's husband, you know. Do you remember him? A very handsome man. Handsome is as handsome does, I say! He didn't come to much, did he?' and she gave a bark of laughter.

'Of course I remember him, Aunt Joan. He was my father,' said Jane gently.

What a strange mood her aunt was in today. Disturbed by memories, all the old resentments seemed to have come to the surface. Why was her poor old charmer of a father always in the firing line?

'I met him first, of course,' Aunt Joan said. 'Your mother never liked people to know that.'

'Did you?' Jane was surprised for a second time. She had always been told that her parents had been introduced at a party.

'Oh, yes. I was seconded to MI5 during the war. It wasn't as exciting as it may sound. I worked in the division that conducted routine personnel security checks. Your father was one of them. He was in London on his own, lonely and bored and waiting to be posted. We went out together for some time—oh, not like *that*! We weren't lovers. I took him to a party and it was there he met Eileen. Oh, as soon as she set eyes on him she was determined to get him. She couldn't believe her plain sister had turned up with such a good-looking man. By the end of the evening she was hanging round his neck.'

Jane sat in silence. She had never heard any of this before but it all made perfect sense. A piece of the puzzle had been missing and now it slotted into place and the whole picture became clear. She could understand the lasting animosity—you couldn't call it hatred, it wasn't that intense, just a grumbling resentment between the sisters. She remembered the old photograph of the two of them walking on a seaside promenade, arm in arm, a picture of sisterly affection, a short time before Timothy came into their lives and set the cat amongst the pigeons. He had made the obvious choice between them—or rather, the pretty one had chosen him and the plain one, destined for spinsterhood, had inevitably been sidelined. Handsome, charming men were not on the cards for Joan.

There was little more that could be said now and besides, Jane wanted to get on her way to Florence. What did it matter, any of it, anyway, she thought again. She hated that stupid expression 'letting go', but it was what Aunt Joan needed to do. She had allowed her whole life to be shadowed by a hurt she could not forget.

But what it also meant, she thought as she drove away, was that Aunt Joan had been there to support her when her mother had turned her back on her, and for that she would always be grateful. Tintin was a direct result of this. If she had given Florence up at birth, she would not now be speeding to help her with her baby. She might never have known the joy of holding her grandson in her arms.

*   *   *

In June Hugh borrowed his mother's car and drove Jane down to Sussex to meet Denby's sister and finalise the details of the cottage. These days he was doing everything he could to look like a revolutionary. His hair was nearly on his shoulders, two sheets divided by a centre parting, out of which he peered through his little round tin glasses. The bottom half of his thin face was furred with pale stubble, which had a long way to go before it became anything like a beard. This morning the fuzz caught the sun and gave him a gilded look. Gilded youth, thought Jane. Perhaps that was what the expression meant, but the rest of his appearance did not conform to this romantic idea. He was wearing torn plum-coloured velvet trousers

202

and a black T-shirt with a white skull and crossbones on the front. Round his neck was a West Bromwich Albion football scarf in royal blue and white stripes. Jane was not allowed to forget that his team had just won the FA cup.

'God, Hugh, you'll have to hide under the seat when we get there. If Denby's sister sees you looking like that, she'll never let me move in. One look at you would confirm her worst fears.'

'Good,' said Hugh. He had devoted a lot of time and effort in the hope of creating exactly that reaction in people like Caroline. It would have been a huge disappointment if he had failed to shock.

By contrast, Jane was wearing a neatly ironed cotton shirt over her maternity jeans. She had washed her long hair and it curled, shining, on her shoulders, held back by a velvet hairband. She looked young, fresh and wholesome, and extremely pregnant. She sat in the front of the Morris Minor with her hands folded over her bump, watching the green countryside flash by while Hugh told her with great envy and admiration of the students in France who had joined with the workers to rock the government. He talked about Molotov cocktails and police baton charges, of the throwing of paving stones, and tear gas, and all the time Jane's mind wandered to dwell on the baby, who was turning inside her.

She didn't want to hear about violence and unrest, about Enoch Powell's speeches in Wolverhampton, which had so enraged his mother, or the shooting of Martin Luther King or Robert Kennedy, or IRA atrocities or Black Panther kidnappings. She wanted to shut out the horrible world and find a small, safe corner in which to hide with her baby, where she would love and protect her, and lead a simple happy life with Bunnikins china plates and sweet little egg cups.

Sadly, it needed a nice, fantasy husband to complete the picture. She had to accept that her mother was right about that. Jane had no feminist stirrings or desire to be independent. She was utterly conventional in her longing for a regular relationship, a wedding ring and the father of her baby by her side. How happy she would be, she thought, if she had only done things properly. As it was, she was just going to have to manage as best she could.

She had never before lived on her own. She was frightened of the dark, for one thing. She hated an empty creaking house, had always been scared when her parents went out for the evening and left her alone. She heard noises, footsteps, tapping on the window and, paralysed with fear, used to lie waiting to hear the car's wheels on the gravel and the beam of headlights that meant her parents were back and she could breathe again.

She would have to get over that if she was going to live with the baby in a cottage miles from anywhere. The nights would be dark and there would be no streetlamp shining its comforting light through her bedroom window. The cottage might be surrounded by glowering woods or a wild common where a mad axe murderer could take cover. Oh, she must stop this. These stupid thoughts made her heart beat and her throat constrict with panic.

In front of her she had the typed instructions that Caroline had sent her. After Haslemere the country was very pretty, with wooded valleys and secluded houses hidden down long drives, and winding roads climbing out of sleepy villages towards distant open downland.

' "Turn left in Wooland after the cricket ground. Second right after the church, and Yew Tree Cottage is second on the left behind a holly hedge." We must be nearly there. I feel sick with nerves. This Caroline person is terrifying. Like a prefect, if you know what I mean. I even cleaned my shoes!'

'You shouldn't kowtow to the petty bourgeoisie!' said Hugh, loftily. 'Here we are. Wooland. What a great cricket pitch, with the pub opposite. Ideally situated for post-match pints.' How bourgeois a remark is that, thought Jane, affectionately, but said nothing. Hugh hadn't quite been able to wean himself off cricket.

'Left!' she said. 'There's the church. We go on past it to the second right.' Cottages lined either side of the road but there was nobody about, and then Jane said, 'This is it. Grove Lane,' and Hugh turned onto a small road, which appeared to lead out of the village. There were no more houses, just field gates and hedges, and a verge deep with grass and cow parsley. Then a substantial house appeared on the left, a fairly modern house with a circular drive, a double garage and a manicured garden. 'Those will be my neighbours!' said Jane. 'I hope they're nice.' There was a bend in the lane and then she could see the holly hedge and the red-tiled roof of Yew Tree Cottage. 'This is it, Hugh. We've arrived!'

*   *   *

To say that Caroline Webster had been doubtful and suspicious would be to underestimate her reaction to meeting Jane. It was a very good thing that Hugh had dropped her off at the gate and reversed down the lane to go to the pub, having arranged to see her there in an hour. If Caroline had met Hugh, even his public school accent and medical student credentials would not have reassured her that Jane was a sufficiently sensible and respectable person to be caretaker of her cottage.

Caroline was a tall, fair girl in her late twenties. She had a large pink face and a superior manner. She was wearing jeans with an ironed front crease and a navy Guernsey sweater, the front of which was filled by a hefty bosom, and flat shoes with miniature snaffle bits on the front. She had what is known as 'difficult' hair, very thick and frizzy, held back by an identical hairband to the one that Jane had thought was a good idea to wear for this particular meeting. Her mannish, rather rough-looking hands were adorned by sparkly and obviously good rings, and she wore a pearl necklace to offset the artisan nature of the sweater. She had a ringing voice and talked fast without properly listening to the answers to her fired-off questions. Her pale eyes were cold behind heavy lids and short lashes coloured with cheap black Outdoor Girl mascara. She embodied that particularly English upper-class contradiction of not caring what one wore but at the same time adhering to a strict code of dress and behaviour.

She had obviously made up her mind to get to the bottom of how and why Jane was pregnant and

206

unmarried, and she clearly found all her answers unsatisfactory. At some point in the conversation she actually said, 'So you have *no idea* who the father is?' and Jane shook her head in shame while inwardly boiling with resentment. If only I was brave enough to say, 'Mind your own bloody business,' she thought, but humility and desperate need sealed her lips.

She was offered coffee, and a tin of shortbread biscuits came out of a cupboard. 'Mummy knows how much my husband loves them!' Caroline said as she put them on the table. At the end of an hour she sighed and said, 'Well, it seems that your referees—your aunt and your employer—are prepared to vouch for you, and I think I've made it clear what we expect. You understand that if you break any clause of the agreement you will be asked to leave without notice?' And she produced a typed contract drawn up by Nigel and asked Jane to sign it. Jane had a moment of panic, and then wrote her large childish signature on the dotted line.

'So that's agreed then,' said Caroline. 'You'll be here for two years, apart from the month that Nigel and I will be home in the summer. We are responsible for general maintenance and the gardener, who comes once a fortnight. You are responsible for all bills except for the rates, and for damages. You can receive incoming calls on the telephone line but you will have to use the telephone box on the green for outgoing calls. You will move in as soon as the baby is born.'

Jane nodded meekly.

'You'd better come and look round,' said Caroline. 'There's a dear little room which will be ideal for a nursery,' and there was a touch of wistfulness in her Pony Club voice.

CHAPTER NINE

The first thing Florence said when she opened her front door was, 'Oh no! You haven't brought the bloody dog, have you?' and promptly burst into noisy tears.

It wasn't the best start, but for once Jane was unapologetic.

'He won't be a nuisance, I promise you,' she said. 'He's very quiet and well-behaved,' but Florence continued crying.

'It's just the last bloody straw,' she gulped, her mouth made ugly and her face red. 'I've got enough to bloody cope with, without having that great dog here. What were you thinking of? No, you weren't bloody thinking, as usual.'

'Florence! That's enough!' said Jane, remaining calm although her heart was beating loudly. 'Now let me come in with all this stuff. There's more in the car. I'll make us a cup of tea, and you'll feel better. Where's Tintin? It's very quiet.'

'He's having the first sleep he's had in twenty-four hours,' said Florence bitterly. 'That fucking dog will bark and wake him up, no doubt.'

'Oh, stop it! Anyway, I had to bring him. I couldn't leave him at home with Enzo.'

All the time, Jane was shifting her bags through to the kitchen where she could see that chaos reigned. There was no room on any of the counters to unpack. 'I'll see to all this in a minute. Just let me put on the kettle.' Florence had one of those state-of-the-art electric kettles that were impossible to fill and it took ten minutes to work out how they switched on, but Jane managed, and washed two mugs and found the tea bags in the cupboard. She filled a bowl of water for Chipper, who drank noisily and went to collapse heavily under the marble-topped table. He laid his great head on his paws and took up a watchful position.

'See,' said Jane. 'He's as good as gold.'

Florence had followed her to stand in the doorway, arms crossed over her chest, hands plucking at the sleeves of her sweater, still gulping sobs, her face a picture of extreme misery.

'Oh God, I'm sorry, Mum. I'm so sorry. I just feel so fucking hopeless. I'm all over the bloody place and it's not getting any better. Look at the state of everything.'

'That's all right, darling. Don't worry. Now I'm here we can get all this lot sorted out. If Tintin is asleep why don't you go and lie on your bed and I'll bring you a cup of tea later on? I'll get him when he wakes. When did he have his last feed?'

'About ten minutes ago. He seems to need feeding every half an hour. I don't know what the matter is. As soon as I put him on the breast he goes to sleep. It's taking me hours to get a feed down him.'

'Don't worry. It's very early days. He'll soon settle down and it will all get easier, I promise. Off you go and have a rest while you can. I'll have to go back down to the car but I'll leave the front door on the latch. Chipper won't let anyone in.'

'The washing machine is broken. I can't get anyone to say exactly when they'll come and mend it. Ha is having to go to the launderette every day. He'll be round later. He may bring something to eat; I can't remember if I asked him to shop. I seem to have lived on toast for a week.'

'Stop worrying about all of that. That's why I'm here. Go on, off you go.'

Flo came over to where her mother was loading dirty crockery into the sink, and laid her head on her shoulder. 'Thank you so much, Mum. Thank you! I'm so knackered I'm not thinking straight. Sorry I was so inexcusably foul.'

Jane felt sympathetic but not overly concerned. This was all as she had expected. Florence was clearly finding it hard to adapt to motherhood. Perhaps Tintin *was* a difficult baby; it was too early for her to judge. She felt a surge of the happiness and affection that comes from helping people. 'Go on!' she said. 'Go and rest while you can. You don't need to thank me!'

For the next two hours Jane worked hard. She cleared the kitchen, washed and dried the dishes and mopped the floor. She examined the washing machine, checked the plug, wondered whether it had fused, looked for a screwdriver and couldn't find one. She tidied and vacuumed the sitting room and cleared away the dying bouquets of flowers that were stuck in various vases in half an inch of green, stagnant water. She put the daffodils that she had brought with her in a large glass jar on the coffee table and set the dining table for supper, including a place for Ha. She put the casserole in a low oven and peeled potatoes.

She checked Tintin, who was sleeping peacefully, and opened the window to let in a bit of fresh air. The central heating was blasting and she considered it far too hot. She tidied his room, moving all the furry toys from the floor to a shelf to make it easy to vacuum. She noticed that Flo had kept her old teddy bear, and picked him up for a moment. His fur was worn and he had lost one glass eye but he was still the same old bear who had accompanied Flo everywhere when she was a little girl.

She heaved the black bag of rubbish down to the ground floor and lobbed it into the refuse collection area. When she got back to the flat she was pleased that it smelled fresh and looked tidy and welcoming. She retuned the radio in the kitchen to Radio Four and listened to a play as she cleaned out the fridge and then started on the bathroom, which was, frankly, disgusting. She sorted out clean from dirty clothes and then into coloureds and whites. She shook her head over the big pile of tiny garments that would have to be hand-washed. How stupid and unnecessary was it for a baby to wear cashmere? Talk about making things difficult for yourself—or other people.

The work was satisfying and tiring, and she made herself another cup of tea and checked the time. It was nearly half-past five and Tintin and his mother were still asleep. She would leave them another half an hour and then wake Tintin for his bath. She had found some extraordinary plastic arrangement in the bathroom, which was supposed to slot into the tub, but she preferred to bath a tiny baby in a bowl, or a proper small baby bath placed on a towel on the kitchen table. Flo's bathroom was a windowless square of steel and marble, all slippery and cold, with a roaring fan—it reminded Jane of a sluice or an abattoir. She remembered bathing Flo on the kitchen table of the Sussex cottage and laying her on a towel to kick in the sunshine that flooded through the window.

Ha arrived some time after six, carrying a bin liner full of crumpled, still warm laundry. His face looked pale green and haggard with exhaustion. Jane kissed him on both cheeks and handed him a glass of wine and a dish of olives.

'God, I'm glad to see you,' he said. 'Flo's been having a really tough time. We never thought it would be like this. The nights have been, well, a nightmare. If I try and get some sleep, it makes Flo resentful, but she won't give Tintin a bottle, so there's nothing I can do anyway. We had a row the night before last and I went back to my house and slept for thirteen hours, which made me feel a selfish bastard.'

'But that was sensible!' protested Jane. 'There's no point in you both being exhausted. It's obvious that if you can get some sleep then you'll be able to support her better. At least there will be one of you who won't be overtired and emotional.'

Ha slumped on the sofa and Chipper heaved himself up from under the window and went to lie at his feet with a sigh. Ha leaned forward to stroke his ears.

'You've brought the dog!'

'Yes. Flo wasn't very pleased, I'm afraid. I must feed him, poor old boy. As soon as I've bathed Tintin, I'll take him for a walk and then we can eat.'

'It's nice to have him here. I like dogs,' said Ha. 'Whatever you are cooking smells delicious. Jesus, it's good to have you here!' Really, he could charm the birds out of the trees, thought Jane. He had the most engaging smile, which dimpled his cheeks and seemed to spread across the whole surface of his face. It was such an expansive smile that his eyes almost disappeared and his very white and even teeth flashed.

They sat for a moment in silence, looking at one another over their wine glasses. Ha seemed suddenly thoughtful and it felt to Jane as if there was something that brooded unspoken between them. Uncharted waters, she thought, into which she hesitated to set sail.

'Do you know,' began Ha, looking down at his glass, 'how Florence sees me in all of this?'

'What do you mean?' asked Jane, although she knew exactly. It was a question she would like to ask him. She couldn't see how *she* could have anything to offer on the subject. She was always in the dark as far as Florence was concerned.

'I just wonder if she's talked to you—you know, about how she sees us, as a *family*, as it were.'

'Surely you've talked about that with her? She never discusses anything personal with me. I am sorry to say that we've never had that sort of a relationship. Not since she was a teenager, anyway.'

Ha sighed. 'We have, in a way. I mean, obviously she told me that she wanted to have my baby and all that, but I've never been that confident of where I am supposed to fit into her life from now on. She's never asked me to live with her, for instance.'

Jane's mind reeled. It seemed an extraordinary state of affairs. It was like ordering a baby over the Internet. She thought for a bit and then said, 'Well, have you asked her to live with *you*?'

Ha smiled at the suggestion. 'That wouldn't work. I share a house with a load of other guys.'

'But you don't *have* to go on doing that, do you? For goodness' sake, you're grown up! You could set up home together somewhere else.'

'Yeah.' Ha sounded doubtful. 'I don't think Flo has that sort of commitment,' he said sadly. 'Not to me, anyway.'

'How long is it that you've been, er, seeing each other?' Was that the right term? She couldn't say 'lived together', or 'been together', because they hadn't. Not on any long-term basis, anyway. How carefully she had to pick her way through the definitions of modern relationships.

'Five years or so. Neither of us has been with anyone else in that time.'

Jane was flummoxed. Wasn't that commitment, if anything was? If you were young and healthy and normally sexually active, didn't fidelity count as a significant commitment? She couldn't begin to guess what Florence wanted, or what effect Tintin's birth would have on her life plan. 'Perhaps,' she suggested, voicing what she had wondered all along, 'now you have a baby, she will feel more positive about what someone of my generation would call normal family life.'

Ha shrugged. 'She keeps changing her mind. If I'm here for more than a day or two she gets fed up with me, says she needs her own space. I think she holds you up as an example.'

'Me?' Jane was genuinely astonished.

'Yeah. She's always saying how you brought her up on your own. She thinks it was really cool, that you were a real sixties chick doing it alone.'

Jane stared at him in disbelief. 'Ha, you've got

214

this very wrong. She is misleading you here. I wasn't a sixties chick, as you put it. I was a terrified teenager. I went through some truly dreadful times. I wouldn't have *chosen* to do it that way, I can tell you. What's more, Florence has always despised me for it. For not providing her with a father. I mean, Enzo has been just marvellous, but it isn't the same thing at all. He's not her flesh and blood.'

Ha now looked as if he regretted starting this conversation. He took a gulp of wine and said, 'Yeah, well . . .' They lapsed into silence again while Jane's mind raced in confusion. Ha had got it wrong, totally upside down. She had never, ever, not once, believed that Florence thought her origins were anything other than disastrous.

She was glad that Tintin chose this moment to make small mewing noises and she put down her glass and got up to go to him. As she passed Ha she was moved to place a gentle hand on his shoulder. She felt that they both needed comforting after the conversation they had just shared.

Tintin was lying on his back in his Shaker cradle, waving his little mottled arms in the air and turning his head from side to side. He was very wide awake and Jane gazed down at him and he gazed back with his blue glare.

'Hello,' she said. 'What's all this I hear about you, Monsieur Tintin?' and she bent to pick him up. The back of his head was wet with sweat. 'You're far too hot, aren't you? We'll have to see about that, won't we?' In fact, the whole bundle of baby felt very warm and damp. She took him through to the sitting room and placed him in Ha's arms.

'Here's your boy!' she said. 'Just hold him for a minute while I get his bath ready.'

She collected what she needed and although he yelled throughout, she thought that the warm bath, taken in the washing-up bowl in the kitchen, was good for him because when he was dried and freshly powdered and dressed in a clean nappy and Babygro, he lay happily against Ha's shoulder and made quiet snuffling noises, stuffing his little fists into his mouth.

'Now,' said Jane. 'I've put the potatoes on to boil and while they are cooking I'll walk Chipper along the canal a little way. You can take Tintin in to Flo for a feed when he starts crying. Tell her I won't be long—not more than twenty minutes. She might like a glass of wine.'

'Actually, lactating mothers—' began Ha in a doctor's voice.

'Oh bollocks!' said Jane. 'Only a glass. It will help her relax.' She picked up Chipper's lead and collected her jacket. 'I won't be long. You'll be all right, won't you?'

Chipper's nails scrabbled on the wooden floorboards and she was gone. Ha sat on with Tintin on his shoulder, enjoying the slight weight and warmth of his son. He looked round the tidy flat and for the first time since Tintin's birth he felt that maybe everything would turn out OK.

*   *   *

Jane walked briskly along the canal path. The warmth of the sun had gone and it was now quite a cold grey evening with scudding, steel-coloured

216

clouds and a brisk wind. She turned up the collar of her coat. The path went along the backs of warehouses, mostly now turned into flats. Some still had the old platforms and chain pulleys for unloading the barges that had once used the waterway.

The canal to her left was a poisonous-looking green. Algae, she supposed. The darting moorhens trailed a wake of clear water behind them. Someone had done a clean-up, though, and the shopping trolleys and great mats of rotted-down rubbish had been removed since the last time she had walked here. Now there were benches set along the path, spindly trees had been planted, some already broken down by vandals, and every now and then a notice explaining the origins of the canal, how it had been built and the trade that had used it, and how the city had sprung up on the resulting commerce. There was even the occasional restaurant with long windows that opened onto the water. This evening they were tightly shut.

Chipper trotted along in front, cheerful and interested in his new surroundings, and when Jane sat on a bench and took out her mobile telephone to ring Enzo he came back to stand beside her, keeping a watch right and left, his ears cocked. There was no reply and so she left a message and then rang Tash's number. That too went unanswered. She tried her mobile but it was switched off. What did that mean? Was it good or bad? Probably she and Denby were at a party— they were always out—or at a concert or the theatre. If Tash had had any news, she would have let her know.

In the end she sent her a text and then sat staring at the green surface of the water, trying not to think about breast cancer and what it could mean. She thought about what Aunt Joan had told her earlier that day and she wanted to tell Tash—to pass it on as if it were good news from the past—but she found that she was still unsettled by the revelation. Maybe it was that her mother had chosen not to tell her two daughters, had not wished to share her anxiety with them, that upset her, but that was no more than what Tash was doing now. Maybe she was just trying to spare them worry, but she knew in her mother's case that was not true. It was more about the distance between them, and the lack of closeness saddened her. She thought of her own daughter and how difficult it was to be close to her.

Chipper laid his large head on her lap and nudged her hand, and she stroked him in return. She was so glad that she had him with her because she suddenly felt lonely and afraid.

She had already been gone for fifteen minutes so she stood up and turned back the way she had come. She had no idea quite how the evening was going to turn out.

*   *   *

When she got back to the flat she found Flo sitting up in bed with Ha beside her, their heads bent over Tintin, who lay peacefully in his mother's arms, wide awake, surveying them both with what Jane thought was rather a beady expression.

'How did the feed go?' she asked from the doorway.

Flo looked up. 'Well, he seemed to take enough. It's bloody agony with cracked nipples but at least the pain wears off after a minute or two. I tell you, I shall be more sympathetic in future. I'm ashamed to think how I used to dismiss new mothers' complaints about breast-feeding.'

'Is he windy?' asked Jane. 'Does he need to burp? Shall I take him while you get ready for supper? Perhaps you want a shower first?'

'Oh, bliss!' said Flo, lying back. 'I haven't had a relaxed bath or shower for, well, it seems months. I've either been too tired or Tintin's been crying.'

'Go on, then,' said Jane. 'I'll see to him and put him to bed.'

She sat on the bedroom chair and took the baby upside down across her lap and gently rubbed his back. Two huge burps followed. In his own room, she changed his nappy and wrapped him tightly in one of Tash's cotton blankets before putting him gently in his cradle on his side. She rolled another blanket against his back to make him feel more secure. In her view the crib was too big for a newborn, used to the closeness of the womb. She was probably breaking all the current rules about baby care but this was what she had always done with her own babies. She covered him snugly with another blanket, drew the curtains, gently stroked his cheek with a finger for a moment or two and then quietly left the room.

The casserole was ready, the table set, and Jane opened another bottle of wine. Ha was watching television and Flo was in her bedroom getting dressed after her shower. She emerged with wet hair and a fresh-looking face in a clean white T-shirt and a pair of tracksuit bottoms.

219

'I feel so much better. Just an hour's sleep makes all the difference. You are a miracle worker, Mum, really you are. I feel like I used to do when I was little and came home from school with a temperature and you used to put me to bed with a hot Ribena, and it was just such a relief to be home and to be looked after.' She noticed the table, the casserole, mashed potatoes and dish of spring cabbage, and said, 'Oh, this looks wonderful. You've even found napkins. Come on, Ha. Come and sit down. I'm starving. Did Tintin settle? If he did, it's for the first time in his not very long life.'

'I think he was too hot. I've taken that great sheepskin thing out of his cot. I hope you don't mind, but really, with central heating . . . it would be all very well for the frozen north, Mongolia or somewhere, living in a yurt, maybe. Ha, pass your plate, would you?'

Later, as they sat amongst the debris of supper, Ha said, 'Who do you think Tintin looks like, Jane? Florence says me, but I can't see it.'

'I think she's right—the eyes, anyway, and perhaps your mouth.'

'Of course, people always see who they want to see in babies. In Vietnam, it's the grandparents who are honoured by a supposed likeness.'

'In Tintin's case there's a large part of his genetic history missing. For all we know he might look just like his maternal grandfather,' said Florence. She took another sip of wine and said carelessly to Jane, 'Do you really have no memory at all of what my father looked like? To be honest, I've never been able to believe that. I've always thought you were deliberately concealing it for some reason.'

220

Jane stared at her daughter. '*Concealing* it? Whatever do you mean? I told you the whole truth when I thought you were old enough to understand. Your father was a boy I met once and once only. At a student party. I'd drunk too much. Flo, I've *told* you all this . . . and the next morning my memory was vague. He was tall and thin and had soft brown hair and, well, was nice-looking. He had a southern voice—an educated voice. That's all I can say with any certainty.'

'But surely you could have traced him when you found out you were pregnant? There can't have been *that* many people at the party. Someone would have known who he was? After all, Cambridge isn't a big place.'

'Flo, I didn't know where to begin to look for him. It was a freshers' party but there were students from other years there as well, and people from other colleges. None of my friends knew him, and neither did their boyfriends, and as far as I was concerned he just vanished afterwards. I gave him my telephone number but he never contacted me again. I wasn't sure of his name. It was something like Nicholas Alexander, or Alexander Nicholas, Peter Gordon, or Gordon Peters—one of those names that work either way. One of my friends managed to get a list of first-year students from the college, but it only had initials for the Christian name, and hundreds of surnames were things like Russell, Richards, Phillips, Stephens, Lawrence. And at those parties boys often went under an alias; girls did the same thing just in case you didn't want to see people again. He was a scientist, though. I did remember that because it meant we hadn't got anything to talk about regarding our

221

work. Nothing in common.'

'When I was a teenager I had this dream that one day I would pass my father in the street and he would know me instantly and we would have this great reconciliation and he would tell me that he had been looking for me all his life.' Florence gave a snort of laughter, but her face was not smiling.

'You don't think that I didn't dream that as well?' said Jane. 'I was a teenager at the time too, remember. After you were born, I used to tell myself that one day he would come and find us. There would be a knock on the door and I'd open it and there he would be. I would know him instantly and he would take me in his arms and say, "At last! I have been searching for you everywhere!" and it would all be a case of lost telephone numbers and misunderstandings.'

'When I was small you used to make up stories about who he was—it made me feel as if I was part of a fairy tale. A handsome prince, a wave of the wand, and *voilà*! The princess has a baby girl! It wasn't so good when I got older. It wasn't easy growing up without a clue about my father, not even his name. Even adopted children can trace their natural parents, but not me. All I had was a blank.'

'But when you were ten, you had Enzo. He was as good if not better than any natural father could have been.'

'Yeah, sure, but it's not the same, is it? It didn't stop me wondering about who I really was. I used to lie at school about how my real father was a spy, or a South American freedom fighter, or a member of the royal family.'

'He certainly wasn't any of those, but he must

have been clever. At least he has given you a good brain.'

'A Cambridge college is a top gene pool, I suppose.'

'I'm sorry, Flo. I'm sorry it happened like that.'

'Yes,' said Flo coldly. 'So you have always said.'

Jane felt a heavy sensation in the region of her heart. This was the first time that Flo had ever talked about her feelings, although how she felt had always been obvious. What can I do, thought Jane, to change how things are between us? Isn't it time we came to a resolution? I suppose I hoped that Tintin's arrival would change things. How can I ever make her understand how much I loved and wanted her?

Ha got up and began to clear the plates. 'That was lovely, Jane, thank you,' he said, and it was his turn to place a hand on her shoulder as he passed behind her chair.

'Oh, yes, I forgot,' he said from the kitchen. 'Your sister telephoned while you were out. She was at a concert at the Barbican, so she said not to ring her back. She'll call you tomorrow.'

Jane sat up in her chair, instantly alert. 'Was that all? She didn't say anything else?'

'No, I don't think so. Just that she'll ring you tomorrow.'

*   *   *

During the last month of Jane's pregnancy she was bidden to attend the hospital prenatal clinic once a week. By now she felt huge and exhausted, and longed for it all to be over and at the same time terrified of what lay ahead. It was no use telling

223

Aunt Joan how she felt because she knew nothing at all about pregnancy and babies, or Mr Kowalski, who was totally absorbed in the rumbles of news from Czechoslovakia, and wouldn't know anything either. Twice she telephoned Hugh's mother, who was brisk and kind and matter-of-fact, and talked her through what she might expect to happen, but she sounded distracted and Jane could hear voices and telephones ringing in the background and she imagined the busy surgery and felt that she was being a nuisance.

'Telephone your mother,' advised Dr Bywater. 'She is the person to talk to.'

'I can't do that,' said Jane awkwardly. 'You know, she doesn't want anything to do with me ...'

'That is ridiculous!' Dr Bywater's voice was sharp. 'I shall go round and speak to her. This must be stopped, this absurd situation ...'

'Oh, no. Please!' said Jane. 'Please don't. I'm all right, really I am. Anyway, I must go.' She tried to make her voice bright and confident. As she put down the telephone she realised it was a mistake to have asked for help. She might have known it would be complicated—the Bywaters and her parents being next-door neighbours and on opposite sides of the Enoch Powell debate. Hugh had told her that the wild-eyed politician had stirred up racial hatred in his Wolverhampton constituency and that his mother was dealing with Pakistani and Indian women abused in the street and now too terrified to leave their homes.

It was a hot summer and the heat radiated off the pavements and buildings, and the sky was a hard relentless blue. Jane still lumbered off to work each morning. She felt she might just as well be there as on her own in the flat. She had packed her bag as directed by the hospital, in case she had to go in a rush, and had a list of taxi numbers by the telephone. There was nothing to do but wait.

'What will you do when I have the baby?' she asked Mr Kowalski. 'You will need to find someone to help you in the shop.'

'Ah, the shop,' said Mr Kowalski sadly, as if he were thinking tragic thoughts about something else.

'Yes. You'll need another assistant, won't you? I won't be able to come back, you know. After the baby, I am moving to Sussex. Look, I've written out the address and telephone number. Oh, Mr Kowalski, you will keep in touch with me, won't you?'

He looked at her with his vague blue eyes and with an effort took in what she was saying.

'Oh, yes! And you will come and see me. I do not want to lose you now, my dear Jane. You are like my family to me, and the joy of your baby is a light in this bad world.'

'Of course I'll come and see you, and I'll bring the baby. After all, Mr Kowalski, if it hadn't been for you, I might have decided to give it away.'

'This you will never regret. This baby will be the most blessed gift.' He clasped both her hands in his and spoke so fervently that Jane felt embarrassed. Really, he rather overdid the joy about the coming birth. He made it sound like Christmas, but she knew that he meant every word and she was touched.

'What about finding another assistant?' she asked again, but he was already scrabbling about amongst the papers on his desk and she felt she shouldn't nag him. She had often wondered if, by the time he had paid her wage, the shop earned enough to make it worth continuing, and over the last few months she had thought that he looked more faded and tired. Perhaps it was time that he gave up, but what would become of him if he did? She could not bear to think of the overwhelming loneliness, his silent flat, the scratched-together meals, his memories of the past speaking more loudly than the voices of the present.

The last days of her pregnancy seemed long and slow. Still strong and healthy, she had no symptoms other than feeling tired at the end of the day and occasional heartburn, but her brain felt soft and muzzy, her thoughts turning inwards. She listened to the rhythms of her body, felt the beating of her baby's heart within the hard drum of her womb. The baby had been quiet for the last day or two and according to the nurse at the clinic the head was in the right position. It could be any moment; today, tonight, tomorrow. Jane tried to imagine what giving birth would be like, the pain, the waters bursting, the horrible stirrups, like something from a torture chamber, which they put your feet into in the delivery room.

The pains started at six the following morning. Jane sat hunched on the edge of her bed in her Snoopy nightshirt, wringing her hands and scrunching up her face as each spasm swept over her. This is it, she thought, and she felt terribly alone and afraid. People died having babies, didn't they? They screamed and screamed and hung on to twisted sheets tied to the bedpost in Victorian novels. She picked up her rabbit nightdress case, which she had had since she was eight, and buried her face in its soft grey fur. She tried to time the contractions but she couldn't concentrate. She would have liked to lie in a warm bath but there would be no hot water. Perhaps a cup of tea would help, but as she stood waiting for the kettle to boil the iron fist of pain grabbed and twisted her inside so viciously that she cried out loud.

When it was over she went to the telephone in the hall and with a shaking hand and tears pouring down her flaming cheeks, she dialled for a taxi. Timidly, she tapped on Aunt Joan's door.

'I am so sorry to wake you,' she said, 'but I think the baby's coming.' She heard her aunt turn on her bedside light and then the rustle of bedclothes and dressing gown. The door opened and Aunt Joan's face looked out, her hair in curlers tied up in a pink net.

'Oh, my goodness,' she said. 'Oh, my goodness me. Dear Lord! Are you sure?'

Jane nodded and then said, 'Well, I don't know for sure but I think so.' She felt light-headed between the contractions. 'I've called the taxi.' She had to hang on to the hall chair while the next pain swept over her.

'Go and get some clothes on, child. I'll get dressed as well. Quick, quick!'

Jane went back to her room and without bothering with underwear, pulled on her jeans and a smock top. She slipped her feet into her new leather clogs, collected her bag and looked round the room to which she would not return. She had already packed her things back into her trunk. Apart from a splodge of nail varnish dropped on the lino by the window and a small ink stain on the bedside table, there would be no trace of her ever having lived here, or her efforts to make it more homely. She waddled out into the hall to wait.

As she sat there on the hard chair, feverish with anxiety, she knew that more than anything she wanted her mother. She wanted her to take command, to tell her what to do and how to do it. She wanted her to reassure and comfort her, to tell her that everything would be all right. But she doesn't even know that I am in labour, she thought self-pityingly. She isn't even able to think of me, and neither is Daddy, or Tash. She wanted to pick up the telephone and dial her home number and plead, 'Help me! Come to me!' but it was Aunt Joan's dry hand that clasped her own in the taxi and it was Aunt Joan who was firm with the unhelpful and unsympathetic nurse on the admission desk.

'No,' she declared, in ringing tones. 'We will not sit here while you finish your cup of tea. My niece needs immediate attention. She is in imminent danger of giving birth here in the corridor. Now are you going to take her in, or am I?'

*   *   *

After Jane and Ha had cleared away the supper and Jane had set the kitchen to rights, she felt weary. It had been a long day and seemed to have been crowded with emotional upheavals. She left Ha and Florence watching television and went through to the nursery and began to tidy up, and put her own things away. She assumed she would sleep in the divan bed pushed against the wall and covered with toys and clothes. She had seen that it was made up with sheets and a duvet. Tintin was

228

fast asleep, still securely swaddled in his blanket, but Florence appeared in the doorway and whispered, 'Mum! Don't wake him. I can't believe he's still asleep!'

'Don't worry!' Jane told her in a normal voice. 'Really, you don't have to tiptoe round babies. They get used to a bit of noise, and then they sleep through anything. It's good training.'

When she had finished she looked at her watch and wondered what Tash was doing. Possibly the concert was just about to finish and she would telephone her again. She checked that her mobile was switched on.

It was time to take Chipper out for his final run. She had put his blanket in the corner of her room beside the huge collection of large furry animals that Florence had amassed for Tintin. He would lie beside a two-foot giraffe and an almost life-sized donkey on wheels. She expected that Florence would object, but she would stand firm. She was sure that she had recently read some research that said babies were healthier for being brought up with animals—more resistant to allergies and asthma or something, like old people who lived longer and happier lives if they owned a dog.

When she went through to the sitting room Florence and Ha were sitting together on the sofa. Florence, with her feet tucked under her, rested her head on Ha's shoulder and he had his arm round her. Jane was touched by their apparent closeness. That's what Florence needs, she thought. She remembered how wonderful it had been when the boys were born and she had Enzo's support and love and how important it had been that his joy matched her own.

At the same time she remembered the loneliness of the early days of Florence's life. It had been all right in the hospital. There was a cheerful Welsh sister, Sister Owen, who persisted in calling her 'Mrs', pretending that she was just like the other mothers, and there was camaraderie amongst the women who befriended her, especially those that had had several children already and took trouble to show her how to pin on the bulky triangles of terry towelling nappy, and how to deal with the terrifying-looking knot of umbilical cord. They were London women from the poor streets of King's Cross and Euston, and they were unconcerned that she had no husband to come and see her at visiting hours. 'Had a slip-up, did you, love? Where's the bastard that got you knocked up? Done a bloody runner? You're a posh girl, though, aren't you? Yer mum and dad will see you right.'

Yes, it had been OK there on the ward where Sister Owen had insisted she stay for ten days, although she had felt like a prisoner and longed for fresh air and freedom. She'd been mad to get out, but how wise that sister had been to make her stay until she felt more confident with the baby and breast-feeding was established. What a wonderful person she had been. Jane remembered with infinite gratitude how she had helped her in the first few days when she had been so pathetic and tearful and thought that she would never manage to keep little Florence alive and well. Sister herself would come and sit beside her and chat while she gently guided the baby to feed. She would tuck a pillow under Jane's elbow as she nursed, and bring her a cup of tea and a custard cream biscuit, and best of all, tell her how well she was doing and what a good mother she was.

You were a saintly woman, Sister Owen, thought Jane as she collected Chipper's lead and let herself out of the flat. If you are still alive you will be an old woman now, but your kindness and true charity still shine brightly in my memory. How different had been Sister Nash, who came on duty for the last few days of Jane's stay, who was well bred, and rushed, and cross, and never had a moment to help anyone, and who treated Jane with ill-disguised contempt.

There was another girl too. She suddenly remembered a poor, thin teenager with drooping shoulders who had been brought in before her due date because there were some complications with her pregnancy. She trailed about in a pink dressing gown and fluffy slippers and seemed hardly able to string two words together, except to beg cigarettes. At night Jane heard her crying in a side ward and even Sister Owen seemed to find her irritating. Later, after her baby boy was born, Jane heard that he was to be adopted and for a whole morning the girl screamed. It was amazing how much noise she made—such a frail-looking creature—and it upset everybody on the ward. The other mothers exchanged knowing looks and sighed. Eventually she was sedated and taken away on a trolley. Jane watched her wheeled past, her yellow, backcombed hair like a mat on the pillow, her thin little hands with chipped pink nail varnish clasping the sheet. It made Jane terrified that something would happen to her and that they would take Florence too. Awful Mrs Thing would come and take her away and give her to the Christians. She couldn't bear to

231

have Florence out of her sight and when the babies were wheeled away in their cribs to the nursery, she would hang about outside the door, watching through the window, on guard.

Jane felt shaken by these memories. She hadn't thought about any of this for years and years, not Sister Owen, nor the poor girl who would now be a woman in her fifties. Somewhere there was a man of Florence's age who would never know how his mother had screamed when he was taken away from her.

Out by the canal, the dimly lit towpath had become a frightening place. The water was a dark, oily glimmer and above the noise of a distant road, the raucous shouts of a group of youths gathered round a bench further ahead on the path frightened Jane enough to make her turn back. It was nearly ten o'clock. When she got back to Florence's flat she would make her a milky drink and help her feed Tintin, and settle him for the night. With any luck he would sleep another four hours and Florence would get some rest.

She put her hand in her pocket and felt the hard shape of her mobile telephone. She wished that Tash would ring. When she took her hand out, her fingers found the coarse hair of Chipper's neck. He was keeping close to her tonight and she sensed that he was wary and watchful. He had never forgotten his dreadful past and she spoke softly to reassure him.

There was Tintin too, now. She knew that she loved him already, just as if he was her own baby. Kinship, blood lines, how naturally they flowed from vein to vein down the generations. How perverse it was to block the line, cut it off, as she had done by accident. It was all wrong, like a badly lopped tree; Florence without a father, Tintin without a grandfather, and a tall, clever scientist in his fifties who would never know that he had a daughter.

Yet how easily things could get in the way and the connections fall apart. There was the time after Florence had been born when she and her parents were estranged—not even a Christmas card, and her father only able to meet her in secret. How was it that her mother's social and moral pretensions had been stronger than her maternal love?

It was too late to regret that although she had loved her parents, she had never really known them, although with age had come more understanding. For her own part, she had to accept that between her and Florence there was a barrier that she did not seem able to bridge and she wondered if they would ever be able to grow close again as they had been when Flo was small and it was just the two of them. Flo had been the apple of her eye—she loved that expression without knowing what it really meant. After they had moved back to London they had shared everything when Flo was old enough to be a companion.

She didn't want to think about the beginning. She didn't want to think about Sussex. That was a chapter she would not reopen.

And it wasn't just the Kindersley family that had been fractured by circumstances. At supper she had asked Ha about his parents, hard-working refugees who barely spoke English but had managed to build a thriving takeaway business in Newcastle, and had realised that he now felt alienated from them, separated by his education and his acquired Western culture. 'I don't get up there as much as I should,' he confessed. 'I saw them only twice last year. It's hard, you know, for my mother, who doesn't speak much English. She's never been able to learn and she's too old now.' He smiled his bright smile and Jane understood that he had described a situation that he regretted, but was unlikely to do much to change. He would only go to see his parents when he absolutely had to, and yet she could tell that he loved them. How proud his mother must be of her handsome, clever, successful son, she thought, and how much his visits must mean to her. She imagined a small brown woman, quick and neat, with Ha's broad smile that, in her case, revealed crooked, peasant teeth, shaking a sieve of chips over a vat of hot fat in a Newcastle chip shop.

Love doesn't really conquer all, she thought sadly, but it's all we have. And only the sort of forgiving love that endures the inevitable hurt that we inflict upon one another.

CHAPTER TEN

It was at visiting times that Jane felt most alone. Husbands and mothers and mothers-in-law, sisters and brothers, poured on to the ward every evening carrying flowers and fruit, and usually a bottle or two, to wet the baby's head. When Sister Owen was on duty the ward became festive and rang with chatter and laughter, and the new arrival was passed from one set of arms to another, kissed and cooed over, while the mothers sat up, as if in state.

Jane, who was also required to stay in bed, as if she awaited the arrival of her own court of admirers, watched sadly. Aunt Joan came most evenings, tired after work, her feet pinched by her shoes and with some little offering for Jane in her briefcase, along with the newspaper. It was hard to be cheerful, briefcase there together, contemplating a bleak and uncertain future, and Aunt Joan never took any interest in Flo in her plastic crib, except to sigh and say, 'Poor little thing!'

She told Jane that she had rung her mother to tell her about the birth and received only curt thanks and no further enquiries, but a few days after Flo was born an enormous bunch of flowers arrived from her father, with a scrawled note: 'Thinking of you, darling. Do be a good girl and change your mind. Your mother and I love you and miss you. Your ever loving Daddy.' She guessed that he had stopped at a florist on his way to work and she had the sense not to write home to thank him. She arranged the flowers in whatever vases she could find in the sluice room and she was glad that Flo had been sent masses of tiny pink rosebuds and sprays of baby's-breath. It made her birth seem as welcome and as much a cause for happiness as all the other babies'.

She announced Flo's arrival to Rosie and Judith, her friends from college, on the postcards bought by Aunt Joan. They sent enthusiastic cards back with hand-drawn daisies all over the envelopes—'A BABY GIRL!! CONGRATULATIONS!! What lovely news!!!!' and 'I wish I had a baby!! Lucky you!! College is awful this term with exams coming up!'—and a little Babygro suit in pink and white

235

stripes.

Her only other visitor was Hugh, who blew in one evening with a gang of medic friends. They had been to the pub and were merry and beery. Hugh leaned over her bed to kiss her and introduced the others, 'This is Dave, Tom, Lance and Enzo,' and each one had kissed her in turn. To begin with they were allowed to crowd round and perch on Jane's bed, on the strength of their medical training, but they eventually got thrown out by Sister Nash for being too rowdy. They made Jane laugh and picked Flo up from her cot and passed her around between them as if she was a rugby ball. Jane sat up in bed with her arms round her knees and saw that they thought the whole thing was a wonderful joke—a visit to a maternity ward—and that afterwards they would go back to the pub and forget all about her.

Between feeds she wandered about the ward, took salt baths, tried to read *Tess of the D'Urbervilles*, but found she could not bear to think of the death of the illegitimate baby called Sorrow, and had to put the book to one side. For the most part she thought about nothing but Flo, who was without doubt the most beautiful baby she had ever seen. She was perfect, utterly, completely perfect, from her pearly pink skin, her large blue eyes and long lashes, to her fair crown of downy hair. Jane could not get enough of her. She was good enough to eat. She was delicious and divine. She wanted to hold her and marvel at her and kiss her and croon over her and never be parted, ever. She could no more give her away than die.

Dear old Hugh came to collect her when she was eventually discharged. He'd borrowed his mother's car again and was going to drive her straight down to the cottage. He had already been to collect her trunk and all her baby things from Aunt Joan's flat, and Diana Bywater had sent a box of groceries, a pile of paperback books and some New Baby packs from her surgery. Jane sat in the front holding Florence, who was wrapped in a lacy shawl that she had found in an Oxfam shop.

She felt almost dizzy with happiness as they drove out of London towards her new life. She could hardly remember how she had been before Florence. I was a different person, she thought. College was just a dream. The months at Aunt Joan's were past history. She couldn't even relive very recent moments, like the terror she felt about going into labour or her fear that she would not be able to cope with a baby. She felt elated and strong and capable.

They stopped for lunch at a pub in Haslemere and ate steak and chips and ice cream. Jane paid with the ten-shilling note Aunt Joan had given her as a parting gift. In her bag she had fifty pounds that Mr Kowalski had put in her last pay packet as a leaving present. For the moment she was rich and she was full of confidence that she was going to manage as a proper responsible person in the adult world.

After lunch, while Hugh was putting petrol in the car, she carried Florence in her arms into the pretty town. It was sunny and warm, and the shops had hanging baskets that overhung the pavements in cascading showers of lobelia and fuchsias. Passers-by smiled at her and she beamed back and one or two women stopped and said, 'May I see? Ooooh, what a lovely baby! She's very tiny, isn't she?' 'Yes, just two weeks old,' said Jane proudly, knowing that just one glance at her extraordinary child would dazzle and bewitch.

Halfway down the main street there was a little bow-windowed toyshop and she went in and chose a beautiful teddy bear, very soft and stout with a gentle stitched-on smile. 'This is for you, my darling,' she told Florence. It was ridiculously expensive but she didn't care. Nothing was too good for her golden girl.

She fed her in a layby while Hugh flopped in the long grass behind a hedge and went to sleep, and when they eventually arrived at the cottage there was an evening cricket match on the green, the white figures dreamlike against the dark trees of the churchyard. They turned into the lane and Jane saw that the verges had been cut on either side, trimmed to stubbly grass and weeds, all the wild flowers over and gone. The gate of Yew Cottage was closed and the hedge was higher than before. It looked closed and secretive.

In just a minute or two, thought Jane, I'll open all the windows and let the lovely summer air blow through. Her fingers found the key that she had put safely in her bag.

She kissed the top of Flo's head. 'Here we are, darling!' she told her. 'This is home!'

Hugh held Florence as Jane turned the key in the lock and opened the front door. There was a pile of post on the hall floor that Jane scooped up and put on the table and looked about her. The cottage, unoccupied for a month since Denby's sister and her husband had gone back to Hong Kong, smelled musty and dank. It faced the wrong way for the sunshine, which hardly found its way

238

through the low, small windows—but that doesn't matter, thought Jane, because we'll be in the garden most of the time.

'Jesus!' said Hugh, ducking his shaggy head under the beams. 'It's a bit olde worlde, isn't it? Has it got any mod cons? Any convenient domestic appliances for the modern housewife? Is there an earth closet somewhere? A trivet for roasting an ox?'

'Don't be silly,' said Jane. 'It's got a perfectly good loo, a bathroom, in fact, somewhere on the ground floor. Off the kitchen, I think. I remember, because it's got Eton team photographs all over the walls.'

The sitting room was dark and the inglenook fireplace was like a gloomy cavern in the far wall. It really did look as if it could accommodate an ox. Large pieces of inherited furniture stood about looking cramped and disdainful of their cottagey surroundings.

'When I light the fire it will be cosy in here!' Jane was determined to be pleased with everything.

The kitchen was the best room, with a door to the garden and a cheery red checked cloth on the table. 'I'll move an armchair in here, I think,' said Jane, putting Flo on the floor in her Moses basket. 'Look, there's a telly on the counter. It will be cosier than sitting by myself through there.'

Hugh bounded upstairs and then came clattering down. 'It's OK up there,' he reported. 'There's a huge brass bed, if you want to have a love-in.' He stood looking out at the back garden, to the untidy lawn that stretched towards the trees of the wood beyond.

'Are you really going to be all right, kiddo?' he asked in a serious tone. 'It is the back of bloody beyond, you know.'

'Of course I will be!' said Jane, still cheerful. 'It's a lovely place to be with a baby. I'm going to buy a second-hand pram and I'll walk everywhere, and Flo and I will have rosy cheeks and be the picture of health.'

Hugh sat at the table and rolled himself a joint. 'It would drive me round the bloody bend,' he said. 'Look, I'll stay here tonight. I'll share that huge bed with you. Keep you company. Help you settle in.'

Jane remembered her conversation with Denby's sister. Hugh's suggestion would meet all the worst of her fears. 'That would be nice,' she said. 'I don't know how brave I'll be when it gets dark.'

*   *   *

The first night that Jane stayed with Florence, Tintin woke at midnight and Jane let him lie and grumble for a bit before getting out of bed and securely wrapping him up in his blanket, then turning him over onto his other side. He can't be hungry again, she thought. She got back into bed and lay listening to his cries, hoping that they wouldn't wake Florence. Chipper came to lie beside her bed and she put out a hand to stroke his head. After a while the cries became less urgent and then all was quiet.

The next time she woke it was half-past four and Tintin was stirring again. Jane got up and changed his nappy and then took him through to Florence, who was evidently awake, moving to sit up beside Ha, who was sleeping soundly. Without speaking, Jane put the baby into her arms and tiptoed out.

She felt wide awake herself and went through to the kitchen to make a cup of tea. Even after all these years, the pattern of night feeding came back to her and seemed very familiar. It was something one never forgot, she supposed, like riding a bicycle. In less complicated societies women of her age would be the family midwives and naturally pass on their knowledge and practice to the next generation.

She took her mug back to her bed, remembering how, as she grew more accomplished as a mother, she could reach out for the hungry baby, complete a feed and be back in the still-warm bed in half an hour. It would be like that for Florence when she got more used to it.

A figure appeared at her door and Florence came in carrying Tintin. 'That was much better,' she said. 'It's the longest he's ever gone between feeds and so he was really hungry and took it fast. I seem to have lots of milk and he's gone back to sleep again.'

'If I were you,' said Jane, 'I would have him in your room, beside your bed, while he's needing night feeds. I hate those baby alarms. They make every snuffle seem like a last gasp. I think you'll find you both sleep better. Then Ha could use this bed in Tintin's room, if he needs more sleep.'

'Yeah, maybe. I'm such a light sleeper, though. The slightest noise wakes me.'

'You'll get over that. After a bit you don't notice the baby noises.'

Tintin chose that moment to let rip with a series

of popping farts. They both laughed softly.

'He does seem better wrapped up in the way that you did it,' said Florence. 'Who taught you all that stuff? When you had me, I mean?' She put Tintin gently back into his crib and came to sit on the edge of her mother's bed, stirring the bare toes of one foot through Chipper's thick fur.

'There was a lovely sister on the maternity ward. I was just thinking about her yesterday. Her name was Sister Owen and she was Welsh. She was a really pretty woman with Celtic colouring—dark hair and very blue eyes. She was terribly kind to me. I was in hospital for ten days, you see, which wasn't that unusual in those days. When she realised that I was keeping you—I mean, that I wasn't having you adopted—she spent a lot of time with me. More than she gave the other mothers. She taught me lots of things, ways of doing things, and gave me the confidence that I could look after you.'

'You were so young. I mean, when I think of what I was like at eighteen . . .'

'I was nineteen, actually.'

'Big difference! God, Mum, however did you manage?'

Jane hesitated. 'Do you really want to talk now, darling? I mean, wouldn't you rather go back to bed and get a bit more sleep?' Florence yawned and stood up. 'Yeah, I suppose so. Tintin'll be awake again in a couple of hours, I bet, and Ha has to be up at seven.'

When she had gone, Jane lay a long time looking into the darkness. Why did I do that? she thought. Why did I cut her off just when she was asking me about the one subject she has avoided

242

ever mentioning? Is it because it is me who's frightened of talking about when she was born?

No, it's not that, she thought. I don't mind telling her about how it was to begin with. The first weeks were all right. It was what came after. I'm frightened of that coming alive again, when there's still no need for anyone to know. There never was, and there's even less reason now, after all these years.

It was hopeless trying to sleep. She shouldn't have had tea, because now she felt wide awake. Don't think about it, she told herself. Put the light on and read your book. Think about Enzo. Think about the boys. Think about Tash. Worry about her, if you must worry about something.

But it was no good. Unruly memories had stirred within her and would not go away. All right, she told herself, you can think about some of it. Think about the first months. Think about Florence lying naked on a rug in the garden, kicking her little legs, which by the end of the summer had grown quite stout and brown. Think about how she sat in her little rocking seat under the tree. Think about . . . but suddenly she had an image of the pram, the big cream old-fashioned pram, and she saw herself pushing it through the silent village in the winter. She remembered every gateway and every drive, and she wanted to stop remembering but could not.

It was Tash she needed to talk to. Tash was the only one who could help, as she had done then. She longed to telephone her now, but it was far too early and she could not allow herself to ask for help from her sister. She was the one who needed support. This old monster that was rampaging in her head had to be battled with and subdued and locked away once more. It was too dangerous to let out.

*   *   *

She must have fallen asleep because when she woke again, Florence was in the room, bending over Tintin's crib, and she could hear a television news programme in the background.

'Goodness!' she said, reaching for her glasses to look at the time. 'It's seven o'clock. Was he crying? I must have dropped off.'

'He was just revving up so I came to get him. He was such a good boy last night. I think I can survive if he does as well as that again.'

Jane got out of bed and put on her dressing gown. 'Where's Chipper?'

'Ha took him when he went out for a run. He was a bit anxious about leaving you, but he went in the end.'

'Oh, that's good. They'll be company for each other. Shall I do some breakfast? Tea, coffee? I brought some eggs with me if you'd like a boiled egg, or maybe scrambled?'

'Mum, look at this.' Flo caught hold of the spare flesh over her stomach. 'I've got to get rid of all this. Don't encourage me to eat.'

'You don't want to diet when you're breast-feeding. It will all melt away in a few months.'

'Months! I'm not spending *months* in this obscene condition. I aim to be back in my pre-baby jeans in six weeks. That's my target. As soon as I can, I'll get back to the gym.'

'I can remember being told that it took nine

months to change shape and you should allow nine months to get your figure back.'

'Hmm. No way. I'm not spending nine months like this. It depresses me just to look in the mirror. I've got a cupboard of designer clothes that cost me a fortune, which I can't get into by a mile.'

'Toast, then? Hello, darling. What a good boy you are!' Jane addressed Tintin, who was gurgling on his changing table, waving his legs about.

'Watch out! He pees straight up in the air. Ha was most impressed.'

In the kitchen Jane put on the kettle and set the table. She had brought a good brown loaf with her and plenty of fruit. There was yoghurt in the fridge. That should be healthy enough. Florence came in with Tintin and began to feed him, sitting at the table. Her mood seemed to have changed.

'I was just thinking,' she said, the corners of her mouth drawn down, 'that I can't stand day after day like this. It makes me feel totally trapped and desperate that I can't get out of the flat. It's all right with you here, but what will it be like on my own?'

'Why don't you get out today if you want to? You can leave Tintin between feeds.'

'Yes, I know, but to do what? I'm not up to going to the gym yet, or getting out for a run. There's no point in going shopping when I'm still as fat as a pig. I can't go to work. I've been signed off for three months. All my friends work. What the hell am I going to do?'

'You could go for a walk today,' said Jane, looking out of the kitchen window at the canal. The morning was bright with a brisk spring wind rippling the surface and ruffling the long grass of the bank. 'Why don't you go out after breakfast? A bit of fresh air would do you good. Take Chipper with you. I'll take care of everything here.'

'I suppose I could, but I'll take the trapped feeling with me. It feels as if I have contracted a state of permanent anxiety.'

'That's motherhood, I suppose. You do get used to it.'

Jane passed a mug of coffee over the table and sat down opposite with her own. Tash will telephone soon, she thought. When she does I will go into the bedroom to speak to her in private. I don't want to upset Florence if it's bad news.

'Tell me about it, Mum,' said Florence. 'Tell me about how it was when you had me. It's not something I've ever felt like hearing before, but I want to know now.'

'Well, when you were ten days old, straight out of hospital, in fact, I moved down to a cottage in Sussex. Yew Tree Cottage. It belonged to Denby's sister and her husband. I was a sort of unpaid house-sitter.'

'Did you know anybody in the village?'

'Not a soul!'

'I don't suppose you had a car?'

'No, I didn't, but I couldn't drive anyway.'

'So you were completely stuck there?'

'Yes. There was a bus twice a week into Haslemere, which I planned to use, but it went at eight thirty in the morning and came back at four in the afternoon, so it was far too long to be out with a tiny baby in all weathers, and I had to bring the week's shopping back with me. Well, you can imagine what that was like, with a pushchair to manage as well. Sometimes the effort of it all made

246

me cry, especially if the bus driver was impatient. Once I banged your head when the driver started up before I was safely in my seat and for the first time in my life I swore at someone in public.'

'What happened?'

'He stopped the bus and turned me off. I had to walk home. It's hard to believe that the other women in the bus didn't stick up for me, or the old men, but nobody said a word. They all just stared. Nobody knew me, you see. They all knew one another, if only by sight, and I was a stranger. They didn't know what to make of me. I saw them glance at my hand to see if I wore a wedding ring and I never pretended I was married. I don't know why but it didn't seem worth the deception. Anyway, I had to walk and leave a bag of potatoes in a hedge because I couldn't carry them.

'I can remember trying to find somewhere to go in the town where I could feed you without causing major offence. I once tried in the teashop because it was full of ladies having morning coffee and no men, but I was told by the waitress to go elsewhere. She said it wasn't nice, feeding a baby in public. I was tremendously discreet with an Indian shawl draped right over your head, but it still wasn't acceptable. She turfed me out into the rain. I remember all the ladies in their headscarves and with their shopping baskets at their feet staring at me stony-faced. And they allowed dogs in! In the end I used to go to the library and sit in the ladies' lavatory, which was kept reasonably clean.'

Flo shook her head in disbelief. 'And this was the Swinging Sixties,' she said. 'I suppose page three of the *Sun* was perfectly acceptable. Breasts were allowed for titillation, but not when used for what they were intended.'

'I can remember reading about *Hair* opening in London that year and realising that nudity was OK on the London stage while I couldn't feed you in a discreet corner of a Sussex teashop.'

'So was there a lot of prejudice because you were unmarried and, I have to say, far too young?'

'Of course there was. Being unmarried, I mean. Having a baby at nineteen wasn't so extraordinary then. Attitudes in England changed very slowly in the sixties. The moral climate, that is. Well, of course, London was different and Tash was leading a totally free life, but it took a long time for the ripples to reach the countryside. People were genuinely shocked and scandalised that I not only had an illegitimate baby but also that I was determined to keep you.'

'So it was hard for you in the village?'

'What was hard was the loneliness. You see, my mother had forbidden me to contact my old friends from home and I only had the chance to make a few friends in Cambridge, who were busy, anyway, being students. So after you were born I had no one, really. Tash was in India, which was the hardest thing.

'When I first went to the village I hoped that there would be other young mothers and that I would soon make friends, but it didn't work out like that. It turned out to be more of a dormitory village, with men driving to Haslemere station and catching the train into London, leaving their wives to play bridge and golf, and garden and do good works. Most of their children were older and away at school. It was that sort of place. There was no village school and nothing much happened in the

248

Village Hall. There was no Mother and Baby Group or anything like that.'

'What about the neighbours? Were people friendly?'

'It was a very quiet place. On the lane there were only two or three houses and next to me there was a retired couple who were rather hostile, really. They had complained in the past about the house-sitters in Yew Tree Cottage and I suppose they thought I would be no better. Caroline, Denby's sister, had warned me about them. She told me that I was not to take the radio into the garden—that sort of thing. Ridiculous, really, because I lived like a mouse.'

'Didn't you go to the pub? That must have been a place to meet people.'

'No, I didn't. Although it looked like a typical country village pub, in fact it was rather a smart restaurant, and locals didn't drink there. It was a place that weekend people used, London people. I couldn't have turned up there with a baby, and I couldn't have afforded to eat there, anyway. I was far too hard up.'

'So what did you do? You must have had some sort of contact with people?'

'One day I met a woman playing with two children on the village green and I asked her about doctors and she told me that there was a practice in a nearby larger village that I could walk to. It had a post office and a small shop, but I had to walk along the main road and there was no footpath. I was terrified that we would get run into because people drove so fast between the villages.

'Anyway, I took you to the baby clinic and got you weighed and all that sort of thing. Of course, I saw other young mothers there, but they came from all over the place and all had cars and so I wasn't able to establish friendships because I couldn't get to them. Public transport was non-existent. One rather sweet girl called Rebecca, who had a little boy almost the same age as you, asked me to tea and when I said that I couldn't because I couldn't get there, she came to collect us and brought us back afterwards.

'She was a nice girl, a bit lonely too. Her husband was a solicitor in Chichester but when she learned that I was an unmarried mother, and that I was only living in the cottage as a house-sitter, she was completely put off. I could see that at once. It meant that I wouldn't fit into her social life, which was all about dinner parties and meeting other young couples. It was how it was then for young married middle-class couples. They behaved exactly like their parents. She did go on seeing me for a bit and then, rather awkwardly, asked me to baby-sit. She said she would collect us and then her husband would run me home afterwards. It suited me because I could earn a bit of money like that, but it meant that we were no longer friends.'

'God, Mum, it all sounds ghastly.'

'No, no, it wasn't. I was actually very, very happy, you see.'

'How could you have been? It sounds a bloody nightmare to me.'

'I was happy because I had you.'

'Bloody hell, that doesn't stack up! You can't possibly have felt that. My arrival ruined your life. That has always been quite evident.'

'It didn't, Florence. It really didn't. Yes, I was isolated and lonely but I loved having a baby and

250

playing at being a little housewife. They were the happiest days. You must believe me. I wouldn't have changed it for anything in the world. Having you suddenly made everything make sense to me. I saw what my purpose was. My mother and father were quite distant as parents—you've heard Tash talking about them, haven't you? She exaggerates, of course, but she's right that we were never made to feel absolutely central in their lives. Having you gave me someone to love unconditionally. It was a wonderful thing. I have never, ever regretted it.'

Florence made a harrumphing noise and changed Tintin to the other side. She sniffed, moving her nose like a rabbit. It was a childlike action and made Jane want to laugh. She could see the little girl that she once was.

'Yeah, so you say, but you are a bright woman and you never finished your education. Actually, you've never done much, have you, Mum? I'm sorry, but it's true. I mean, look at your job: working as dogsbody to that clapped-out old pop star. If it hadn't been for me you would have finished your teacher training and you could be a headmistress or something by now. Why didn't you get on with it and go back to college? You could have sent me to a childminder, couldn't you? A lot of the women I trained with had to juggle child care with their studies. It can be done, you know.'

Jane felt the sting of this criticism. 'I couldn't go on with my training,' she said. 'But there were other reasons why I couldn't, and it wasn't so easy then. I just took whatever work I could get without having to farm you out.'

'Yeah, I know that you did what was best for *me*. That's not what I'm saying. I'm asking why you didn't make more effort to do something for yourself. Why were you so self-sacrificing? I mean, that's what I feel you've laid on me—that my arrival spoiled your life. And I'm saying, it needn't have done. You could have done something if you'd wanted.'

Jane was silent. There were so many things that couldn't be said. How could she explain how different things were then? Could Flo understand that being a good mother had seemed achievement enough? Of course, these days, it wasn't considered sufficient. There were all those women who had six children and were successful bankers at the same time as hand-smocking party dresses and growing organic vegetables.

'I'm not getting at you!' said Flo in an exasperated voice. 'Please stop looking hurt. I'm just asking why you didn't. I mean, look at Tash. She got herself off her arse, didn't she?'

'It didn't feel as if I was on my arse,' said Jane, with some spirit.

There was a silence and then, 'Sorry,' said Flo, suddenly repentant. 'Sorry, Mum. Why am I such a cow? It must be hormonal. I seem to want to be unkind to anyone who's kind to me. Poor Ha has taken a terrible tongue-lashing. I keep saying things I don't really mean.'

Jane got up and put her mug in the sink. 'I'll go and get dressed,' she said calmly. 'Then I'll tidy up, and then I'll take Tintin for you. Why don't you finish his feed and then get out, if that's what you want to do?'

In the bedroom her stomach fluttered and her breath was shallow and fast. She felt as if she had been brought to the brink and had only just saved herself. There was so much more to tell and so much to avoid. Then her telephone rang and as she picked it up she saw that it was Tash's number and then Tash was saying, 'Jane? Jane, it's me. Listen, darling, I'm sorry to say that it's not very good news.'

*   *   *

Jane found the pram—the great stately cream pram that Flo was pushed round in like a potentate—advertised in the post office window where a number of classified ads were handwritten on postcards. The writing on this particular card was large and rambling. 'Coach-built pram for sale. Well used, but in good condition. £10', and a telephone number. Jane went straight to the call box outside the post office and rang the number.

'I wondered if the pram was still for sale,' she asked a young female voice. 'I've just seen the advertisement in the post office in Ardington.'

'Hang on!' Jane could tell that her call had been a disappointment. She was not the person to whom the girl was obviously waiting to speak. Then there came a great shout, 'Nadia! There's some female on the telephone about a pram, or something!' Then a long pause, and at last a soft, vague voice said, 'Hello?' and Jane had to repeat herself.

'Oh goodness, yes! The pram. I'd almost forgotten I had put a postcard in the window of the post office. Nobody has called, you see. Young mothers have to have everything new these days, don't they? But it is a lovely pram. I have had six babies and they've all slept in the garden in it and then gone everywhere round and about. I could put one in each end and there was even room for a whippet. It's a Silver Cross and the only pram Nanny would consider. She was terribly difficult to please, dear Nanny, but such a darling.'

'Could I come and see it? I just have a pushchair and it's rather flimsy, and there's not enough protection for such a new baby. She can't really lie down in it very well.'

'Of course you can! Come now!'

'But where are you?'

'Here! In the village. Next to the church. The Grange. Do come! Have you got your baby with you? I do so love babies. Just the smell of one makes me broody!'

The woman was mad, thought Jane. Completely potty. But she hurried to the church and found the house behind a high red wall, and when she went through a tall outer door she was met by three barking whippets. There followed a shout from the open front door and then a slender woman appeared dressed in strange floating garments and with wild dark hair sprinkled with silver threads, scooped up on the back of her head by a tortoiseshell slide.

'Oh, darling, darling baby!' she cried, seeing Florence. 'May I?' and she plucked her out of Jane's arms and went into the house with her, the whippets swarming round her legs. She seemed childlike with her soft, youthful voice and slight frame, but her brown eyes were sharp and bright and surrounded by a network of fine lines. She wore a great deal of black eye make-up and huge, golden hooped earrings added to the bohemian air.

'Only the kitchen, darling. I do hope you won't

mind!' she said as if Jane was an honoured visitor.

The kitchen was large and sunny and very, very untidy. It reminded Jane of the Bywaters', except theirs was rather dirty-looking and shabby, and this was overflowing with colour and brightness from piles of cheerful pottery plates on the dresser, to heaps of clothing on every chair. The walls were the yellow of butter, and lime-green and pink checked curtains hung at the long sash windows.

'I'm Nadia,' said the woman, holding out a slim brown hand on which large rings glinted. 'This darling baby of yours—a love child, of course!'

Jane was unsure what she meant, but Nadia seemed not to worry whether she was understood. 'I had my first when I was seventeen! He's thirty-two now, and a fat banker! Oh yes! I was a child bride, snatched from the cradle. Like you, darling. My youngest you talked to on the telephone. Persephone is sixteen. Poor Sepho is like an only child because there is a gap of ten years between her and Miranda.'

She gazed at Jane vaguely, as if wondering what she was doing there, and Jane felt obliged to say, 'About the pram . . . ?'

'Oh, yes! Look, it's here in the back hall. Watch out for all the mess on the floor, all the bloody boots—it's all bloody coats and boots, you know, having so many children. Here! Here it is. Look, it's fine. Wonderful! See the springs? You can have the pram blankets too and this little lace pillow. And look, this cover goes over the top to keep everything snug and dry. All perfect. Nanny chose it, of course. We had to have what the Queen used—nothing was too grand for Nanny. Poor darling! Did I tell you? She went back to her sister in Scotland when Sepho went to board and she was dead a few months later. As if we were her lifeblood, and when she wasn't with us she shrivelled up and died. She should have stayed with us but Hughie wouldn't have it, and what Hughie won't have, Hughie won't have!'

Jane's mind reeled. She could only follow the half of all this and had to guess the rest.

'Look, pull it out. That's right. I'll open this door, and *voilà*! There, you can go out this way. But, darling, ten pounds? Is that really and truly all right? It seems a lot of money, but you know, it is The Best. Quite literally, The Best. You'll use it for all of your babies. Every one of them.'

She watched beadily as Jane counted out the notes, and then tucked them into a pocket of the strange floating skirt. 'My running-away fund! Oh, yes, it is! Hughie wouldn't give me a penny, you realise. He might be a rich man but he wouldn't give me a penny!' She gave Jane a saucy wink.

Jane found herself shown into a small courtyard at the side of the house, but she still had to retrieve Florence, whom Nadia was cradling in her arms as if she intended to keep her.

'I suppose I must give her up!' she said, reluctantly handing her over and then lifting the smallest of the plush-coloured whippets into her arms instead. 'So sweet, darling! Please, please, come again!' and with a wave, the door in the wall was shut behind her. Jane just had time to glimpse a pale and sulky teenage face at a first-floor window.

She never even asked my name, thought Jane. Or Florence's. Or asked me a single question about myself.

Jane didn't know whether she felt relieved or affronted, but as she started to walk home with the pram running smoothly in front of her, she felt a little bit disappointed and as if she had lost a chance of some sort.

*   *   *

The pram made all the difference that summer. Each morning Jane settled Flo to sleep in the garden, even if it was raining, while she tidied the house and did the washing. Nappies were the worst chore. Every other day they had to be hauled out of the bucket in which they soaked and put through the twin tub washing machine, which was filled from a hose attached to the kitchen tap. They were then fed through the mangle. They dried stiff as boards pegged on the line outside, or draped on a clothes horse in the kitchen if the weather was bad. Then there were all the little garments that had to be hand-washed in Lux soap flakes. The skin of Jane's hands became red and chapped and painful.

Later, if Florence was still asleep, she wrote letters at the kitchen table. Letters were her lifeline. She wrote regularly to her father at his office and although he rarely replied, she liked to think that he was being kept in touch with the progress of his granddaughter. Once a week she wrote to Aunt Joan, a chatty letter full of talk of the countryside and her trips into Haslemere and making much of her friendship with Rebecca.

She wrote racier letters to Rosie and Judith, describing the cottage and making it sound as idyllic as possible. Gradually she wove a fantasy

257

life for herself that she began to people with interesting and promising characters. Nadia became central to her fiction—a warm, eccentric woman who had taken Jane under her wing and was now a firm friend. For love interest she introduced a young unmarried doctor, and the son of the couple who lived next door. Phil, she called him, and she made him a solicitor, like Rebecca's husband, and suggested that he was showing a decided interest in her and had come round and drunk white wine in her garden one warm evening.

While Florence slept, Jane engrossed herself in her fiction, and then would seal and address the envelopes and push the pram to the post box on the green. What she didn't do was open the letters that Aunt Joan forwarded from the bank at which her father had opened her an account when she was eighteen. She had enough money to live on for the moment and the health visitor had told her about claiming Family Allowance. As soon as she could she would find some sort of job that she could do with Florence—cleaning, maybe, or baby-sitting, or addressing envelopes at home.

The telephone very rarely rang. On a Sunday evening it was usually Aunt Joan, and occasionally Hugh, who although he had promised he would come down and see her soon, never quite made it. Every week Jane went to the telephone box on the green and telephoned Mr Kowalski and had a conversation with him in which he asked repeatedly how she was, and how was the baby, and Jane asked how he was and how many books he had sold and he laughed and said, 'Oh, my dear. None at all since you left.'

One afternoon during her customary walk she

pushed the pram through the lich-gate of the churchyard, parked it in the church porch and, trying the great studded door, found that it was open. She picked Florence from the pram and went in to the chilly, gloomy interior that smelled of cold stone and mice. It was very quiet and Jane felt frightened by a sense of being watched. There was nobody there, but it felt eerily occupied. She read the names on the tomb in a side chapel and on the plaques on the chancel wall. 'In loving memory of Stephen Bowden of this parish, departed from this life on 6 May 1642 aged 53 years and of his wife, Priscilla, departed 22 August 1634 aged 28, and of their six children.' Six children, all dead in the first year of their lives! She held Florence closer. Poor little babies, she thought. Poor Priscilla. How sad her short life must have been. Stephen had gone on to marry someone else. There was a second wife, Margaret, added to the list, but no mention of more children.

She picked up a copy of the parish magazine and hurried out, hastily pulling the door shut. Outside she was blinded for a moment by the sunshine and then she was aware of someone coming up the path, a woman, who when she got close stared at her suspiciously. She was late middle-aged and plump, with greying hair arranged in stiff ridges. She was dressed in a pink polyester blouse and a bunchy floral skirt and carried a wicker basket over her arm.

'I just thought I'd look in the church!' said Jane, feeling that she had to explain herself. The woman nodded but said nothing and passed her in a busy manner as if she had things to attend to. Jane was halfway down the path when she reappeared in the church porch, and called something out to her.

Jane stopped and turned round.

'It's one and sixpence!' said the woman. 'The parish magazine is one shilling and sixpence!'

'Oh!' said Jane, flustered. 'I'm so sorry. I thought it was free.' She sought for her purse amongst the blankets of Flo's pram. 'Here!' she said, going back with the money in her hand.

'I'm always saying,' said the woman, holding out a wooden money box in her hand, 'that we should keep the church locked. There are a lot of funny people about these days. Nothing's sacred, not any more.' She glared at Jane, who blushed.

'I'm so sorry,' she repeated. 'I didn't realise.'

The woman stood in the porch watching her go.

*   *   *

After Tash's call, Jane sat on the bed weighed down with fear and anxiety. The worst had happened and Tash, indomitable Tash, had cancer. She was going into hospital the following week for surgery. The doctors would not be drawn to give any prognosis, except to say that they had caught it early. The best they would promise was a fifty-fifty chance of survival. She was being characteristically brave and had told Denby, who was stricken with guilt and remorse for all his shortcomings as a husband.

'Silly old thing,' said Tash fondly. 'He doesn't realise I am long past caring.'

'But how are you feeling?' asked Jane desperately.

'Absolutely fine. Perfectly normal. Extra-ordinary, isn't it, that I am harbouring this dreaded

260

thing and yet feeling quite OK? Anyway, darling, onwards and upwards. I am just going to crack on with it now, and get this bloody op out of the way as soon as poss. How are things with you?'

'Lovely, really. Tintin is lovely. Florence is a bit up and down, but she's glad I'm here, I think.'

'So she should be! Look, Jane, I would really like to see you. I've wanted to see you ever since they told me. I wish I had let you come with me after all, because I felt very weedy and feeble afterwards. No, don't come here. I find I don't much want to be at home at the moment. I thought I might come to you, to Florence, see the baby. All of that. I don't want to be the spectre at the feast but I don't think Flo would mind, do you?'

'Oh, come! Please come. I'll tell her now. I know that she'll want to see you.'

'Well, not tomorrow. I'm seeing the girls tomorrow in London. I'm going to take them out to dinner and tell them. There's not really any way round it. They have to know. I've sent an email to Robin in California asking him to telephone. Julius knows already. Denby saw him last night in Birmingham. He took it on the chin as you would expect him to.' Tash reeled off her children.

'Maybe Thursday or Friday. Would that be all right? I want to see Aunt Joan too. I feel I owe her an apology for disliking her all these years. I'm obviously set on saintliness. I wonder if this is a common reaction to being reminded that one is far from immortal.'

'Oh, Tash!'

'Don't start. I need to have very stiff upper lips around me at the moment. Denby is permanently in floods! See you soon, then, Jane. Love to

261

Florence and co. I'll bring food, so don't worry about any of that.'

Jane went through to where Florence was admiring Tintin, who was lying on the sofa, waving his arms in the air and gazing up at her in a transfixed way.

'He's so sweet, Mum, isn't he? I just adore these little creases on his wrists, and the little scoop at the back of his neck—and the smell of him. He's too good to be true. Heh! What's the matter? You look as if you've seen a ghost.'

'That was Tash on the telephone. It was bad news, I'm afraid. Flo, she had this lump, and . . .'

'Don't tell me. Cancer?'

'Yes.'

'God, I'm sorry. I'm so sorry. Tell me all you know.'

CHAPTER ELEVEN

As the autumn drew on into winter, things started to go wrong. Florence, who had so far been a picture of health and had gained weight very satisfactorily, caught a bad cold. The cottage began to feel chilly and damp, and lighting the sitting-room fire proved quite beyond Jane. The room filled with choking smoke and the logs she had found in the shed smouldered evilly rather than burned. She turned on the night storage heaters and was grateful for their warmth but realised that when it got really cold—frost and snow, proper winter weather—they would hardly be adequate. She would need to find some sort of extra heater, for one room at least.

Mr Kowalski was not well, or he was so stricken by the news from Czechoslovakia, where the stirrings of freedom behind the Iron Curtain had been brutally crushed by Soviet troops, that he appeared to lose what little vitality he had. His voice had become a faraway whisper and although he always asked when Jane was coming to London to let him meet Florence, he hardly sounded as if he meant it.

'I will come, I promise. I'll come at Christmas. I'll catch the train. The baby's not well at the moment. She has a cold, but she will be better by then and I will come.'

Then the next time she went into the bank in Haslemere to take out some money, the woman cashier looked hard at her cheque and said, 'Excuse me one minute.'

An older man in a suit appeared and unlocked a door to the side of the tills and said, 'Miss Kindersley? I am Mr Burns, the manager. Would you be so good as to come this way?'

Quaking, Jane followed him to an office where she sat facing him across his shiny brown desk. Florence started to cry.

'I see, Miss Kindersley,' said Mr Burns smoothly, 'that your current account has become overdrawn. Whilst not, at the moment, causing me any concern, I thought it best we should have a little chat. Perhaps you would like to discuss temporary overdraft facilities, or maybe you have already made arrangements to pay off the deficit?'

Jane felt hot and confused. Florence continued to cry. How could she have gone through all the savings she had put into her account? There must be some mistake.

'I don't understand,' she gulped. 'I should have money left. I—'

'Have you studied your recent statement, I wonder?' asked Mr Burns. Jane thought, panic-stricken, of the pile of unopened envelopes from the bank.

'Well, I can't exactly—'

'If you would be so good as to wait a moment, I will get a copy for you.' Mr Burns pressed a button on his desk, which was followed by a knock at the door, and a woman put her head into the room. 'Mrs Wilson, would you fetch Miss Kindersley's file, please?'

The woman withdrew and they sat in silence while Florence continued to cry, louder now. She's hungry, thought Jane. I should try and feed her but I can't do it here.

The woman returned and laid a buff folder in front of Mr Burns. She glanced across at Jane with a cold, unsympathetic look. Mr Burns opened the folder and slipped out a sheet, which he passed to Jane. She looked at it uncomprehendingly. There was a figure at the bottom in red.

'Eighteen pounds six shillings,' pointed out Mr Burns. 'Let us see, you have been making regular withdrawals over the last weeks, but I see your account has not been credited for some time. What are your current means of support, Miss Kindersley?'

'Well, just at the moment, with the baby and everything, I haven't been able to work. I have my Family Allowance, but it's not very much. I can see I need to get a job, but it's not easy with a baby. I think, if I ask him, my father will lend me money.'

'May I suggest you do that, and perhaps you would make an appointment to pop in again next week to inform me when you will be in a position to repay the Bank? Meanwhile, I will make arrangements for you to have temporary overdraft facilities. Unauthorised borrowing is not permitted and I request that you do not exceed the limit.'

'No, no. Thank you, thank you. Don't worry. I mean, I will repay what I owe.'

'What sort of budget are you currently living on?' asked Mr Burns. He had greasy grey hair swept back from a bullfrog face. Jane was starting to hate him. She felt he had judged that she was a hopeless case and was at pains to prove it.

'Budget? Um, I'm not sure . . .'

'May I suggest that when you get home you make a list of your current outgoings over the last month and set that against the money that you have coming in? This is a very simple form of budgeting, which you may find helpful in giving you a better understanding of your position.'

'Yes, yes, I will, I'll do that.'

Mr Burns stood up and held the door open. He winced and stepped back as Jane went past with the screaming Florence. The other customers stared and tutted as Jane retrieved her pushchair and blundered out of the bank. She walked up the street without thinking where she was going. Florence was crying so much that her face was scarlet, and so hot that her hair was damp and her forehead beaded with sweat. Jane couldn't take her into the library like this and she found herself turning into the only place to escape the street, and saw it was a churchyard. After her last experience she was too nervous to try the church door to see if it was open, so she sat on a bench overlooking the leaning grey gravestones, which bloomed with hard crusts of orange lichen. Florence was too upset to feed, and turned her head away crossly.

Jane felt tears welling in her throat. She tried to think clearly, to deal sensibly with the waves of panic that threatened to overwhelm her. Mr Burns was right, of course. She should have worked out a sensible budget. She would go home and do what he suggested. She would get things back under control and then everything would be all right. Above her head the dark yews blotted out the grey sky, and lack of light and the chill made Jane shiver. She looked at her watch. There was an hour and a half before the bus left. She didn't know what to do with Florence when she was like this, screaming and inconsolable, so she began to walk up and down, jigging her against her shoulder. I could leave her here, she suddenly thought. I could leave Florence here in her pushchair, and just walk away. I could give her to the Christians.

The thought frightened her so much that she began to cry with tight little sobs. Please, she said to Florence. Please stop. I can't bear it. Look, you've made Mummy cry now. Mothers shouldn't behave like this, she thought, or say such things to babies. Maybe she understands in her own little way and it will upset her even more. She sat back down on the bench, feeling lost and hopeless.

Eventually Florence accepted a feed and fell asleep, and Jane felt calmer and started to work out what she would do. All the way home on the bus she held her against her shoulder and stroked her little hot face with her own cheek and asked to be forgiven. Back at the village, she got off the bus and went straight to the telephone box and put a call through to her father's office. When Mrs Weston answered Jane asked to speak to her father without saying who she was, but Mrs Weston said, 'It's Jane, isn't it? Didn't you know, dear, that your father isn't here any more? He retired two weeks ago. He still comes in to board meetings, but that's only once a month. Oh, I do miss him. I shan't stay, I can tell you. I'm just working out my pension and then I shall retire. Things aren't the same. The whole country's going down the drain. We've had lock-outs here. Wild-cat strikes, the lot. Wherever have you been, Jane, not to know all this?'

Later that evening, when Florence was asleep, Jane sat at the kitchen table and made herself rip open the envelopes and look at her bank statements. Of course, it was true. She had been extravagant—buying herself a pair of winter boots for 69/11d and unnecessary toys for Florence. She had run through nearly all her money and now she had nothing left to live on, except twenty-five pounds remaining from Mr Kowalski's gift. She went upstairs and searched through all her coat and jacket pockets but found only a few coins.

She made a list of all the things that she could do. She could clean people's houses or she could garden and do odd jobs, or take in ironing. She could help look after children as long as she could take Florence with her. She would have to put a postcard in the post office window. She would do it the very next day. Meanwhile she would write to her father and ask him if he would help her. He wouldn't turn her down when he realised how desperate she was and she would promise to pay him back.

It was a moonless and windy night, and even with Radio Caroline playing in the background she could hear strange thumps and groans and the garden gate banging. She was scared to go out and fasten it. It was too dark and threatening with the trees tossing their branches into the sky and the last of the autumn leaves scudding and circling, and skittering down the lane. She could hear them rattling against the window, like tiny bony fingers.

Mummy was right, she thought, I've taken on more than I can manage. I can't do this on my own. I'm like a child myself. I've spent all my money, I'm frightened of the dark, frightened of being alone, living on fish fingers and toast, and yet I think I can look after a baby.

Stop it, she told herself. Stop feeling sorry for yourself. Grow up. She heard her mother's voice. 'You've made your bed, now you must lie in it!'

*   *   *

She wrote,

Darling Daddy,

I know that you told me that I mustn't think that I can come to you for help, but I really have no one else to turn to and I am feeling a bit desperate, to say the least.

I am afraid that I have run out of money, and although I am hoping to find work soon, it's not easy with a baby. I am writing, you may have guessed, to ask you if you could make me a loan to see me through until I can get a job. I don't need very much—no more than the allowance you gave me as a student, because we live very cheaply, Florence and me.

Daddy, I wouldn't ask you if I wasn't desperate. I know that it may make things difficult with Mummy, but perhaps you could do it secretly? I do wish that you could see Florence—you would both love her, she is such a lovely little girl. Do you think one day you might be able to meet her?

I spoke to Mrs Weston on the telephone and she told me that you have retired from the works. She said that it wasn't the same without you and that there has been a lot of trouble with the unions and strikes and things. I wonder what you do all day. It must be funny not to go to work after so many years.

I hope that you and Mummy are well and I send you my love. I think about home very often, although really, Yew Tree Cottage is my home now. It's a pretty little place but it is getting quite cold now that the summer is over. I am going to have to find a heater of some sort to keep at least one room warm enough for Florence. She has had a nasty cold that makes her cry a lot. Normally she is very good. I take her to the Mother and Baby Clinic nearly every week and she is doing very well.

Please could you send me a cheque as soon as you can? I don't have much money left and am getting a bit desperate!

All my love,
Jane

When she read it through she realised she had said 'desperate' too many times, but she was too tired to rewrite it and, anyway, that was how she felt.

*   *   *

The next day, when she was on her way to post the letter, something happened that was to change her luck, as she thought then. She passed her neighbour's gate and glanced in, as she did every time she walked by. There were so few signs of life in the lane, and the house next door always looked empty. There was never a window open or any sign of life, although a polished car was often parked on the gravel and sometimes the garage door was open, revealing a tidy array of gardening tools and a chest freezer at the back.

This morning, however, a brown and white spaniel was loose in the garden and when it saw Jane it came running over, barking. She stooped to stroke its head. She had always loved dogs and it had been one of her childhood disappointments that she had never been allowed to keep one.

'Hello!' she said. 'You're a very handsome boy!'

'Sam! Sam! Come here, you naughty dog.' A stout grey-haired woman appeared from the side of the house. 'He shouldn't be out here,' she shouted across to Jane. 'He's not supposed to come into the front.'

'Oh! You'd better go back, then, Sam!'

The woman came over, her fat feet in navy court shoes making little stabbing steps in the gravel. She was wearing a smart coat and dress in checked tweed, and a felt hat with an ugly pearl brooch pinned to it. She had a jowly face caked with a furry sort of pancake make-up and drawn on brown eyebrows. Her small mouth was defined by a line of pink lipstick.

'Are you the girl from next door?' she asked, looking hard at Jane, sizing her up. 'Caroline said there was a girl coming to live there. We were rather upset, my husband and I. She's had some very unsuitable young men as house-sitters, but I have to say, we haven't heard a sound from you. Not even cars going backwards and forwards.'

'Oh, well,' said Jane diffidently, 'of course I'm quiet. I mean I'm there all on my own, so—'

'She did tell us about the baby,' said the woman. 'I have to say I don't approve of all this modern permissiveness. A child needs two parents, I say, but no doubt you're a good mother.' Her face softened as she looked in the pram. 'Oh my, what a bonnie little thing. Just look at her lying there with her eyes shut and thosc long lashes.'

Jane warmed to her. 'She's called Florence,' she said, 'and I'm Jane.'

'I am Mrs Garbutt. Florence—what an old-fashioned name!' said the woman, bending down to take the dog's collar. 'Now, come on, Sam. You come with me. He doesn't want to come in because he knows he'll be shut up all day. Mr Garbutt and I are going to London. He's not a well man, I'm afraid, and we're going to see his specialist. Poor Sam hardly gets out at all these days, not since my husband was taken ill. He had a little stroke a few months ago and is a semi-invalid.'

'I'm sorry about that,' said Jane, and then added impulsively, 'I'll take Sam out for you, if you like. I love dogs and I walk all over the place, taking

271

Florence in the pram.'

'Well!' said Mrs Garbutt, taken aback. She appeared to be undecided. 'I'll have to ask Mr Garbutt, but I think he might be pleased. He's worried that the dog doesn't go out enough.'

'I'm just on the way to the postbox,' said Jane. 'I'll call in on my way back, if you like, and if you want me to, I'll take Sam for a walk. Do you think he'd come with me?'

'Oh, yes. He's a very friendly dog.'

Jane posted the letter to her father and walked back thinking more about the letter than the dog. She thought of the envelope lying on the mat in the hall, which was so familiar to her that she could imagine herself there again, running her hand down the smooth wood of the banister, smelling the beeswax floor polish, seeing the gleam of the brass plate left on the rosewood chest to receive the morning's post. Which of her parents would stoop to collect the letters? Either of them would recognise her writing immediately. She remembered how her mother had kept Tash's letters from her. Would she do the same with hers to her father, if she found it first?

She was so preoccupied that she nearly walked past the Garbutts' gate, but remembered in time to push the pram to the front door and ring the ding-dong bell. The panel in the front door was made of swirly patterned frosted glass and the windows on either side were obscured by sheer net curtains. It was a very secretive-looking house, with a strictly tidy garden. Everything had been trimmed and clipped into submission.

Mrs Garbutt answered the door, carrying a dog's lead in her hand. 'My husband thinks it would be a

272

good idea,' she said. 'I am going to show you where to put Sam when you get back. There's a kennel behind the garage. You could give him his tea later, if you didn't mind. We shan't be back until early evening and it will stop Mr Garbutt from getting into a state, if he knows the dog's fed.' She led the way back across the gravel to a wrought-iron side gate, which led onto a little concrete yard in which there was a wooden dog kennel and run. 'Here he is,' she said. Sam was already at the wire, wagging his stump of a tail and jumping up enthusiastically. 'To tell you the truth, I think the dog should go,' she said in a confidential tone. 'We should get rid of him. He's too much for us, a big energetic dog like this. But my husband's fond of him.'

'Well, I can help you with him,' said Jane, and then taking the initiative added, 'I was going to put an ad in the post office offering dog-walking services and that sort of thing. I'm in need of money, you see.'

'My husband did mention ten shillings, if you agree to come back and feed him at five o'clock and let him out again.'

'But he can stay with me all day, if you prefer,' said Jane. 'Wouldn't that be better?'

'Well, yes, probably it would be. I'll show you where his food is kept and how much he gets.'

So Jane went back to Yew Tree Cottage with Sam tugging on his lead, and for the rest of the day he stayed happily with her and Florence, lying under the kitchen table and following Jane wherever she went. 'You're a nice dog,' she told him, stroking his long, soft ears, 'and I don't feel nearly as nervous with you about.'

Sam had a deep bass bark and ran to the gate when the postman came down the lane. It seemed he already felt protective towards her and Florence.

*   *   *

Jane thought of Sam for the first time in years as she took Chipper and Tintin for a walk into town. Pushing a baby with a dog running ahead must have stirred old memories although Chipper was much better behaved than Sam, who had pulled at the lead and tried to rush off in every direction. Poor Sam. To begin with, though, she had certainly given him a better life.

Florence had drawn her a rough map of how she could first of all take the towpath and then cut through the town into the pedestrianised shopping centre. She was nervous of leaving Chipper outside the shops but Florence laughed and said, 'Mum! No one's likely to steal him! He's not exactly a Cruft's champion, is he? Frankly, who, apart from you, would want him?' Jane felt offended on Chipper's behalf. He was the best dog in the world as far as she was concerned.

As she walked she thought about Tash. It was hard to think of anything else, knowing that her sister was facing a battle with cancer. The injustice of it was hard to accept. She had to fight the desire to telephone her every few minutes and ask, 'How are you feeling now?' and she was grateful that being with Florence and Tintin gave her something to do. Being helpless was hard.

Enzo had been wonderful. After she had telephoned him with the news he had asked if he

274

might speak to Tash herself, and then he telephoned Jane back with all sorts of buoying statistics and a much better prognosis than she had dared to hope for. 'You have got to be positive,' he told Jane firmly. 'That's the best way to support her. You two are so close that she can be honest with you and tell you when she feels down, as she is sure to do, especially when she starts the chemo. It's good to have someone who you don't have to be strong for, and that will be you, Jane. You are the one to whom she can confess all her fears and she can tell you when she feels like shit.'

'Yes,' said Jane, feeling it was not enough and wishing she could do more.

'Now, would you like me to come to you? To Florence? I'd like to, you know. I miss you, darling. I even miss the bloody dog. I've got a full day in the theatre tomorrow, but I could come on Friday?'

'Oh, Enzo, I'd like that. I miss you, too. Yes, please come. Tash is planning to come over as well. I think we all feel that we need one another just now. Somehow, when you get bad news like this, you want to be together.'

Oh, Tash, she thought as she let Chipper off his lead and he trotted off to inspect the line of spindly trees. She wasn't sure that she was going to be strong enough to be any kind of support. She was frightened that it was going to be her who was the needy one. If the worst came to the worst, Tash would die and she would be left to deal with life without her.

Tintin was wide awake this morning and grizzling into his little fists. It was better to get him out and give Florence an hour or so of peace. She had talked about going to get her hair washed and

275

blow-dried. 'It will make me feel more human!' she said.

Jane was glad to be out. She had started to dislike the flat, with its echoing wooden floors, banging doors and uncomfortable furniture. Unless it was kept ferociously tidy it looked awful, and yet there was nowhere to put anything. It was so obviously not a place to have a baby and still less a toddler. Jane thought with dread of all the sliding glass doors and perilous balconies.

Why didn't Florence and Ha move to somewhere more suitable and live together and share their child in the normal way? Ha had been so sweet with the baby this morning, carrying Tintin about with him and asking to be shown how to change a nappy. He evidently was coming round to the idea of being a hands-on father and was keen to be involved.

But it was no use speculating on their relationship or what the future held, thought Jane. What Florence wanted would always be a mystery. Like this morning when she had talked about how she was already looking forward to going back to work and then burst into tears at the thought of leaving Tintin with a childminder.

'But isn't that what you want?' Jane had asked. She couldn't help adding, 'It was only the other day that you were saying it is what I should have done with you when you were a baby! You told me I should have got off my arse, to be precise.'

Florence had flown into the attack. 'Don't always throw my words back at me. I don't know how I feel about anything at the moment. I am so tired, Mum. Does it go away, this total exhaustion? I can't do these broken nights. They're just making me crack up. But one thing I can tell you is that I can't stand being stuck at home. No way am I going to do that. Maybe a nanny would be the answer, but we can't afford it. It wasn't part of the plan, and I certainly don't want anyone living in.'

'But couldn't you have opted for longer maternity leave?'

'Look, Mum, I've been training for years to get where I am. I'm not sacrificing my place for changing nappies and wiping up sick. Any idiot can do that. No, the time I spend with Tintin will be the good time. I know it's a cliché, but it will really be quality time.'

'Oh, I see.'

'Money is a serious issue too, you know. I have a socking great mortgage, a car to be paid for, credit card bills. You don't realise the pressures these days. I've only just finished paying off my student loan!'

Earlier that morning she had tried to fit into a pair of trousers and they looked uncomfortably tight, cutting into her bottom in an unflattering way. 'Look at me!' she said, punching at her hips. 'Lardy arse! No way am I spending all day at home, eating biscuits and waiting for six o'clock to have a drink.'

How complicated people made their lives, thought Jane, sitting for a moment on a bench by the water. Empty lager cans bobbed about in the reeds amongst the moorhens, and since the last time Jane had walked this stretch, the remaining trees had been torn down, their weedy roots ripped out of the ground. What a pity, she thought. They were little birches and would have been so pretty on a summer's day with their silver trunks and flickering leaves. Why were people so determined to spoil things? How blighted were their own lives that they needed to destroy genuine attempts to make things better?

Tintin set up a wail as soon as the buggy came to a halt and Jane smiled down at him. 'You're not hungry, so I'm not taking any notice of you, little man,' she told him. She wiggled the buggy backwards and forwards with her foot. It was an enormous thing with huge tractor-type wheels, and impossibly difficult to fold or carry. How Florence thought she could get it into the back of her car, Jane couldn't imagine. Everything about babies seemed to have got so much larger and more complicated in the last twenty years.

Chipper trotted back to sit beside her. He watched the moorhens with interest, occasionally licking his lips as if they represented a rare, but denied, treat. A man appeared in the distance with a strimming machine. He was dressed in orange overalls and a helmet with a mask. He looked more like the grim reaper than a gardener. He began to attack the long grass on the edge of the bank, sending the moorhens darting across the thick green surface of the water. It must be so disheartening, thought Jane, looking after a nature trail or whatever this was, and then finding your hard work wrecked by hooligans.

She got up again and walked on, and as she passed him he stopped to adjust his machine.

'What a pity about those trees,' she said. She saw he was a young black man with a rather surly expression.

'It's them bloody Asians,' he said. 'Them fucking Bangladeshis.' He had a strong Midlands

278

accent. This was not a conversation Jane wanted to continue so she shrugged and gave him what she hoped was a sympathetic smile.

'They should go back to where they fucking came from!' he said, pulling down the mask and starting the motor again.

*   *   *

When she got back Flo was sitting on the sofa with her laptop, checking on her emails. 'I've had lovely messages from Marco and Sandro,' she said, looking up. 'They want to come and see Tintin. Marco says he's getting him a Wolves T-shirt! They both send love.' She got up to take Tintin from Jane's arms. 'How did you get on?' she asked. Her freshly washed hair shone and swung in a blond curtain. She looked much more cheerful.

'Oh, fine, but he's been awake nearly all the time so he should sleep well this afternoon. I couldn't fold up that great chariot, I'm afraid. Not with Tintin in my arms, anyway. I've had to leave it at the foot of the stairs.'

'I'll go down and get it,' said Florence, putting Tintin into his rocker chair on the floor. He immediately began to cry. She grasped her breasts with both hands.

'That's set me off!' she said. 'I seem to have gallons of milk now. I've turned into a dairy cow.'

'The buggy's hung about with shopping bags. I walked all the way to Sainsbury's in the end and I ploughed up and down the aisles with the buggy as if I was driving a Chieftain tank.'

'You did go a long way. I've never walked that far since I've lived here. What's the matter, Mum?

279

You seem a bit down.'

It was Jane's turn to feel as if tears were threatening. 'I'm sorry. I didn't mean to sound like that. It's just that I'm so worried about Tash. It's all I can think of.'

'Oh, Mum!' Florence put her arms round her mother. 'I'm so sorry. Poor old you. It's awful when there is nothing you can do to help, except be there, as they say. But you must be optimistic. Women whose breast cancers are detected early enough have a normal lifespan these days.'

'Yes. That's what Enzo told me.' Jane sat down wearily on the leather sofa. She had worn an unsuitable pair of shoes for walking and her feet hurt.

'Let me get you a drink. Have a glass of wine?' Florence went to the fridge, brought out a bottle of white wine and poured Jane a glass. She left it on the slate coffee table before going downstairs to bring up the shopping and the buggy.

'I'll feed Tintin now,' she said when the supermarket bags were unpacked in the kitchen. 'And you can tell me about Tash when you were young. Were you always close? She was really supportive, wasn't she, when you lived together in London when I was a baby?'

'Yes, she was. I wouldn't say we were *that* close when we were growing up. We were so different, you see. Later on, after you were born and she came back from India, we saw much more of each other and I can never thank her enough for the support she gave me. Things got very difficult where we were living in Sussex and she helped me more than I can ever say. I couldn't have managed without her.' Jane paused and looked down.

Florence felt the emotion of that moment and, ignoring Tintin's cries, went to sit beside her mother and took her hand.

'She helped me to keep in touch with my father too. He used to come up to London and meet us both. Our mother wouldn't allow him to have anything to do with me, you see, so it had to be done in secret. He combined his visits with lunch with his stockbroker, or something.' Jane paused and took a sip of wine. Her face had fallen into lines of sadness.

'I'm sorry, Mum,' said Florence. For the first time she looked at her mother with proper attention and saw that she seemed faded and tired and really quite old. She had never really seen her like this before. She thought of the miles she had walked and all the shopping she had borne back to the flat, and felt a surge of love and gratitude. 'I'm sorry I bit your head off this morning. You know it's just me and my foul temper, of which I am ashamed. I am so grateful to you, you know. I should keep telling you how wonderful it is to have you here.'

'Well, that's good!' said Jane wearily. 'Now please feed that starving son of yours!'

Florence got up, fetched Tintin and came back to sit on the sofa. In a moment there was silence. Jane took another sip of her wine. 'I'll go and make something for lunch in a minute. I bought a screwdriver and a set of fuses and I'll have a look at the washing machine plug.'

Florence looked at her in amazement over Tintin's head. 'How do you know about things like that?'

'We had to. My generation. We sewed on

buttons and darned socks. Even from our privileged background we learned those simple things. We could knit too, and crochet, and make a sponge cake. Our mother was very determined that we should go to a finishing school and learn how to arrange flowers and get out of a sports car without showing our knickers. Tash was a lost cause, of course. She ran away to London and became a flower child, and I got myself pregnant. Our poor mother . . . What disasters we were.'

'When you talk about Granny you make her sound like a head case. The way she reacted to you getting pregnant, I mean. All that cutting you off and never wanting to have anything more to do with you. What was all that about, for God's sake?'

'It was like that then. That's how most people reacted to illegitimacy. The disgrace was too much for her to deal with. The loss of standing and shame, I suppose.'

'Funny old times,' said Florence, shaking her head. 'I have to admit, I liked her. She was fabulously glamorous, wasn't she? She used to let me try all her scent and stuff. She certainly wasn't like other people's grandmothers.'

'No. That's true.' Jane sat in silence for a moment, watching her daughter's head bent over her baby. She felt there was an easy closeness between them and on an impulse felt bold enough to say, 'Florence, there's something I'd like you to try and understand.'

'What's that?'

'I want you to believe how, from the moment you were born, I wanted you more than anything else in the world. Somehow, and I realise it must be my fault, I don't seem to have convinced you of that.'

'So you were glad to have a little bastard, were you, with father unknown? Come on, Mum! All right, don't look so pained. I'm not saying it unkindly. It just happens to be the truth.'

'Oh, Flo. It might be the truth, but I wish you could look beyond it and realise how much I loved you and what joy you brought into my life.'

Florence did not reply. Then, dropping a kiss onto Tintin's downy head, she said, 'You know, Mum, after all these years of not being able to forgive you, I'm beginning to accept that possibly you did want me. Maybe having my own baby has made a difference—experiencing feelings that overwhelm everything else.'

'I'm really sorry, Flo, that you felt so disadvantaged by your birth; that you have always felt so burdened and angry about it.'

'Don't be sorry. Honestly, Mum, it's all right. Just let it go, will you? It doesn't matter any more. You were a bloody good mother, you know you were. If anything, it's me who should be sorry, for being so tough on you.'

In the silence that followed Jane felt some sense of relief, but also sadness. She's saying that because she feels she should, she thought. She still doesn't understand. Not really. Perhaps it is asking too much that she should.

*   *   *

A reply arrived a week after Jane had posted her letter to her father. The sight of the envelope on the doormat made her heart beat very fast. She knew at once that it would be bad news from her point of view because it was addressed in her mother's handwriting, which meant she had intervened, and that it was very unlikely that there would be any help forthcoming.

It was a particularly bleak November morning and the cottage felt chilly and damp. Outside, the trees were shrouded in a thick wet mist and Jane couldn't see to the end of the garden. It was eerily quiet, she thought, as she stood at the back door to let Sam out, just the rooks quarrelling in the tops of the elm tree, and the drip of water from a broken gutter.

Florence had been grizzling on and off all the morning and Jane was anxious that she wasn't well. She felt restless and nervous herself and was glad to have Sam to keep her company. It was spooky knowing that the house next door was empty and that she was the only person living on the lane. Mr Garbutt had suffered a second stroke a week ago and had been moved to a London clinic. Mrs Garbutt had gone to stay with her daughter. She visited her husband every day and needed to be within easy travelling distance.

Jane sat down at the kitchen table with the letter. If she had been desperate when she wrote it, she was even more desperate now. The previous morning she had had a letter from the electricity board, a last demand printed in angry red letters, saying that if she did not pay within seven days the supply would be cut off. It seemed that the night storage heaters ate up electricity, even though they seemed to be barely warm throughout the day.

She had found some work, though. She had spotted a new advertisement in the post office window seeking help plucking turkeys the week

284

before Christmas, and someone else wanted a cleaner for holiday cottages between Christmas and New Year. She had gone straight to the telephone box, rung both the numbers and found out the turkeys were on a farm just outside her village, to which she could walk, and that the farmer's wife had no objection to her taking Florence with her. 'It'll be cold, mind. You'll have to wrap her up warm,' she said.

The holiday cottages were too far for her to walk, but the man said that he would come and collect her. He couldn't have had many replies, Jane thought, because he didn't ask for references or anything.

'You're experienced, are you, as a cleaner?' was all he had asked. 'Yes,' Jane said. She was, in a sense, because she had learned to clean the cottage and could remember the various tricks that Mrs Clegg, the daily woman at home, had shown her, like wiping windows with vinegar and newspaper.

She slit open the envelope and took out the letter written in her mother's neat, even handwriting. There was a folded cheque inside as well, and Jane opened it at once and saw that it was made out for twenty pounds. She began to read the letter.

Darling Jane,
Daddy and I were disappointed that you had to write to us asking for money. I think we made it clear to you that if you chose to keep your baby against our specific wishes and advice, then we could no longer continue to support you. The situation that you find

yourself in is exactly what we warned you of, and comes as no surprise to us.

However, we are your parents and we love you, as you know, and because it is Christmas, I am sending you a cheque to buy yourself a present from us both.

Should you decide to change your mind about adoption, you know that you will have our fullest possible support. It is not too late, you know, and you can be assured that you will be doing the best thing possible for your baby, and for yourself. To give up your little girl would be by far the most responsible course of action. To keep her is pure selfishness on your part.

Your loving, Mummy

PS, we have news of Tash! She and Denby are due back before Christmas. Thank heavens they are flying home and leaving the dreadful old minibus in India.

Jane put her face in her hands and wept. Any strength that she had felt in the past when she had decided to keep Florence seemed to have left her. Perhaps Mummy is right, she thought. Perhaps it would have been better for Florence to have had adopted parents and to have been growing up in a family. But I can't give her up. I can't. I'd rather die. I'd be better dead.

She picked up the cheque. At least it would cover the electricity. She would just have to live as well as she could until she got paid for the turkey plucking. She emptied her purse on the table. She had twenty-two shillings, plus the three pounds a week for looking after Sam.

She got up and looked in the cupboard. There was some pasta and tinned tomatoes, two small tins of beans and some potatoes. She would just have to make that do. Thank goodness she was still breast-feeding Florence, though now she worried that her milk would give out. The clinic nurse was always on about a healthy diet. It was a good thing she couldn't see what Jane was going to have to live on. If she found out the truth, anything could happen. She could get Florence taken away from her, put into care, or something.

Jane felt another wave of panic and despair. She got up and went to look out of the window at the dismal winter garden. She felt utterly alone. A long time went past before she realised that there was no sign of Sam. She would have to go and shout for him. He was always wandering off.

She got Florence well wrapped up, placed a hot-water bottle in the pram, put on her overcoat and pushed the pram down the lane, carrying Sam's lead and calling as she went. Perhaps he had gone back home, she thought, but when she got to the Garbutts' house there was no sign of him, so she hurried on.

It was then that the stealing started. She passed the two cottages at the top of the lane. Both looked deserted, but there were four pints of milk on the doorstep of the first. Jane saw the milk and without really deciding to do it, she opened the gate, walked up the path and calmly took one bottle. She walked back to the pram, hid the bottle under the blankets and walked on. There, she had done it! It had been easy. She felt suddenly happy. 'See, Mummy will look after you,' she told the sleeping Florence.

She caught sight of Sam on the village green. He was disappearing round the side of the pub where the rubbish was put out in a little yard at the back of the kitchen. Jane followed him and caught him trying to get the lid off a dustbin. She put him on his lead. 'You bad boy,' she told him.

Then she noticed that a box of potatoes had been put out by the pig bin and it was easy to put four of the largest, only a little sprouted, under the blanket with the milk.

There was a sudden bang on the window that overlooked the yard. Jane's heart stood still, but then the window opened and a man's voice called across to her in a friendly tone, 'Do you want those for your chickens? I've got a bag of rolls here. Any good for you?'

'Oh, yes, please,' said Jane. Her voice was high-pitched with fright and her knees wobbled beneath the skirt of her coat.

The man came out of the back door. He was quite young, wearing a pair of checked chef's trousers, and carrying a plastic bag of rolls in his hand. He stopped to light a cigarette and then ambled across to where Jane was waiting.

'Here!' he said, holding them out. 'It's a crying shame, all the food we waste. Take what you like. Monday's the best day, when we clear out after the weekend.'

'Oh, I see. Thank you.'

'Keep a lot, do you? A lot of fowl?'

'Sorry?'

'Chickens. You said they were for your chickens.'

'No, no. Only a few.'

'Well, if you ever have extra eggs, let me know.

We can always do with eggs.'

'Oh, yes. OK. Yes, I will.'

Jane walked back home feeling sick with terror but also elated. She had proved something. She had proved that she could survive, that she would survive. It was just a question of being brave.

She ate four rolls for lunch with a tin of beans and felt full and satisfied. While Florence slept she got out her writing pad and began a letter to Rosie and Judith. There was a pile of them by now—lying unposted on the kitchen counter.

Dear Girls,

There is such a lot happening in this village that it's hard to find the time to write, but now Florence is sleeping—at last—I thought I'd let you know how things are going.

I have made quite a few new friends, apart from Nadia, mostly other young mothers, and it's fun to have people to share all the worries of new babies, like teething and weaning and nappy rashes!! Are you jealous?!!

I also share baby-sitting with another friend, and she has come here a couple of evenings to be with Florence while I go out, and I do the same for her. Phil, the bloke I mentioned in my letter, has asked me out!! I went to the cinema with him but as soon as the film started I went to sleep! I only woke up when he put his arm round me! It's nice to have a bit of love interest, although nothing serious. This morning I met another guy while I was out walking my new dog—a lovely spaniel called Sam. He is a chef at the pub in the village and he came out of his kitchen to have a chat. He asked me to go back next week—Monday is his day off—so who knows!!

The cottage is lovely, and really cosy now it's getting colder and dark quite early in the afternoon. I have a great big crackling fire and . . .

The light of the afternoon faded and Jane got up to turn on the lamp. She pulled her cardigan closer round her and chewed on the end of her biro. Writing always made her feel better. It doesn't matter if it's all made up, she thought. It doesn't matter at all.

Suddenly she remembered the postscript to her mother's letter. Tash would be home before Christmas! Tash would be home and then everything would be all right.

CHAPTER TWELVE

Enzo had not enjoyed the days of Jane's absence as much as he had promised himself he would. He had had a couple of rounds of golf but played badly and pulled a muscle in his back, which was causing him pain and would make his long days in the operating theatre uncomfortable.

He had telephoned both Marco and Sandro, suggesting that they might like to come home for a few days, or meet somewhere for a good meal and a night out, but neither of them was available.

'Sorry, Dad. Things are very busy here. I'm campaigning to be president of the Union. Can't really get away,' said Marco.

'Dad! You know I'm in serious rowing training. I've got a place in the First VIII,' said Sandro. 'I've had to commit to early nights and no booze!' They both adopted what Enzo felt was a placatory tone with him, as if they were conscious of disappointing the old man and feeling bad about it. When had that happened, he thought. When had his sons moved so imperceptibly into adulthood that they now felt their responsibilities towards their father?

He tried to get on with his work at home but he disliked the empty house, with its still rooms and its air of waiting for something to happen. It made him feel restless and unable to concentrate. He found he kept listening for the sounds that he realised were the sounds of Jane—the radio, the washing machine, the Hoover, the telephone, the sound of her voice talking to Chipper. Even if she were out at work, or shopping, there was the sense of waiting for her return: her car tyres on the gravel, the slam of a door, her step on the stair.

There was the smell of her too: cooking, obviously, or coffee, freshly made, and the lovely lemon smell of the bath oil she always used, or her scent that lingered after her in their bedroom and wafted down the stairs in the morning.

There was something so calm and reassuring about Jane, Enzo thought as he swung on his desk chair and looked out of the window at the garden that was hers as well. She had worked on it for all the years that they had lived in this house: planting, weeding, putting in the paths and the greenhouse and the sheltered places to sit in the summer.

His mother and sisters were so different, so loud and demanding and demonstrative. The minute his mother found that he was alone for a few days she had wanted to come down on the train with his eldest sister, Raffella, who had recently left her husband, and look after him, but he had fobbed her off. They were like an invading army, his family. They took over, filled the house with their shouting voices, their shrieking television programmes, their pungent, clattering cooking, their demands that he should eat this, drink that, wear his hair differently, buy a new suit. They were wonderful, he adored them, but he didn't want to have to live with them ever again.

Jane was quiet and gentle; she allowed people to be themselves when they were with her. She made them feel valuable and worthy. She was never pushing herself or her own views forward. She was self-effacing, but she was not meek. She was strong, enduring, about important things. She was wholly reliable. She was transparent in the way that good people are. Enzo felt he could go on and on, but he didn't want to, because it made him feel more miserable about being alone.

She had sounded so relieved to speak to him about poor Tash. It made him feel pleased that she needed him. He had to own up to being aggrieved that she had seemed so dismissive of going to San Francisco with him and the fact that she had rushed off to be with Florence. He knew this reaction was unworthy, but he couldn't help it. He liked to feel at the centre of her world and sometimes she did not seem to realise it. Lately, she had remarked quite often that he hardly seemed to need her. How could she really think that?

Enzo stood up and wandered back to the window, then caught sight of himself in the mirror over the fireplace. How grey his hair had become, and deeply lined his face. It looked like a dried, rocky stream bed. I am nearly an old man, he thought mournfully. Soon I will be sixty years old. His back hurt when he moved. Oh, Jane, he thought. Jane, Jane . . .

*   *   *

Ha came back for lunch. He admired Florence's hair and she received his compliments by putting her arms round his neck and kissing him on the mouth. Jane, busy with a salad at the kitchen sink, was glad. She found that she was looking for signs of warmth and mutual dependency between them. Unlike her own mother, she didn't mind about the stigma of illegitimacy. It was just that Tintin stood a better chance in life, she was sure of it, if his parents were lasting lovers and friends.

Perhaps she was unfair to her mother. After all, she had only wanted what she really believed to be best for her and Florence. It was the punishment that was cruel, the cutting off, the withdrawing of love and contact, the enforced separation from her father, whose love was so much less conditional.

Jane, catapulted into the past, stared, unseeing, at the lettuce in the sink. It was still painful to remember her nineteen-year-old self, to be taken back to how she was. All the years in between had conspired to help her forget. There were better times to come, there was Enzo waiting for her, the birth of the boys, the happiness of having a family.

It was the birth of Tintin that seemed to be reawakening memories of things she had left behind.

Now, here was Ha with Tintin in his arms, telling her something, holding him out to her, and she turned back to the present with relief.

'Florence has gone out for a breath of fresh air before lunch,' he said, 'and there's something I want to tell you. My parents are determined to visit. They are very impatient to see Tintin. Their first grandson! He means a lot to them.'

'Yes, of course he does. Of course they want to see him. When will they come?'

'Oh, soon, I think. They're Catholics, so there is a bit of an issue, though. Me and Florence, I mean. They are not really very happy about us.'

'Oh, I see.' Jane had not imagined that Ha's family would be Catholic. She wasn't sure what religion she had expected—something to do with temples and goddesses with a lot of arms. How ignorant she was.

'They'll want him to be baptised and all of that. I think that they'll put on a lot of pressure.'

'But he's your baby! You don't have to be pushed into anything, do you? You've plenty of time to make up your own minds.' Jane suddenly thought of the problem of the name. Could anyone called Tintin be baptised? It seemed unlikely.

'They are strong-minded people,' said Ha. 'They had to be, to make a go of things. They don't go in for indecisiveness. They came here with nothing and speaking no English. Now they own their own business and my brother is an accountant and I'm a doctor. That doesn't just happen by accident. They are what you could call single-minded.'

'I see. Yes, I suppose they would have to be.' She thought of Enzo's family, struggling to make a life in Musselburgh, an alien, far-off, bleak grey town where the bitter winds blew in from the Forth and the people were cold and suspicious. Yes, you had to have a determined streak to survive as an immigrant. Your family was all you had and it was through the efforts of your family that you sank or swam.

'Have they met Florence?'

'Yes, a couple of times. They like her a lot. They're pleased that I have an English girlfriend. To them, it's a sign of success. It's something that they can boast about. But all the same, they don't like it that we have had a baby and aren't married, or engaged. It was quite difficult to tell them, in fact.'

Hmm, I can see it would be, thought Jane.

'Actually,' said Ha, smiling down at Tintin, who stared back at him with his wise old man expression, 'what I wanted to say to you is that I have been thinking of asking Florence to marry me. You asked me if I ever had, didn't you, and it made me think, well, why didn't I?'

'Oh, Ha!' Jane beamed at him. Something lightened inside her.

'I don't know what she'll say. I feel quite nervous about it, but having Tintin makes a big difference. I want us to be together. It seems important.'

'You could always just live together,' said Jane, playing the devil's advocate.

'Yeah, I know, but it's harder to ask her to do that. It's like asking, well, can I move into your flat and share your life, whereas asking her to marry me means something different. We both have to be prepared to start something new—you know, move and all that. Set up a proper home together.'

'Yes, it does. Actually, it's been one of the things that has worried me—that this isn't a good place to bring up a child. This flat, I mean. I can't see it working well; the stairs, the sliding doors and that dreadful canal.'

Ha laughed. 'Dreadful?' he said. 'I think it was the unique selling point for Florence!'

'Well, maybe as a single, childless professional it seemed attractive—a sort of lifestyle statement—but not for a mother. But truthfully, it's a horrid old canal, isn't it? You couldn't take your eyes off a toddler for one second along that towpath. You want somewhere safe, a little house with a garden.' She knew she sounded absurdly middle class, but she couldn't help it.

'Yeah, well. It'll be a big change for us, if it happens.' Ha spoke solemnly. 'We'll have to get a bloody great mortgage. Up until now I've never been in a position to save much. It'll be a big change.'

'But you are both well paid. You'll never be out of work, either of you. Surely you can afford it?'

'Well, yeah, in theory, but we've both got a lot of debts. We're neither of us very good at saving.'

How *old* are they, thought Jane. Ha made himself and Florence sound like unemployed teenage parents living in a bed-and-breakfast hostel. As far as she could judge they were the same as most of their generation who had grown up thinking that luxuries and an extremely high standard of living came before anything else, especially boring things like living within a budget, or saving for a rainy day. It made her feel quite impatient.

'If you want it enough, you'll find a way,' was all she said.

*　　*　　*

Jane did not steal on a regular basis. Leading up to Christmas she took what she could until she got paid. A pint of milk here and there, a few eggs from a farm where trays were put beside the road, ready for collection by a van. It had been easy to slip four into the folds of the blanket at Florence's feet.

She grew clever and cunning and watchful. Up and down the back lanes of the spread-out village she walked, noting the comings and goings and the houses that were empty during the day. There were two in particular where garage doors were left open and there were chest freezers at the back. It took only a moment to push the pram into the garage and open the lid of the freezer and whip out four fish fingers or a bag of peas or a half-loaf of bread. She began to carry little plastic bags with her so that she could take just small amounts of things, unlikely to be missed.

People wouldn't mind, she told herself. They would understand if they knew. They would surely give her what she was taking if she asked them, but that was the one thing that she could not do. No one must ever know how desperate she was, because if they did, Florence would be taken from her. The police and social workers would move in and she would be found unworthy to be a mother. She was already wary of the district nurse, who came round every now and then and asked questions about how she was managing, running her eyes round the kitchen for damning evidence, examining Florence for signs of neglect. Jane was haunted by the screams of the girl in hospital when they came to take her baby away.

Sam was to be her excuse if ever she got caught. 'My dog ran into your garage, and I had to follow him to put him on his lead.' No one would search a pram where a baby lay asleep, the picture of innocence.

As it happened, she never came near to being caught—not even a close shave—and the turkey plucking saved her as far as Christmas was concerned.

*   *   *

It was bitterly cold in the long shed and she worked from eight o'clock until three o'clock in the afternoon for five days running. She wrapped Florence as warmly as she could with a hot-water bottle at her feet, but on the first day the farmer's wife came out from the house to where she was waiting in the freezing dark to clock on in the farm office and said, 'Here, I'll take that baby into the kitchen with me. I'm icing Christmas cakes all the morning. I'll come and find you when she needs feeding.'

'She should be all right until eleven o'clock,' said Jane, gratefully. 'Then she has some groats and a feed. I've got the packet in the pram. It just needs a bit of warm milk to mix.'

'What are you doing?' grumbled the farmer to his wife. 'Running a bloody nursery? They'll all be

298

bringing their kids next.'

'Oh, be quiet, you!' said his wife. 'It will be lovely to have a baby about the place for a while. Don't worry, love, I'll look after her.' Jane could have wept with gratitude because she was frightened that she would get reported, or that Florence would catch a cold.

The pluckers were mostly women, earning a bit of Christmas money, or elderly men, all wrapped in layers of old clothes and fingerless gloves. They were collected from the neighbourhood by the farmer's son driving an old Transit van and they worked sitting or standing at long tables, which were soon mounded with feathers and down. The turkeys were still warm—they had just been killed—and Jane was shown how to remove the tough wing feathers with a pair of pliers by an old man called Robbie, who worked next to her. She could hardly understand a word he said but she gathered he was Scottish and that he lived in a caravan on the farm.

Some of the pluckers preferred to work with the birds hung on a hook from a wire running down the length of the shed, but others plucked them lying on the table in front of them.

Jane hated plunging her hands into the warm feathers, and the smell and clammy touch of turkey flesh. She was terribly slow to begin with. Her first bird took her nearly an hour, while Robbie was starting on his third.

'You'll get faster!' said a girl called Sharon, who stood on her other side, turning up the Monkees on her transistor radio. She was seventeen, she told Jane, and hadn't had a proper job since she had left school in the summer.

'Ain't nothing to do round here,' she said, tossing back her long brown hair. 'Come the summer I'll do hotel work. Disgusting, this is, ennit? I did it last year with Paula, me best mate, but she wouldn't come again. She'd rather sit on her backside all day. She's engaged, see, to a boy in the RAF. She reckons now she's got a ring on her finger, she's too good for grotty work like this!'

It was the closest thing to friendship that Jane had known since Rebecca from the baby clinic. Sharon made her laugh and Jane liked her style, all the black eyeliner and the skintight jeans and her irreverent manner. She reminded Jane of what it should be like to be young.

She showed Jane her love bites and sat amongst the feathers smoking a banned cigarette, swinging her legs and giving Robbie two fingers when he told her off. They walked home together after the first day and Jane invited her in for a cup of tea.

'Not bloody likely, not smelling like this,' said Sharon, pulling a face. 'It clings terrible, the smell of turkey. I'm off home to have a bath before me mum gets back from work. I'll get the hot water that way. Then I'm out with me boyfriend. He's got a car, see. We're going to the flicks in Haslemere.'

She showed little interest in Jane's situation. 'You're a bit young and posh, ain't yer, to be on yer own with a baby? What went wrong, then? What bastard got you up the duff?' Jane gave the sketchiest of explanations, with which Sharon was quite satisfied. There was an acceptance from the first that hers was the more interesting life. However, she seemed genuinely to love Florence, asking to hold and cuddle her.

'I want one of me own,' she confided. 'I want a

baby, like, maybe next year. Me nan will look after it while I go out to work. I want to train in a hair salon, see. We'll get a council house, if I get pregnant. Dave'll have to marry me.' How simple she made it sound, Jane thought. Babies, marriage. It didn't seem to matter which came first.

*   *   *

A week before Christmas, Tash telephoned from a coinbox in a café on the Boulevard St-Germain in Paris. Jane felt quite overcome to hear her voice and had to sit down on the hall chair. They kept talking at once and then stopping and both starting again, and laughing and saying, 'It's so good to hear you!' and, 'I can't wait to see you!'

'Come to us in London for Christmas,' Tash said. 'We've got a house! One of Denby's ancient relatives has left him a house in Notting Hill. It's fairly dilapidated and full of tenants in bedsits, but apparently there's a flat we can just about live in. We're flying back tomorrow. I'll telephone again from London. See you very soon, darling. Can't wait! There are the pips! See you, Jane. Dear little mother Jane! Tons of love . . .'

*   *   *

The turkeys were finished four days before Christmas and Jane caught the bus into town with a roll of dirty banknotes in her coat pocket. She did her final Christmas shopping with a light heart. She had knitted Tash and Denby and Mr Kowalski long striped scarves, Aunt Joan some gloves, and made Florence a little white felt mouse with pink

301

ears, but she couldn't think of anything that she could make to send to her mother or father. In the end, she bought her mother soap, and her father a Penguin detective novel that could pass as new, which she found in a charity shop, where she also found a warm snowsuit for Florence in bubblegum-pink nylon.

It was fun to browse through the brightly decorated shops and listen to the carol singers in the marketplace. She held Florence up in her little knitted bonnet to see the lights sparkling on the Christmas trees. 'Your first Christmas, my darling!' she told her.

There were other excited small children on the bus home and Florence watched them, spellbound, while Jane listened to their mothers chatting about their plans for Christmas and complaining about visits from their in-laws. That's one thing I don't have to worry about, thought Jane, looking out of the window at the black night jolting past. It was a comfort to know that Sam was waiting for them back at the cottage and that she would hear him barking a welcome as she opened the garden gate.

She felt guilty that she couldn't take him to London with her, but had arranged that Mrs Garbutt's daughter would come to collect him to put him into kennels over the holiday. When she arrived, on the Monday before Christmas, the news she brought of Mr Garbutt was not good.

'I don't think he'll ever be well enough to come and live down here again. It's not fair on my mother. He needs a lot of nursing and this place is so cut off. The dog will have to go, I'm afraid. It's asking too much for me to have to come down here especially to deal with him. I've had to take the whole day off work.' She was a thin, impatient-looking woman in a trouser suit and a fur coat and a lot of jangling gold jewellery. She jerked at Sam's lead and he turned his head longingly towards Jane and whined. 'Get in the car, you!' she said. 'I've arranged for the gardener to fetch him after Christmas. I can't keep coming backwards and forwards from London and I don't want him in that kennels any longer than necessary. It costs an arm and a leg, having him there. Well, that's it. I'll be off. Happy Christmas!'

On the same afternoon Jane got a taxi from the cottage to the station. She hated spending the money but she had no alternative. There were no buses and she had Florence in her pushchair, and a suitcase. It was very cold and the countryside looked beautiful with every hedge and tree and fencepost iced with frost and the sky lit with a pale orange glow as the sun went down. The train was late. There was no heating in the waiting room and Jane tucked Florence into her coat to keep her warm. When at last the train arrived, a kind man, the same type of man as her father, well wrapped up in a tweed overcoat and a trilby hat, helped her into an empty carriage. He had a suitcase of his own and a brace of pheasants, their necks tied together with a piece of orange baler twine. He got in as well and put his case and the pheasants in the rack, then sat opposite her and asked if she would like anything from the buffet car. She thanked him but said she wouldn't. She didn't tell him that she did not have the money to spend on such luxuries.

'Would you keep an eye on my things?' he said, indicating the rack. 'I don't want to lose my Christmas dinner!' and he went out into the corridor. When he reappeared he was carrying a mug of tea and a square of fruit cake. 'You look half frozen,' he said. 'I thought you could do with this. I put sugar in the tea but I didn't stir it.' When he bent over to give her the mug she could smell whisky on his breath and then she saw a miniature bottle in his hand and he was asking if she would like a drop in her tea to warm her up.

From somewhere down the corridor there was a burst of laughter and then young male voices singing 'White Christmas' and then 'Lily the Pink'. It was off-key and raucous, and they didn't know the words beyond the first two lines, but the cheery noise lifted Jane's heart and she smiled at the man and said, 'Yes, please.'

'Your baby is very good,' he said, settling down opposite her.

'Yes,' said Jane, beaming. Praise for Florence was the best compliment anyone could give her, and she *was* being good. She slept all the way to London, although Jane herself felt electrified with excitement. Soon she would see Tash again and all the months of feeling so alone would be over.

It was dark by the time the train drew in to Waterloo and she couldn't bear to wait another moment. She dragged down the window and stuck her head out to look for Tash, and then she saw her, standing on the platform, wearing an ankle-length coat and a felt hat and looking different from everyone else, very thin and brown and more striking than ever.

'Tash! Tash!' Jane called out of the window and she saw her sister turn and then she was waving and shouting too, and galloping to meet her as the train came to a halt. She wrenched the carriage door open and Jane fell into her arms, while the kind man lifted her suitcase and the pushchair onto the platform and then stood patiently holding Florence's carrycot in one hand and the brace of pheasants in the other while the sisters clung to one another in a laughing embrace.

Denby was there too, also thin and brown, with long hair and a fur coat and wearing a huge number of silver necklaces. He took the case while Tash commandeered the sleeping Florence.

'She's so perfect,' she said, peering into the carrycot. 'Like a pink and white doll! But, Jane, you are so pale and tired-looking. Is that what babies do to you? Denby, I'm not having any, do you hear? What you need, dearest, is some food and drink and some FUN! Come on, Denby, get a move on, it's freezing. We've borrowed a car to collect you so Denby will go on ahead and get it. It's parked on a yellow line somewhere. We've got a Christmas tree in the back with the end sticking out of the window. I shall have to sit amongst the branches.'

*   *   *

Notting Hill was an area of crumbling down-at-heel terraces populated by West Indian immigrants. The house Denby had inherited, once rather grand and stately, had been divided up into tiny bedsitting rooms with a horrid dirty little bathroom and a lavatory on each floor. Jane looked at it in dismay, at the broken wall in the front and the garden full of bricks and other rubbish. The hall was depressing, with dirty lino and brown paint, but in the very short time that

Tash had been in London she had made the little ground-floor flat habitable.

'Denby's great-aunt lived here, until she went into hospital about six months ago. It's been empty since then. Denby and I have given everything a real scrubbing and filled a builder's skip with rubbish, so although it's all a bit grim, at least it's clean. We moved some of our own stuff over yesterday. You'll have to sleep on a mattress in the sitting room, I'm afraid. We've piled all the junk we can't get rid of into the spare room.'

'It's not grim at all. It's lovely,' said Jane, who felt that compared to the frugal bleakness of Aunt Joan's flat it was bohemian paradise itself. Brightened with patchwork floor cushions and Indian bedspreads, and lit with candles, the rooms glowed with colour. Denby had made fires in the grates and it was warm and cosy, and the air was scented by the Christmas tree, leaning at a precarious angle in an old bucket in the corner.

That evening Denby went out to meet some friends and Tash and Jane lay by the fire and talked, filling in the gaps since they were last together. When Jane told the full story of how she got pregnant, Tash sat up and looked at her indignantly.

'But why?' she demanded. 'Why the hell did you let that boy have sex with you? Were you drunk?'

'A bit, but not very. He certainly was. I've asked myself the same question over and over and really all I can come up with is that I didn't have the confidence to make him stop. I was too polite. I think that there was so much emphasis on good manners at home, on doing what one was told, of pleasing people, that I hadn't got the gumption to stand up for myself.'

'How come we are so different?' exclaimed Tash. 'God, I'd have knocked his teeth out, I can tell you. The fucking jerk.'

'You got all the courage when it was handed out,' said Jane, sadly.

'Well, you've got a lovely baby out of it—that's the positive thing—and it's obvious that you're a wonderful mother. It seems to come naturally to you. Later on, when Florence is older, you can begin again, can't you? I mean, you'll still be young when she starts school.'

'Yes, I suppose I can, although Mummy has convinced me that my life's over; that I've wrecked it completely.' Jane suddenly wanted to tell Tash the truth about how desperate things had been, about the stealing, but she was too ashamed, and anyway, all that was in the past. She had her cleaning job waiting for her, and at the moment she had some money. Things were going to be better, she was sure of it.

'I've already quarrelled with her!' said Tash, lying back again. 'We rowed about you, of course. She tried to tell me that I shouldn't see you. Can you believe it? She wanted Denby and me to go home for Christmas. Now she's found out that Denby is posh—from "a good family", she calls it—she wants to ingratiate herself. I told her the truth—that I'm not going home while she refuses to see you.'

Jane sighed. 'I've broken up the family, haven't I?'

'No, *she* has.'

*   *   *

307

There was a little television set in the flat and on Christmas Eve, when outside the window rain turned to drifting flakes of snow, they watched the Apollo space shot. For the first time the pitted and barren surface of the moon was visible to human eyes in fuzzy black and white, and the three of them sat, entranced, while Florence lay awake on a rug in front of the fire. They held their breath when the little spaceship went out of contact. It had been such an awful year in other ways—riots, assassinations, the Vietnam war, Soviet troops invading Czechoslovakia—that Jane hardly dared to believe that the spacecraft would return safely. She picked Florence up and held her tight and prayed silently, while her daughter thrust her little fists into her hair and gurgled in delight.

Then from the dark side of the moon came the crackling signal that the ship had successfully achieved orbit, and she could breathe again. When the astronauts took it in turns to read from Genesis and ended with, 'God bless you all—all of you on the good earth,' even Tash and Denby, as new converts to Hinduism, did not object, and Denby surprised himself with a loud, 'Amen!'

'It's like a sign of a better world to come—a new beginning,' said Tash, with shining eyes. She took Florence out of Jane's arms and tickled her until she laughed. 'Moon shot baby!' she said. 'It's going to be a better world for you to grow up in!'

*   *   *

On Boxing Day morning both Tash and Denby felt unwell, protesting that their time in India had left them unprepared for the turkey and Christmas pudding that they had shared with friends the day before. They stayed in bed, smoking dope and sleeping, while Jane got Florence dressed up warmly and took her out.

It was the strangest Christmas, thought Jane as she pushed the pram along the empty streets. She had never spent it away from home before, and her mother had always staged a very traditional day, with church and then a huge lunch, followed by the Queen's speech, then present opening, tea, and a slice of Christmas cake, and the pulling of crackers. Last Christmas had been miserable, of course, but that had been her fault.

It was wonderful being with Tash and Denby, but having Florence, being a mother, set her apart from them and the friends who had come round to help them celebrate. The drugs and smoking and drinking, the shambolic arrangements with people turning up and drifting out again, did not suit the routine that Jane had imposed on her own life. Last night, for instance, two other girls had crashed out on the sitting-room floor, and this morning they were still asleep with the curtains tightly closed. Florence had woken at six o'clock and a crying baby was the last thing anyone wanted about the place.

I'm not a hippie, Jane thought. Not by nature. I worry too much. I like order and early nights and a clean kitchen.

Florence was fretful today and turned her head away when Jane had tried to feed her some mashed banana in the kitchen, amongst the debris of the night before. Perhaps she has started teething, she thought, and wished that she had

309

someone she could ask for advice.

Thank goodness the motion of the pushchair lulled her to sleep. Jane walked on through the slushy streets. It wasn't a pretty white Christmas, just cold and raw, with the pavements icy and slippery. Soon her boots were sodden. She had forgotten her gloves and her hands were red with cold so she pulled down the sleeves of her jumper to cover her wrists. It was eerily quiet. Some pigeons batted their wings, quarrelling on a rooftop, and a large ginger cat sauntered across a road that would normally be busy with rushing cars. Every now and then a solitary taxi swooshed past, leaving dirty tyre marks in the wet snow.

This was a part of London unknown to Jane. Most of the large old houses were decaying and dilapidated, with threadbare curtains strung across grimy windows and ugly modern front doors replacing the shabby originals, which would have once opened onto freshly painted railings and scrubbed steps. Every now and then scaffolding and builders' skips indicated that renovation was going on, and at the far end of the street there were several houses already done up, with shining brass door handles, bay trees in tubs and Christmas tree lights twinkling in handsome drawing rooms.

In one window Jane saw a young woman with long dark hair wearing a pale dressing gown, holding a baby of about Florence's age to look out at the white street. Their eyes met and the girl smiled and half-lifted a hand to wave. Jane looked away and hurried on. Lucky baby, she thought. It doesn't have to be pushed round the streets in the cold because its mother has nowhere else to go. Suddenly she felt anxious and sad, as she so often did these days. I've got to make things good for Florence, she told herself. I must, or Mummy was right. I should have had her adopted if I can't make her safe and happy.

She walked past a row of shabby little shops, all closed and shuttered, and began to long for a cup of coffee and something to eat, but Florence was sleeping peacefully and so she kept going. Perhaps she would find somewhere open further on.

Her thoughts turned to home again. Every Boxing Day her father went shooting, tall and handsome in his tweed suit and waxed jacket. Her mother and the other wives would join the guns for a late lunch of thick brown stew and baked potatoes. This year would be no different. Nothing would change because she and Tash were not there. We were never really anything more than extras, she thought, remembering how they had lolled around at home watching television all day and eating cold turkey and mince pies and working their way through the bowl of nuts. They had been happy to be left on their own, and now she felt nostalgic for those days, and homesick for a time when life had been so simple.

Turning a corner she suddenly recognised where she was. Another ten minutes and she could be on Marylebone High Street. Aunt Joan was staying with a friend for Christmas but maybe Mr Kowalski would be at the shop. He ignored holidays as a rule, saying that they meant nothing to him. Perhaps he would be in the back room, with the electric fire and a pot of hot coffee. Jane smiled at the thought and hurried on. It would be a long walk back but it didn't matter, she had nothing else to do and she had promised him that

311

she would bring Florence to meet him.

*   *   *

Enzo couldn't wait to get away. He was still feeling oddly unsettled and adrift, and he had an urgent sense that it was Jane whom he needed to regain a proper sense of himself. He had a long day in the operating theatre with hip replacements and resurfacing booked in from early morning onwards. The work was routine—any car mechanic could have carried it out, or so he felt—and this was the first time he had experienced this level of disenchantment.

There was something going on with his nurses too, his well-trained and dedicated team, and he couldn't put his finger on it until he realised that the giggling in the scrub room and the occasional, momentary failure to interpret his needs during an operation was something to do with the new surgeon he had taken on. He was a very handsome young Indian, educated in England, smooth and clever, and there was just something in his manner that Enzo found mildly disquieting. He was polite, deferential almost, but Enzo detected that he was being treated, very slightly, as a grand old man, rather than an exciting pioneer, at the forefront of his profession.

Of course, there were new techniques in orthopaedic surgery, and Gavinda had trained with one of the top orthopods in London, and while he had never directly challenged Enzo, he had an impressive air of youthful authority. Enzo had recently noted the frequency with which his patients turned to Gavinda to ask questions during

312

preparatory examinations. It was right it should be thus, and Enzo always smiled and nodded his head in acquiescence when Gavinda politely glanced at him for permission before he answered.

Enzo could afford to be generous, given his experience and reputation, but nevertheless he felt a chilly foretaste of the future, his declining years—and what an apt description that was. Declining eyesight for one thing. During operations it was getting harder to see as clearly as he once had. A shaking hand would be the next handicap, and forgetfulness, as well as this damn back that he had tweaked playing golf.

Enzo had never lacked confidence, and he recognised that what he was feeling was something new but not entirely unexpected. After all, he was nearly sixty and things were sure to change as one got older. The secret was to embrace change, not fight it, and see the advantages in easing up a bit, taking more time to do the things that he enjoyed, moving over professionally, without resentment. It was all obvious, really, but harder to put into practice than it was to recognise and think about.

He needed to talk to Jane, discuss how he felt with her. She would understand, as she always did, and they could plan for the future and make sensible decisions. The house and garden were far too big, for a start. They could down-size and have more freedom to travel. He had, for some time, nursed a desire to revisit his Italian roots, which for the most part of his life so far he had had little interest in. It's all part of getting older, he thought, this desire to know oneself. Jane would use the dog and Tintin and the boys as a brake against this new freedom, and, of course, she was right. One's family mattered most. Even the bloody dog. For God's sake, he'd missed the dog as well.

He also wanted to see Florence, for whom he felt a real affection. He couldn't pretend that his feelings were the same as for his own boys, but he loved her in another sort of way, which was just as true. There was something so forthright and direct about her, and always had been ever since she was ten years old when he had first met her. She had never been one of those wily, manipulative small girls who use their femininity to get what they want. She had been glowering and cross, and later, when she had forgiven him for moving in on her life with her mother, she had become a devoted companion, stoically accompanying him to freezing rugby matches and on long walks along the Thames in the winter, while Jane was occupied by the baby boys. They had sat together outside pubs in Chiswick with their coat collars turned up, while Enzo drank a pint and Florence had a ginger beer and a packet of crisps.

She was as good company as any of his mates, and when she announced that she wanted to be a doctor, it had touched his heart, it really had, because he recognised that it was a tribute to him.

Later on, she had grown away, which was as it should be. It would have been too easy to have taken advantage of her, as older sister, to baby-sit and supervise the boys, and he had taken trouble to encourage her independence. She had moved out of home when she was eighteen and never came back, except for the occasional weekend. Jane minded this, he knew, but Enzo thought that it was healthy and that their relationship was robust enough to weather separation.

Now here she was with a baby of her own, and the idea of Florence as a mother intrigued Enzo. The fact that she had asked Jane's help signalled a change about which Enzo was not surprised. Everyone turned to Jane when they needed support. As he felt now, in need of her calm attention.

It seemed to be a thoroughly modern arrangement Florence had with Ha, and if it worked, well, that was fine. He didn't share Jane's anxiety. For goodness' sake, they were practically middle-aged and taking parenthood seriously enough. They would always put Tintin's interests first and, anyway, one shouldn't underestimate the power of tiny babies and how they can transform the best-laid plans.

He always told Jane that he had fallen in love with Florence first, when, more than slightly drunk, he had held her in his arms in the maternity ward.

CHAPTER THIRTEEN

It had started to snow again when Jane turned into Marylebone High Street. It had taken her longer than she had thought and Florence was awake and hungry, starting to grizzle and stuff her fists into her mouth. When at last Jane reached the bookshop she saw that the window was exactly as she had left it five months earlier and now looked dusty and neglected. Some of her display had toppled over and books lay face down where they had fallen. Mr Kowalski had evidently been speaking the truth when he said that he hadn't sold a book in her absence.

There was no sign that he might be inside, no light in the shop, and she could see there was a pile of post in a heap inside the door. Her heart sank.

She knocked on the door, and then called through the letterbox, 'Mr Kowalski? It's me, Jane! Are you there?' Nothing happened, so she tried again. Not only did she want to see her friend, but where was she to feed Florence if he wasn't in? She would have to sit on a bench in the snow. She could see the door to the back room was firmly shut. If he was in there, she doubted that he would hear her anyway. She knocked for a third time, and then saw the door open and a dark, familiar figure was making its way to the front of the shop, feeling its way, really, using outstretched hands to seek the path between the bookshelves and the till.

Mr Kowalski looked more frail than ever and it took a while for him to get the door open, and then she had to negotiate the pushchair into the shop, and then at last she could turn to him. He embraced her as a grandfather might a granddaughter and she was shocked to find that his little bent body had shrunk to a frame of bones draped in a heavy coat, but his voice was firm and his welcome as warm as she had hoped.

'Come, come,' he said, and then she was hit by the heat and old man's smell of the back room.

'Oh, my dear, my dear! Let me see your baby, your little one!' he said, wiping tears from the corners of his eyes, and Florence stopped crying and looked up at his face with curiosity. Jane thought that she might take fright, Mr Kowalski looked so strange and unfamiliar. She saw that his

316

hair had grown almost to his shoulders and his fingernails were long and neglected, but Florence returned his gaze and then smiled back her best, dimpled smile, and reached up to touch his face.

Jane fed her then, sitting on one of the broken-down chairs while Mr Kowalski made coffee and found a packet of biscuits amongst the papers on his table. From the state of the room Jane could see that he was no longer running a business, and he said as much as he fumbled about with the cups and jug. 'I am no longer able. It has become too much for an old man. I come here every day and sit with my books and my thoughts, but the shop is closed.'

He seemed so far removed from the real world that when he enquired, Jane could not begin to explain how things were with her. It was easier to say, 'Everything's fine, thank you. Fine.' She spoke the truth when she added, 'I am so glad that I kept Florence, Mr Kowalski. That's the main thing, and I have you to thank for that.'

'Did you watch the moon shot on Christmas Eve?' she asked later as she sipped the strong sugary coffee. 'Do you have a television where you live?'

'No, but I listened to it on the wireless,' he said. 'It is an astonishing achievement. Man is capable of so much that is good. It cheers my heart. Perhaps it is a new beginning. A new page of history.'

'That's what my sister said. It makes it seem even more special that it happened on Florence's first Christmas Eve.'

After she had finished feeding Florence, Jane surreptitiously looked at her watch. She would

317

have to go. It was a long walk back and Tash might be worried about her. On the way out, and despite her protests, Mr Kowalski put two twenty-pound notes in her hand, and at the same moment she saw the little packet she had sent him, containing a Christmas card and the scarf that she had knitted, lying unopened amongst the post on the floor of the shop.

*   *   *

It was hard going back to the cottage after Christmas. Jane dreaded the cold and the loneliness, but she knew that she couldn't stay with Tash and Denby. There wasn't room, for one thing. Their lives were too irregular. Tash was already busy arranging appointments with Liberty's and Harrods to show off samples of some of the clothes she had had made up in India, and Denby was supposed to be developing the jewellery line. Also, Jane had a job to go back to, cleaning the holiday cottages, and poor Sam would be missing her.

Nevertheless, it was horrible opening the front door, knowing the cottage was dark and empty. There was a little pile of post on the mat, including the packet she had sent her parents. Confused, Jane picked it up and saw that it had been returned to her, unopened, readdressed in her mother's handwriting.

She sat at the kitchen table with the packet in her hands and cried in tearless sobs, while Florence watched her, propped in the armchair. The feeling of not being strong enough was overwhelming, and also the guilt of behaving like this in front of her baby. All the happiness of Christmas and being with Tash seemed to flow out of her in the absence of tears. You've only yourself to blame, she told herself. All this is your choice.

After a while she blew her nose, got up and put the packet away in a drawer she never had reason to open. She would forget it existed because there were no options here. She had got to make the best of things. Now it was time for Florence's tea and bath. Her baby needed her and she would not let her down. Tomorrow Sam would be back and that would make all the difference.

*   *   *

Cleaning the holiday cottages was fine. The owner came to collect her three mornings in a row and he did not object to Florence coming along in her carrycot. Jane wedged her with cushions to sit on a sofa while she vacuumed and dusted, and later fed her her lunch, like a little picnic. The clinic nurse had advised that as well as mashed banana she could now have stewed apple and sieved vegetables, and Jane had bought a small hand-turned sieve and made little sloppy messes for Florence each day.

She was such a pretty baby, with pink cheeks, curly fair hair and her one little white front tooth—a picture-book baby—and Jane only had to look at her to feel glad and proud. She's the best thing I've ever done, she thought. The best and most important, and for the time being it was all all right, with her turkey money and the cleaning job, and Mr Kowalski's Christmas present.

As the new year wore on into February, it got

hard again. It was very cold and she had to buy an electric radiator for the bedroom to keep Florence warm enough at night. She worried about the quarterly bill and whether she would be able to pay it. She telephoned the farmer's wife and asked if she had any work, or if she knew anyone who wanted a cleaner, but she said, no, they wouldn't need anyone on the farm until the potatoes were harvested, and that wasn't work for a girl.

The holiday cottages were empty until Easter. 'We might need you again then,' said the man. 'I've got your number. I'll give you a ring.'

Jane even went to see Nadia. She found her in a studio at the back of the house wearing a paint-splattered apron and with her hair up in an untidy bunch. 'Darling!' she cried. 'How lovely to see you. Oh, the delicious baby!' She was vaguer than ever, unable to drag herself away from the huge canvas on which she was splodging paint with a sponge. The three grey whippets lay in an armchair in velvety, elegant disarray. It seemed that today they couldn't be bothered to bark.

'I was wondering if you had any work for me?' asked Jane. 'I'd do anything. Cleaning, gardening, painting. Anything.'

'Oh, sweetheart! Mrs Baker would have a fit if I employed anyone else. She's done for me for twenty years. And I have Ken in the garden. Can you cook, though? Could you cook for parties?'

'I could help,' said Jane, 'but I don't think I could do it on my own.'

'But you need money, do you, darling? Like us all! Goodness, what I would do if I had some lovely money.'

Jane stood, feeling awkward.

'I know what. I *have* got something for you. Come!' Nadia held out her hand as if she were leading a child. Jane, unable to take it and also push the pram, followed her round the house to the back door of the kitchen. Nadia went inside and came out with a large, square cake tin. 'Here!' she said. 'Have it!'

It seemed rude to open the tin and examine the contents, so Jane thanked her effusively, and prised off the lid only when she was well out of the gate and down the lane. Inside were the crumbly remains of a rather dry-looking Christmas cake.

Sometime after that, when she was particularly desperate, she had a short letter from Mrs Garbutt enclosing a cheque to cover Sam's food for a few weeks. Mr Garbutt was still in hospital and she planned to remain with her daughter in London for the time being. Jane sat at the table looking at the letter, wondering. She had often thought of the deep freeze in the Garbutts' garage and how the garage key was left out for the gardener, under a stone beneath the rainwater tub. She knew that Mrs Garbutt had a well-stocked freezer. She was nervous of driving to the shops on her own and so she filled it with ready-prepared meals and small packs of meat and vegetables.

Jane wasn't sure which days the gardener was there—he seemed to suit himself now the house was empty—and so she decided to visit after dark, being careful what she took: one chicken joint, a small pack of mince, some stewing steak, two fish cakes. She rearranged the sections so that they looked only slightly depleted. She didn't think of it as stealing. One day, when things are better, she told herself, when summer work is to be had, I can

321

put all this back.

Of course, that day never came.

*   *   *

Jane woke suddenly with a beating heart. There was a baby crying and she sat bolt upright with a gasp of fear, but, thank goodness, a moment later she realised where she was, in Florence's flat, and the baby was Tintin. She lay back on the pillows. It was the dream. She had been in the grip of the terrible dream again and it was so fresh in her mind that it had been like living through the terror first-hand.

She looked at her watch in the pale morning light and saw that it was six o'clock. She must lie still for a while and try to shake off the residual fear and dread and reassure herself that all that was in the past. It was obvious that being here with Florence and the baby had triggered the nightmare but it alarmed her that it was all still there in her mind in every vivid detail. Why hadn't the happiness of the intervening years wiped away the fear? Was she never going to be able to put it behind her?

Tash had once told her, herself undergoing cognitive therapy at the time, that she had never worked through the full consequences of what happened, that until she was prepared to open up, the trauma would remain with her, but Jane did not hold with that view. She saw it as her duty to protect those she loved with secrecy, and not visit her past upon them. They were innocent. If her punishment was to be tormented by dreams, so be it. But then the nightmares had dwindled and

322

stopped and she had been left in peace until recently, when they were back with a vengeance. Tintin's birth had brought her joy and a new closeness with Florence but it seemed that she must still be reminded of how much she had once let her down.

After a while she felt sufficiently calm to close her eyes and drift back to sleep, and when she woke again it was broad daylight and Chipper was touching her hand with his nose, and she realised that the fear had left her and she was completely herself once more.

Florence was cheerful too. Tintin had had a good night, waking at two and six o'clock.

'I never knew what it would be like—this lack of proper sleep,' she said, wolfing down a bowl of cornflakes. 'I'm only getting three hours between feeds, but it's so much better than it was. I feel only half human, though. I don't think I could drive a car, for instance, or hold any sort of intelligent conversation.'

'You get used to it,' said Jane, passing her daughter a mug of tea, but thinking that age had a lot to do with it. It was easier when you were very young. 'Why don't you go back to bed for an hour or two after Tintin has had his bath and feed?'

'I might just do that. What will you do?'

'I'll tidy up a bit and put some washing on and then I'll do a bit of cooking. It would be nice to have a pot of soup for when Tash comes. I'll take Chipper for a good walk later on.'

*　　　*　　　*

It was after lunch before Jane could get out. It was

quite warm again and she felt it was good to be out and to take lungfuls of the fresh air and walk fast, swinging her arms. Chipper deserved a proper walk—he had been so good—and she wanted time on her own to think about Tash, who would by now be on her way to join them.

She walked further than usual to where the canal inched sluggishly past some still derelict buildings and the bank was overgrown with brambles and nettles. She noticed there was a gang of youths ahead; 'hoodies', lounging around a bench with some bicycles thrown down on the path. There were four or five of them, taking drugs or sniffing glue or something, Jane thought, and she regretted walking along in a dream. Chipper had trotted on and was already approaching them suspiciously and two had noticed him and were pretending to be frightened, jumping on the bench and flapping their arms.

'Chipper!' she shouted. 'Chipper! Come here!'

Chipper hesitated and looked back at her, and then turned again to survey the youths.

'He's all right!' Jane shouted, hurrying on. 'He won't hurt you!' But something was going on. There was a flurry of movement that she could not really distinguish, a struggle of some sort, shouting, and then a loud splash.

Instinctively, Jane started to run. Now the boys were picking up broken bricks and lobbing them into the violently churning water. There was laughter and jeering. Jane knew that something horrible was happening. Was it Chipper in the water? Then she saw him again on the bank and he was barking and agitated, and she realised that there was a boy in the canal, floundering and trying to get to his feet, dripping with weed, and toppling backwards under the hail of missiles. 'Stop it!' she shouted. 'Stop that! Leave him alone!'

She was close now and she could see them properly. They were old enough to have stubble on their chins; tall, lanky youths with baggy jeans that hung off their hips. 'What are you doing?' she shouted and hearing the alarm in her voice Chipper became defensive, making little dashes at the boys, his hackles up, his teeth bared.

That did it. Laughing and falling over each other, they loped away, picking up the bikes, turning to shout abuse, kick out at Chipper, or scoop a stone to throw into the canal.

Jane arrived at the point on the bank nearest the boy in the water. He was crouching at the edge among the reeds, young and frightened, wreathed with bright green, spongy-looking weed. He was coughing and crying at the same time. He was just a terrified teenager.

'It's all right!' cried Jane. 'They've gone. I'll help you. Here, give me your hand.'

*   *   *

Tash was on her way. It had been hard to get free of Denby, who was still overdoing the caring husband role, bless him, and could hardly bear to let her out of his sight. His guilt was touching. His various indiscretions had been painful at the time, occasionally bringing their marriage to the brink of destruction, but she had the wisdom to see how valuable she was to him, and how enduring was their love. Imperfect, but enduring. She had to allow him to fuss, to speak of her with welling eyes, because he meant every word and it was important to allow him the distinction of caring for her now.

She had played the whole cancer thing down madly with the children and they had been surprisingly easy to placate. She had overwhelmed them with positive statistics and although both the girls had wept—they were still at the age where they saw themselves at the centre of every drama—they were able to smile weakly by the time she left them. Probably deciding what to wear at my funeral, thought Tash, fondly.

Now it was Jane she wanted and needed, and en route she was going to visit Aunt Joan. There was unfinished business that she would like to see to before she went under the knife on Monday. It was a silly, slightly hysterical way to react to her illness, but Tash knew that the impulse to put things right was strong in her. She liked things to be tidy. 'Sorted!' was one of her most used expressions.

Aunt Joan, she had shoved to one side for years and years. She didn't have the time or the interest to think about her too much, but the web of family connection held her more strongly than she had bargained for, and now that she had been forced to look at her life as an entity, there were things that she wanted to know, and forgiveness that she felt she needed to extend and receive.

All the months that she and Denby had been in India, Aunt Joan had supported Jane, and Tash had never thanked or acknowledged her for that. She might be a desiccated old maid but she had never been chillingly narrow-minded in the way that their mother had been. She needed to know about her mother too, and Aunt Joan was the only person alive who could help her. The necessity to understand seemed pressing because Tash felt that the day that she was booked into the clinic was like a deadline. She wanted her life to be in order by that date.

Since she had received the news from her specialist she seemed to have become both calm and impulsive in turn, and it was the latter that made her insist that she would take her aunt for an excursion, a trip in her car to meet her great-great-nephew.

'I will bring her back tonight!' she told the care home manager. 'Don't worry! I'll look after her, and she will be in good hands. Three of the family are doctors.'

Aunt Joan made no protest at all. She expressed surprise to see Tash, who had not visited her for three years, and allowed herself to be put into her warm jacket and helped out to the large comfortable car in the car park.

'You would like it, wouldn't you?' insisted Tash. 'To see Tintin? To visit Florence?' She couldn't wait to be outside in the fresh air. She felt stifled in the enclosed, heated atmosphere of the home, which seemed to deaden the mind and the body. Too much like bloody hospital, she thought.

It was a slow process, tottering to the car, and getting Aunt Joan into the front seat and the seat belt done up. The old woman peered into the daylight like an underground creature brought into the light. Her face was surprisingly unlined, just crumpled and fuzzy with age, and her once vigorous hair was lustreless and dry and sparse, revealing pink, baby-like scalp.

Tash was not dismayed by any of this. When you were that old, what did you expect? What lasted for nearly ninety years without showing its age? And she admired her aunt's large, practical hands, her strong grasp and her beady eye. There's not much that gets past you, old girl, she thought, admiringly.

'Jane told me,' said Aunt Joan, when they turned out of the drive, 'she told me that you have cancer.'

There you are, thought Tash. So many people could not bring themselves even to say the dreaded word.

'Yes. It's a bore,' said Tash, instantly thinking, what a ridiculous thing to say. A bore is the one thing it's not. It was quite exciting, in a way. Exhilarating almost, like a project or a challenge— all the things she enjoyed. At this stage anyway, before the ghastly treatments began.

'I told Jane that your mother thought she had cancer. She was booked in to have a lump removed when they got back from France. She was ill-advised to go. The specialist wanted her to have immediate surgery but she wouldn't. She wanted that last holiday, she said.'

'Jane told me,' said Tash. 'It's strange to think I'm going through the same thing. Only mine is for real. For goodness' sake, we shared little enough when she was alive.'

'You are not unalike.'

'What?' Tash shot a glare at her aunt as she drove. The old bat always managed to annoy her. 'Nobody could be less alike! We were at daggers drawn most of the time.'

'That doesn't prove anything. Often people who are alike don't get on.'

'Well, in what ways, then? Tell me that!'

'Strength. Obstinacy. Tenacity. Loyalty. Determination to get what you want.'

'Hmm.' Tash was not sure how she felt about this list. You could say the same about Hitler or any other despot or tyrant. 'I see. Well, I suppose I can't argue with that. I just hope that we use these qualities differently.'

'Yes. You do. Eileen's were all directed towards controlling and possessing Timothy.'

'You're so bitter about them, aren't you? About their marriage? You have always talked about it as if it was a personal affront.'

It was Aunt Joan's turn to be silent. The atmosphere in the car bristled with hostility. This was a mistake, thought Tash. Why on earth did I think it would be a good idea? Rancour and bitterness were the last things she needed now.

'I found it hard to forgive my sister. I knew Timothy first, not that he would have looked at me romantically—I was a plain, awkward girl with no style, unlike your mother—but we formed a true friendship. She put a stop to that. You knew your father well enough. He was charming, but weak. She manipulated him. Finally, of course, she killed him.'

*   *   *

The stealing couldn't go on. Jane knew it in her heart, but she did not allow herself to stop and think about it. The village was too small for people not to exchange gossip, and one particularly bleak March day as she was out searching for milk she found a hand-written note pinned to the gate of a house from which she had previously lifted a bottle. 'WATCH OUT,' it warned in large capital letters, 'THERE'S A THIEF ABOUT!'

Jane felt a spasm of shock and disbelief. A thief! She was described as a thief! It was only a bottle of milk from a doorstep, for goodness' sake. Now she did not dare take another. She felt watched and under suspicion from every door she passed, although when she met a woman coming out of her house a few yards on, the woman smiled and said, looking at Florence, 'What a pretty little girl!' Florence was sitting up now, and had two teeth, and waved her hands and banged the wooden spoon Jane had given her to play with against the side of the pram.

'Thank you!' said Jane, but tugged at Sam's lead to pass on quickly.

'Are you the girl living next to the Garbutts? That's their dog, isn't it?' persisted the woman.

'Yes,' said Jane, feeling her face go hot under her beret, which she had pulled down round her ears.

'Someone was talking about you the other day. I'm trying to remember where I was . . .' The woman had a pleasant open face. 'Oh, I know! It was the district nurse. Margaret Clegg. She's a friend of mine. She mentioned you lived on your own. She didn't think you had made many friends. I said I'd call round one day, or have you for coffee. My children are all at school now but I can remember what it was like to be at home with a new baby. Not that she's new any longer, are you, darling?'

Jane could not meet the woman's eye. She coughed and pulled a tissue out of her pocket for something to do. 'Thank you,' she said, awkwardly.

330

Was this a trick? She didn't trust the nurse. She made her feel inadequate and guilty for being a single mother. Her enquiries about Florence always seemed coloured by suspicion. It made Jane feel as if she was on her mother's side; that she thought Florence should have been adopted.

'I'm Gilly, by the way. Gilly Forrest. I'm off to work today, so I can't ask you for a cup of coffee now, but maybe one day next week?'

'I'm not sure,' said Jane, panicking, feeling cornered. 'I might be away. I might be staying with my sister.'

'Well, call in when you're passing, if you like. You're always out pushing that pram, aren't you? I've seen you quite far afield.'

'It's the dog,' said Jane, defensively. 'I have to walk the dog.'

The woman laughed. 'There's no law against it! This isn't the friendliest of villages,' she added as she got into her car. 'I lived here for two years before anyone spoke to me!'

Jane walked on, regretting the conversation and still feeling shaken by the warning on the gate. When she reached the village green she sat on a bench overlooking the cricket pitch. The wind was from the east and bitterly cold. There seemed to be no sign of spring, and the grass was greyish, tired-looking and littered with twigs and dead leaves. It was hard to remember that first day when she came to Sussex with Hugh and there was a match going on in the dreamy summer sunshine.

She looked across at the pub, which was no longer an emergency source of food. The car park had been tidied up and the bins were now locked in a yard of newly erected fence panels. She hadn't seen the young cook for weeks. Perhaps he had left.

What can I do, she thought. I can't go on like this. She ticked people off on her fingers. Her father? No. He had said that he could not help her although she knew her parents would do anything for her as long as she gave up Florence. Aunt Joan? No. Jane had given her her word that she would not ask for support. Aunt Joan had done enough for her already. Hugh? She didn't even have his current address or telephone number. Hugh had disappeared in the vortex of student dissent. He certainly wouldn't have a spare penny. Tash? Tash would do whatever she could, but Jane felt a reluctance to ask for help and she knew that currently Tash and Denby were very hard up for cash and working every hour that God gave. Mr Kowalski? He was the only one who might send her some money—a small loan to see her over this crisis. It would have to be to him that she turned.

The red telephone box was on the other side of the green. Jane parked the pram and rearranged Florence's cap and woolly gloves. It was really too cold to have a baby out for so long, but she felt driven by desperation. Unless she got some money over the next few days, she didn't know what she would do. She had another electricity bill to pay and there was very little food. There was enough for Florence—she would never let her go short—but she herself would have to go hungry and her hunger was terrible, raging and ravenous. She couldn't sleep at night she was so hungry, and she was terrified that she would get ill and she would be unable to look after Florence.

She took off her clumsy woollen mittens and

332

dialled the number for the bookshop. It rang and rang, unanswered. She checked her watch, puzzled. Mr Kowalski should be there, sitting in the back room poring over his catalogue of titles. She tried again. Still no answer. She stood in the box, trying to think what to do, and then it occurred to her that she could ring the premises next door, the funny old-fashioned ironmongers. Mr Kowalski often passed the time of day with Mr and Mrs Barker, a tall, bald man in long brown overalls, and his tiny, busy, darting wife. Jane found the number from Directory Enquiries and, feeding more pennies into the slot, dialled again. This time the call was answered almost immediately.

'Hello!' she said, anxiety making her voice rise on a childish note. 'This is Jane, Mr Kowalski's last assistant. I have been trying to get through to him at the bookshop but there's no reply. I wondered if you knew where he was, or if there is something wrong?'

'Oh, dear,' said Mrs Barker, 'didn't you know? Mr Kowalski passed away last week. We've just got back from his funeral, Mr Barker and me. There was no one there but us and a few from the Catholic church. Very sudden, it was, although as I said to my husband, he'd gone downhill ever so much lately.'

Jane had to replace the receiver without speaking. Sudden tears filled her throat. She pressed her forehead against the cold glass of the telephone box. For the first time in her life she felt overwhelming sadness for someone other than herself. She wept for the friend she had lost, the tragedy of his life and for that little girl in the creased black-and-white photograph. She wept for her mother and her unborn child, whom Mr Kowalski had never held in his arms. She wept because now there was no one left to remember them. She wept because she felt she had let him down.

* * *

That evening she went to raid the Garbutts' freezer for the last time.

* * *

'What on earth do you mean?' demanded Tash. Was Aunt Joan suffering from dementia that she could make such a wild claim? But she looked perfectly composed and rather satisfied that her words had caused such a reaction.

'Didn't it ever occur to you? I have always been convinced that Eileen was driving on the evening of the accident. They had been out to dinner, hadn't they, to some very special restaurant in the mountains? That was so much her style—always stage-managing things, insisting on romance. No doubt Timothy drank too much. He did at that time, and no wonder. It was the only way to escape the pressure she put on him. After dinner, she would have driven back to the hotel. She was an excellent driver, if you remember. The winding road, those legendary hairpin bends wouldn't have bothered her.'

'They never established who had been driving, did they? It was always assumed it was Father. Didn't the lorry driver say it was someone in a panama hat?'

334

'Yes, he did, but that doesn't mean anything. Your mother often wore Timothy's hats. She knew they suited her.'

'Does it make any difference, if it was her? It was an accident. It hardly matters now.'

'I don't believe it was an accident. I never have.'

'Hang on. I'm going to find somewhere to stop. I can't drive and listen to all this!'

She's completely barking, Tash thought as she pulled into a layby beside the road. Her mind is wandering. Jane said she sometimes imagines she's back in the Home Office.

'So, what are you saying?' she asked when the car came to a stop and she turned off the engine. She looked at her aunt, who was quite unruffled, staring ahead, her face set in its long, horsy expression. Her large hands lay still in the lap of her skirt.

'It was the cancer. She was quite convinced that this lump they had found was malignant. The moment she and Timothy got back she was booked into hospital to have it removed, and perhaps a mastectomy. It was a very radical procedure back then—disfiguring, leaving terrible scars. She had told Timothy but no one else knew apart from me. She couldn't bear the thought of ill health or ageing, especially not fighting a disease that robs you of your feminine allure. I think she thought it was better to die in rather a splendid and dramatic way, enjoying life to the end, and taking Timothy with her. An accident on that particular road would almost certainly be fatal and could happen without involving anyone else. The lorry driver was completely unhurt, just shocked by the car coming round the bend and swerving over the edge at one

335

of the steepest places.'

'She couldn't have done that!' exclaimed Tash. 'No one could plan something like that!' but as she said it, she thought, yes, she could. She had that sort of steely resolve.

'She could not bear the thought of dying and leaving Timothy. She knew it would not be long before he was comforted by some pretty woman or other.' Aunt Joan's tone was contemptuous. 'I think it makes perfect sense.'

Tash sat looking out of the window trying to separate her feelings. The crash had been a terrible shock and although she had not been close to her parents, to lose them both like that had been a dreadful thing to deal with. Dreadful, and traumatic, but not unbearable. She had her own family, her own worries, her business. Of course she had grieved, especially for her father, and missed him for years afterwards, but it had not been a tragedy in the true sense. Not like losing a child, or as if something had happened to Denby or Jane.

Could her mother really have planned and executed such a thing? She remembered the remarkable orderliness of her parents' affairs. How the solicitor handling their wills had praised their foresight and organisation, with everything neatly filed and labelled, but that was her father's doing, surely, not her mother's?

She tried to imagine what her mother would have felt about the possibility of cancer. She thought of her immaculate appearance: well groomed, beautifully dressed, her shapely legs in smooth stockings and polished court shoes, her slim wrists jangling with charm bracelets, her manicured hands with painted nails. She could not conjure up any memory of her face or her voice, so it was like seeing in her mind a well known and instantly recognisable model or film star; someone whose appearance was the key to their identity.

She would have loathed the indignity of illness. She would have been terrified of losing her looks and Aunt Joan was right about how she would not have wished Timothy to have a life without her.

What sort of love was it that could destroy the loved one? It was as savage and as dangerous as jealousy or rage or any of the other motivators of dreadful crimes of passion. How could it even be called love? And yet her mother had truly worshipped her husband. He was the centre of her life. But it was a selfish love that ensnared and couldn't let go. It was a controlling and utterly possessive love. It had been the same with her and Jane. Eileen had wanted to control their lives.

Tash thought of how she had broken free because she knew she had to. Even when she was quite young she had known that her mother did not have her true interests at heart and that if she wanted a life of her own she had to leave. And look what had happened to poor Jane. What perversion of mother love was it that could cast her out when she most needed help and support?

'I can see it was possible,' she said at last. 'I can see that. It's a horrible and disturbing thought, but I can see it could be true.'

Aunt Joan stirred in her seat. 'It's far too long ago to matter,' she said. 'But I believe she took Timothy's life as much as if she had stabbed him with a kitchen knife. And unnecessarily, as it turned out.'

'It does matter,' said Tash, speaking slowly and resting her head on the steering wheel. 'It does matter because Jane and I are her flesh and blood. It's like how the offspring of alcoholics are always counting their drinks. You've already said I'm like her in some ways. For God's sake, you kindly listed all the qualities we share. It makes a difference to how I think of myself, and it will make a difference to Jane as well. It's a warning. I don't mean we are either of us likely to do anyone in, but it tells us something about loving wrongly and selfishly.'

And Jane, she thought. Dear Jane. Gentle and unassuming, and yet look what happened when she had to fight for Florence.

'You probably imagine,' said Aunt Joan, moving her mouth as if she were chewing a toffee, 'that I know nothing about life or love. Arrogance is another of your qualities, I am afraid. I understand that it's easy to imagine a dull, plain woman like myself, unmarried, with an overdeveloped sense of her own importance, as being forever unloved and unlovable. But such women have as many romantic yearnings as anyone else. They feel no differently, you know. The need to love and be loved is just as strong. They may be more tentative about their feelings, less confident, less ambitious, with lower expectations, but they can love, hopelessly or otherwise, with just as much passion, despair, joy, as you who are fortunate enough to be born beautiful.'

'Oh! Yes . . . well, OK!' said Tash, surprised and defensive. Where was this all leading?

'I loved, intensely, as it happens, for most of my adult life. First your father. Later, a man for whom I worked for many years. He was married and

338

utterly unattainable but I offered him something that was in short supply at home—uncritical, undemanding devotion. He used to come to my flat perhaps once a week, right up until his retirement, when all that had to stop. Except, of course, when I had Jane living with me.'

Tash drove on. She was speechless with surprise, and anyhow did not know what was appropriate to say. The small glimpse of her aunt's unknown and unexpected private life had opened in front of her and she felt bewildered by the revelation.

It was true what Aunt Joan said. She would never have dreamed that the ugly, bad-tempered old woman had ever known what it was to love—to have been in any way a sexual being. She still couldn't quite believe it now. She thought of the lover, imagining a heavy, important-looking man in a three-piece suit. She could picture Aunt Joan making him a cup of tea, handing it to him with a custard cream biscuit balanced on the saucer. She could imagine her kneeling at his feet and tenderly removing his polished black shoes, but she couldn't think of any services beyond that.

But she was glad that Aunt Joan had known what love was like, and sorry that it had been a lost cause. She ventured to say as much but Aunt Joan snapped back, 'Don't be sorry! It suited me very well. He wasn't an easy man. I shouldn't have wanted to live with him. In fact, I felt quite sorry for his wife.'

It made Tash smile. Was love always such a complex thing? On the one hand, a product of selfishness and self-regard, and on the other, devotion and sacrifice? She thought of her friends and how the least selfish and most understanding

339

of wives sometimes seemed to derive a sort of smug self-satisfaction at being so worthy, and what about those downtrodden and betrayed wives of politicians, standing so bravely at the sides of their cheating husbands? They surely got their kicks from forgiving, and being put on a pedestal by the bastards who had been caught screwing their secretaries? For that matter, what about her and Denby? She had chosen to stay with him, and he with her, out of a mixture of habit and dread of family upheaval, amongst other things. Their marriage was a balance of need and dependency and yet they both thought of it as love that held them together.

The journey had not turned out as she had expected and they drove in silence for some minutes. When she glanced at her aunt again she saw that she had fallen asleep, her chin on her bony chest. She had delivered enough salvos to tire her out.

Tash drove on, thinking of what she had said, remembering that she had denied her lover for the months that Jane was living with her. That was unselfish, she thought. That was bloody unselfish.

*   *   *

'She's been gone for ages,' said Florence to Tash. 'She took that awful old dog of hers along the canal. She said she would only be ten minutes or so.' She passed Tash a mug of coffee. 'Thank you for all of this stuff!' She indicated the two champagne bottles on the counter, the packs of smoked salmon, the cool box of fillet steaks from an expensive organic butcher, the bag of early

340

vegetables from Denby's polytunnel. 'Mum was going to go to the supermarket. She doesn't have to now.'

Tash put her arm through that of her niece. 'I'd rate Tintin a five-star baby,' she said. 'Jane told me he was beautiful but I thought she might have been wearing her granny specs, but he is. He really is, and you look good too. How are you doing, babe? You gonna make it?'

'Yeah, I think so. I feel bloody awful some of the time but mostly I'm much better now. Mum's been amazing. She's got the little tyrant into something like a routine and I'm not so terrified now if he cries. Ha's been pretty fabulous too. I suppose I wondered how hands-on he would want to be, but he loves him, you know, he really does, and he's very good with him now hc's got a bit used to it all. He changes nappies like a pro.'

'That's good,' said Tash. 'It doesn't always happen like that. I think people underestimate the business of coming to terms with the first baby.'

'Nothing,' said Flo vehemently, 'but *nothing*, can prepare you for it. Not any number of prenatal classes or baby manuals.'

'Of course not. It's one of the few really life-altering events,' said Tash, thinking that birth and death were in so many ways still a mystery. There was a lot of surface activity and fuss surrounding them, but not much real understanding. Maybe that's what I'm looking for, she thought suddenly. Something calm and spiritual and unfashionable. Perhaps she should become a Quaker. She imagined sitting silently in a whitewashed chapel, and feeling the peace of surrender. It would be such a relief to feel that there was Someone

341

organising things better than she could.

'Look at Aunt Joan rapping with her great-great-nephew!' said Florence, turning to the sitting room. Aunt Joan, who had been manhandled between them up the stairs to Florence's flat, was now enthroned in a leather armchair with her feet up on an improvised footstall. Tintin was awake in his Moses basket by her side. They appeared to find each other mutually fascinating.

'How about you, Tash?' Florence put her arms round her aunt, who was so small and seemed so frail, despite the youthful brightness of her clothes and the animation of her face.

'I go in on Monday for the op and I'll know much more afterwards, obviously, but at the moment they are all very optimistic, and so am I.'

'You should be. If the lymph nodes are clear, you can expect a normal lifespan. Even for the most aggressive types of cancer the survival rates are improving.'

'Yes, I know. Enzo told me. He gave me all the figures. He's been great too.'

'He telephoned just before you arrived to say that he's coming tonight, when he finishes in theatre. I'm longing to see him, to show him his grandson.' Flo used the term with no artifice or pretence.

'I don't expect we'll still be here. I'll have to get the old girl back. I can't very well push her up the fire escape after midnight.' They both smiled.

'She was good to your mother, you know,' said Tash, in an altered tone. 'She was really good to her when she was expecting you. She told me the most astonishing thing on the way here. I'm still trying to work it all out in my head.'

'What? What did she tell you?' Tash hesitated and Florence glanced at her great-aunt, now soundly asleep, and said, 'She can't hear you. She's out for the count.'

'She told me that she has always believed that our mother deliberately drove off that road in the South of France. She thought that she had cancer and so she decided to take her life, and our father's too. It's a preposterous story, but it does make sense on one level. She hated getting older and the thought of breast cancer would have horrified her. All that I can see. Whether she had the guts to kill herself and our father is another matter. She was terribly possessive of him and I can see that she wouldn't have wanted him to live without her, so it does make sense, but it's pretty mind-blowing all the same.'

'Jesus! You'll never know, will you? You'll just have to arrive at whatever seems the most likely truth.'

'Yes. It takes some getting used to, though. I don't know what Jane will think. She also told me something else—that she had had a lover for years and years! A very well-kept secret, that one! I would never have thought it possible!'

'Well! To be honest she is so old, and always has been in my eyes, that I can't imagine it, but good luck to her, I say!'

'Exactly, but what secrets to hang on to all these years!'

'You can never be sure that you really know people, can you? They only let you see what they want. There's always something hidden, kept to themselves. It needn't be anything dramatic. It could just be private thoughts that they would never tell even their nearest and dearest.'

Tash looked out at the slice of green canal from the kitchen window and thought of Jane. What Florence had just said was so near the truth. 'Your mother,' she began, 'has she ever told you what happened when you were a baby?'

'What do you mean, "happened"? She told me that her decision to keep me wasn't very popular.'

'Hmm. That's quite an understatement, you know.'

Florence shrugged. 'Yeah, well. It was different in those days. More shocking, I suppose. Sure, it must have been difficult.'

'You should ask her. You should get her to tell you.'

'I don't want to. What's the point? I don't need to hear what a hard time she had. I mean, what am I supposed to do about it? We have talked about it, actually. I told her I was sorry that I used to hold it against her. Oh, come on, Aunt Tash, you know what I mean. I was a resentful brat.'

'It's not that. It's not about *you*, Florence. This is about her. She's carried a burden of secrecy since then and I wish she would tell you. Enzo too.'

'What are you talking about?' Florence shook her head in bewilderment.

'I can't tell you. It's up to her.'

'Are you going to tell me that she really knows who my father is? I've *always* thought that she did, that she was keeping it a secret on purpose.'

'No, nothing like that. I'm sorry, Florence, maybe I shouldn't have said anything. It's not for me to tell you. Ask her. I should.'

'She'll have to tell me now! It's not fair for you to have told me this much, for goodness' sake. It makes me feel uneasy.'

'Just ask her,' said Tash, wondering what she had started, but not regretting it. 'I might just go along the path and see if I can find her. I'd like a little walk. Do you mind if I leave you with Aunt Joan?'

'Of course not. She's not exactly demanding company. When she wakes up perhaps she'll start giving me some hot sex tips! Nothing seems unlikely any more.'

'Do you want me to take Tintin in his buggy? I was always grateful when anyone offered to take my babies away for an hour or two. I was almost able to believe that I was myself again.'

Florence smiled. 'I know what you mean. Yeah, well, that would be great. I could go and have a shower. I need to change my clothes about six times a day. His Imperial Highness shouldn't need a feed for a while. I'll take the buggy down for you. You need a degree in engineering to work out how to put it together.'

Ten minutes later, Tash was pushing Tintin along the towpath. It was the dead time of the afternoon when few people were about. It was too early for mothers with school-age children and too early for people wanting to take a stroll after work.

There was no sign of Jane or Chipper. Now the canal path narrowed and the banks were overgrown. Regeneration had not got this far and the buildings on either side were broken down and roofless, with windows that were jagged holes. As she walked Tash thought of her conversation with Florence and wondered if she had said enough, or too much. Just because she felt she wanted to put her life straight did not mean that Jane would want her interfering in hers. Well, it was too late now. She had set Florence on the trail like a bloodhound.

Ahead there were some broken trees and two figures sitting on a bench and then she saw it was Jane, talking to someone, and she quickened her step and called out, 'Jane! Jane!' Tintin woke with a little start and began to cry.

*   *   *

Jane saw Tash coming and jumped up. Involuntarily, awkwardly, the sisters ran towards each other: Jane, middle-aged and flat-footed, Tash trundling the buggy and the crying Tintin in front of her. They met and embraced, arms tight round each other, heads buried in the other's shoulders with Chipper right beside them, wagging his tail, wanting to be included.

'I'm so glad to see you.'

'Me too.'

'How are you? How *are* you?'

'I'm all right. Really. He's a lovely baby. Flo seems OK. No, more than that—Flo seems *fine*.'

'Yes, yes. Things are better. Ha wants to marry her!'

'He does? Wonderful! Has he asked her?'

'Not yet. He's waiting for his moment. But, *really*, how are you?'

Slowly they walked back towards the bench on which the young man still sat, watching them from under the edge of his hood.

'This is Quasim, Tash. I've just met him. We were talking about things. He'd been thrown into the canal by his cousin's gang. I helped him out.'

346

'As one does,' said Tash, taking in the youth, his sodden clothes, his downtrodden expression.

'He's been telling me about his life,' said Jane, her face animated by compassion.

Quasim got up, his trainers squelching green slime. 'I'm off, then,' he said. 'Thank you, and all that.'

'Take care!' said Jane. 'Really, it was all true what I told you.'

'Yeah, OK. Cool, man,' and the youth shambled away.

'What was all that about?' said Tash, tucking her arm into Jane's. 'Little sister, little saint.'

'You used to call me Little Mother,' said Jane. 'Do you remember?'

'Yes, of course I do.'

'That boy has had a terrible start in life. He's illiterate and has never had a job and been in trouble with the police. He was in prison last year.'

'So what were you tclling him?'

'About me,' said Jane simply.

CHAPTER FOURTEEN

Nothing could have been worse than that night. It was pitch-dark and blowing hard. Jane was terrified by the sound the wind made as it roared down the lane. The hedges seemed to rear and heave on either side as if something wild and furious was trying to break through. Fallen branches went skewing across the road and under her boots there was a litter of twigs and stones washed down by the earlier rain. It was hard work

347

pushing the pram into the wind and she had to bend her head and use all her strength.

She'd left the dog at home. It was easier without him in the dark and she hadn't far to go. She was nearly there now. The double gates were open, which was strange. The wind must have forced the catch that held them closed.

She knew where to go. She didn't need the torch, but the dark, looming house frightened her, and when she stepped out of the wind it was worse, listening to it howling through the trees at the back.

She had the key ready in her pocket and the door opened smoothly. The light switch was just to the right. Her fingers felt across the rough cement and it was a relief to turn it on and be able to see again, everything familiar and in its place, and to bang the door shut on the wild night.

She had opened the freezer lid, with her back to the door, when she heard a sudden noise and turning round, her heart leaping, she saw Mrs Garbutt on the steps from the house.

'Caught you red-handed!' she cried. 'I knew someone was stealing from the deep freeze as soon as I looked into it this evening. You're a thief. You're not fit to have a baby. It's a disgrace!'

Jane leaped round and in her panic made the mistake of trying to flee but Mrs Garbutt had taken hold of the pram. 'No, you're staying here. I'm calling the police!' Her pouchy face was contorted with anger. 'What else have you stolen? What else have you helped yourself to?'

Jane yanked the handle from her grasp and pushed it violently away from her. 'Let go! Let Florence go!' she cried. She rammed the pram at

the outside door, which swung open, but Mrs
Garbutt was grabbing at her. Jane pushed against
her with all her might and the elderly woman, off
balance, took a step back, tottered and fell.

Then Jane was running through the crashing
night the way she had come, a sob of fear in her
throat. The pram careered along the pitch-dark
lane, jolting and bouncing. She must get back to
the cottage and lock herself in from the terror of
the neighbouring house and a few minutes later
she was there, fumbling with the front door key
and shoving the pram through into the hall. She
slammed the door behind her, shot the bolt, and
with a racing heart ran to snatch the curtains
across all the windows. Sam was barking from the
kitchen and Jane threw the door open and pushed
the pram inside. Trembling, she crouched in the
armchair while Sam slobbered at her hand in
ecstatic welcome.

What now? What should she do now? She must
think. She must stay calm. She buried her face on
the top of Sam's head and folded his long ears
against her cheeks.

She was home, but she wasn't safe. Mrs Garbutt.
What had happened to her? She had seen her fall,
but what then? Was she already telephoning the
police? Maybe she was hurt, lying in a pool of
blood? She could be dead, even. If she was dead,
then she, Jane, was a murderess. But no one would
know what had happened. It would seem that the
old lady had stumbled down the steps. Jane wished
with all her heart that she was dead. If she was
dead, then everything would be all right. But what
if she wasn't? What if she was just lying there,
injured? Jane couldn't leave her, on her own, in

pain, her heart full of anger and fear.

She would have to go back. She would. There was no other way. She would have to go back to the garage and if she was still there, lying in a heap at the bottom of the steps, she must get help. Jane's hands shook and her breath still came in little, exaggerated gasps but Florence was peacefully asleep. She would leave her here, in the kitchen with Sam. She would creep back on her own. No one would see her. Maybe, if Mrs Garbutt was all right, uninjured, she could plead with her, explaining that she had only taken what she needed, only small amounts, and that she would pay her back.

She stood up and hesitated for a moment. She knew, in her heart, that something irreversible had taken place and that now she was just being swept along by circumstance. Like someone cast into a torrent she must find something to cling to, to save herself.

She kissed Florence's warm cheek and slipped a finger into her little half-clasped fist. 'Sam, you look after her,' she said, kneeling beside the dog who whined, made nervous by the tension. He followed her to the door, wanting to be with her, and she had to shove him back with her knee as she slipped out.

She ran as fast as she could back up the lane to the house. It was still in darkness and the gates were open but from under the garage door there shone a sliver of light. Jane felt her way to the back until she reached the door. Very gently she turned the handle and pushed. The door moved a little and she peered in.

Mrs Garbutt was where she had last seen her,

crumpled on the bottom of the steps. Jane went in and crouched by her side. Oh my God, she thought. She was either unconscious or dead. She couldn't tell which. It was hard to tell if she was breathing. Please be dead, she thought. But she wasn't. She rolled her head to one side and began to breathe loudly in a frightening rasp, and her arm twitched.

What now? She mustn't move her, she knew that, even though she was lying so awkwardly with one leg buckled beneath her. Her face had a whitish blue tinge and there was spittle collected at the corner of her mouth.

She must telephone for an ambulance, find a rug to cover her, sit with her until help arrived. She stood up and went to the door to the house, which opened onto a utility room off the kitchen, with washing machine and drier and a tidy row of coats. There would be a telephone in the kitchen, surely. She pushed open the next door and saw a wall-mounted telephone above a row of units.

First she must speak to Tash. With fumbling fingers she dialled the number. Please let her be in, she prayed, and then she heard her voice and it was such a relief that she couldn't talk for a moment and Tash was saying, 'Hello? Hello? Who is it?'

'It's me,' she whispered. 'Tash, it's me, Jane. Tash, you must come. Please come. You must come and take Florence.'

*   *   *

She went back to Mrs Garbutt with a bundle of coats and folded one under her head although she

351

did not want to touch what looked like a death mask with crisp grey hair and lipsticked mouth. She covered her with the others and then sat on the steps and waited, listening to her breathing and terrified that she would wake up.

When at last the ambulance came, Mrs Garbutt had regained consciousness but was bewildered and confused.

The ambulance men wanted to treat Jane as next of kin. 'No!' she said. 'I'm just a neighbour. I hardly know her. She has a daughter in London. You must contact her.' And in fact, Mrs Garbutt, lying on the stretcher, didn't appear to recognise who Jane was, and stared at her with a blank expression.

'Lives on her own, does she? She was lucky you found her,' said the ambulance man. 'She could have lain there for hours. Been a lot more serious for her, then.'

*   *   *

Tash came. She and Denby jumped into a car and drove straight down to Sussex. They arrived as dawn broke. Jane had already packed all of Florence's things, her toys and clothes, and they were stacked in the hall with the teddy bear she had bought her on the day Hugh had driven her to Yew Tree Cottage when she was ten days old.

They sat at the kitchen table and talked while the wind howled and banged outside, and Denby made tea and searched for something to eat.

'You must take her,' said Jane, her eyes sunk and staring in a chalk-white face. 'Take her now. Before the police come for me.' She went to the

352

pram and lifted out the baby, who snuffled in her sleep and stretched, without opening her eyes. She wrapped her tightly in her blanket and then held her out to her sister. Her face was a blank of anguish and Tash looked at her in great alarm.

'Go at once! I want her to be safe and out of this. I've written out everything: her routine, and all that. She'll drink milk now from a cup. There's nothing to eat, Denby, so there's no point in searching.'

'All right! I'll take her. When all this is sorted out in a day or two, we'll bring her back. We'll bring her back to you. Jane, do you hear me?'

Jane stood at the door watching Tash climb into the back of the little car with Florence in her arms. She looked so small and insignificant—nothing more than a little sleeping bundle—and yet she was the whole world.

Denby folded himself into the driving seat and then reversed and turned in the lane. Jane saw Tash's anxious face flash past for a moment, a raised hand, and then Florence was gone. She watched the bright taillights disappearing up the lane and then the darkness of the terrible night closed in again.

Now it was done, Jane went back to the kitchen and sat in the armchair with her arms round her knees. She was unable to cry or even think very much but every now and then her body was racked by violent shaking that rattled her teeth in her head. After a few minutes she realised that she couldn't be in the same room as the empty pram. She got up and pushed it into the hall, but even that did not seem separation enough, so she opened the front door and shoved it outside into the garden.

There. It was over now. In her heart she had known all along that she would be found wanting. Her mother was right. Before she sat down again to wait for whatever would happen next, she picked up the little plaid blanket from where it had been left on the kitchen table. It smelled of Florence and she held it to her face as a child would a comforter.

Sam crept up and put his head on her lap and then, with a sigh, flopped down by her side. She took no notice of him but was grateful to have his company. She was still sitting there, holding the blanket, when the police came in the morning.

She heard them knocking on the front door and rose to let them in with an expressionless face. When she saw the two policewomen she felt a sort of relief. It was as if she had been moving towards this moment for a long time. Now she could surrender, give up. She didn't care what happened to her as long as Florence was safe.

The two women constables followed her into the kitchen. They were not unkind, but firm and insistent in their questioning. One of them made coffee while the other sat opposite Jane and made notes in her notebook.

'We're going to have to take you into custody,' she said. 'Mrs Garbutt has made an accusation against you of theft and common assault. We need to take you in to make a statement under oath. We understand that you have a baby?'

Jane nodded.

'Is the father here?'

'She has no father.'

The two women exchanged glances. 'In that case

we will have to make arrangements with the social services to take her into care.'

'No you won't. She's not here any more. She's with my sister. I've sent her to my sister. She's looking after her.'

The policewoman gave her a long look. 'I'll need her name and address,' she said, and wrote it down. 'And the dog? It's not yours, I understand?'

'He's Mr Garbutt's dog. I expect the gardener would have him. For now, anyway.' Suddenly Jane felt terribly sorry for poor Sam. She had forgotten all about him.

The policewoman nodded. 'I've got his number here. We'll get in touch with him.'

She snapped shut her notebook. 'I'll give you ten minutes to get your things together. Is there anyone you want to speak to before we take you in?'

'No,' said Jane. 'No one.'

All the way to the police station she sat in the back of the car, dry-eyed and stony-faced. She had not asked after Mrs Garbutt and did not care. 'Remorseless,' the policewoman later described her in court and that was how she felt. The only things she cared about were Florence and the dog. She hadn't spent a minute apart from her baby since she was born and the pain of separation was like a physical wound.

When she was put into a cell and given a blanket, she lay curled up, facing the wall. In the cracked paint a few inches from her face, she saw an image of Florence. She saw her sitting in her high chair, laughing, banging her spoon, her eyes full of trust and confidence. In her head she heard her cries, louder, louder, more insistent, crying for her mother, crying because she was frightened and confused. The pain in her chest was so bad that Jane wondered if it was her heart that was breaking.

*   *   *

Some time later she was given a cup of tea and a sandwich, which she left untouched beside her bed, and then she heard a familiar voice. It was her mother, arguing with the policeman on duty. Ah, she thought bitterly. She comes to me now. Now I have lost Florence.

*   *   *

'What did you tell Quasim?' asked Tash, leaning back on the bench and closing her eyes in the afternoon sunshine.

'I told him that I'd been in prison for three months when I was his age. He couldn't believe I had been charged with unlawful entry and assault. He actually said, "Cool, man!"'

'Well, you're not exactly anyone's idea of a criminal.'

'No.'

This is the moment, thought Tash.

'You know, darling, I wonder how is it that you can tell a stranger, but not your daughter? Or your husband? It's time, Jane. It's time you told Florence. She is a mother herself now. She would understand.'

'I only told him because I've been thinking about it so much lately. I dream of that night. It comes back to me, Tash, as vividly as ever.'

356

'It comes back because you have shut it up inside you, as if you thought you could seal it over. It won't go away, you know.'

'Tash, I can't tell Florence! I have thought about it these last few days because we seem so much closer since Tintin was born, but *I can't*. She would think less of me than she does already.'

'But you will never be close if you keep the truth from her. It will always lie between you like an unexploded bomb. She senses that there is something that you're not telling. She thinks it's to do with the identity of her father. I agree there are some things better kept from people you love, things that they don't have to know, things that would cause them too much pain, but all the times Denby was cheating on me, what hurt more than the affair was the secrecy. There always came a point when I knew perfectly well what he was up to, and the fact that he was lying to me was the most hurtful thing of all.'

Jane sat with her head in her hands. 'That's totally different. Please, don't bully me. I can't do it. Not after all this time. How can I tell Enzo? We've been married for twenty-five years. He thinks he knows me.'

'Why would the truth change what he feels for you? I never really understood why you didn't tell him from the beginning.'

'Oh, Tash! Don't you remember how it was? I couldn't believe he had come into my life. It was like a miracle that here was this lovely man who wanted both me and Florence. I was terrified that if he knew I'd been in prison it would drive him away. He was working so hard to be a surgeon, to get established. I didn't have the courage to tell him.'

'He should know the truth.'

'I don't lie to him.'

'Yes, you do. What about going to San Francisco? You told him you couldn't go because you were worried about me. I know because he told me. That was a lie. Not that you're not worried about me, but that you couldn't go anyway. You wouldn't get into the States with a criminal record, would you?'

'Please, Tash! Don't.' Jane had started to cry soundlessly. Large tears slid down her cheeks. Chipper whined and touched her hand with his nose and she stroked his head with nervous fingers.

'Tell them the truth,' Tash persisted. 'Clear it up once and for all. And tell the boys. They should know too. They are grown-ups and they love you. They can handle it. After all, what you did was nothing to be ashamed of. It was silly and childish, but it wasn't wicked, and it stemmed from love, darling. From your desperate love for Florence. They will be touched and moved by it more than anything else.'

The sisters sat in silence and then Jane said, almost angrily, 'For years I haven't thought about it. It was safely in the past. Laid to rest.'

'Secrets are never safely in the past. Aunt Joan and I were talking about our mother on the way here. She told me the most extraordinary story about how she thinks that she was driving on the evening of the accident, and that she deliberately went over the edge. She thinks that she wanted to kill them both.'

'She hinted as much to me. I found it upsetting, hearing something like that after so many years. It forces us to look again at how we think of our parents, and none of it can be proved one way or the other. I didn't want to speak to you about it. Not now, anyway, when you aren't well yourself. You've got enough to deal with.'

'Actually, it wouldn't surprise me if she was right. Our mother was an extraordinary woman. Do you remember how she rallied to your side when you were charged? How she insisted on Daddy getting you the best lawyer? She was prepared to cut you off for keeping Florence, but then fought for you like a lioness when you were in custody?'

'Yes. She was like the Mounties coming over the hill. Unstoppable.'

'And there's something else I've just heard about. Aunt Joan told me on the way here that she had a married lover for years and years. Did you know that?'

'No!' Jane looked at her sister in disbelief.

'She did! All the time you lived with her too. She had to stop seeing him while you were there!'

'No wonder she was so crabby! Honestly, though, I can't believe it. You should have seen her underwear! Peach-coloured knickers to the knee.'

'I'm terribly glad she had a lover,' said Tash, smiling. 'Not that he was married, but that she had a chance at life.'

'Yes.' Jane nodded. 'A chance at life. When Florence was little, that first Christmas, do you remember the Apollo moon shot? I took her to see old Mr Kowalski. It was the last time I saw him before he died. He thought that Florence would have the best possible chance at life in a new world, a better world, where spacemen could travel

359

to the other side of the moon and look down on planet earth.'

'Yes. We all hoped for great things back then. We were so full of ideals. What have we done with that fresh start? Ballsed it up, I'd say. We've grown up to be as greedy and grasping as any generation that came before.'

'No! Look at you and Denby. You've tried to change things. And think of Enzo, and the difference he has made, and people like Hugh Bywater. Do you remember him? The boy next door with the radical mother, who was always on marches and demos? It was him who brought Enzo to see me when I was in the maternity ward with Flo.'

'Yes, I remember. What about him?'

'Oh, he's head of some medical charity that's always involved in war zones and famines. He's lived those ideals all his life.' Jane looked down at Tintin, who had gone back to sleep. 'Now it's up to Florence and Ha. It's their world now.'

'I suppose we should be getting back. It's not really fair to leave Aunt Joan all this time.'

'Come on, then.'

The two sisters got up and Tash linked her arm through Jane's. Chipper, glad to be off again, trotted cheerily along in front.

'I was thinking this morning about that dog,' said Jane. 'Sam, he was called. When Mrs Garbutt came out of hospital, she had him destroyed. I think she knew that it would be an extra punishment for me.'

'Mean-spirited bitch!' said Tash. 'I'm glad she had that stroke which finished her off.'

'You can't say that!'

'I bloody can!'

*   *   *

They had not gone very far before a figure appeared far ahead of them on the towpath. Chipper ran forward, wagging his tail in greeting.

'It's Florence,' said Jane, squinting into the low afternoon sunshine. 'Do you think something has happened?'

But when they were within hailing distance, Florence called out, 'Ha's back from work, so I thought I'd come and meet you. I've got some news for you!' and she began to run.

'We've put the champagne in the fridge!' she said when she reached them. Her face was very pink and young-looking. 'Guess what? Ha's asked me to marry him! He just has! About ten minutes ago. Down on one knee in the kitchen, with Aunt Joan snoring like a warthog next door.'

'Oh, darling!' said Jane. 'What did you say?'

'Yes, of course! I've been wanting to get married for ages but I didn't think he did.'

'Well, it's wonderful news. Goodness, we do have a lot to celebrate.'

The three of them walked on slowly until, when they were passing a bench in the sunshine, Tash suddenly said, 'Look, I am going to sit here for a minute. You two go on.'

Jane turned to her in immediate concern but she made a face at her and said. 'No, you go on! I'm fine and you have a lot to talk about.'

This is it, then, thought Jane. She expects me to tell Florence now. It could wreck the happiness of her day. It could ruin everything. She took a deep breath.

'Darling,' she said, 'there's something you should know and I don't suppose there will ever be the right time to tell you . . .'

*   *   *

In the end it did not take as long as she had expected to speak of the events that had haunted her for so long. Flo listened in total silence, her head bent, her eyes on the ground, and several times they stopped walking altogether as Jane talked. Somehow Tash had forced open the door to the past and now there was no stopping the story breaking out into the open.

'And what happened in the end? After you were charged?'

'My mother and father got me out on bail and I went to stay with you and Tash in London. Then I was put up for trial and despite the efforts of the best lawyer my father could find, I was sent to prison for three months.

'My mother was amazingly supportive throughout. She took over the case, wanting my lawyer to prove that I was not of sound mind, that I was unfit to stand trial because I was suffering from postnatal depression, but I wouldn't allow that. I was too frightened that the court might decide at the same time that I was an unfit mother. I insisted on pleading guilty.

'While I was in prison you stayed with Tash. There was an elderly Jamaican woman called Ruby in one of the bedsits in their house, who used to look after you. She had been a real thorn in their side up until then because they had tried to get her evicted so that they could begin doing up the house, but she wouldn't go. She just ignored the solicitor's letters, and in the end it was the best thing that could have happened. She was the most wonderful baby-sitter.

'Your grandparents came regularly to see you. They fell in love with you, Flo, and although they still felt I had made a terrible mess of things, they supported me from then on.

'While I was in prison I learned that Mr Kowalski had left me the remaining years of the lease on his bookshop. That made the most tremendous difference because I was able to let it out and live on the proceeds when I was released. It meant I could begin my secretarial training, leaving you with Ruby during the day.'

'Mum, why didn't you tell me all of this? *Why didn't you?* I've always known there was something else, something you wouldn't talk about.' Florence's eyes were full of tears.

'I didn't have the courage.'

'But I would have been *proud* of you! You *did* have courage! You were the bravest person I can think of. You were only nineteen, for God's sake. I'm so glad that I know now.' Florence reached for her mother's hand and held it to her own face. 'Mum! I love you so much. You do know that, don't you?'

Jane nodded, thinking, yes, I do, and also that it was the first time that she dared to believe it to be true.

They were nearly back now, crossing the car park of the apartment building. A large, expensive car was reversing into a space and they halted for a minute to let it complete the manoeuvre.

363

Florence caught a glimpse of the couple in the front and put a hand on Jane's arm. 'Wait a minute, Mum. I think this could be Ha's parents. He said that they were longing to come and meet Tintin. It would be typical of them just to arrive with no warning.'

The car doors opened and a small oriental woman got out of the passenger seat. She was beautifully dressed in a lightweight suit and her hair was set in a glossy dark helmet that was more of a fixture than a hairstyle. She carried an expensive handbag on the crook of her arm. Her nails were lacquered scarlet. From the other side stepped a tiny grey-haired man almost hidden behind an enormous bouquet of flowers done up with a huge blue satin ribbon, and a very large teddy bear.

'Goodness!' said Jane. 'They look like the royal family. I thought they owned a chip shop?'

'They do—several. She's a Vietnamese version of Mrs Thatcher. We are a grandmother! I expect they have come to tell Ha and me that we must get married.'

'Just a minute!' said Jane, taking Florence's hand. 'You go on and meet them, darling. I'd like to wait for Tash, if you don't mind. We won't be long.'

Flo turned to give Jane a hasty hug and kissed her cheek. 'Best mother in the world,' she said. 'Cheesy, but true.'

'And, Flo, I'm so happy for you.'

Jane watched her daughter push Tintin towards his grandparents and heard their cries of delight, and then turned back the way they had come to find her sister. Tash was still sitting on the bench where they had left her, staring at the green water of the canal, her elbows on her knees.

'So?' she said, looking up. 'You've told her, I hope?'

'Yes,' said Jane sitting beside her and putting her arm round her. 'I did. She was amazing. Loving. Forgiving. Proud of me, even.' Jane couldn't stop the tears now. They flowed down her cheeks and she wiped them away with the back of her hand.

'What did I tell you? Now you must tell Enzo.'

'Yes, you have given me the courage. I already feel as if a huge weight has lifted from my shoulders.'

'So it has.'

'Tash. It's you now. It's you.'

'Yes, I know. I'll be OK, don't worry. I'm a mean little fighter. Ask Denby. Mean as an alley cat. I'll have it licked in no time.' She dropped her head on her sister's shoulder and Jane stroked her hair.

They sat like that for some moments and Jane felt a sort of peace descend on them from the tender blue sky. The ugly green canal sparkled in the sunshine and the moorhens darted busily in the reeds. It wasn't over, of course it wasn't, thought Jane. There were things in the future she could not contemplate, despite Tash's reassurance, and she dreaded telling Enzo what she had just told Florence, but her daughter's reaction had given her heart. Forgiveness was a wonderful thing.

'Come on!' said Tash, getting up with a little shake. 'That champagne will be cold by now. We should go and join the party!'